"Enticing and original . . . I'd be hard-pressed to conceive a more intriguing plot."

—Barrett Tillman, author of *Warriors*

"Brilliant . . . Mixes adventure with bloody intrigue in a desperate race against the clock. A great read."

—Martin Caidin, author of *The Final Countdown*

"One of the most fascinating books I have read in a good long time . . . Combines all the best qualities of suspense, adventure, and techno-thriller novels . . . Joe Kogan is one of the most interesting and attractive characters in contemporary fiction. It is impossible not to root for him."

—R. E. Harrington, author of *Marvels*

"Military fiction, romance, political intrigue—one surprise after another. Runyan really delivers."

—Allen Appel, author of *Till the End of Time*

THE
FLIGHT
C.F. RUNYAN

A Novel

Bantam Books
New York · Toronto · London · Sydney · Auckland

THE FLIGHT

A Bantam Book / July 1991

All rights reserved.
Copyright © 1991 by Clair Runyan.

Cover art copyright © 1991 by Robert Hunt.

Book design by Guenet Abraham

Library of Congress Cataloging-in-Publication Data
Runyan, Clair.
  The flight / Clair Runyan.
      p.   cm.
  ISBN 0-553-35305-5
  I. Title.
PS3568.U49F57   1991
813'.54—dc20   90-24589
                                           CIP

*Published simultaneously in the United States
and Canada*

Bantam Books are published by Bantam Books,
a division of Bantam Doubleday Dell Publishing
Group, Inc. Its trademark, consisting of the words
"Bantam Books" and the portrayal of a rooster,
is Registered in U.S. Patent and Trademark Of-
fice and in other countries. Marca Registrada.
Bantam Books, 666 Fifth Avenue, New York,
New York 10103.

PRINTED IN THE UNITED STATES OF AMERICA

FFG   0 9 8 7 6 5 4 3 2 1

ACKNOWLEDGMENTS

I am profoundly grateful to all who gave me reassurance and advice (often impious) during the writing of this book. Special thanks, however, go to:

Martin Caidin, whose encyclopedic knowledge of World War II aircraft—both Japanese and American—saved me from several grievous errors.

Kelly Scarborough and Jesse Huerta—good friends and airline captains—for sharing their professional expertise with me.

Denise Marcil, my agent, for her strong advocacy of my work.

Betsy Mitchell, my editor, for her wisdom, encouragement, and sustaining phone calls.

And not least, to Mary... *Marie.*

═ PROLOGUE ═

Somewhere in the large Georgian house a phone rang.

Brigadier General Scott Armitage entered his study, tossed his briefcase onto a side table, and cocked his head peevishly at the insistent ringing.

Answer it, Freddy, for God's sake!

The sight of the cluttered room made him almost physically sick. Maybe he should wait for the new man, whoever he was. The realization that he needed help—damnit, *had* to have it— made him even sicker. Hell, there was no guarantee they'd even find a new man—not one with the kind of knowledge this god- damn operation needed. He stumbled to his desk, blinking his eyes rapidly to clear them of what felt like coal dust. The desk calendar mocked him. He glared back, blaming it for the dull headache that had taken up permanent residence. Time, that was the killer. Like in the song, the days were dwindling down to a precious few. Dah dah dah-dah-dah, dah dah. . . . He must be going batty. If only he could throw back three stiff drinks, take a hot shower, and sleep for twelve solid hours. . . .

Gotta get back to that damn book. He hated the title— *Logistical Analysis of the Philippines Campaign, 1941–42*—six pounds of tables and graphs and footnotes. But out of that maze of figures, he had to devise a plan. How many had he come up with and then tossed out? He didn't want to think about it.

Come on, now, no need to slam the book. Nerves a little raw? Maybe one of those pills—nope, he absolutely had to cut down. Just take it nice and easy. Check the index, "Aerial Resupply," and find the northern terminus. Check it out on the big Philippines map. Uh-oh, that won't do. Need one of Luzon. Okay, got it. Much better, gives definition to Manila Bay, but Corregidor is still just a speck. Dammit, gotta have a larger map than that.

Will that phone ever stop ringing?

The right map has got to be here, mixed up with about a million notes and studies. Okay, found it—Manila Bay nice and detailed, with Bataan dangling down like a bull testicle. Ah, now Corregidor—the "Rock"—stands out, just east of the bay entrance. Looks like a fierce tadpole guarding Manila. Where's Kindley Air Field? It must be there. Yes, yes, good! Right there— how could he miss it?—planted squarely on the tadpole's tail, oriented east and west. But is it really that short? Pray it's not so. Where's the map scale? Yeah, okay, careful now, let's see what we've got—hey, don't let those hands shake. Come on, Armitage, settle down, remember tan Canh, and the rockets that never stopped coming in? Not a tremor, then. Like a rock. Sure, but that was twenty-five years ago and the president of the United States wasn't all over your ass.

All right, easy does it. No mistakes. Want to make sure we've got enough landing room . . . shit! Kindley is only a lousy thousand feet long. No way that can work. Unless . . . yeah, yeah, try to remember, think, get the old bean working. Ah, it's coming back now. Planes, small planes. A rinky-dink air force they called the . . . bamboo something. Bamboo Fleet, that was it. All MacArthur had left. Saw something about it in a note . . . where? On his desk? Gotta check it. Look at that pile of papers, must be a foot high. So keep digging.

Maybe he should have learned to use that damn computer mocking him from across the room, but generals don't use computers—wasn't that what he'd told Freddy? And his slim-hipped, broad-shouldered driver had just laughed, his handsome head and Greek god profile thrown back—now whoa, this wasn't the time to start thinking about that sort of thing.

The study door opened. Armitage finished the note and looked up. Freddy leaned casually against the back of a chair with that arrogant, beautiful smile on his face, wearing that irritating rock band T-shirt.

Freddy pantomimed a phone call.

"Who is it?"

"Dunno, they wouldn't say."

"Take a message, please." Armitage gestured at his desk. "I'm really very busy." God, what an understatement. But that's the way you talk to subordinates, even a special one like Freddy. Don't let them know you're in trouble.

The corporal didn't move. "I've got a feeling you better take this one."

For an instant, their eyes met, then Armitage nodded. Freddy was about the poorest soldier he'd ever run into—a dog-robber who traveled on his looks—but he was street-smart, with a sixth sense that seldom erred.

Suddenly, he was anxious to take the call. His spirits lifted, really soared. Maybe it was the White House. They couldn't find anyone, so they were canceling the damn thing. The thought made him realize how much he hated this absurdity called Operation SUCCOR. He longed to get away from here, back to an assignment that made sense. Jesus, even the Middle East would be an improvement. And besides, there was the matter of Freddy.

He wouldn't order him to go along—the thing was too dangerous. And Freddy would never risk his superbly tanned hide by volunteering.

Reflexively smoothing his close-cropped hair, Armitage marched out of the study. Though he tried not to, he couldn't resist letting his arm brush the corporal's. In the hall near the front door, he picked up the phone, noticing idly the brown-paper package lying next to it with his name on it. He held his hand over the mouthpiece.

"What's this?"

The corporal shrugged. "Dunno. Came a little while ago. Want me to open it?" Armitage shook his head and gestured for Freddy to leave.

"General Armitage." He listened as a voice spoke strongly accented English with a rapidity that made it difficult to follow. He muttered an annoyed curse; the last thing he needed right now was a crank call from Count Dracula. He nearly slammed down the phone, but the caller's words suddenly began to have coherence, creating images that had no business being spoken over the phone or anywhere else—images that struck the most profound terror in him. He listened, gripping the phone tightly, not quite believing this was happening.

Finally, the voice stopped.

The general held the phone in a hand wet with sweat. "I've never heard anything so goddamn ridiculous . . . this is crazy. Just who the hell are you?"

The voice, calm and unemotional, told him it did not matter. What was important was that the work he was doing must proceed more slowly. Unforeseen obstacles to its completion must be put in place, plans must go awry—

Armitage broke in. "Listen, you sonavabitch, you don't scare me—"

Don't interrupt, the man warned, exhibiting irritation for the first time. The general should listen carefully because his career was on the line. Did he expect to add three stars to the single one on his shoulder? What chance would a queer—the caller chuckled as he emphasized the word—have of becoming army chief of staff? All was not lost, however. He had only to ensure that Operation SUCCOR did not go forward. Did he understand?

Armitage felt his guts roil with nervous gas. He licked his dry lips, took a raspy breath, and fought back. Wiping the sweat from his face with his sleeve, he deepened his voice, putting all his outrage into his response.

"I refuse to be blackmailed. The charges are totally unsubstantiated. You haven't a shred of proof—"

A chuckle of genuine amusement mocked his words. Correction, please. Within the past thirty minutes, a package had been delivered to his quarters. If he were to open it, he would find videotape cassettes containing pictorial evidence that the general himself had touchingly recorded of some very tender moments between him and his enlisted aide. The cassettes had been *borrowed*, the voice continued, for just long enough to make copies—

The telephone dropped on the table with a clatter as Armitage ripped open the package. There they were, labelled in his own handwriting: "The Beach House," "Todd's Party," "The Jacuzzi." Coming from the receiver, the man's voice reached his ear thinly. He picked up the telephone, unable to speak, but his gasping breath must have been heard by the demon on the other end.

Would he, the voice asked smoothly, care to have these tapes delivered to the general's aged mother, to the joint chiefs of staff, and to every major metropolitan newspaper in the nation? Of course not.

Armitage spoke in a voice that he hardly recognized. "You don't understand. I cannot do what you ask." He searched his battered brain for an argument. "I took an oath a long time ago. In all my years in the army I've never violated it. Look, I have some money. I can give you eight, nine thousand right away. Let me have a few days and I can borrow another twenty thousand—"

Forget it, the man said contemptuously.

Armitage tried again. "All right, here's what I'll do. I'll resign the command...say I'm in ill health, anything."

The response was unequivocal. He must stay on the project to see that it did not succeed. That was the mission assigned him. If he expected to have a future in the army, the operation had to fail.

Two words blazed in Armitage's mind. "*Mission assigned*? By who? Tell me, goddamnit, who's behind this?"

Without another word, the man broke the connection.

Armitage's breath rushed out of his lungs. The tall clock in the hall struck the quarter hour and he was surprised at how melodic the chimes sounded as they pealed a death knell to his hopes—his life. It was true, something like this really did sharpen the senses.

He put down the phone and stumbled back to his study. Locking the door, he walked to his desk and with a savage sweep of his arm sent the pile of books and papers crashing to the floor. His eyes swept the room, seeking an escape hatch, an answer. Nothing there, nothing anywhere.

The doorknob turned once and turned again. Then came knocking. Freddy called out, "What the hell's our videos doing laying out here?"

"Get rid of them."

"Scott, what happened? You all right?"

He swallowed hard and tried to keep his tone normal. "I'm okay. No problem."

"Then why's the door locked?"

"I said I'm okay. Now forget it." He listened for the corporal's footsteps, but Freddy wasn't leaving. The doorknob turned against the lock again.

He tried to regain his composure. There must be some way out. But he knew different. He knew it as surely as he was Brigadier General Scott Withrow Armitage, rising star in the U.S. Army; number one man at Staff and Command, Leavenworth; number three at the National War College; battalion commander at twenty-nine; regimental commander at thirty-seven, and certain to become army chief of staff before fifty. His options closed one by one like slamming doors. The star had become a meteorite, burned out as it plunged downward. Thank God for that locked door, because he found himself fighting back tears he had not shed since he was ten.

He yanked open the desk drawer and took out his service pistol. Hefting the weapon, he leveled it at a large photo on the opposite wall, captioned CLASS OF 1967, U.S. MILITARY ACADEMY, WEST POINT. He steadied the front sight on a vague figure in the front row. Yes, that was the answer, the final, irrevocable answer.

But first . . . He pulled a sheet of paper in front of him. Taking a few calming breaths, he wrote a dozen words in his precise hand, folded the paper and carefully printed a name and phone number on it.

Freddy was calling out, a shrill note in his voice. The kid was sharp. He probably guessed what was happening. The knob turned and rattled, then the heavy panels shook under urgent pounding.

As his thumb snapped off the pistol's safety, Armitage whispered, "Good-bye, Freddy."

Very quickly, he placed the muzzle of the pistol in his mouth and pulled the trigger.

$\equiv$ **CHAPTER ONE** $\equiv$

Washington, D.C.

September 15, 1994

During much of the Cretaceous period, the land on which the national capital now sits had been a vast, swampy sea, along whose shores the allosaurus and other nasty specimens prowled the fiery, supermoist climate. The reptiles have disappeared (although some Washington observers might argue otherwise), but as the year A.D. 1994 approached the September equinox, the climate had reverted to pure primeval.

At dawn, an angry late-season sun vaulted out of the Atlantic, searing the lower Chesapeake Bay, roiling the methane and carbon dioxide into an opaque, suffocating blanket of haze. As the sun rose higher, tourists gripped their guidebooks in sweaty hands and set out doggedly for the next air-conditioned repository of American history. Washington bureaucrats eyed the

ocher sky and prayed for autumn rains to arrive. Foreign dip-
lomats huddled behind the thick walls of their embassies and
wondered why the crazy Americans had ever chosen this miserable square of land as home for their government.

And on the Maryland side of the Potomac, two non-VIP, run-
of-the-mill lovers prepared themselves for another blistering day.

To the groaning of a window air conditioner in a modest
apartment just inside the beltway, Fay Donello, GS-9, wearing
only panty hose, arched her back sinuously, slipped on her bras-
siere, and adjusted the straps to carry the load. She stood sideways to the mirror and punched the slight convexity of her
stomach, a small but worrisome reminder of her twenty-nine
years. After slipping a light green linen dress over her head, she
leaned forward and applied makeup while inspecting for any
lines that might have etched themselves on her admirable skin
during the night. Finished, she stood back and gave her reflection
a deprecatory moue. Then she swept assorted beauty aids into
her purse and hurried off to the kitchen.

There she found Lieutenant Colonel Joseph Kogan, U.S.
Army, Retired, leaning against the dish-filled sink, drinking coffee and watching a thin line of ants trek across the scuffed
linoleum. He held up the coffeepot and sloshed the liquid around
seductively.

"Uh-uh, it's late." Fay moved in close and kissed his cheek.
"Gotta run. We used up our breakfast time in bed, remember?"

He thought about it, blinking at the ceiling. "Can't say as I
do."

"You dog." She punched his arm. He resumed his study of
the ants.

"See you later?" Fay picked up her purse and walked to the
door. She looked back at him over her shoulder, her eyes warm
and sensuous.

"You betcha." He watched her go, coppery hair swinging in
rhythm with body movements that were a hundred percent
woman, thinking that he was lucky to know her, lucky to be her
lover, and damn lucky she had made the first move because he

probably wouldn't have had the guts. He was forty-five, hair thinning, with features that were on a downward course, going from rugged to craggy. In spite of a good marriage that had ended tragically, he still felt insecure around women. He guessed twenty-five years in the army had done that to him. Lot of things he didn't know about people with high voices and no beards.

Another problem was that income-wise, he was playing it awfully close. The money for romance just wasn't there. A retired lieutenant colonel ate all right, could keep a car running and pay rent, but this research trip to Washington had soaked up his reserve capital. Courting rituals such as good seats at the theater and expensive dinners with wine were off-budget items.

Time was another thing he didn't have. Kogan had given himself one calendar year to write his doctoral dissertation, which left only the remaining months of 1994 in which to do it. The thought gave him considerable pain.

He had met Fay Donello when he first started his research at the National Archives. She had been hard to miss. An assistant archivist in the Modern Military Affairs branch, she brightened his mornings just by being there. Usually, before he opened his laptop and cracked the first letter file box, he sat at one of the chrome-legged tables and took a few minutes to finish his coffee and read the *Washington Post*. By sneaking furtive looks from behind the paper, he was able to enjoy one of man's greatest pleasures—watching a pretty woman who just might know she was being watched. Sure, he felt both raunchy and guilty, but he hadn't stopped looking, and not long after, the thought began to cross his mind that maybe, damnit, life did hold more worthwhile things than digging through musty letters.

At first, Kogan had struck up a friendship with Fay's boss, Michael Witkowski, a chunky, conscientious man with keen, wise eyes behind gold-rimmed glasses. A walking encyclopedia, Mike was, performing yeoman service in charting Joe's research into the defense of the Philippines in World War II. Then, a month or so ago, for no good reason Kogan could understand, this friendly young woman with the sensational smile had volunteered to lend a hand. One day after a grueling, productive day in the files, she offered to buy him a drink at a dark little bar in Suitland. The next day he bought her one, then two, and a little later she suggested that it would be cheaper to buy a bottle and go to her place. Now they alternated a couple of times a week and Kogan found he was wrong about being able to afford romance. Fay was good for him—she brought him back into the human equation out of which he'd slipped three years ago. That was when a ten-ton tractor-trailer had jackknifed and killed his wife, Jean, on Interstate 5 south of Bakersfield. He grunted with an almost physical torment at the memory, and forced himself back to the present. And Fay.

She had been understanding of the way long unused organs defy desire, no matter how intense. But they'd worked at it until he was pulling his share of the load, so to speak. Even so, he once asked her what a really pretty young woman like her saw in him.

"Oh, I don't know," she had answered. "You're real. Not one of those romance novel heroes with a crooked little smile and a big dick. Or is it the other way around?" She grinned wickedly as her hand did a gentle grope. "Nope, sure isn't," she pronounced. Her smile teased. "Not to mention..."

"Keep going, you've captured my interest."

She tapped a knuckle against his head. "Smarts. You don't go around walking into doors. I hate dummies." She threw her head back, staring at the ceiling. "I dunno. You give me space, I guess. Some guys want to take over your life—tell you what to think, what to wear, how to make love, how to scramble their goddamn eggs...they want all the goodies without picking up the tab." She kissed the corner of his mouth. "That's not you, lover."

Her hand trailed up his belly to play with his chest hair. "And somewhere under all that fur, I'm damn sure there's a heart."

• • •

Kogan flipped on the TV to catch the morning news. A newscaster was giving the lead-in. "And now let's go to Hal Jacobsen at Andrews Air Force Base for coverage of the president's departure for Hawaii." The picture changed. The presidential helicopter dropped down beside Air Force One, but it was a long shot and Kogan moved closer to squint at the TV screen. Because of the distance, the figures leaving the helicopter were unrecognizable, causing him to wonder why they even bothered with this news bit. The shot zoomed in to show a group of figures shaking hands. The one recognizable person was the White House chief of staff, whose great height masked the president, except for one well-tailored shoulder.

Kogan snorted and reached out to change the channel, but stopped as the screen filled with Jacobsen at Andrews, his face a study in controlled irritation. "Sorry, ladies and gentlemen," he intoned with a bleak smile, "that we couldn't get an interview with President Moody, but both Secretary of State Talbott and Martin Rodale, the White House chief of staff, are seeing the president off on this rather sweltering day. Perhaps we can get a word from them." He wiped his brow with a handkerchief, then suddenly pressed the miniature receiver in his ear. "Yes." He smiled into the camera. "I've received word they should be here in a few minutes."

While the station cut to a commercial, Kogan walked to the bedroom, put on his shirt, and got back in time for the interview with the towering Rodale. In the background, he could see the sturdy figure of the secretary of state, an aide whispering to him.

"Mr. Rodale," Jacobsen began with more than a hint of acerbity in his voice. "Inasmuch as this is virtually the eve of the DOE—excuse me—the denuclearization of Europe summit, we were hoping that President Moody might give us a statement. He *is* planning to be in Brussels next month, is he not?"

Rodale stood with his frame slightly bent, a habitual posture enabling him to see into the faces of persons of average height. "Of course he is, Hal. It's important to understand that without Simon Moody, there would be no comprehensive plan today for taking all nuclear arms out of Europe. The president is looking forward with great anticipation to what he, as well as the American people, must consider the capstone of his administration."

Hal Jacobsen briefly showed his teeth. To Kogan's eye, he looked like a wolf about to drag down a badly wounded deer. "Last night, sir," the anchor continued, "Vice president Spencer Pyle made a speech in which he referred to the proposed treaty as stripping Europe naked. He got quite a laugh when he referred to DOE as 'Bambi.' Does this indicate a rift in the administration's position on disarmament?"

Rodale's chuckle sounded a bit hollow. "Let me just correct you there, Hal. The vice president said DOE *could* go too far if Europe were *demilitarized*. Simon Moody has no intention of removing any more of our conventional forces from the Continent—at least not now. He is quite satisfied with the Conventional Forces agreement as it now stands." In the background, Talbott looked up sharply, then, as if recognizing he was within camera range, turned back to his aide.

"Excuse me if I seem importunate, asking these questions, but you understand that since President Moody hasn't granted interviews or held a press conference in some time..." Jacobsen let the unasked question hang in the air.

"Of course." Rodale's angular face had a touch of condescension. "But there really hasn't been a whole lot happening of significance recently—"

Jacobsen interrupted. "You don't consider significant the quite negative statements on the summit we've been hearing from Europe lately? Mr. Rodale, getting rid of the bombs and missiles on the Continent may not be the piece of cake President Moody seems to think it will be."

"These so-called negative statements, Hal, have come from unnamed officials of countries scattered across the length and breadth of Europe. They have no geographical or political coherence that we can see. They represent a certain bellicose minority that we are convinced will fade away once the DOE conference begins." Rodale started to move off toward a waiting limousine.

Jacobsen edged around to block the big man's departure. He looked up into the chief of staff's face. "Do you include the vice president in that 'bellicose minority,' sir? If so, are we seeing a situation in which the future of disarmament depends upon whether the president or the vice president represents the United States at the summit?"

The camera closed on Rodale's face, and Kogan thought he saw a flicker of something—anger, indecision, perhaps even fear—before the chief of staff's smile broadened and he managed a chuckle. "That's a really suspenseful scenario, Hal. I congratulate you on injecting some drama into a dull interview. But President Moody *will* go to Brussels."

"But supposing his health—the president *is* all right, isn't he?"

"His health is fine. He's had a few minor ailments recently and right now he has a touch of the flu. A few days lying on the beach and breathing good, clean air will take care of that." Rodale pushed by the newsman. "Sorry, I have to rush. I'm due for a meeting on the Hill." He entered his car, and the camera shifted back to confront Hal Jacobsen's sardonic smile.

Kogan turned off the TV, rinsed his cup in the sink, and stepped into the tiny living room. Something about the interview troubled him. The newscaster was right. Now that he thought about it, the president had not been particularly visible recently. A mental image of the vital, outgoing Moody flashed before him. No politician in recent years enjoyed public appearances more than the handsome, ebullient president. Hiding out wasn't his style. Maybe Moody *was* sick, but if so, why not admit it? If it's serious, let the vice president pull his share of the load.

He crossed the room to the drop-leaf table that served as his desk. On it were his Toshiba laptop computer and stacks of computer paper, a printer, and a foot-high jumble of books. He grabbed a handful of his latest notes and stuffed them into a battered briefcase, closed up his laptop, and was putting on his poplin jacket when the doorbell rang.

Two men stood there, clothing and demeanor announcing "We're federal agents, pal." What the taller of the two, a man with bored eyes and salt-and-pepper hair, actually said was, "Colonel Joseph Kogan." It was a statement, not a question.

Joe wondered how this guy could be so sure. Then he wondered why they had come looking for him. Couldn't be his tax returns. With his income, he used the 1040A—short and not so sweet. The statute of limitations had run out on the jeep he'd left behind in the fight for Hué.

"I'm Joe Kogan," he said.

"Wonder if you'd mind coming with us?" Both men held out richly embossed gold badges with blue striping.

"Matter of fact, friend," Kogan said, "I *do* mind. I've reached the stage of life where I don't tag along with just anybody. You guys got a warrant?"

Before the agent could answer, Kogan's phone rang. Leaving them at the door, he walked to the bedroom. It was Mike Witkowski at the Archives. "Joe," his voice was tense, "we had visitors this morning."

Kogan rubbed his forehead, hard. Fornicating on an empty stomach must cause brain damage, because he was sure as hell having trouble staying abreast of developments. He tried to keep the annoyance out of his voice. "Wonderful, Mike, I'm really happy for you."

"No, no. These were federal agents. Uncommunicative and not very friendly. All they said was they wanted to talk to you. I had to give them your address." Witkowski chuckled lamely. "Why do I feel like a character in an old movie?"

Kogan tucked the phone into his shoulder and buttoned his shirtsleeves. This was going to be a long day. "Too late, Mike. The G-men have got the place surrounded. They're lobbing tear gas through the windows. I can't hang on much longer. Tell Ma I went out fighting." He hung up and returned to the federal minions. The sun beat down on them and Kogan noticed with some satisfaction the sweat on their faces. "Now, gentlemen," he said, "what can I do for you?"

"As we said, we'd like you to come with us."

"Where?"

The taller agent again took out his badge and held it up. "Take a closer look, Colonel."

The badge was emblazoned SECRET SERVICE. Below that was the agent's number, 624, and at the bottom, WHITE HOUSE DETAIL. "We'd like to tell you more, but all we're authorized to say is that your cooperation would be greatly appreciated."

Witkowski replaced the phone and stared at it, perplexed. When Kogan had first arrived to work on his doctorate, Mike had pegged him as a straight-arrow, retired army type. A bit abrasive at times, but once you got to know him, you found beneath the tough exterior a sense of humor and a good mind. Deadly serious, too, about finishing his research on the Philippines debacle of 1942, and appreciative of Witkowski's help. Joe seemed like the last person in the world to be in trouble with the Feds. Maybe he wasn't. He didn't sound too worked up on the phone.

He checked the clock. Fay was going to be late again. He knew what was going on between her and Kogan—could tell almost from the day it began. Well, he'd had his fling with her. Three years ago she had come to work in the branch as his assistant. She was capable, sexy, and without a guy in her life in a town where there were thousands of women in the same boat. Maybe that's why she had taken up with an overweight, low-level bureaucrat. For a year they had gone together, and it had been about the best time he could remember—so good that he couldn't believe it would ever stop. He even talked obliquely about marriage, but she had shushed him up.

"Come on, Michael, my Polish prince," she had said. "A piece of paper will kill it."

It hadn't taken a piece of paper, just a lawyer in HUD. Fay had met the guy—how, he never found out—and on one teary night (for Mike, at least), she told him it was over between them.

The world ended for Mike, or so he believed, and the atmosphere in the Modern Military Affairs branch was definitely polar for a while. But he coped, and they became just two co-workers once again.

It wasn't too long afterward that Fay came to work with red-rimmed eyes. Surprise! The attorney's wife and two children had joined him in Washington.

But Fay, he had come to understand, didn't take much to celibacy. It was only a matter of weeks before she indicated in subtle ways that she wouldn't mind seeing the status quo ante restored. But by this time, Mike was seeing a history instructor at Georgetown—a quiet, very bright, average-looking woman several years older than he. No white-hot romance, but comfortable. He obtained considerable satisfaction from playing it cool—maybe even a trifle supercilious—in rejecting the offer.

He looked up and there was Fay, looking very, very happy as she poured a cup of coffee from the machine. It must have been a good night. Walking to her desk, she waved at him. She glanced at her watch, looked aghast, then held her finger to her temple and pulled the trigger.

"Sorry, Mike," she said. "I'm going to do better, really. Oh— soon as I finish my coffee, I'm going to get some logistics records out for Joe. He'll be along in a little while."

"Don't be so sure," he answered.

"I'm William Passmore, director of White House security."

The Secret Service official extended his hand and Kogan took it, surprised at the power in the grip. Along with the erect stance of most short men, Passmore had the alertness of a wolverine hunting in a forest set with deadly traps. He moved around his office on the balls of his feet, neat and careful. "Thank you for coming," he added, not seeming terribly grateful.

"Yeah," Kogan said, not terribly impressed. "Mind telling me why I'm here?"

Passmore walked around a desk that was as uncluttered as

the rest of the Spartan office. He seemed annoyed, as though Kogan had violated an orderly world where *he* asked the questions. "In the next few minutes, Colonel, you will be shown something that affects the security of the United States."

"That doesn't answer my question."

"Let me finish. You will not—I repeat, *will not*—reveal to anyone what you are about to see. Is that clear?"

Kogan felt irritation surface through his puzzlement. The Secret Service agents who convoyed him to the White House had not been enlightening, or even amiable, rebuffing his attempts at conversation with polite but firm head shakes. As far as he was concerned, an explanation was long overdue.

"Hold it, Mr. Passmore," Kogan said. "Who said I want to see anything? If I hanker to take in the White House, I'll book a tour."

Passmore bristled, his eyes boring into Kogan's, then visibly relaxed. "All right. Here it is." The Secret Service man sat on the edge of his desk. "The president wants to see you."

Kogan felt Passmore's eyes watching him closely, and tried, without notable success, to appear unimpressed. The president of the United States wants to see Joe Kogan? What the hell is going on? What does a retired army grunt ass-deep in doctoral research have that Simon Moody wants? He was pondering that when a thought struck him.

"Mr. Passmore, you've got to be kidding. Hey, look, the president left for Hawaii this morning. I saw it on TV."

Passmore jerked a thumb over his shoulder. "He's not in Hawaii. He's less than a hundred feet away. Now do you understand why you're to keep your mouth shut?" Kogan, his capacity for surprise overloaded, nodded. Passmore stood up. "Let's go. I'll introduce you to Martin Rodale, the chief of staff."

The introduction had been perfunctory, the chief of staff saying only that any questions he might have would be answered later. Afterward, as Rodale gestured for him to follow, Kogan caught the looks exchanged between the big man and the Secret Service director. Neither seemed happy.

They left the elevator. To the right, down a long, broad hall, Kogan could see a large Palladian window with furniture clustered around it. Rodale tapped his arm. "This way," he said, and turned left. They passed an oval-shaped room furnished in yellow, opening onto the Truman Balcony. The next door was closed. Rodale knocked softly before entering. It was a small library, furnished richly with Victorian pieces—Grant era, Kogan guessed—the most prominent being a magnificent walnut table. At one end of the room, two windows overlooked the South Lawn. Facing one of the windows was a huge leather chair. Because of its position, Kogan could see just the shoulder and arm of its occupant, but he guessed he was in the presence of the president of the United States. The chair swiveled and the rest of Simon Elihu Moody appeared, smiling at his visitors, gesturing to them to be seated.

The last time Kogan had seen him on TV—and that was some time ago—the president had been his usual dynamic self, maturely handsome, with broad shoulders on a stocky, powerful body. What now remained of the fifty-four-year-old chief executive was a shell, shrunken inside his pajamas and dressing gown, good teeth too large for his wrinkled lips, his head appearing too heavy for the scrawny neck. Cancer, Kogan was pretty sure, and metastasizing like wildfire. He steeled his face to immobility.

"Mr. President," Rodale said, "may I present Lieutenant Colonel Joseph Kogan, U.S. Army."

Kogan couldn't resist. Glancing at Rodale, he added softly, "Retired."

The president, reaching out painfully, extended his hand. To Kogan it was like shaking hands with a sack of dried twigs. "Thank you for coming, Colonel." Moody gestured at his body. "Sorry about the deception I'm forced to play." Kogan wondered about that. Why would a president as ill as Moody obviously was be "forced" into a deception?

"Colonel Kogan," the president continued, "I'll get right to the point. I understand that you're an expert on the Japanese assault on the Philippines in World War II."

Surprised, Kogan hesitated. "I'm familiar with it." He assayed a chuckle. "I'd better be, sir, since I'm writing my Ph.D. dissertation on it."

"We know that. Just what do you intend to do with a doctorate?"

Kogan thought the question lacked presidential quality—what the hell does one generally do with a Ph.D. in history? He shrugged. "Teach. Small college somewhere."

Moody seemed to study him, his surprisingly blue eyes staring intensely into Kogan's. Then he shifted his gaze to Rodale, and Kogan had the feeling that a silent message had passed between them. The president picked up a folder from the table at his elbow.

"Let's see," he said, opening what Kogan saw with a shock was his 201 file. "Two tours in Vietnam," Moody read. "Five years in Special Forces; two years senior adviser, Southern Front; three years with Rapid Deployment Forces, Persian Gulf Command." He flipped a page. "Two Silver Stars, a Bronze Star, a Purple Heart. Three Letters of Commendation." He looked farther down the file and vocalized mild surprise. "And a Letter of Admonition. Seems you got a bit abrasive with a senior officer." He put the file down. "Well, you seemed to be on your way to much higher rank, yet you voluntarily requested retirement. Mind telling me why?"

Damn right, I mind. It's none of your business. You'd probably get pissed off if I told you that after I grew out of the kid who went to Vietnam it made me physically sick to think that LBJ could kill thousands of Americans and hundreds of thousands of Vietnamese, then go back to his goddamn ranch on the Pedernales and die peacefully in bed. No impeachment for his "high crimes and misdemeanors"—just a nice pension and a big library. So I stayed on while the army engaged in heroic and hard-fought battles against military superpowers like Grenada and Panama. That did it. I took a walk. But I made damn sure to get my little green check every month.

He had to answer the president some way. "Well, sir, I guess after twenty-four years I got a bit tired of wearing a uniform."

"I see," the president said, and his smile said he didn't believe it. "Isn't teaching going to be a bore?"

"Peace and quiet, sir," Kogan said. "That's all I ask."

The study was hushed. "Yes," Moody said, "I guess that's what we all want, but sometimes...." He didn't finish, and fatigue seemed to overwhelm him. With an effort, he shifted in his chair. "In some respects, your work here in Washington has paralleled our own. Did you know that we did a very thorough search of the MacArthur files several months ago?"

Kogan concentrated. "Not really, sir. Although Mike...uh, the archivist at the records center, did mention some recent interest by a government agency."

"That was us. We found what we were looking for. A letter—a very important letter. Marty has a photocopy." Moody motioned to the chief of staff.

Rodale pulled a folded sheet of paper from an inner pocket. "Read it," the chief of staff said curtly to Kogan.

He glanced at the photocopy and remembered the letter. Yellowed by age and in places indecipherable, it had been written by a senior surgeon on Bataan in the last days before the peninsula had fallen to the Japanese. It claimed that a young doctor, using indigenous plants, had found a usable substitute for the quinine the U.S. Navy couldn't slip through the Japanese blockade. He had shown the letter to Mike, saying he thought it was interesting enough to make a good footnote. The archivist had been enthusiastic. "Hey, Joe," he'd said, "better than that. This is truly great stuff. Can't you just see this young guy out in the swamps of the Bataan Peninsula, maybe under Japanese fire, gathering his weeds, boiling the damn stuff, trying to come up with an antimalarial drug? And according to this," Mike waved the wrinkled old letter, "he succeeded gloriously."

"You sound like a minor poet," Kogan had said. "I happen

to know they never found anything that worked. Interesting, but not worth a historical damn."

Rodale interrupted his reverie. "Read the letter, Colonel," he repeated.

Kogan nodded at the chief of staff. "I read it several weeks ago," he said.

"Read it again, Colonel," the president said. "Aloud."

"Yes, sir." He held the letter to the light coming in through the red velvet drapes. The words on the fifty-year-old typewritten letter were barely legible. "It was sent by Colonel Winfield Ritter, chief medical officer of the forces on the Bataan Peninsula," Kogan said, "addressed to Brigadier General James Fleming, chief surgeon of MacArthur's command on Corregidor, just across Manila Bay."

He started reading.

112355 March '42

Sir:

Important, unbelievable news! Upon receiving your message early last month indicating that no more quinine or atabrine could be expected to make it through the Japanese blockade, I assigned a Dr. Roger Babcock to investigate the recurrent rumors of an antimalarial substitute used by the aborigines. Although recognizing the probable futility of this course of action, we had to do something, for as you know, our troops are rapidly approaching zero combat effectiveness.

Working with indigenous plants, Babcock has synthesized a liquid he calls B-juice—a wretched name—which seems to be remarkably effective against malaria. I know this is difficult to believe, but the foul stuff really works!

God may be on our side after all.

A few faded, handwritten words were scribbled at the bottom of the sheet. Kogan angled the letter and squinted. "Dr. Ritter wrote a postscript in longhand, Mr. President, that's only partially legible," he said. "It says: 'Jim, even though I have not seen proof, I cannot keep this information to myself any longer. Babcock tells me of an extraor....'" Kogan folded the copy and handed it back to Rodale. "I assume that last word is *extraordinary*, but that's all I can make out, sir. The remainder of the writing has faded badly."

The president smiled. "Colonel, we can tell you what the missing words are." At Kogan's look of surprise, he added, "You see, we were looking for this letter, or something like it. You don't, at this time, have to know why." His voice dropped and he leaned forward, staring intently into Kogan's eyes. "But I can tell you that I deemed this letter to be so important, so fundamental to our future well-being, that it was essential to recapture every word, every pen scratch on it. So we ordered the FBI to do an amplification and enhancement procedure, and came up with this."

Rodale pulled another sheet of paper from his pocket and offered it to Moody, who waved it aside. "I remember it very well, Marty. I quote: 'Babcock tells me of an extraordinary and utterly marvelous side effect. The stuff cures *cancer*! Completely and very, very quickly! But for the time being, old friend, please say nothing to anyone of this.'"

The president's smile broadened. "The postscript is signed *Win*."

Kogan suddenly wished desperately to be somewhere else, for it was all becoming too damned uncomfortably clear to him. The sick man sitting before him believed the formula for B-juice could be found in the MacArthur files. Find it and he'd be cured! The whole thing was so pathetic that Kogan wanted to take Moody by his thin shoulders and shake him.

"Well, Colonel," Moody said, "what do you think?"

I think, Mr. Chief Executive, that you need a head doctor. But Kogan's annoyance at the president vanished as he looked at the man's wasted body. His eyes were hooded with fatigue, heart-rending in their silent plea for confidence in his scheme. He wanted desperately to say, *Yes, Mr. President, there* is *a chance the panacea might be found in those musty files.* But he couldn't. Sooner or later, and not too much later, Moody would have to face the truth. Better now.

"Mr. President," Kogan spoke sympathetically, "consider the circumstances. Dr. Ritter was a desperate man, and so was this Babcock. They were working under incredibly harsh conditions on Bataan, fighting one of the toughest armies in the world. It would have been easy for them to misinterpret something like this." Kogan stopped, yet he knew he hadn't said enough. "Sir," he continued, "your people have gone through the MacArthur files with a fine-tooth comb, just as I have. If there was more to this, such as the formula for the medicine, it would have been found. But that's all there is—this one letter. B-juice was a delusion. It didn't cure malaria or . . . anything else." He expelled his breath. "Believe me, sir." There, by God, he'd laid it on the line.

The president's reaction came as a surprise. No dismay or consternation showed on the gaunt face, just a faint, imperturbable smile.

"How can you be so sure?"

"Well, for one thing, sir, if this B-juice worked, why didn't anyone talk about this marvel? What happened to it?"

The president's expression sobered. He nodded his concurrence. "Yes, we thought of that, too. So far as we know, three officers were in on the cure—Babcock, Ritter, and by virtue of Ritter's letter, General Fleming. Yet, there is no record that they ever spoke or wrote of this wonderful cure. Why? Well, we've tracked them down and here's what we found. First, Dr. Babcock was captured by the Japanese and died in a POW camp." He glanced at Rodale. "I've forgotten. Where was that, Marty?"

"Shizuoka, sir. In the summer of 1945."

"Okay, that explains his silence. We next turned our attention to Dr. Ritter, who wrote the letter. During the Bataan Death

March he stopped to assist a fellow prisoner. A guard bayoneted him. The doctor was awarded the Distinguished Service Cross posthumously."

The president paused, and his fatigue was evident. "Now," he said in a low voice, "we come to the unexplainable—General Fleming's silence." He passed a shaking hand over his eyes. "Colonel, I'm going to ask Marty to finish this for me."

The chief of staff leaned forward. "Mr. President, why not save this for another time? You need to get some rest."

"No, no." Moody gestured impatiently. "I'm all right."

Rodale turned reluctantly to Kogan. "General Fleming is the problem. He wasn't captured. When Roosevelt ordered Mac-Arthur out of Corregidor to Australia, he took a few officers along with him. Fleming was one of them. He served with MacArthur throughout the remainder of the war—"

Kogan's head jerked up. Rodale noticed. "Anything wrong, Colonel?"

"Uh, no . . . sorry." Kogan needed time to think about what he had just heard. For he was pretty sure he had the answer now. He knew why Fleming had never talked about B-juice, but should he tell the president? The formula, if it *was* anything beyond a crazy screwball idea, had been lost beyond recovery anyway.

"Am I boring you, Kogan?" Rodale's smile was razor thin.

"Sorry." He decided to let the chief of staff spin out his tale.

"Okay. Well, Dr. Fleming retired in 1952 with the rank of major general, and died in 1967 at the age of eighty. He had every opportunity to speak—officially, informally, or both—about B-juice, but he didn't, and we can't figure out why, unless," he glanced at Moody, "there was no cure."

The president sipped a dark liquid that looked like a cola. "It's a puzzle," he said. "Old soldiers love to talk, and General Fleming would have had a wonderful, fascinating tale to tell about the greatest medical discovery in history—a panacea lost tragically in a POW camp during World War II." Moody set his drink down with something like a groan. "Damn, I wish we knew why he didn't talk!"

Kogan felt he should say something. "A remarkable story, sir. But in a sense, isn't it better that it end this way? Suppose you had *absolute proof* that a cure for cancer had existed back there and was lost. It could drive you crazy."

"A very cogent observation, Colonel." Moody smiled. "But we think it did exist. I guess," his face clouded over, "that the only doubt in our minds is General Fleming's silence."

What the hell, Kogan thought. If they had brought him here to shoot the shit with the president of the United States about World War II and a cockamamy idea like this B-juice, the least he could do was hold up his end.

"That's no problem, Mr. President," he said. "The reason General Fleming never talked about B-juice is because he never knew about it."

=== CHAPTER TWO ===

Only the faint, muffled roar of a jet taking off from National Airport broke the silence. The president and Rodale exchanged stunned glances, then the chief of staff threw his pencil angrily on the table. "Damnit, Colonel, you haven't been listening."

Kogan looked up in surprise, then his own temper flared. "Oh, I've listened," he shot back, then reined in; this guy *was* the White House chief of staff. "All right." He extended his hand and spoke with as much calm as he could manage. "Let me see that letter again." Rodale stared at him, still angry, then slowly handed the paper over. Kogan glanced at it and tapped it with his finger.

"That's what I thought. The date-time group is 112355 March. Ritter wrote this just before midnight on the eleventh of March."

Kogan turned to the president. "Sir, it's a matter of record that MacArthur and his party—with Fleming along—left by PT boat at about 2100 hours on twelve March, the following day. This letter never reached him."

"What do you mean?" Rodale demanded. "If Ritter wrote this the night before Fleming left...Corregidor's only a short distance across the bay from Bataan."

"Five miles," Kogan interjected.

"Five miles, okay. They had boats, didn't they?"

"They did. But the Japanese bombed anything that moved during the day, so the mail boat made its run after dark—probably no earlier than seven on the evening of the twelfth. Get the picture?"

Rodale's mouth set stubbornly. "Fleming didn't leave for another three hours. I don't see the problem."

Jesus, this guy is really bullheaded. Kogan tried to keep the irritation out of his voice. "Mr. Rodale, we're not dealing with a well-oiled machine here. The Japanese bombed and shelled the Rock continuously for two and a half months. By March every man and woman there was woozy, disoriented, unwashed, underfed, and miserable. They'd been abandoned by their country, so there was no help on the way. It was only a matter of time before the Japanese took the island. Military routine got sloppy. They just didn't give a shi...a damn. They got a bundle of mail, it got distributed in the morning—maybe."

Watching the stubborn, closed lines of Rodale's face, Kogan could see that his supposition wasn't playing well. He'd have to spell it out. "But okay," he continued, "for the sake of argument, let's say that everyone on the Rock feels wonderful, has had a good steak, mashed potatoes, and apple pie dinner under his belt, showered, put on starched khakis, and follows routine religiously. We've got optimum conditions. Here's still what would have happened. The mail from Bataan arrives at Corregidor's north dock by seven in the evening at the earliest. It's off-loaded, hauled up to Malinta Tunnel, and taken to message center for distribution, probably about eight o'clock. High-priority tactical stuff *might* get distributed. Everything else waits, including a letter from one doctor to another. The next morning this letter *can't* be delivered because Fleming sailed off to Australia the night before. So it sits in message center. Six weeks later, just before the Japanese take the island, all the headquarters files are put on a submarine and taken to Pearl Harbor and stored until the war is over. The files are then forwarded to the National Archives. Fifty years later, that's where we find the letter."

Glad the long explanation was over, Kogan waited warily for Rodale's rebuttal. It didn't come. The chief of staff smiled ruefully and nodded his head at Moody. The president winked back, then turned to Kogan.

"Colonel," the president said, "you've done us a great service. I can't tell you how much we appreciate it." He glanced at his chief of staff. "What do you think, Marty?"

Rodale nodded. "He's got my vote. I think the general will be very pleased."

"Have you told him we might have a candidate?"

The big man shook his head. "Tried to call him this morning, but I haven't been able to get through."

Moody turned quickly, his face suddenly clouded. "Nothing wrong, is there?"

"No, sir. He's damn busy. Has just one enlisted aide, and sometimes he doesn't bother to answer the phone."

Moody considered this, then turned to Kogan. "Joseph," he said, using Kogan's given name for the first time. "We're going to find B-juice—" As Kogan opened his mouth to object, the president waved him down. "No, not in the MacArthur files. We're sending a small group to the Philippines to look for it. We have a commander and a support group, but we'd like you to go along as...well, sort of a technical adviser. We need your expertise badly." He stopped suddenly and bit his lip. A strange, haunted expression shadowed his face. "I...uh, must tell you that there is danger, great danger, in this."

Moody paused and looked out over the trees of the South Lawn shimmering in the heat before quickly turning back to Kogan. A sense of urgency seemed to propel his wasted body.

"I won't insult your intelligence by belaboring the rewards to mankind if this effort is successful."

There was something going on here Kogan didn't understand. Recruiting an expert on the Philippines of World War II didn't make any sense, especially since he couldn't tell a petunia from an African violet. He decided not to keep quiet any longer.

"Mr. President, I'm sorry—"

Moody held up a restraining hand. "Please. I don't want either your acceptance or refusal now. Before you make your decision, I want you to understand fully what this project is about."

Rodale leaned forward solicitously. "Sir, you're tired. We'd better wrap this up."

The president sighed acquiescence. His smile had faded and his skin had turned putty gray. "You're right, Marty. But finish Kogan's briefing." He looked at Kogan and a small glint of humor chased the shadows from his eyes. "Bear with us, Colonel. This is not a loony bin, I assure you."

He pressed a button beside his chair. Instantly, Passmore entered. Standing by the door, the agent nodded to Kogan. "This way, Colonel."

Kogan ignored him. "Sir," he said to the president, "I'm serious about this. Don't waste any more of your time on me. Swatting mosquitoes and wading around in the swamps on Bataan isn't on my program. Besides, you don't need me. I'm not a botanist, or a . . . chemist."

Rodale was helping Moody out of his chair. He glowered at Kogan. "Will you show a little patience and understanding, Kogan? All we want you to do right now is look and listen. Is that asking too much?"

The president tapped his chief of staff reprovingly. "Now, now, Marty. We've imposed on the colonel without fully explaining what the project is." He peered at Kogan around Rodale's shoulder. "I'd appreciate it, Joseph, if you will at least listen to what Dr. Hiraga has to say."

•   •   •

The distinguished-looking Oriental was tall, about Kogan's own height, and his handshake was cool, dry, and firm. "Dr. Otis Hiraga," Passmore had said by way of introduction, "has got something to show you, Colonel Kogan. Afterward, the president would like to see you again..." He looked at his watch. "About one, let's say." The Secret Service man left, and Hiraga pointed to the front row in the small projection room.

"Please be seated," he said, then busied himself with a sophisticated VCR off to one side of the small stage.

Kogan watched Hiraga's long fingers flash confidently over the controls. He exuded competence—the kind you'd definitely want in a guy who was doing your triple bypass. About forty, he guessed, with smooth black hair touched with gray at the temples, face healthily tanned from outdoor sports rather than ethnicity. Kogan was no expert on expensive clothing, but he'd bet Hiraga's slacks and jacket cost about half of his own monthly pension check. He was wearing loafers that must have come all the way from Italy, and what looked like a gold Rolex glittered on his wrist.

"You an MD?"

Hiraga picked up a cassette and inserted it. "Physicist," he said economically, then walked across the stage and adjusted the controls on a large TV screen. That didn't make a lot of sense to Kogan. A hunt for therapeutic weeds shouldn't require a physical scientist.

"Mind telling me what the feature is, Doc?"

The remark didn't amuse Hiraga. He stood in front of Kogan, looking down at him as if pondering a decision.

"This video will take about fifteen minutes. If you have any questions, just speak up. When it's over, I'll go into as much detail as you like." He pointed a remote control at the VCR and it made soft clicking noises. The presidential seal appeared on the screen, followed by a terse warning in large red letters:

THE MATERIAL IN THIS VIDEO IS CLASSIFIED
EXECUTIVE TOP SECRET AND WILL BE RELEASED

ONLY UPON ORDER OF THE PRESIDENT OF THE
UNITED STATES.

Without further explanation, the film began, surprising Kogan
with its crudity. Although in color, it lacked commentary, and
the editing, continuity, and camera work were primitive, as if
the importance of whatever was taking place took precedence
over such minor details as a film record.

Kogan had to guess at much of what was happening. A long
shot showed a camp enclosed by a very high wire fence set in a
deep forest of northern pines. Heavily armed sentries and guard
dogs patrolled the periphery. Inside the fence, people wearing
hard hats moved quickly and with purpose between mobile
homes and larger structures. Except for the guards, no one wore
uniforms. Shorts, sleeveless shirts, and an occasional white coat
seemed appropriate for the bright, sunny day. There were quick
shots of large power units, overhead dollies, cranes, and thick
power conduits lying haphazardly around the enclosure. The
camera entered a Quonset hut. Rows of cages holding small
animals—dogs, cats, rats—lined the walls. Kogan was getting a
headache from the bouncing camera.

"Hold it, Doc," he said. "You've lost me. What's going on?"
Hiraga didn't answer; he kept his eyes on the screen. The camera
approached a group of white-coated men, who looked up in
apparent annoyance at the camera's intrusion. One of them, a
young Oriental, looked directly into the lens. Kogan could have
sworn he'd seen him someplace before; then he got it.

"Hey, isn't that you?"

Hiraga stopped the VCR, and smiled for the first time. "My fa-
vorite young physicist," he said. "One year out of graduate school
at MIT." He folded his arms and leaned back against the wall.

"Colonel, this was filmed sixteen years ago, during the Carter
administration. I'd been offered a government contract to work
on something really supersecret. I wasn't all that impressed because DOD's known for throwing a lot of hype around to get
top grads from the big schools. But I ended up working on what

turned out to be the most electrifying, innovative development ever brought to the point of engineering." Hiraga's obsidian eyes seemed to soften as he remembered.

"Yeah, what?"

The physicist took a deep breath before he spoke. "What you'd call unidirectional time travel—moving back in time."

Shocked, then amused, Kogan covered his mouth with his hand. Hiraga seemed too sincere to appreciate being laughed at. Time travel. Even a scientific illiterate like himself knew it wasn't possible. Well, he'd play it straight.

"How far did you get with it?"

Hiraga wasn't fooled. He must have sensed that Kogan was unconvinced. "My friend," he said, and his voice wasn't friendly, "we got all the way. You hear me? All the way." He pushed away from the wall, walked to the VCR, and rapped a knuckle against the machine. "You're thinking it isn't possible, but I'm telling you it is. I could say that what I'm about to show you will prove it, but you're intelligent enough to realize that this tape could be faked. It is not. Why should you believe that? Consider the circumstances. One, this is the White House; two, the president of the United States wants you briefed on this; and three, I'm not selling snake oil. I hold a very prestigious research chair at MIT—you can check that out."

"You're serious about this." For a split second, the key to the president's project dangled tantalizingly before his eyes, then vanished as Hiraga spoke again.

"I'm serious." Hiraga looked thoughtful. "And in all candor, I don't know whether that's to the good. The potential for great things are here, but there are great dangers, also. To tell you the truth, I feel a bit like Oppenheimer and Szilard did—wonderful science, disastrous results."

"Such as?"

Hiraga shrugged. "Forget it." He aimed the control at the VCR, then lowered it. Kogan thought he was about to say more, but then he raised the remote control again. Kogan sighed. This had been a hard morning.

"Doctor," he said, giving Hiraga his full title, trying for sweet reasonableness, "I'm a professional historian, and the idea of time travel excites me as much as working on it did you. I'd give anything to see a real live Neanderthal, or King Harold deploying his house carls at the Battle of Hastings, or tape the Sermon on the Mount, but why waste my time showing me a botched job? If the results were disastrous, why pick at it?"

"My choice of words was bad. You'll understand when I run the rest of the tape. As I said, we *can* do it." Hiraga paused to let that sink in. "But you have to forget the old stuff. No ancient history. We can go back to maybe the late thirties, but for reasons that I'll demonstrate, that's our limit. Now please." Hiraga's face became stern. "I don't want to show this damn tape any more than you want to watch it, but I have my instructions. Let's get through it, and then we'll have a chance to talk."

What the hell is going on? Kogan's brain whirled with half-answers to his nagging questions. *The president is terminally ill, a cure may have existed in the past, and let's say for the sake of argument that time travel is possible.* Okay, the answer that had eluded him was getting through. He was pretty sure he now knew what Simon Elihu Moody was planning. *Solve the world's greatest medical problem—and his own—by going back to 1942, picking up this miraculous cure and delivering it safely to 1994. Sort of like Federal Express. You betcha. Forget the probability that Messrs. Ritter and Babcock were whacko from malaria and tropical heat. Forget such small impedimenta as World War II, the Japanese, and Murphy's immutable law.*

Kogan tried to concentrate on the screen. A young dark-haired woman, her pretty face shadowed by a billed cap, wearing khaki coveralls belted around a tiny waist, was evidently being given instructions by a middle-aged man with an authoritative manner. Others stood by, listening deferentially as the older man spoke to the woman.

"The project director," Hiraga said, pointing to the screen.

The director took the woman's arm and led her toward a steel-gray capsule about five feet in diameter that resembled a diving bell. Three thick-paned glass ports gave a 360-degree view to anyone inside. The camera closed in on the gleaming white interior, which contained only a leather-covered pilot's seat and a set of headphones hanging from the bulkhead.

Interested now, Kogan leaned forward. The project director squeezed the woman's slim shoulders, smiled confidently, and helped her seat herself in the capsule and fasten her seat belt and shoulder harness. The camera took a last look at the woman's face. She was frightened, Kogan could see. Her luminous dark eyes blinked rapidly and her smile told the world she was trying hard to be brave.

"That gal doesn't look like she's having a bucket of fun," Kogan commented. "Why's she doing it?"

"Money," the scientist said tersely. "Fifty thousand for this one shot." Kogan whistled and Hiraga scowled, adding, "Fifty million wouldn't have been enough." They both turned back to watch the capsule hatch clang shut. The director knelt, looked through one of the ports, and waved, an almost childlike gesture.

Behind Kogan and Hiraga, a door opened at the rear of the projection room and a woman slipped in, her bearing regal. Had Kogan entered the White House through the East Wing lobby, he would have seen her portrait, the very latest to be hung among all the other First Ladies.

Even in the dim light, Lillian Moody glowed with a mature, classical beauty. She was perfectly groomed in every detail, her shining ash-blond hair pulled into a chignon. Yet, in spite of the perfection of her features, sadness and fatigue showed in her large gray eyes. After quietly seating herself in the rear row, she adjusted glasses that hung around her neck and watched the screen, where the camera had zoomed in on a massive dull-gray object that resembled a heavy artillery piece.

Hiraga anticipated Kogan's question. "The tachyon beam projector."

"The what?" Kogan asked.

"I'll explain later."

A bluish-orange beam of light erupted from the snout of the

projector and splashed on the capsule. When it died away, the capsule had disappeared from its tripod rest. In an orgy of delight, the project personnel clapped, laughed, and embraced round-robin style. But something Kogan had seen was out of kilter—an anomaly that flashed on and off so fast he couldn't have said what it was.

Perhaps caught up in the exhilaration, whoever was handling the camera tried to do the moment aesthetic justice by shooting upward at the brilliant summer sky. But the heavens chose exactly that time to switch gears. The upper branches of pines swayed frantically as dark thunderheads marched across the sky, blocking out the sun and plunging the enclosure into shadow. A few drops hit the ground, raising tiny puffs of dust. Then, as people ducked under cover, heavy rain drenched the place.

The scene shifted to a control booth, squat and massive, apparently the only permanent building in the complex. Three technicians sat before a remarkably simple console; the project director stood just behind them. In front of them, through a wide window splashed with the driving rain, the empty tripod rest and the tachyon beam projector could be viewed. The scientists shifted their attention to the second hand of a wall clock as it swept toward twelve.

"We planned to give her thirty minutes in the past before bringing her back." Hiraga's voice was hushed.

The second hand moved straight up. A technician placed his finger on a red firing button on the console, then glanced back at the project director, whose face showed none of its previous exhilaration. Grimly, he nodded. The technician leaned on the button. The same flash of intense blue-orange light from the projector played on the empty tripod, then faded. The structure remained empty. Obviously stunned, the control personnel looked again to the director. Kogan could read his lips as he said, "Hit it again." The projector flared again. Nothing. And again. The tripod remained empty. The director pounded a clenched fist on the console. Four more times the strange colored beam erupted in vain from the muzzle.

Hiraga stopped the VCR. "It took us a while before we figured out what happened. It was a real bitch—something we'd never anticipated." He sighed heavily.

Kogan's eyes were still focused on the blank screen. He didn't *know* why the capsule had not reappeared, but inexplicably, he had a strong hunch. "I've got a feeling," he said slowly, "that the boss man broke out a whole lot of shovels."

"What did you say?" Surprise vied with respect in Hiraga's eyes. "Jesus, you're quick, Colonel. You must have picked up the movement of that tripod as it shifted upward. That's really amazing. We had to rerun this very video twice before we caught it." He shifted in his chair and pointed the remote at the VCR. "I don't like showing the rest of this, but it's important that you understand completely."

Night had fallen. Portable spotlights ringed the enclosure around the tripod as men in rain gear dismantled the structure. A trench digger lurched into position, lowered its steel claw, and scooped up mud. A cut eighteen inches deep had begun to stretch across the site, when the digger suddenly stopped and men dropped to their knees to dig with their hands. The camera moved in closer. Through the mud, wet gray metal gleamed dully. A crane arm lowered its hook, engaged a lifting eye, and the cable went taut. Slowly the capsule broke through the damp loam, big clumps of dirt falling from its sides. The project director shouldered his way to the capsule, his face agonized. While hands steadied the suspended ball, he grasped a handle and, with some difficulty, wrenched open the hatch. The eerie glare of a spotlight revealed the body of the woman, still strapped to the seat, her once pretty face ugly, etched with an expression of agony and fear.

Behind Hiraga and Kogan, still unseen, Lillian Moody shielded her eyes with her hand.

"Damn," Kogan growled. "What a screw-up." It was pretty plain that the capsule had rematerialized ten to fifteen feet below its original position. He winced inwardly as he imagined the woman in the sudden dark—the blackness of a tomb—and the terror gripping her as the air became thicker, suffocating, and she realized she was going to die horribly.

"You guys *did* send animals back, didn't you?" Kogan didn't try very hard to keep the sarcasm out of his voice.

"Yes, of course." Hiraga sounded lifeless, as though he wouldn't even try to defend the indefensible. "And got them all back. Of course we ran more experiments—dozens—after this happened." He gestured toward the screen. "And quickly, I might add, because we suspected they were going to close us down. We discovered an unpredictable, unmeasurable variable in the vertical dimension. We could go along with four, five, or more transferences and the rematerialization would be perfect, then a rabbit or a rat would come back under- or aboveground. We sent a cat back ten years, its capsule came hurtling out of the sky and crashed into the compound. Wonder no one was killed."

"But you got closed down?"

"Yes. President Carter himself made the decision." Hiraga ejected the cassette from the VCR and tossed it into a briefcase. "I think he was right."

"Is President Moody thinking of opening it up again?"

Hiraga looked at Kogan sharply. "I'm not at liberty to say."

"How much more experimentation would you need to travel back in time for, say, fifty years?"

A phone rang. Hiraga answered it. "Yes?" He listened. "Not quite through. What's the problem? . . . Well, yes, if it's that serious, I'll be right there." He hung up and turned a worried face to Kogan. "I have to leave."

"Got time to answer my question?"

Hiraga nodded. "As I told you, we might be able to get back maybe fifty, sixty years, without any further testing. All that's required is to have the subjects in an aircraft thousands of feet in the air."

"What about this—what did you call it—projector?"

"Tachyon beam. No problem." Hiraga picked up his briefcase and moved to the door. "Sorry, I've got to run." He closed the door behind him, then stuck his head back in. "You know how to get to Passmore's office?"

Kogan nodded and slouched back in his seat, trying to separate substance from illusion. Hiraga hadn't explained how time travel worked, but it probably would have been only high-tech gibberish to him. Not that it mattered. If he was right in his assumption that President Moody was trying to get back to pick up this B-juice, and wanted Kogan along as sort of a tour guide—uh-uh. Noble it might be, but it wasn't for him. He'd volunteered for Vietnam. He didn't need to go back and catch up on wars he'd missed.

"Colonel Kogan." A soft voice from behind him spoke. He whirled around, then jumped to his feet as he recognized the woman walking gracefully toward him.

"Mrs. Moody!"

The First Lady's smile was somehow both radiant and sad. She extended her hand and Kogan took it, conscious of its slimness and fragility. "It's been a difficult morning for you, hasn't it?" She spoke the simple words with such sympathy that he caught himself feeling sorry for poor, abused Joe Kogan.

He had seen Lillian Moody a hundred times in magazines, newspapers, and on TV, but to be close enough to sniff her delicate fragrance and look into those remarkable eyes helped him understand why interviewers described her as "mesmerizing." She was undoubtedly the loveliest First Lady since Jacqueline Kennedy; many gave Lillian the edge in that department. In bearing and dignity, she was supposed to have matched Grace Coolidge, while her intelligence and humanity were compared to Eleanor Roosevelt's. Despite what a biographer called her "natural aristocracy," Lillian's life had begun in the valleys of Rockingham County, Virginia. This moved the president's political advisers to crow about the virtues of Jacksonian Democracy, and how only in America could a woman, by her own talents, rise so far above her humble origins. What those talents had been were of course the subject of considerable speculation, since her vita listed only the somewhat euphemistic job title "model" before her twenty-fourth year when she surfaced in Roanoke as an anchorwoman on station WDBJ. However, the most diligent investigative reporting had been unable to find any lurid secrets. Since becoming First Lady, her popularity had skyrocketed. It would take one brave son of a bitch, Kogan thought, to suggest, even if true, that Lillian Moody had perhaps jumped into every important bed between the Blue Ridge and the Tidewater.

He looked at the forty-one-year-old First Lady with her beautiful face and firm body, and in spite of the tough morning and a certain stubborn loyalty to Fay Donello, wondered how this magnificent woman would be in bed.

"You've figured this thing out, haven't you?" Lillian asked.

"I think so," he answered.

"Let me spell it out for you," she said. "Simon is sending an expedition—code-named Operation SUCCOR—back to 1942 to find Dr. Babcock and bring back the cure." Her tone was flat, undramatic. She could have been ordering groceries. Neither looked at the other. The words hung in the air, gathering force and challenging Kogan to react. He sat quietly, controlling his emotions, denying her the advantage of surprise. What the president wanted, she wanted, and right now Kogan felt like the last tortilla in Mazatlán. He had to keep his head, and it wasn't going to be easy.

"You heard me?"

He nodded. "Yes."

"What are you thinking?" He looked at her standing before him, feet primly together, her hands clasped in front of her, only the whitened knuckles betraying her inner turmoil.

He shrugged. "I wish him all the luck in the world."

"That's not what you're thinking." Her voice became a fierce whisper. "Forget your manners, Joseph Kogan. Tell me."

It was not good manners that kept him from speaking his mind. He simply did not want to get deeper into this thing. That, and a reluctance to shoot down something which was so important to this lovely woman. Whichever, she had asked—no, demanded—an honest answer.

"All right, Mrs. Moody," he said. "I don't think it's going to work. There's nothing back there."

He watched her closely. And just as the president had shown no emotion, neither did she. He wasn't getting through. She even smiled, a slight, knowing upturn at the corners of her full lips.

He groaned. "Ma'am, listen. One old letter—that's all they've got. Nothing else. You want to risk lives on that?"

Her expression didn't change, and he could see that her convictions were as rock-hard as her husband's. Well, he'd done all he could. Time to get the hell out of there. But depart on a friendly note.

"So, Mrs. Moody, if you'll excuse me, I've got a lot of note-taking to catch up on. I'd appreciate it if you'd pass on my good-byes and best wishes to the president." He started for the door saying, "Ma'am, it's been a pleasure meeting you. I mean that."

"Wait!" Her eyes and body implored him to stay. He stopped. "Please," she continued, "don't make a judgment yet. It's so terribly important, not only to Simon, but to the world. We have this one chance of ridding ourselves of this filthy thing, this horrible disease. Colonel, just moments before I came in here, Simon described to me how skilled you are, how familiar you are with the Philippines of 1942. That's the kind of knowledge the expedition needs and doesn't have." She took another step toward him. "Don't, I beg you, turn your back on us. There *is* a cure back there. Just listen, please."

Kogan leaned against the door and folded his arms. All right, he'd listen, disguising his apprehension, and then he'd have to batter down her fool's tale with logic. He knew how it would end—with her lovely face crumpled and tearstained because he had placed the final nail in her husband's coffin. He, feeling like the ultimate asshole for having done it. But if that's what it took to get the hell away from this madhouse, so be it.

"Okay, Mrs. Moody, I'm listening."

She started to tremble. One arm went to a table to steady herself. Kogan jumped forward and helped her into a seat. He poured a glass of water from a decanter. She drank gratefully and handed the glass back.

"Are you all right?"

"Yes. It's just that, well . . . we've been under such a strain these last weeks." She breathed deeply, then smiled. "I'm sorry for being so . . . nineteenth century. I'm fine now." She dabbed at her lips with a lace handkerchief. Whether the performance was genuine or not, Kogan admired the deftness with which she had gotten him to come back into the room, to want to help her, to sympathize with her and her husband.

Her pale face was composed, but she wet her lips and swallowed nervously. Before she could speak, the door behind her opened and Passmore stood there. His face was a stoic lump, but Kogan thought he saw trouble in his eyes. He nodded to the First Lady.

"Mrs. Moody, the president wants to see you."

"Is something wrong?" Lillian asked, looking at the agent closely. Passmore nodded, tight-lipped. The First Lady drew in her breath sharply. "Operation SUCCOR?"

"Yes, ma'am."

The agent opened the door and Lillian Moody stepped through, then turned back. "What about Colonel Kogan?" she asked Passmore.

"We won't be needing the colonel any longer." There were deep furrows on Passmore's brow as he turned to Kogan. "Sir, a car will be waiting at the east entrance to take you anywhere you want to go." He extended his hand. "Thank you for coming. We all appreciate it. Forget what you've heard. Matter of fact, just pretend you were never here, okay?"

═ CHAPTER THREE ═

Kogan got in the sedan and looked at the back of the driver's neck. About an eighteen and a half, he estimated, with shoulders that filled half the front seat.

"You a White House driver?"

The big man gave a reluctant grunt, a shake of the head, and held up a black leather case holding a Secret Service badge. "Where to, Colonel?"

"Federal Records Center, Suitland...no, wait." The day was more than half gone. Besides, scrabbling around in dusty letter boxes had lost its attraction. It wasn't every day an average guy like Joe Kogan got a chance to schmooze around with the president and the First Lady, or get privy to a couple of real deep secrets. Secrets that if they got out would make every newspaper in the country read like the *National Enquirer.*

He felt sort of bad about his talk with Mrs. Moody. She was the sort of woman that made men really want to help her—a perfect damsel in distress, beautiful and vulnerable, but still able to push all the right buttons. Even though he'd passed up a chance to play hero—and the temptation was great—he guessed he'd done the right thing.

"Oh, hell, take me home." He gave the driver the address and leaned back as the car exited through one of the east gates and headed south on Fifteenth Street. The air-conditioning worked perfectly, but the sun beat in through the windows and Kogan moved into the shade on the other side of the car. He was thirsty and his shirt felt clammy.

He leaned forward and tapped one beefy shoulder. "Violate any laws if we pick up a twelve-pack of beer along the way?"

The agent shook his head. Talkative devil.

Lillian Moody, a half stride in front of Passmore, hurried down the hall toward the secluded study. In spite of her haste, she forced herself to slow down. It wouldn't look good if any of the staff saw her running through the White House with fear in her face. She threw her shoulders back and placed each foot precisely before the other as she had been trained in modeling school. That was before landing the TV news job in Roanoke almost twenty years ago. God, those were carefree days. Her aspirations at the time were a jump in salary to $25,000 a year and marriage to an account executive she was dating.

It all changed when she had to do an interview with a stocky, graying-blond congressman from Maryland, whose blue eyes flashed like beacons when he saw her. Simon *Mooney*, she had called him. Later, he had laughed at her gaffe. "You are going to know my name very, very well," he said. "I promise you." He was right. The account executive faded ungraciously away and the job and money didn't seem to matter. In six months they were married.

"Mrs. Moody," Passmore interrupted her thoughts. "Here we are."

In her preoccupation, she had walked by the Treaty Room. He held the door for her as she retraced her steps and entered the room that had been adapted to planning for Operation SUCCOR. The president's chair had been pushed around so that he sat at the head of the big walnut table covered with writing materials and detailed maps of the Philippines. The chief of staff stood to one side, gazing out one of the windows. Leaning over the table, the secretary of state studied a map. The president's oncologist, Dr. Sidney Eccles, a thin, sixtyish man in a well-tailored suit, sat near the end of the table, making notes with a gold pen.

The president barely glanced up as the First Lady entered, then went back to aimless doodling. To Lillian's eye, the change in her husband since she had last seen him was shocking. The despair in his face was that of a drowning man who had seen a lifeboat suddenly turn away. Dr. Eccles lifted his head from his notes, saw Lillian, and started to rise.

"Please don't get up, Doctor," she said, waving him down, then looked at the president sharply. "Simon, dear, what's wrong?" Moody shook his head, less a negative than a motion of hopelessness.

Martin Rodale started to seat himself in the chair to Moody's right, then caught himself and held it for the First Lady. "Please sit down, everybody." His voice was grave as he looked at Moody.

"I have an announcement to make," the president said, his hand reaching out for Lillian's. "General Armitage is dead."

Lillian cried out. The others—except for Passmore—muttered in shocked tones. Before the questions could come, the president continued. "According to the information Bill has gotten from the army," he nodded toward Passmore, "it appears that Armitage committed suicide. Why, I don't know."

The president tried to clear his throat and failed, coughing heavily. His hands shook as he sipped from a glass of water. He continued. "Everything seemed quite simple when we began planning ten weeks ago. I remember talking to General Armitage at the time he agreed to take command. I remember his confidence then and how his wonderful 'can-do' attitude buoyed my own spirits. As time went on, though, I watched him change. I sensed a frustration in him, and not long ago I asked him what was wrong. The general was quite forthcoming. He told me he hadn't realized how difficult it would be to learn how to cope in a whole new world—one with different rules, mores, machines, and enemies.''

Moody stopped and sipped more water. "But the general's overriding concern was a problem he wasn't able to solve—getting Babcock and his formula off Corregidor. As I understand it, there were no airfields there that could handle the jet we're sending back. The plane would have to land somewhere else. That left the problem of getting to Dr. Babcock unsolved.''

Dr. Eccles's gold pen made a sharp noise as it struck the table. "Incredible. Surely the general *must* have had a plan,'' Eccles said. "SUCCOR *must* leave soon. It's imperative!''

"Yes it is, Doctor,'' Moody said grimly. "You and I know why, don't we?'' He glanced around the room. "But as far as I know, Armitage was stumped.''

"How about it, Otis?'' Rodale asked Hiraga. "Did the general ever crack that problem?''

"The general had not taken me into his confidence.'' The physicist snapped off his words.

"Jesus,'' Rodale said disgustedly. He turned to Moody. "Mr. President, you think he might have taken his life over this?''

"No.'' The president spoke positively. "He wouldn't have chosen that way out. He would have come to me and admitted failure. Armitage was tough and loyal and he was doing the very best he could.'' He looked around the table. "I tried hard not to pressure him too much, but time was running short, as you all know.''

Lillian's head came up sharply at the past tense in the last sentence. Time *was* running short, not time *is* running short? Surely Simon couldn't mean—

"Beyond the personal loss that I feel," Moody said, "his death means—this comes hard, my friends—that we must close down SUCCOR."

Oh, God, he couldn't. "Simon," Lillian wailed, "this is wrong. You can't stop now." Her husband, her love, was giving up their only hope, surrendering. Shock and anger mixed with her grief. She looked for the man she had married and he was gone. Simon had been so vital, so strong, so capable of carrying through with any task, no matter how demanding. Before she could guard against it, bitterness swept over her at this shrunken shell of a stranger who refused to fight on. The perfidy of her thoughts made her catch her breath.

"Darling," she said, her voice tender and under control, "we must go on. You know how important it is."

"How?" The president spread his hands helplessly. "What are the alternatives? Besides, I've found that when something starts to go bad, it's usually...irredeemable. For me, the general's death was the end. I see no point in continuing."

"No! You can't quit." Lillian's eyes flashed as her voice filled the room with her anger and anguish.

"Lillian, please." The president chided her gently. "Let's not flog a dead horse. I guess that maybe it just wasn't meant to be." He leaned toward her, one hand outstretched in a gesture of conciliation.

"No!" She jumped back from his touch as though it might soften her resolve. "I won't accept that. We *won't* give up." Her small fist banged the table. "Now, damnit, listen to me, all of you. We've got a problem and we've got to lick it." Her eyes, desperate, swept around the room. "Marty, you're a corporate lawyer, a problem solver. People paid you millions to get them out of trouble." She turned to Quentin Talbott. "Mr. Secretary, can't you come up with something, anything, that will keep our hopes alive? Come on, everybody, for chrissakes, think!"

No one spoke. Rodale rubbed his long jaw and avoided Lillian's eyes. Talbott lived up to his nickname of "Quiet Quent," but even his rocklike taciturnity seemed in danger of shattering. Finally, his reedy voice broke the quiet.

"Mr. President," he said, then nodded in a courtly fashion to Lillian, "I have no solution to the technical problems this . . . effort you have mounted faces. But you and I have been friends for a long time. I cannot tell you how much I pray for you to get well. Beyond that, I have to think of the great effort we are mounting that may eventually lead to the elimination of all nuclear weapons in the world. You and I have worked toward this goal for years—long before you became president. The first step is DOE. As your secretary of state, I have to emphasize the importance of your leadership at Brussels next month. Unless our allies can be assured of American support for denuclearization in Europe, the entire effort may collapse."

"I know that," the president said tiredly. "Quent, I've factored everything—I mean everything—into my decision. I just don't see how . . ." His voice faded.

Dr. Eccles stirred himself and cleared his throat. "Sir," he said to Moody, "I must insist that you get some rest now."

Moody nodded assent, but one hand signaled for patience. "Quent," he said to Talbott, "I'm afraid our group will be going under the leadership of the vice-president—who may just be president in October."

"Then I," Talbott's voice rose slightly, "will not be there, either. Simon, you and I know what Pyle's position is. The conference will be thrown into a turmoil. God knows what will happen."

Lillian covered one of Simon's hands with her own. "Dear, you *must* fight on. We must let the flight go."

The chief of staff's heavy voice broke in.

"Sir," Rodale said, "maybe we should explore this more. The pilot, Jake Longford, is an air force colonel and nominally second in command. Why not let him take over?"

"No." Moody's voice was positive. "Longford's a good man, but he knows nothing about the Philippines, and very little about

World War II. There isn't even a plan for him to get a handle on."

"Then, what about this guy Kogan?" Rodale continued. "Maybe he could come up with something."

"Yes, Simon, oh, yes!" Lillian grasped the president's hand in both of hers. "Talk to him, make him see the light."

The image of Kogan as the two of them stood close together in the projection room invaded her mind. Strong and potent, as she wished Simon again to be. Not attractive—at least, not at first glance—but when she had nearly fainted, his big hands on her arms had sent alternate chills and warmth through her. Suddenly she hated her body for distracting her mind from what was important. Kogan had thought the project stupid, but he didn't know the whole story—maybe he could be convinced. Surely, if the president of the United States asked it, he could hardly refuse.

She shook her husband's arm gently, trying to prod him into action, but the lines of his face had gone slack and his eyes stared, empty blue shells. It was almost as though he had lost consciousness. For long seconds, the study was absolutely quiet. With visible effort, the president roused himself. He looked at Dr. Eccles.

"How much time have I got?"

Eccles seemed startled at the abruptness of the question. Pulling himself together, he spoke slowly and deliberately. "Hard to say, sir. You see . . ."

Moody's thin hand slapped the table. "Damnit, Eccles, don't waffle! I want an answer!"

Eccles took a deep breath. "Mr. President, if I knew, I would tell you. These things are simply not subject to accurate forecasting." He made a few vertical lines on a pad in front of him. "I can say only this: you will not be able to go to Brussels next month. I'm sorry."

Moody glanced around the room. "There you have it. The time element. I don't have that long to live. Colonel Kogan has already refused to go. Even if we could change his mind, we'd have to say to him, 'Oh, by the way, we don't yet have a plan.' " He seemed to lose his train of thought. With a confused look, he turned to Hiraga. "Otis, what else has to be done?"

"A few modifications to the plane. CINCPAC at Pearl Harbor will give us a hand with them."

Rodale jotted figures on a pad. "How long at Pearl Harbor?"

"I don't know," Hiraga answered. "General Armitage knew. Maybe Jake Longford."

Rodale spoke in a low rumble. "Then the stop at Guam, the rendezvous with the carrier group, going back and finding Dr. Babcock, getting him off Corregidor..." His voice faded.

Moody shook his head. "Heaven help us. I guess that maybe it was an insane idea to begin with."

Lillian knelt beside his chair. "Oh, Simon, there's still time left. You're tired. Don't make the decision now. Sleep on it. You'll be rested tomorrow."

"Rested?" A hollow chuckle came from the thin chest. "Maybe. But I'll still be dying. I'm sorry, my dear." He looked up at Talbott. "It's over, Quent. I'm sorry. It just isn't in the cards." He got laboriously to his feet and started out of the room, Dr. Eccles following. Lillian watched her husband go. Rodale stepped close and put a hand on her shoulder.

Passmore moved quickly to open the door for the president, but Moody stopped and looked back at Rodale. "Oh, yes, make an appointment for the vice president to see me."

Kogan glanced at his wristwatch. It was five twenty. He slumped back in his old Eames chair and sipped his beer moodily. He'd showered after getting back to the apartment, put on a T-shirt and shorts, flipped open his laptop, and started to work on his notes. But the day's events banged away relentlessly inside his skull. Here he was, three hours later, still staring at the blinking cursor.

He tried hard to take Passmore's advice and forget he'd ever seen the dying president or heard of Operation SUCCOR. Crazy stuff. Hard to believe that people in the White House could go for a plan where the objective was so dim and the chances of failure so high. He'd been in dozens of situations in the army where the odds were real good, but the operation had still turned sour. He wouldn't bet a nickel on this madness. Well, it was apparently over. Something had gone wrong; Passmore's face had revealed that.

Anyway, if Moody's appearance was any indication, it wouldn't be too much longer before the nation would have a new president—Spencer Pyle. It had sort of a nice rhythm to it, but he wasn't sure the man was what the country needed. He was mega-rich, with lots of smarts—he'd torn the opposition apart in the vice-presidential debates—but he came on kind of sour, a guy without a helluva lot of integrity. Moody, he had trusted until today; seemed like the country had gotten a very up-front president for a change, but this was one big whopper he was laying on the people. What had happened to plain old honesty? Where the hell had all the Washingtons and Adamses and Jeffersons gone?

The doorbell rang. He jumped, then sat motionless, angry at the jarring insistence of the sound. He was in no mood for company. There was more ringing, then a hollow knocking that said *I know you're in there.* He cursed whoever it was, and went to the door.

Fay Donello thrust a paper bag into his arms, then segued lightly into the apartment, outflanking him. A whiff of Szechuan struck his nostrils.

"Close the door," she commanded. "It's hot outside. And while you're at it, close your mouth. I know it's not one of our nights, but I thought you might appreciate a little spontaneity." She looked up at him, suddenly intimidated by his silence. Her bravado vanished. "I'm sorry. It is all right, isn't it? My being here, I mean."

"Sure, I like surprises," he lied. It struck him that he didn't want her around, not now. Even as he carried the bag of food into the kitchen, the thought of her warm, willing body in his arms was an intrusion rather than a pleasure. Maybe if he had the rest of the night to drink and think, he could wipe the day out of his mind. Right now, he sure didn't want to have to make a lot of talk.

Fay looked for more assurance. "I'll leave if you want."

"No, of course not." It was hard to say that and harder still not to make an excuse for her to leave, though right now he couldn't think of one.

Fay turned quickly at his flat tone, her eyes seeking his. "You're really not glad to see me, are you?" She didn't wait for him to reply. "I'm sorry. Oh, damnit, why do I keep saying that? But when you didn't come in today, I thought something might be wrong."

He ignored the implied question and planted a kiss on her moist forehead, then he looked in the bag. "Ah, my keen nose never fails—Chinese."

She opened the refrigerator and passed out two cans of beer. He flipped them open and they both drank, awkwardly avoiding eye contact. Neither seemed able to get comfortable. He set the food on the table and made a ritual of folding the bag and stowing it under the sink. Fay toyed with the cartons, then faced him, and he saw for the first time the strain in her face. It was more than a lover's upset—something very close to an uncomprehending fear.

"Joe, something's wrong." Her voice was hoarse with tension. "We're not the same people we were this morning." She shook her head. "No, that's not right. *You're* different."

He made another attempt at lightness. "Man of a thousand faces." He chuckled lamely. "Hey, come on. It's been a tough day, that's all. A little fried rice and some sweet and sour and I'll perk up."

"You haven't said where you were today."

Her words brought him close to open anger. What made her think he had to account to her? Then he repressed his annoyance. *Come on, Kogan—for chrissakes, lighten up. So you got to talk to the man in the White House. You're still nothing but an over-the-hill army retiree with a cash flow problem. Fay Donello is a good gal. Give her a break.*

He set his beer down and got plates out. "Want to bring the forks and napkins? It's cozy in front of the air conditioner."

She moved forward quickly, placing her hand on his arm. "I'm sorry, I don't mean to pry. I'm not jealous, for God's sake—really, I'm not. Forgive me, will you?" Her eyes pleaded with him. He nodded and walked into the other room. He wasn't angry—even his irritation had disappeared—he was just startled. She couldn't know of *his* weird day, so why was she frightened?

"Come on," he said, "let's eat."

He heard Fay putting things away in the kitchen. He picked up the remains of a fortune cookie and nibbled while trying to read the message, but the light was too dim. Maybe it said "Go west, old soldier." Good advice. He should pack his bags and point his old car toward California. He might even have enough research stashed away on his Toshiba's sixty-five megabyte hard disk to finish his dissertation.

He sensed Fay standing in the doorway watching him. She spoke in a small voice. "Can we talk?"

He patted the seat beside him. She sat and reached for the other cookie. "What did yours say?"

"These are the times that try men's souls."

She tossed hers down untasted. "And women's." A pall of unease settled over them again, but this time it was worse. "You don't want me to stay, do you?" Her hair shadowed her face. She didn't look at him.

He reached out to touch her shoulder, but dropped his hand. She moved uneasily, seeming to sense his indecision.

"Okay, I'll go, but first tell me something. You don't have to, but I wish you would."

He made an impatient gesture, wanting to deflect what he sensed was coming. "Don't ask me about today. I can't tell you."

She turned and he could see her face, chalk white, the large, uptilted brown eyes filled with unshed tears and a nameless fear. Her voice was nearly a whisper. "Your not being at the Archives wasn't why I came here. There's another reason."

"Yeah? What?"

"First I want to ask you something."

"Listen, I've told you." The irritation came back. His voice was insistent, biting. "Drop it. Today's off-limits."

Fay shook her head. "Okay, okay. It's not that. It's a very simple question." She laughed unconvincingly. "I feel so stupid asking, but tell me, your father served in the army in World War II, didn't he?"

"Boy, now that's changing the subject." Puzzled, he nodded. "Yeah, for a couple of years. Why?"

The lines of her face relaxed. Sighing with relief, she reached out and took his hand in both of hers. "I knew that must be it. And I'll bet he served in the Philippines. I suppose that's why you're doing your dissertation on it."

This talk was becoming tough for Kogan. Fay's sudden swings of emotion and her conversational flip-flops weren't making the evening much better than the nightmare day. He wished very much for her to leave.

"Sorry," he said, "but you got the wrong scenario for Dad. He didn't get to the Pacific. He was wounded at Bastogne and discharged in 1945."

She looked as if he'd slapped her. "You're sure?"

His snort was disbelieving. "We're talking about my father, for chrissakes, not some third cousin."

Her lips trembled and all the light went out of her eyes, replaced by the dread he had seen there before. He reached out and cupped her chin gently. "Fay, come on, what is it?"

"I don't know, I really don't." Her voice was a whisper. "But I'm frightened, Joe—scared out of my mind."

Again he felt shock. If Fay wasn't psychic, then she must have heard something. Ah-ha, he had it now—he should have guessed. "Mike told you about the little visit I had this morning—about the Feds, right?"

Her brow knit in puzzlement. "Feds? No, Mike said nothing." She pounded her knee in exasperation. "Damnit, can't we say one straight thing to each other? We talk like two people who just met on a bus. Federal agents? What did they want?"

"Forget it. It wasn't important."

She looked at him blankly. He could see that she didn't believe him. "All right," she said, "you're calling the shots tonight." She pulled at a gold chain around her neck and a locket emerged from the front of her dress—a piece of jewelry Kogan had not seen her wear before. "I'm going to show you something." Opening the locket, she leaned forward. Kogan held it up to the light, then smiled when he saw his own likeness.

"Dear me," he said. "I didn't know you cared." As he released the locket, his smile vanished. "Hey, I don't remember you taking a photo of me." Fay watched intently as he frowned and reached for the locket again. Even though the photo was in black and white and a bit grainy, it was clearly of him. He was in a uniform—one that was familiar to him, though he knew he'd never worn it. "Hmmm..." He was genuinely puzzled. "What is this?"

"You don't know?" Her eyes were wide with apprehension. He shook his head. "Oh, God, Joe, don't say that—it terrifies me." She laid her face alongside his and he could feel the dampness of her tears.

He gripped her shoulders and gazed into her eyes, astounded. "But why? Because of this?" He managed a grin. "Sure, I take a bad picture, but crying won't help." In spite of himself, this thing was making him nervous. It was like he'd had amnesia. He really didn't remember that photo ever being taken, and who, for God's sake, still took black-and-white snapshots?

Fay wiped her eyes, breathed deeply several times, and tried to speak calmly. "You know what I think?" she asked. "I think you should pack up and get back to California, right now. Do your dissertation next year." She tried to smile, but her eyes still sparkled with tears. "Better yet, do it on another subject."

Kogan would have laughed, had not her words been so close to his thoughts. It was eerie. She could not have known what had gone on today in the family quarters of the White House, and her fears seemed to be connected to this strange picture. "Look, honey." He forced a calmness he didn't feel and pointed to the locket. "Tell me, what gives with this thing?"

She shook her head. "I just *can't* tell you. I'm not sure why, but I don't think I should."

Fay drove through the night, blinking back the tears. The traffic on the Whitney Young bridge was light, for which she was grateful, because emotionally she was in no condition to drive. That damned, miserable photo frightened her so. Why hadn't she told him where she had gotten it? Why hadn't she shown him the original picture? Was it because she didn't want to know the answer—or because she was afraid to find there wasn't one?

She hadn't even shown it to Mike Witkowski—well, not the entire picture.

About midmorning, Mike had called her in. "Fay," he had said, "the boss man wants us to get all the MacArthur files in tip-top condition. Top priority. There seems to be continuing White House interest. That includes photos."

She'd started with those. It was interesting at first, looking at the stern young faces of the fighting men on Luzon and Mindanao confronted with impossible odds and a dubious future, but later it became depressing. Most of these fresh-faced youths had died either in the fighting or in Japanese prison camps. The survivors who might still be alive would be old—in their seventies and eighties.

A little after three, tired and bored, she'd opened a dusty box labeled AG 411.23—PHILIPPINES CAMPAIGN—PHOTOS and started segregating. She was about half finished when she pulled out an undistinguished picture of a group of women dressed in khaki, standing three-deep on the steps of what appeared to be a veranda. They were young, in their twenties and thirties, but what set the photo apart from the other grim portrayals were the women's happy smiles.

Fay turned the picture over. On the reverse was a caption: GROUP OF ARMY NURSES—MINDANAO, 1942. She looked at the picture again, idly wondering why, in the middle of the Japanese conquest of the islands, there existed this one group of cheerful women.

Then, behind the nurses, she saw a man, apparently in the act of turning away from the camera. He was hatless, in an officer's uniform. It was not just any man—it was Joe Kogan. Not someone who looked like him, but *him*. She dropped the photo as if it were hot. She picked it up, forced herself to look at it again, then turned it facedown. For long moments she stared sightlessly at the Civil Defense emergency directions stenciled beside the door. She got up and circled the room, with its dirty cream walls and gray-green furniture, welcoming the familiar surroundings, postponing going back to the skin-prickling thing on the table. Finally she flopped down, gingerly turned the picture over, adjusted the light, and minutely examined the man on the veranda.

She pulled a magnifier over. He hadn't changed. She wasn't wrong. There could be no mistaking the way his head sat on his large shoulders, or the strong features in three-quarters profile. Wait...wait. On which side of his face was that dime-sized mole—the one above his eyebrow he called his bullet hole? His right eyebrow! She looked at the photo. The man had turned to his left. She grabbed the magnifying lens and focused. Faintly, but indelibly, there it was—a tiny mark above his eye. The blood drained from Fay's head and she knew she was close to fainting. With every ounce of will she forced herself to be calm. There had to be a logical answer. She flipped the picture over and reread the caption. The date "1942" jumped out at her. Of course, that was the mistake. This had to be a photo from Vietnam, captioned incorrectly and filed in the wrong place. Relief flooded through her. These things happen. But wait—again she peered closely at the image—Joe looked exactly as he had when she had kissed him good-bye this morning. How old would he have been in Vietnam—in his early twenties? Suddenly she doubted her own senses. Someone else should see this.

Fay pulled a sheet of heavy bond from her desk and placed it over the photo. With scissors, she cut away just enough paper so that Joe's likeness was exposed. The nurses remained concealed. Then she headed for Witkowski's office.

Mike was just hanging up the phone. Holding the paper carefully in place, she laid the picture in front of him. "Did you ever see this?"

Mike barely glanced at it. "What the hell are we doing with a photo of Kogan?" With a sharp intake of breath, she snatched the picture away and ran out of the office. Behind her, Mike shouted for an explanation.

Back at her desk, she decided that no matter how crazy it seemed, there had to be an answer. A soldier in a fifty-year-old photo who looked that much like Joe Kogan had to be his twin. No, of course not, she wasn't even thinking straight. His father, then. That must be it. Oh, God, it had to be. Maybe that small mark in the photo wasn't really a mole after all. She started down the hall to Reproduction, but a glance at the wall clock told her she was too late. But she had to get this awful thing cleared up. Returning to her office, she closed the door, again took out her scissors, and committed a federal crime.

CHAPTER FOUR

Kogan watched from his front door stoop as Fay's car pulled into the street and disappeared in the early autumn mist. A light rain had drifted in, cooling the air. He raised his face to the dark sky and breathed deeply, welcoming the change in the weather. Maybe his luck would improve, too, but a tightness around his midriff warned him not to count on it. The Chinese he'd eaten had upset his stomach. He belched and wondered if the Alka-Seltzer bottle was empty. Another day like today, and he'd be buying it by the case.

He turned to go in, but stopped as he saw a movement among the trees. A burly figure stood near the curb, trying to move back into the shadows. Kogan yawned elaborately and stretched, slammed the door behind him, flicked off the living room lights, and hurried to the bedroom. He turned on his bed lamp, closed the blinds, then quickly returned to the front of the darkened apartment. Through the window he could see the man, now leaning against a tree to the left of the building. A moment later he spotted another man across the street by a parked car. He didn't bother to look further. The Secret Service was still with him, maybe checking to see that he didn't make a visit to the editorial offices of the *Washington Post*. To hell with it—he needed another shower and some sleep.

As he was toweling off, he heard the doorbell ring again. *Come on, Fay, give me a break.* Throwing on a robe, he went to the door.

The rain was coming down harder and he could hear the soft patter as drops fell on the rain hood hiding the woman's face. He knew it wasn't Fay—or rather, he sensed it.

"I'm sorry to bother you."

Jesus Christ! The softly accented voice was Lillian Moody's. Instinctively pulling his robe closer around his body, Kogan looked over her shoulder. No one was in sight.

"May I come in?"

He stepped back from the door and gestured dumbly. As she moved past him, he caught the scent of her perfume, mixed with the fresh smell of rain. Kogan closed the door quickly and locked it. Lillian had moved out of the cramped hall and stood in the darkened living room. He hurried past her, checking to see that the blinds were drawn before turning on a floor lamp. Conscious of his hairy legs and bare feet, he wished to God his robe was longer.

The First Lady threw her hood back, and in the dim light her face was chalklike, her eyes strained and darkly underlined. She glanced briefly around the small room, taking in the worn carpet, the bargain prints on the walls, the books and papers scattered on the cheap, Herculon-covered furniture.

"I wasn't expecting . . . uh, any company," he managed to get out.

"You mean *more* company." She managed a wan smile.

"Excuse me, Mrs. Moody. I'll just throw on some clothes." He started toward the bedroom.

She shook her head. "No, wait, don't bother. I really haven't the time. May I sit down?"

"Oh ... sure." He leaped forward and gathered up books from the couch, dumping them on the floor. Lillian opened her raincoat. It surprised him to see that she wore the same dress she had this morning. Somehow he figured First Ladies changed outfits hourly. She sat down, leaning forward, and he could see around her tired eyes the shadow of defeat. He could only guess at what had brought her to the crappy apartment of a virtual stranger, and if his hunch was correct, he wasn't looking forward to it.

Kogan pulled a chair away from the dinette set and seated himself, keeping his legs together while trying to pull down the short bathrobe, realizing that his movements must look effeminate.

"Can I get you something?" He asked because he couldn't think of anything else to say.

She shook her head absently. "Simon is calling the project off."

He said nothing. Passmore had already said nearly as much, so her words came as no surprise.

"Do you want to know why?"

He shrugged. "It's none of my business." Of course it had been, earlier today, and he'd fought to get the thing off his shoulders. Technical adviser to this damned crazy plan. Ha!

Lillian looked at him. "It *is* your business," she said calmly. "It's the whole world's business. And my dying husband has had to bear the entire burden. I'm going to tell you what happened. I want you to understand everything." She coughed slightly. "I'm sorry. My throat is suddenly dry. Could I have a white wine— or a Coke?"

He was in the kitchen before he remembered. He stuck his head around the door. "No wine or Coke, I'm afraid. Would you like a beer?" She nodded. He found a glass and polished it on the dish towel before pouring. He brought the glass in and handed it to her, along with a paper napkin.

He spoke as she sipped the cold liquid. "Why do you want me to understand? If it's over, it's over."

One slim hand gestured impatiently at his words. "Just listen," she said, her tone edged.

Then she told him what had happened after he had left. It took about ten minutes for her to finish. Something about the operational commander dying; she didn't say who he was or explain how he had died. Her voice seemed about to break when she described the president's reaction to the man's death, but other than that, she didn't let her fatigue or emotions affect her recital. It was as though she had rehearsed every syllable. Kogan was impressed—and fascinated.

Lillian Moody glanced down at her hands as she stopped speaking. At that moment, with fatigue dragging at her features, she looked older, yet her bereft expression made her seem somehow childlike, bewildered, and hurt.

"So it *is* over," he said.

She raised her eyes, and there was a resolve there that surprised him. "Maybe," she said, then raised her glass to her lips and gulped the liquid. "It all depends."

"On what?"

"On you, Colonel Kogan."

He started to chuckle, then cut it short. "Please, Mrs. Moody, help me. I'm just an ex-grunt who isn't very bright. You surely can't be trying to recruit me again."

"I am."

"But . . . damnit, ma'am, the operation's been called off."

"You're our only hope. Without you, Simon's decision will stand. If you show up at the White House tomorrow, willing to take over, I think he'd change his mind."

Kogan sighed. How many goddamn times must he tell her there was nothing back there? She was a noble woman—brave, loyal, and a fighter—but he was losing patience. Taking a deep breath and trying for calm, he spoke as reasonably as he could.

He began, "Mrs. Moody—"

"Lillian," she interrupted.

"I don't think I should use your—"

"Lillian, Joe," she repeated. "Tonight we're on a first-name basis."

"Okay," he conceded. "Lillian, both you and the president believe in this B-juice. I don't. That one scrap of paper, that single old letter, just isn't enough to risk lives for. I've told you that before."

"Yes, you have. Now let me tell you why we believe." She held up her empty glass. "Could I have another beer?"

Kogan detoured into his bedroom and slipped into a sport shirt, slacks, and sandals, no underwear. When he returned with two beers, she arched her brows and said, "My, my, aren't we the proper gentleman."

"Never realized what you women went through in skirts," he said, swinging one leg over the other. He really didn't want to hear any more about B-juice or the Philippines or why she thought the whole crazy idea made any sense, but after all, she *was* the First Lady—she rated a little reverse noblesse oblige. "Okay," he said. "Shoot."

She became businesslike. "I'll be as brief as I can," she said, then stopped as though organizing her thoughts. The rain intensified, beating strongly against the windows, muting the sound of traffic outside and heightening the intimacy of the small apartment.

Lillian put the glass down on the laminated surface of the coffee table, placing the napkin beneath it as carefully as though the piece of junk were a valued antique.

"Well," she said, "the story begins in late 1941, when a young army captain was assigned to the Philippines. Because of the possibility of war with Japan, he left his wife and infant son in the States. A few weeks after he arrived, and about the time of the Japanese attack on the islands, he became ill, very ill. The diagnosis was leukemia. His wife was notified by the chaplain of Hospital Number One on Bataan."

She paused and sipped her beer. When she continued, she spoke deliberately, for emphasis. "The identification of the hospital, Joe, is most relevant to the rest of my story. As I said, the wife was notified that her husband's cancer was terminal. His condition had worsened to the point that he could not live for more than a few days. Shortly after that, Bataan fell, and the young wife was left with only her young son and her memories."

The First Lady shifted so that she could look directly into Kogan's eyes. "Now the story becomes interesting. In the autumn of 1943, more than a year after the fall of Bataan, something incredible happens. The wife receives a letter—from her husband, who is now a POW on Hokkaido. The letter is heavily censored, but the captain says he is well. Naturally, the young woman is overjoyed. His cancer must have been cured or gone into remission. But that letter is the last she gets. In late 1945, after the Japanese surrender, a telegram arrives from the War Department, stating regretfully that her husband had died in December of 1944, from pneumonia."

Lillian stopped and Kogan could see the question in her eyes— wasn't this proof enough? *Christ, no, lady, you aren't even close.*

"Lillian," he said, "I have no training in medicine, but even I know that it could be exactly as the wife believed—the captain's leukemia went into remission."

"You know the chance of that happening in a terminal case?"

Kogan shook his head. This was going nowhere. What the hell did one cure—if that's what it was—prove?

Lillian answered her own question. "Less than one in ten thousand. That's a proven statistic. And consider this. Bataan Hospital Number One was where Babcock was doing his research! Joe, do you understand what that means? The captain went in terminally ill, and walked out cured at the very same time Babcock was working on his B-juice!"

Yeah, he could see it now, and it made sense. But it was a

long way from being rock solid. He tried to veer away from the subject. "I'm curious. How were you able to do so much research on this patient in so little time?"

It seemed to him that she had been waiting for the question and relished it when it came—savoring each word of her answer. "We didn't have to research him. He was my father-in-law. Captain Peter Moody was the president's father."

Oh-oh. He had walked into that one, and it was good—really good. Now he understood her—and the president's—complacency in the face of his disparagement of the letter. He could understand that when Simon Moody came face-to-face with his own mortality, the story of Captain Peter Moody, probably implanted by his mother, had kicked in, initiating that search of the MacArthur files. The First Family's hopes, Kogan now understood, had never been solely based upon that single, fragile piece of evidence, the surgeon's letter.

With a wary look at him, Lillian reached out to set her glass on the coffee table, and something bright tumbled to the floor with a tiny metallic sound. She picked it up and Kogan saw that it was the locket Fay had shown him—the one with the strange picture he couldn't remember being taken. He reached out and Lillian dropped it in his hand. He didn't need to look at the photo again; he remembered the detail—the grainy black and white, the uniform shirt with the kind of epaulets not worn since World War II.

His hand closed on it tightly. Then it hit him—there was only one answer. The explanation was so obvious, yet so frightening. As it sunk in, the hair rose on the back of his neck, and for an instant, the room moved giddily.

"Joe? What is it? What's wrong?" Lillian leaned forward and put a hand on his arm.

He fought his way back to the room and to Lillian, who was watching him closely. Once more in control, he took a deep breath, but his mouth was dry, and the hand holding his beer shook slightly. Quickly taking a swallow, he got to his feet. Lillian stood with him, her hand still on his arm.

"Are you all right?"

He nodded. "How soon was the expedition to leave?" he asked.

Puzzled, she said, "I'm not sure. Within a few days." A look of joy, still hesitant, spread over her face. "Joe! Will you go?"

"I'd have to be in command."

"Oh, yes, I'm sure Simon would—"

"I'll have to approve all plans."

"Of course."

"They're complete—down to the last detail? Everything ready to roll? No hitches?"

A shadow crossed her face. He could see her reluctance to speak. She shook her head. "I hate to say this—we've got a big problem. Apparently, General Armitage was never able to figure out how to get Dr. Babcock off Corregidor. It has to do with the plane—the landing field being too short or something."

He understood the problem instantly. "Oh, boy," he muttered, his mind racing along the peripheries, seeing the obstacles, finding at that moment no solution.

He took her arm and led her, protesting, to the door. "I've got work to do," he said, and reached for the knob.

"Wait," she said, and stood close to him. "Something happened in there. What was it? What changed your mind?"

He gestured with his head. "Tell Passmore's boys out there to have a car here—well, whenever the president is ready to see me. And Lillian," he touched her shoulder gently, then dropped his hand, "see you tomorrow."

"Joe." She placed her hand lightly on his arm. "I could be wrong. Simon may decide to close it down regardless."

As he leaned forward and opened the door, their faces were just inches apart—so close that he could see a slender blue vein under the translucent skin of her temple. She shifted her hand to his shoulder, and it seemed to him that her face moved even closer. This couldn't be happening. With an inaudible groan, he steeled himself. He didn't need another problem.

"No," he muttered to her. "Operation SUCCOR will go. Trust me."

The rain had diminished to a steady drizzle. She looked into his eyes for a long moment, then turned swiftly and left, her heels tapping on the walk. Near the curb, two figures stepped forward. A third man moved out of the shadows and opened the door to a large sedan. Kogan watched until the car pulled away, then came back inside, closed the door, and walked over to the table holding the sum total of the work he had done since leaving California. He checked his watch. It was almost midnight.

He picked up his half-empty bottle of beer, walked to the kitchen, and tossed it in the trash. He got the jar of instant coffee out and put water on to boil. Then he went back into the living room and switched on his computer.

September 16, 1994

8:34 A.M.

Her arms clamped tightly around her body, Lillian stood stiffly against the wall of the study as though trying to occupy the least amount of space and attract the least amount of attention.

"Join us, Lillian?" the big chief of staff asked lightly. He sat at Moody's elbow, his ubiquitous yellow pad before him.

Lillian gave a quick, negative jerk of her head and Rodale shrugged. Strange, Kogan mused. Was it a reaction from last night? Was she rethinking the rather dangerous game the two of them had played? Or was she just tired and suddenly frightened at playing Wonder Woman? Maybe she and Moody had had a spat over how far she should go in running this weird business. Whatever, her vivacity and charm were being held closely in check this morning.

Dr. Eccles sat across from the president, eyeing him, tapping the table with his gold pen. Otis Hiraga kept watching Kogan quizzically, as if to say, This is one big tiger you're about to ride, fella.

A night's rest hadn't improved Moody's physical appearance, but maybe, Kogan considered, he hadn't had much rest. The liver-spotted hands trembled as he took the cup handed him by the light-skinned, middle-aged steward with the name "Charles" embroidered over the pocket of his beige jacket. Sipping the coffee, the president looked up at Kogan with watery eyes, then twisted his head in his wife's direction.

"It was a little after midnight, wasn't it, Lillian," Moody said, "when you gave me the news that Colonel Kogan was willing to go along?"

Joe sensed the sudden interest among the others. Hell, that was understandable. Just how was it that the First Lady had gotten that information during the evening from this down-at-the-heels army type? Had Moody made a point of it to embarrass her?

Kogan also noted the pallid phrasing of the president's question. There was no mention of the command he'd insisted upon. He glanced at Lillian. Charles offered her coffee, but she shook her head. She didn't answer the president, nor did she look at Joe.

"Anyway, Joseph," Moody continued without pressing her, "in light of your offer to help, I've reconsidered my decision to shut down SUCCOR. I must tell you, though, that I still have reservations about going ahead with it. Colonel Longford has been summoned, and as soon as he arrives, we'll make a final judgment. If it's a go, we'll also decide whether to give you command of the operation or ask you to go along as executive officer." He paused, gazing at Kogan as if to give him a chance to respond.

Again Kogan glanced at Lillian. She was watching him, but dropped her eyes when he looked her way. Passing along the news that he intended to command might not have been the right way to waken her husband. Or maybe she hadn't told him. But Kogan intended to have that command, or he'd damn well tell Moody to stuff it. He wasn't going to trust his neck to some plane jockey who didn't know an '03 Springfield from a mess kit. As anxious as he was to pass that word along, he realized it might be better to wait and see what developed.

There was a discreet knock on the door, then Passmore entered, followed by a big, broad-shouldered redhead in a sport coat and open-necked shirt. Colonel Longford, Kogan guessed, and surprised himself at the instant feeling of kinship he felt for the flier.

Pink-skinned, blue-eyed, and amiable-looking, Longford reflected an inner stress as he shook the president's hand and murmured his regrets over Armitage's death.

Moody gestured toward Kogan. "Jake, this is Lieutenant Colonel Joseph Kogan, retired army." Longford looked puzzled as he shook hands, but said nothing. Kogan could understand his confusion.

The president got right down to business. "You have any idea what happened?"

"No, sir," Longford replied. "I spent several hours with the general a couple of days ago. He gave no indication of any... emotional problem. Of course, I could see he was under a lot of pressure, but not enough to—"

"Jake," the president interrupted, "Colonel Kogan is an expert on the time period and the Philippines. We're lucky that he happens to be here in Washington working in the Archives. For his information, would you review in general terms the plan as it now stands?"

Longford's face brightened as he glanced at Kogan. "He's going along with us?"

The president said sharply, "The plan, Jake."

"Yes, sir." Longford took a deep breath and pulled a map from the pile on the table. "All right," he said. "It's simple enough, as far as it goes. We're set up into two components— an operational group of seven men headed by... well, it *was* headed by General Armitage. We're the ones who will actually go back. The other component is a support group of about thirty scientists, engineers, and technicians that has done the stoop labor getting everything ready.

"Briefly, our plane—a Boeing 737—will rendezvous with an aircraft carrier provided by CINCPAC at a predesignated point near the Philippines. The tachyon beam projector has been mounted on the carrier's flight deck. Using the GPS satellites—the global positioning system—for proper alignment, we make the jump back. If all goes well, we rematerialize on—" He turned to Hiraga. "Sorry, Doctor, but what's that window again?"

"April seventeen to nineteen, 1942." Hiraga spoke without hesitation.

"Yeah." Longford nodded. "And we come in just east of Mindanao." He pointed to the map. "This big island here. We fly in after dark and land at Del Monte Airfield. Boy," he interjected, his expression dubious, "that's not gonna be a lot of fun. Then we present our credentials—faked, of course—to General Sharp's headquarters."

"Why Mindanao?" Dr. Eccles asked. "That's a long way south of Corregidor."

"About five hundred miles," the pilot answered. "You see, the Rock—Corregidor—sits in the middle of Manila Bay. It's got only one airfield—Kindley. Too small to handle our 737, and constantly under Japanese artillery bombardment. Mindanao has a crude airfield MacArthur ordered built on the pineapple fields owned by Del Monte. It's long enough to handle us."

The president turned to Kogan. "Any questions, Joseph?"

"Well . . ." He had a lot of questions, but this was not the place to flog staff work. There was one thing he wanted to get straight in his mind, though. "I'm curious as to why you picked the Boeing 737. I understand the transit vehicle has to be a plane, but why that one in particular?"

Longford seemed eager to tackle his question. "I worked with the support group on that one, Joe. First off, we needed a heavy lifter that could handle tons of scientific equipment. And we need speed. We've got to be able to outrun trouble. Okay. The 737 got the nod because it's configured fairly close to the heavy transports of the time. We couldn't use any monster 747's or 727's with tailmounted engines, or Concordes. We don't want to blow their minds."

"You don't think flying in without propellers might do it?"

Longford's face split into a grin. "We think we can lick that problem."

Kogan was about to ask how, but the president broke in.

"Thank you, Colonel," Moody said. "That's the good news. Now let's move along to the bad news." He glanced at the faces around the room. "Jake, the last time you saw Armitage, did he tell you how you were going to get to Dr. Babcock?"

"No, sir. At that time I don't think he knew, although he was working on it. He was always working on it—or them, because he had a bunch of different plans. I kept telling him we were running out of time, and he kept biting my head off."

"Wait, excuse me," Kogan said quickly. "Mr. President, this Armitage—was he the commander who died?"

"He was."

"Scott Armitage?" Memories evoked by the name came in a flood.

"Yes. Did you know him?"

"Yes, sir, in Vietnam. I was a boot lieutenant in his rifle company."

"That's interesting. How well do you remember General Armitage?" The president leaned forward, putting an arm on the table.

"Quite well, sir, although it was, oh . . . twenty-four years ago." Yeah, he remembered Armitage. A real hotshot. Everyone knew he was going places in the army. Remote, though. No one got close to him.

"You don't have to answer this, Colonel, but it might help us understand this tragedy a bit more. Did Armitage handle stress well?"

Kogan nodded. He didn't mind answering. "He was a very solid soldier, Mr. President. Nothing seemed to bother him." He recalled one time in the highlands, a few miles east of the Ho Chi Minh Trail. The company had been ordered out to stop infiltrating units coming off the trail from the north. An hour into the march, while pushing through the dripping mountain foliage, the company radioman had stepped on a land mine. The explosion threw the man into the air and showered debris on both Armitage and Kogan. By the time they got to him, the radioman had lurched erect, and Captain Armitage helped him stumble along for a few steps. Then Kogan noticed something strange. The radioman had been taller than Armitage; now he was shorter. Kogan looked down and was sorry he had. The man's feet and lower legs had been blown off. He was walking on white, bony stumps foliated with shreds of bloody flesh and tendons.

They put shoestring tourniquets on his legs and called in a helicopter, but the man died in Armitage's arms. During the entire incident, Scott might have been lecturing in a Fort Benning classroom: unhurried and calm, issuing exactly the right orders.

"No, sir," Kogan said, "under pressure, he was an iron man."

"I wonder," the president said musingly, "whether that kind of ungiving control is healthy. To keep one's emotions so closely bound it may seem like strength, but it could conceal an underlying flaw."

"I wasn't aware of any, sir," said Kogan. "Everyone respected him."

The president drummed on the table. "I doubt we'll ever find out what happened to General Armitage. What a tragedy." He expelled a deep breath. "Well, Jake, to move on, how do we get Dr. Babcock off the Rock?"

To Kogan's surprise, Longford's face creased in a grin. "I'm happy to say, sir, that I think the general found the answer. I'm still not absolutely sure, but I've got a glimmer. Last night the head of the army CID team investigating the general's death telephoned. He said he had something for me. I told him to bring it over. It turned out to be a note from Armitage. Could have been the last thing he ever wrote. The CID people found it under his hand."

Longford paused, obviously striving for dramatic effect.

"Well, damnit, Longford, what did it say?" Rodale growled.

"I guess you might say it's a vindication of the general. He *had* discovered a way to get to Babcock." The pilot pulled a sheet of paper from an inner pocket and unfolded it. "Not much to it, though—less than a dozen words. It says," he started reading, " 'Longford—Use Bamboo Fleet to get Babcock off Rock. Good luck. Armitage.' "

Longford held the paper up for all to see.

With an audible sound of satisfaction, Moody leaned back in his chair. His eyes, kindled with new enthusiasm, sought Kogan's face. "Well, Joseph, things may be looking up." He turned back to the pilot. "Jake, explain this Bamboo Fleet to us."

Longford's face fell. "Right now I can't, sir. This is the first I'd heard of it."

"Jesus!" Rodale slammed his hand on the table.

All eyes turned to look at Kogan.

"Joseph?" the president asked.

Kogan sighed inwardly. The question underscored the help-lessness of these powerful people. They were wandering through a strange world, grasping at straws.

"The Bamboo Fleet," he said slowly, recalling the circum-stances behind the obscure term. "Well, after the B-17s had pulled back to Australia in December, there were no bombers left in MacArthur's command—and only a handful of fighters."

Rodale erupted. "You must be crazy, Kogan. America was building thousands of war planes about that time."

"Yeah, Mr. Rodale, but not one—I repeat, not one—ever got to the Philippines. Roosevelt sent them either to England or Russia."

Kogan looked around the room. "Let me explain this Bamboo Fleet." He held up the fingers of one hand. "There were five or six planes—patched-up crates, most of them civilian models. Let's see, there was a Waco, a Beechcraft, and a Bellance, I believe, along with another piece of junk I can't recall. And oh, yeah, an antique P-35 pursuit plane. Mr. President, that was it."

Kogan watched the vitality leave Moody. He slumped in his

chair, his eyes glassy and unfocused. Eccles hurriedly produced a pill from his bag, then poured a glass of water and handed it to Moody.

"But, Mr. President, that's the answer!" Longford grinned in relief. "Any one of those planes could land and take off from that little airfield on Corregidor. We could fly Babcock from there to Mindanao. That's what Armitage meant."

For a moment, dashed hopes revived like parched flowers in a rain. But Lillian, watching her husband, placed her hand on his arm. "What's wrong, dear? Don't you think it will work?"

Moody leaned forward. "Don't you understand? Would you put the greatest medical advance in history—and its discoverer— in an old, unreliable airplane and fly five hundred miles through skies controlled by enemy aircraft?"

The silence in the room was almost tangible. Lillian finally broke it. "But, Simon, if it's the only way—"

"Forget it," Kogan said, his voice curt. "Dr. Hiraga, you said the group was going back in April?"

"Our window is between April seventeen and nineteen."

That did it. Kogan remembered reading something—what was it, Ind's book, or Craven and Cates, or the Malonée diaries? Didn't matter. The answer was the same. "Too late," he said. "All those old planes were long gone by then. They had either crashed or been shot down."

"You're sure?" Longford asked.

Kogan nodded. For the last year and a half, his waking life had been tied up in books, reports, memoirs, and journals on the fall of the Philippines. "I'm sure," he said. The words settled over the room like a funerary mantle. Then Rodale got to his feet and leaned forward, both hands on the table.

"All right, Colonel Kogan," he rasped. "Since you know so much about it, how would you get to Dr. Babcock?"

"Wait." Lillian had moved to the middle of the room. She stood there a moment, as if to gather attention. "I don't think Joe—the colonel—would be here if he didn't have a plan." She walked to her husband's side and placed her hand on his shoulder in a comforting way. "Simon, we're wasting time. We've got to know," she said.

Without waiting for a response, she turned to the pilot. "Colonel Longford, General Armitage is dead. Time is getting to be absolutely critical. The expedition has to have a commander. Could you lead Operation SUCCOR?" Her eyes left Longford's face and sought Kogan's.

"Just a minute." Kogan came to his feet and faced Longford. Lillian was right. It was time to quit bullshitting. They were either going to accept him or throw him out. The others watched him, startled.

"Longford," he said, "you know anything about the Philippines in 1942?"

"Not too much, I'm afraid. That was Armitage's department." The pilot pursed his lips in thought. "Americans were fighting a losing battle against the Japanese."

"You ever lead troops in combat?"

"Ground troops?" Kogan nodded. "No, sir," Longford said, unconsciously adding the *sir*. "I'm an air force officer."

"You outrank me. You have any objection to serving under my command?"

Rodale's booming voice filled the room. "Now, see here, Kogan—" The president cut him off with a motion of his hand.

Moody's voice was calm. "Answer the question, Colonel Longford."

The pilot gave a pleased little smile. "I'd be damn happy to," he said. "If you know the territory, and it appears you do, that gives me a real comfortable feeling. With all due respect to General Armitage, that would be a welcome change. I . . . well, my answer is an enthusiastic hell, yes." Then his face sobered. "But, Joe, I'd still like to know how we get Babcock off the Rock."

"There's a way," Kogan said.

The president jerked upright.

"Joseph, you mean it?"

"Yes, sir."

"Well, damnit," Rodale interjected, "let's hear it."

Kogan leaned forward, bracing himself with his hands. His eyes swept around the table and came to rest on the president. "Am I in command, sir?"

Moody nodded eagerly. "You are, Joseph."

"All right." Kogan spoke deliberately. "I've gotten the impression that time is short. I'm going to suggest that you trust me and we get cracking."

The president reached up and grasped Lillian's hand on his shoulder. He smiled up into her face. "It's been a wonderful morning, my love. Thank you."

For weeks now, the president had slept in a small guest bedroom in the Family Quarters. Lush plants partially blocked from view health-monitoring devices and equipment for life support, while fighting the sharp smell of medication for control of the air. It was an unhappy compromise between a normal place of rest and an ICU.

Eccles and Beth Diego, a plump young Hispanic nurse, eased the president onto the bed and covered him with a light blanket. Rodale entered and watched from the doorway.

The doctor felt Moody's pulse. "This has been a strain on you, Mr. President," he said. "I'll give you a mild tranquilizer."

"Marty." Moody spoke.

"Sir?"

"One more thing. That appointment you set up with Spencer Pyle? Call him. Put it off."

"Okay. What'll I say?"

"Stall him." The president's voice was weary. "You know how." His eyes were already closed.

Beth closed the blinds on the bedroom's single window. For a moment in the dimness, the big man in the doorway watched the quiet figure on the bed, then left.

CHAPTER FIVE

Martin Rodale watched warily as Spencer Pyle eased his slender, slightly potbellied frame into a chair beside the chief of staff's desk. Last evening, he had telephoned Pyle that the president couldn't see him today, but the vice president's response was a demand to see the chief of staff. Rodale had agreed reluctantly. This little visit this morning, he figured, wasn't going to produce a jolly exchange of views.

"Mr. Vice President," he said with false heartiness, "I guess you and I are the only two people in the executive branch doing business at seven in the morning."

"Marty." Pyle's tone indicated that he was in no mood for small talk. "I'm sure as hell pleased to be able to talk to the chief of staff. Not only pleased, but honored. Of course, it would be just wonderful if I could ever get to see the man himself, but a simple, humble vice president shouldn't expect too much, I suppose."

"Coffee, Spence?" Rodale poured from the carafe and set the cup in front of the vice president. Pyle eyed it without enthusiasm and returned to his subject.

"Another thing. I would very much appreciate, if it's not too much to ask, just a little more visibility. A couple of days ago, when you guys put that bozo on the plane to Hawaii, why couldn't I have been notified? I'd have gone out to Andrews and played my part to the hilt—Olivier risen from the grave. Tell me," the vice president's tone became hard, "why do I get this feeling I'm an outsider in this administration?"

Rodale's smile was as cold as the Dakota winters he had grown up in. This was going to be something more than just a little hand-holding. Pyle's labored sarcasm was coming very close to outright hostility.

"Hey, we're doing you a favor, do you realize that?"

Pyle didn't look grateful. He said, "Pursue that a bit further."

"Simple enough. Simon is very, very ill—"

"That's another thing, damnit. As vice president, I want to be brought up to speed on the president's health."

Rodale held up one big hand. "Please. One item at a time. The president, as you have been told repeatedly, is taking a calculated risk in not informing the public just how sick he really is. We have the absolute minimum—fifteen, sixteen people here in the White House—who know. Passmore has detailed one agent to ride herd on them, but God knows how much longer it will be before someone spills his guts. Or until Simon . . . well, when the time comes that we have to give up on this charade. What's going to happen then?" Rodale hurried on. "I'll tell you. Everyone connected with the deception is going to have to take his lumps."

"You and Quent Talbott were out there at Andrews grinning and waving and picking up brownie points."

"Sure. But we're not elected officials. We don't aspire to any further political office. Speaking personally, after this is over, I never want to see this fucking town again."

Pyle took a sip of his coffee. "I see your point, but my ass isn't completely covered. Who's going to believe that I didn't know the president was sick and was using a double?"

"Spence, at the risk of boring you, let me fall back on a real old cliché: one picture is worth a thousand words. By keeping you under covers, so to speak, the opposition party is never going to be able to run a videotape of you shaking hands with that rent-a-prez we're using." The chief of staff faked a yawn. He wanted very much to cool the situation and get Pyle out of there.

"I'm afraid," he continued, "this is about the best we can do for you. The spin on this thing should be that your motivations were purely humanitarian. You loved Moody and wanted to protect him. It was only with the greatest reluctance that you went along with this business. Got it?"

Spencer Pyle sat back and drummed his manicured nails on the polished wood of Rodale's desk. "I'm deeply touched by your concern for my political future. Now I'd like to see the president, if you don't mind."

Rodale nodded. He tried an agreeable tone. "No problem with that, Mr. Vice President, but we'll have to find a good time for it."

"You mean I've got to have an appointment." He pointed to the phone. "You can't just pick up that instrument and say to His Holiness that the vice president would like an audience?"

Rodale glared at him. "You're in my office, *sir*, so just load that sarcastic shit back on the wagon and dump it somewhere else."

Pyle took the warning with an opaque look. "All right, Marty, no offense intended. Now, how about it?"

Rodale lowered his hackles. He'd made his point. "Sorry, can't do it," he said, trying for reason. "He's not up yet. Simon is a sick man—you know that. He has to have medication, therapy. We have to work you in."

"You're a good chief of staff, Marty, but I want to warn you—

don't shut down communications between me and the president."

Rodale knew that he could go only so far in keeping Pyle away from Moody. But he'd do everything in his power to see that the vice president didn't get in often. He upset the president. Simon had told Rodale that from the minute Pyle walked in until he left, he felt like he was getting measured for a coffin. His "How are you?" sounded like "How long have you got to live?" Well, Rodale wouldn't shut down communications, but he'd do what any good chief of staff would do to protect his boss.

Why couldn't Pyle just be an old-fashioned vice president who accepted the job for what it was meant to be—political oblivion? But he was a wild card, put there at the last minute by those whiz kid assholes masterminding National Committee strategy. "Balance," they kept repeating. "We've got to appeal to the nation's business and industrial leaders. Run one of their own on the ticket and they'll overlook Moody's liberal bent." Well, they had, and now all that Simon Elihu Moody and a substantial bulk of the Western world had worked for so long was being put in jeopardy. So much for representative democracy.

Rodale remembered the party convention. In the hotel, after the nominations were locked in, someone had asked Spencer Pyle how one got to be a billionaire.

"Nothing to it," Pyle had said, holding the same drink he'd started with. "You need to do two things: one, start with fifty million dollars...."

The questioner waited, then asked, "What's the second thing?"

"I forget," Pyle answered. "But if you've got the fifty million dollars it doesn't matter."

That had gotten some obligatory laughs. Encouraged, another party hack asked why, when he had everything in the world he could possibly want, Pyle sought a job that promised so little. Moody was the picture of health, the man said, and barring accident, Pyle could look forward to four years of doing damn little except attending funerals and laying wreaths. Rodale had been talking with Simon when the question was asked, and although the room was crowded and noisy, it got suddenly quiet, waiting for the vice presidential nominee's answer. Simon sipped his drink and watched his running mate out of the corner of his eyes.

"Friend, there comes a time," Pyle began, "when a man recognizes his own mortality. Money is a poor heritage to leave behind. It embitters and vandalizes relationships, and even in large amounts, it doesn't last long." He had chuckled, and Rodale wondered whether the man was sincere or a consummate actor. "No, some would agree with old John Garner's statement that the vice presidency isn't worth a bucket of warm piss. I don't agree. To me, it's a way of paying back in some small measure all the things this wonderful country has given me. If I can just stand close to the most powerful office on the face of the earth, that is enough for me. If the president wants my advice, he will have it. If he wants me to perform a task, he knows it will be done to the best of my ability. If he wants neither my advice nor my labors, so be it."

Except for Pyle's words, the room was quiet now. He no longer spoke just to his questioner, but to all present, his voice deftly raised.

"So, you may say, what a fine man this Spencer Pyle is, who wants nothing for himself except to serve. Bullshit." He grinned at the good-natured laughter. "There are not many ways to get in the history books, my friends. You can invent something, invade a country, or hold political office. I'm no good at the first two, but future generations of schoolchildren will know that Spencer Pyle was president of the Senate of the United States, a member of the National Security Council, and vice president of this great country."

Simon Moody led the wave of applause that followed Pyle's words. Then he turned back to Rodale and said, "Not a bad little talk."

Rodale peered into the depths of his glass, but said nothing.

"You don't agree?"

"I agree with one word of it—bullshit." Rodale had then turned serious. "It's true, Simon, that you're the picture of health, but let me tell you something—there are a lot of nuts out there, and Spencer Pyle knows it."

Later, on the plane for Florida, where they were going to spend a few days planning their campaign strategy, Moody had brought it up again. "You know, Marty," he had said, "I think Pyle was sincere. When you've got a lot of it, money can become a bore. I don't think he'd take the nomination on the very slim chance that something is going to happen to me."

"Maybe not," Rodale answered. "And I don't want to sow seeds of dissent between you and Pyle, but he'd love to be president, I'm convinced of that."

"So what? If political ambition were a crime, I'd have gone to the chair years ago. So maybe he's got his eye on 2000, or 2004."

"Ha." Rodale indicated his feeling for that. "On his own, Pyle couldn't get elected county clerk. Look, Simon, I don't mind him riding on your coattails, but this man has an agenda, and it's a long way from yours. I think vice presidents should have the same political vision the main man has. If something happens, the policies go on. Ever think about that?"

"Of course. But we don't practice mind control in this country. Our constitutional system says that if there's a death in the family it's a new ball game." Moody had reached over and rapped Rodale's leg. "We have to live with that."

A death in the family. God, if they could only have seen what the next thirty months would bring, they would have been somewhat less cavalier about choosing a running mate. For here he was, this morning, and Rodale wanted to get rid of him.

He got to his feet. "Sorry, Mr. Vice President, but I've got a breakfast meeting at the Pentagon. I'll get back to you as soon as I can set up a time." To his surprise, Pyle leaned back in his chair, making no sign of leaving.

"You seeing the Joint Chiefs?" Pyle held his cup out for a

refill. Rodale hesitated, then poured coffee. Pyle put it down without tasting it. "Talking about DOE?"

"It will probably come up." He didn't resume his seat. He wanted this man out of here.

"Sit down, Marty, the troops will wait."

"I have a full schedule today. I don't want to fall behind."

"Okay, suppose I come with you. We can talk on the way. I'd like to get my views on record with the Chiefs." He looked smug. "Simon's not getting a lot of support from the Pentagon on DOE, is he?"

Rodale stiffened. He hadn't seen that one coming. He put everything into reverse, forced a smile, and sat down, because what Pyle said was true.

Bedford Shaw, the secretary of defense, had fought DOE tooth and nail, giving in reluctantly only when the president agreed that for the time being he wouldn't reduce conventional forces in Europe. Shaw's arguments were about the same as those developing among a loose confederation of second-level officials in a half-dozen European ministries, led by what the CIA called the Czech cabal. According to what Rodale had learned, a Czech, Dr. Josef Gebauer, who had some shadowy connection with the Skoda Munitions Works, was the unofficial leader of this dissident movement.

The cabal and its adherents professed terror at what was happening in the Middle East. With Israel tenaciously holding on to her nuclear capability, the Arab nations—particularly in view of the Persian Gulf crisis—had insisted they had a right to develop their own. Why, Dr. Gebauer had reportedly said in leaking his agenda to European papers, should the United States encourage Europe to strip naked while the most volatile region in the world brandished new and devastating weapons?

And this was essentially what the hawks in the Pentagon were asking.

With Bedford Shaw and Pyle dangerously close in their thinking, Rodale had no intention of letting the two of them gang up on him this morning.

"I'll take a few minutes." Having lost that skirmish, Rodale slumped down in his chair. "What do you want to talk about?"

"That's better." Pyle crossed his legs and brushed imaginary lint from his sleeve. The signals were, he wasn't going to be rushed. "Now I'm going to tell you what I intend to tell Moody when I see him. It's criminally stupid not to keep me abreast of what's going on—particularly in the field of foreign relations. You want me to take over like Truman did? Hell, he didn't even know there was such a thing as an A-bomb."

"You may not *have* to take over."

The vice president's head jerked up sharply. "What do you mean?"

"Damnit." Rodale was having trouble holding his temper in check. "The president's not dead yet. He's getting treatment. There could be a remission. What the hell, these things happen." It seemed to him that Pyle relaxed at his words. Rodale wondered if the vice president had somehow heard of Operation SUCCOR. Secretary of State Talbott had been told of the effort, only because he and Simon were old friends. The rest of the cabinet, including the vice president, had been kept totally in the dark.

"Well," Pyle answered smoothly, "we can only pray for the president's full recovery. That would be wonderful. Still, I hope you and he are sufficiently pragmatic to look at the odds." He set his cup down carefully and got to his feet. He looked at Rodale without smiling.

"So, my friend," Pyle said, "from now on, I want to be included in all discussions relative to DOE, particularly with State and Defense. Is that understood?"

Rodale winced. Pyle was beginning to push hard. Bringing him into the sensitive preparations now going on would create chaos. The summit team wouldn't have a clue as to who was calling the signals, or even what the signals meant. But Rodale had no grounds on which to debate the issue. He'd have to fall back to a firmer position. He got up and was at the door in two strides.

"Pyle," the chief of staff said sternly, "being the second man in the land, you rate nineteen guns and all kinds of respect, but I'm not *your* boy. I take my orders from the president. And may I point out that *you, too,* still take orders from him."

Spencer Pyle's eyes narrowed at the rebuke. His voice had a nasty edge to it. "It's been a pleasure talking to you, Marty, a real pleasure. I'll be expecting a call—real soon."

The vice president passed through the doorway, the balding crown of his head barely reaching to the chief of staff's shoulder, and stalked firmly down the hallway. Rodale, feeling a bit sick inside, watched him go. Somehow, they had to hold the ramparts for a while longer. The blows had been unremitting in the last thirty-six hours—Armitage's death, Jake Longford's unwillingness and unfitness to lead SUCCOR, and a brand-new, untested leader. He didn't like—hell, he resented—the way this guy Kogan was throwing his weight around. On the other hand, he seemed to know his business. One thing was certain—the man was sure no wimp.

Rodale went to his telephone. "Nellie, have my car brought around, will you?" He picked up his briefcase, then reached back into a drawer and pulled out the Tylenol bottle.

Charles, his café au lait face gravely composed as always, entered and gave the First Lady an inquiring look. She shook her head and he exited as quietly as he had come. Lillian picked up Kogan's cup and filled it from a silver coffee urn, then warmed her own and sipped it.

The tension both felt gradually eased. The emotions of two nights ago, the conflict of wills, the sexual attraction, the incongruity of the highest woman in the nation drinking beer with a half-naked man in a stuffy little apartment, now seemed a remote happening in a remote time. If she remembered the heat and the primal rhythms of the rainy night and whatever else it was that had pulled at them, she didn't show it. This morning it was Mrs. Moody and Colonel Kogan.

Kogan pushed the last morsel of his eggs Benedict away. It was damn good, but somewhere out of his past a feminine voice spoke warningly, "Joseph, when you're out in company, it is not polite to clean every last bite off your plate!" Maybe his mother, now gone, would be pleased to look down and see her gangling son grown up and having breakfast with the First Lady in the White House. Well, bless her, but he was still hungry. He speared the bite and shoved it into his mouth.

Lillian Moody rearranged the fruit on her plate. Her deceptively simple green housecoat gleamed against the gold of the upholstery, and the sunlight streaming in through the tall windows of the solarium was very kind to her skin and hair. She sat across the table, facing Kogan. An empty chair at the head of the table was for the absent president. Simon was with Dr. Eccles this morning, Lillian had explained, but should be available by the time they had finished breakfast.

Since they sipped their first cup of coffee, she had done most of the talking, first about how grateful she and the president were that Kogan was taking the job, then, with the skill of a natural hostess, turning the conversation into personal channels, delving tactfully into his life, but with never a hint or gesture that her interest was on a personal level. Now, hesitantly, she murmured her regrets about his wife's death.

"Did that have anything to do with your leaving the army?"

The question revealed that she must have read some background reports on him. Kogan washed the Canadian bacon and eggs down with a swallow of orange juice and answered. "Yes, ma'am. Life in the army wouldn't have been the same without Jean. She liked it—the tradition, the social part, the travel—maybe more than I did, I guess. I thought it was better that I make a clean break. Besides," he added, "I'd had about all I wanted out of the army, and I guess the army felt the same way about me."

She smiled reflectively. "And now you find yourself back in the army. How ironic."

That startled him. Back in the army? On active duty? Yes, he guessed that was what he'd volunteered for. "Going to be a little unusual, I guess," he said. "I'm only a lieutenant colonel. Jake Longford's a full colonel."

A familiar voice sounded behind him. "Good morning, General." Kogan whirled in his seat and rose hastily. Simon Moody motioned him down. The president wore a white cotton sport shirt and gabardine slacks that were painfully large around the waist. He eased himself into his chair, eyeing the food on the table with distaste. Lillian quickly poured coffee, added a heaping spoon of sugar, and set it before him. "Ah-ha." Moody managed a chuckle that had little humor in it. "I find my wife having breakfast with another man."

Kogan glanced quickly at the president's face, trying to interpret the remark, but Moody's expression was guileless as he continued talking.

"At least she has the good taste to choose a major general."

"I don't understand, sir," Kogan said.

"Simple, Joseph," the president replied. "I have the power to make temporary appointments for special circumstances, subject to confirmation by the Senate. The rank may come in handy." He sipped his coffee, made a face, added more sugar, then turned his strained and bloodshot eyes on Kogan. "Thank you again, my friend, for taking this command. Whatever happens," he spoke slowly, "I want you to know that you have my eternal gratitude for leading Operation SUCCOR to whatever destiny awaits it. Now," he added, forcing a smile, "when do you leave?"

"Tomorrow, Mr. President. I've spent two days working with Jake Longford and Dr. Hiraga. We'll wrap it up today. In the morning, Longford will fly us to New Jersey to meet the rest of the crew and orient me on the 737. We'll be on our way to Pearl Harbor by noon."

Lillian reached out and rested her hand on Kogan's. "This is all happening so fast. Joe, take a few minutes and call Martin Rodale's office. One of the White House attorneys is standing by. A will, power of attorney, your car, apartment, personal property—anything you need to have taken care of will be." Her eyes shone suspiciously bright. "I don't mean to sound dismal. Just a precaution...." She stopped there.

"Thank you, ma'am. I might just do that," he answered. He swallowed the last of his coffee and used his napkin. Mom would be proud. The mood was getting pretty heavy. Maybe he'd better exit on a confident note.

"We should be back in a few days, sir—we'd better be. I'll have a lot of note-taking to catch up on."

The president nodded absently. If he noticed the whimsy, he gave no indication. He glanced at Lillian. She pointed to her watch.

"Joseph," the president said, "you're witness to something amazing—a politician who suddenly doesn't want to make a speech. All I have to say to you is go do the best you can." He seemed suddenly ill at ease. "Now I'm afraid you'll have to excuse us."

Kogan got to his feet. He was being dismissed. Lillian rose, too. "I'll see Joe out," she explained to her husband.

"Yessir, looks like they came up with another sucker." Looey used the slang to show his fluency. And to show his contempt for the new man. "Guy by the name of Kogan, retired army."

"You're sure, Louis? I don't pay you for guesswork."

Looey wondered briefly why the vice president insisted upon calling him Lou-iss, but then, this was not an ordinary man he was dealing with. Never, even while working for Communist officialdom in Prague before the Great Change, had he encountered such exacting precision. He was prepared for the question.

"The time we could gain in making our move now, sir, should compensate for the very slight possibility that I may be misinformed." It was the kind of answer, Looey knew, that Pyle would accept. Besides, he had used his considerable connections to make certain he was correct. He continued. "Kogan is an expert on the Philippines. He has received a visit from the Secret Service. During the last few days, he has spent much time at the White House. This morning he is there again."

"I see." The phone was silent. "Can he be scared off?"

Looey chuckled. "Like General Armitage? Do you suggest, sir, that we expose him as a heterosexual?" Suspecting his heavy humor had carried him too far, he didn't wait for a reply. "No, sir, he cannot. As a matter of fact, I understand his principal problem in the army was that none of his superiors could intimidate him. We can, of course, take him out of the picture."

He sensed only a momentary hesitation on the other end. "Yes, that will have to be done."

Looey waited, saying nothing. These little conversations had a pattern. Always some advice, no matter how simple the task. It was aggravating for a professional of his caliber to be lectured by an amateur, no matter the money involved.

It had been chance more than anything else that Looey had caught the attention of the vice president of the United States. What had happened was that an old acquaintance of his in the Czech embassy in Washington had called him and asked how he was doing in the country of his dreams. After Looey had swallowed his shock at being traced, he admitted that things could be better—he had yet to figure out how to obtain a position in a society where crime was privatized. His countryman had not only commiserated, but said he knew of something that would pay very well. It seemed that a very high-ranking American official had recently attended a reception at the embassy and had expressed his need for a man of discretion and talent.

Looey was given a number to call as well as a code name to use. After a series of interviews conducted in guarded language, Looey found the employment that he had sought.

So for the past three months, things had been much better, much closer to the excitement and the rewards he had always expected from life in the United States. The work given him by Mr. Pyle had been easy; the openness of American society rendered transparent what would have been opaque in others. And the pay! The only drawback was Mr. Pyle's insistence upon guiding his hand. Just describe the result you want, Looey wanted to shout at his employer—let me decide how it is to be done. You want this Kogan thrown from a tall building, found dying in the arms of a dead mistress, shot, garroted, poisoned, impaled on a cathedral fence? The last was a nice touch, he had seen it in an old movie a few nights ago. Only say the word and it shall be done. But no. Looey rolled his eyes heavenward. That was not how things went with Mr. Pyle.

Ah-ha, here it comes. The vice president's voice carried a cautionary note. "No killing, no rigged suicide, you understand? Two in a row would be unacceptable. Some sort of an accident, perhaps. Serious enough to incapacitate him."

"For a month, a year, or permanently?"

"I'll leave that up to you."

"Is there anything I can do? Any personal calls that I—" Lillian Moody gave that a little thought and backed away. "—or one of the people on my staff could make for you?"

He shook his head and thought of Fay Donello with a pang of regret for how badly their last evening had gone. He'd have to call her.

Lillian touched his arm lightly and they started down the broad, carpeted hall, side by side, walking very slowly. "About the other night," she began. "I came close to making a fool— or worse—of myself. I am so very grateful that you acted as you did."

"Mrs. Moody—" he began.

"No," she interrupted. "I'd really prefer that you not comment. All I need to say to you is that I love my husband very much. He is the light of my life, even though—"

The slight hum of the elevator reached them. Hurriedly, she extended her hand. "I'll say good-bye here. Good luck, Joe." Kogan found her hand surprisingly warm. "And please, please hurry back," she added.

Kogan watched her go, then turned and continued on down

the hall past the great Chinese coromandel screen. As he approached the elevator, he heard the metallic clank of the door opening. Martin Rodale and Spencer Pyle stepped out and walked toward him, the former haggard and displaying no recognition except for a terse good morning. Kogan had never seen the vice president in the flesh, but he recognized the small, neat figure, the ovoid head, and the alert, dark eyes that glanced at him sharply. As Kogan stepped into the elevator, he looked back. The vice president, walking slightly behind the tall chief of staff, was staring over his shoulder at him.

Rodale knocked on the mahogany double door. Bad luck to run into Kogan like that. It was obvious that Pyle was interested in him. Maybe it was just the vice president's insatiable curiosity, or—

"Who was that?" Pyle asked.

"Old friend of the Moodys," Rodale answered, and was grateful when Charles opened the door and ushered them in.

"I'm disappointed, Mr. President," Spencer Pyle said. His coffee remained untasted at his side. "To put it mildly. And pardon me for speaking with such candor. But as I told Marty, I think it's time for me to become more engaged in the day-to-day functioning of this administration."

The president's hand trembled as he doodled on his writing pad, but his voice was firm. "I agree, Spencer." He looked up at his surprised chief of staff. "I see no problem with that, do you, Marty?"

"Well—" Rodale began.

"Providing, Spencer," Moody interrupted, "that you understand and adhere to the policies I have set forth. That speech you gave to the Press Club a few days ago was out-of-bounds. I do not appreciate my vice president denigrating the DOE talks by referring to them as *Bambi*."

"Just a joke, Mr. President. Whatever happened to freedom of speech?" Pyle spoke lightly and smiled, but his eyes challenged the rebuke.

"You've spoken at length in cabinet meetings, NSC meetings, and with me privately," Moody said. "You've had every opportunity to set forth your views, and I have considered them carefully. But once I have made my decision, you and every other official in my administration will speak with one voice."

What the hell, Rodale thought. If it's Pyle-bashing time, he'd like to get in on it. "There's another thing, Mr. Vice President. We're certain there's nothing sinister in it, but you seem to have gotten a little cozy with the Czech embassy people recently—"

Pyle turned, his face flushed angrily. "Who I see in this town is my business, Rodale."

The president chuckled, but the sound had no humor in it. "Normally I'd agree with you, Spencer, but there's too much at stake here. If we have trouble in Brussels, you can bet the eminent Dr. Gebauer I've been hearing about will have had something to do with it . . . no, don't interrupt. You say you want to be part of my administration. That's fine. Just get on board and stay with my policies. If for some reason you cannot do this, then I suggest you resign."

Rodale looked up, surprised. He hadn't thought Simon would go this far, but hell, it was a great idea. The problem was, it came too late and both the president and Pyle knew it. The vice president wouldn't have dared make that Press Club speech even a month ago, but now he was in the driver's seat. Moody's threats didn't bother him.

The vice president paced to the window, then turned to face Moody. "Let's get one thing clear, Simon. I don't like being treated as a pariah. When the cabinet first agreed to go along with this . . . deception, we were promised that a cure was in the offing and it would be just a matter of time before you'd be back on your feet. But you've gone downhill—to the point that you no longer make public appearances. We were asked to say nothing about the double, to do nothing that would alarm the public. We were again told that soon the cure would be forthcoming."

Rodale watched Pyle as he moved back and forth across the sun-filled room. There had always been a descending curve to this game they were playing. Some days might be better than others, but at the end of each week the curve was lower than at the beginning. The line went steadily down, like one of Eccles's medical charts on Simon. Too many losses, too few victories. Now, like a skilled trial lawyer, Pyle was laying the groundwork for a palace coup.

"I've watched you this morning, Simon, and I'll be blunt. You're ill—desperately ill. We've carried you beyond where I or any member of the cabinet thought would be necessary. And still the cure remains as mysterious and as far away as ever. Right now, I don't think you could lead this country in a crisis. Unless a miracle occurs, I don't think you will be in Brussels. Were I to follow my constitutional role to the letter, I would invoke the Twenty-fifth Amendment tomorrow."

Rodale watched Simon and Lillian. Their faces were frozen, drawn to Pyle's and held there by fascination. The man was in command. What he intended to do with it might soon be revealed.

"Now," Pyle continued, "you suggest that I sit like a dummy while you go about the emasculation of western Europe."

"This is still my administration."

"Didn't you hear me, Simon? Read the Twenty-fifth. I can have you out of the White House within forty-eight hours."

Rodale glanced at the president's putty-colored face. The boss needed his help, his intervention. "Now, hold it, Mr. Vice President," he said. "You and the cabinet agreed to stay the course as long as the president can function. Are you going back on your word?"

Pyle glowered at the chief of staff. "*Function* is a very subjective word. I think any *objective* medical authority would say that right now, the president can no longer perform the duties of his office."

"That's enough!" Lillian's full lips were drawn in a tight line over her teeth. "Let me tell you something, Spencer Pyle. We have moved much closer to the cure. There is a chance—a very good chance—that Simon will be cured in time for the DOE conference."

"Mrs. Moody, we can only hope so. But where *is* the cure? Are you sure you haven't created a will-of-the-wisp, an illusion to keep your hopes up? If a cure is available, put it to use." He fidgeted and shook his head in apparent frustration. "Excuse me for putting the question so bluntly, but is the president not worse off today than last week? When can we expect him to get better?"

"Soon. We may be just days away from getting the treatment Simon needs." Lillian's mood changed. A small smile broke over her face. "It's a wonderful, incredible thing. We only wish we could tell you more."

"Yes, that's what you've said from the beginning. Why don't you tell me? Tell the cabinet? Why not tell the whole world?"

"Because," she answered, "of the uncertainty. It would be criminal to tell the people that we have a cancer cure unless we are absolutely positive."

Pyle turned to the president. "All right. But your health . . . the situation has gone too far to be put off by vague promises. How long before you know positively?"

"I'm not sure. Just give us a little more time."

The vice president made a circuit of the room as though deep in thought. Finally, he stopped. "I'm going to call the cabinet into session, Simon, sound them out. I may have to tell them that I cannot shirk my constitutional responsibilities indefinitely."

"Mr. Pyle," Lillian said, "it's Simon's cabinet. He'll have a few words to say to them also."

Rodale groaned inside. *Hold it, Lillian. Back off—this is a trap.* He watched Pyle smile, rather like a cat eyeing a lame mouse. "That's true," Pyle said smoothly. "Simon, if you like, we could meet together with the cabinet to present our respective positions." He waited for the president to reply, then jogged him a bit. "Would you prefer that?"

"I'll let you know." The words were barely audible.

"Yes, Mr. President, you do that. And above all, let me know if you find the cure. Good day." He stalked out, shoulders squared in presidential style, Rodale thought.

For a moment after Pyle left, the room was silent. The president collapsed further inside his clothing, his face drained of vitality. Lillian, her expression agonized, reached for the nurse's call button, saying, "Simon, you've got to rest."

The president waved his hand in feeble protest. "Wait, please." He looked up at Rodale, his expression entreating. "It could have been worse, couldn't it? He's not doing anything right away."

Rodale didn't answer. Pyle had let them off the hook and he had a cold, uncomfortable feeling that he knew why. Lillian watched him, suddenly fearful. "What is it, Marty?"

"I don't trust him. He knows a lot more than he lets on."

The president attempted a chuckle that ended in a croak. "Aren't you getting a little paranoid? Pyle could have blown the whole thing sky-high. But he didn't."

"That's what bothers me." Rodale slammed one big hand into the palm of the other. "Simon, we've talked about this before. Your vice president didn't take the job because he wants to be in the second spot. He intends to become president."

"But, Marty," Lillian said, "he gave his word."

"Don't give him any credit for that. The cabinet went along with the plan, so Pyle had no choice. A vice president too eager to take over has the same social standing as a ghoul."

Moody rested his head in one hand. He was visibly exhausted. Lillian stepped to his side quickly, her hands on his shoulders. "Come on, dear, you have to get some rest."

"No, wait," Moody said. Taking a deep breath, he seemed to draw on reserves of strength. "Spencer Pyle is right. I couldn't handle a continuing crisis. He's given us some time to get the cure, but if it doesn't come soon, I'll—"

Lillian wouldn't let him finish. "SUCCOR will be back soon. I'm sure of it," Lillian said.

"Maybe. But my God, it's an awful long shot."

Rodale stood over the president, his expression sour. "There's something else. I think Pyle knows about SUCCOR."

"What are you talking about?" Lillian asked.

Rodale's face broke into a cynical smile. "Just before Pyle left, he made a little slip of the tongue. He said he'd do nothing until our 'effort to find the cure failed.' Not one of us said anything about 'finding' anything."

The curtains had been drawn in the president's bedroom against the late afternoon sun. Moody lay in his bed, an open book lying unread on his chest. The nurse, Beth Diego, stepped in noiselessly and peered at him. His eyes were open.

"Mr. President," Beth said, "Mr. Passmore is here."

Moody gestured his assent and the agent entered.

"Good afternoon, Mr. President."

"You have the information?"

"Yes, sir." Passmore opened a folder.

"How long was she at the apartment?"

Passmore ran his finger down a paper. Before he could respond, Moody spoke up. "No, Bill, never mind, I don't know what's come over me." He waved his hand in dismissal. "Let's forget it."

"Yes, sir," Passmore said, and he seemed to relax. "Will there be anything else, Mr. President?"

"No."

Passmore closed the folder and started toward the door. He had almost reached it when Moody spoke again, his voice strained. "Wait."

"Yes, sir?"

"I'm sorry, it's not . . . I guess all I want to know is how long was she there?"

Passmore stood quietly for a few seconds, the folder in one hand. Then he opened it, his eyes quickly scanning the agents' report.

At 2202 hours, transportee entered Apartment 21B, 928 Foresman Way, Suitland, Maryland. At 2306 hours, transportee departed the apartment and was returned to the White House. Elapsed time while beyond observation of the Service—one hour, four (64) minutes.

"Well? How long?" The president's voice was urgent.

Passmore swallowed, then said firmly, "Mrs. Moody was in the apartment for eighteen minutes, sir."

The faint hint of a smile played around the president's mouth. He inclined his head in a gesture of thanks and dismissal.

Passmore turned on his heel, and left through the anteroom that had been adapted for a nurse's station. Beth Diego glanced up as he passed. It was with some surprise that she noted a film of sweat on the agent's face.

CHAPTER SIX

Spencer Pyle leaned against the fireplace in the master suite of the big brick turn-of-the-century building in northwest Washington, swirling very old brandy that glowed sensuously in the subdued lighting.

"I made a serious tactical error," he said gloomily.

"If it's about that . . . general," Yvonne said, "I prefer not to hear it."

Pyle sipped his brandy and watched his wife strip the rings from her fingers, knowing that the vigor with which she performed this task was a measure of her state of mind.

Of course, it had been a long time since her moods had really concerned him—long before they had moved here to their official home on the grounds of the U.S. Naval Observatory. Once the quarters of the Chiefs of Naval Operations, it was now the home of the vice presidents of the United States, but never, not even when Nelson Rockefeller had lived here, had it looked like this. After taking over, Spencer and Yvonne had ordered every stick of the functional, government-provided furniture removed. Bringing in a young go-getter of a decorator from New York, they had authorized what to her was all the money in the world, the only caveat being that when the Pyles gave their first party, in the not-too-distant future, every infinitesimal, beautiful detail must be complete. Working furiously with an army of assistants, the young woman had met the deadline, and this huge bedroom, with its subtle palette of colors, superb fabrics, and minor masterpieces on the walls, reflected what genius and money could do.

"I just didn't expect Armitage to do away with himself," he muttered. She twisted around to look at him, both hands at the nape of her neck, undoing the clasp of a magnificent, multi-stranded diamond necklace. In Zurich, ten years ago—or was it eleven?—he had written an $800,000 check to pay for it.

"What *did* you expect from a man whose career was about to be destroyed?" She stopped wiping her face, threw the cotton pad down, and eyed him in the mirror. "How can you discuss character assassination and suicide as though they were stocks and bonds? When we married, I knew you were cold and maybe even ruthless, like a lot of people said, but I told myself that you were basically decent." Yvonne leaned forward and clutched at her chest as if having trouble breathing. "My God," she gasped, "how could I have been so wrong?"

He winced, not at her words, but at the ugly lines of her neck and jaw. Yvonne was ten years his senior, and although it hadn't seemed all that important twenty years ago, when they had married—particularly since she had style and breeding—it irked him that with all the beauty his wealth could now command, he had to put up with her unattractiveness. She *did* have her usefulness, though.

Pyle eyed her calmly. "You speak rhetorically, of course." He slumped into the pull-up chair, his brandy dangerously close to spilling on the Brittany faience covering. "I usually enjoy our talks, my dear. I really have no one else I can trust. But these attacks of self-righteousness can become quite dull. Understand what I am saying. We are very close—unbelievably close—to a permanent move to better quarters." He glanced around with mock disdain at the fine old room.

"*We?*" Yvonne said. "Supposing I just opt out of this marriage? How do you think the public would take that?"

Pyle waggled a reproving finger at her. "Back to middle-class respectability in Hamilton, Ohio? Think about it. No more jewelry by Shlomo Moussaieff, underwear by who is it—Oggioni?—or dresses by that monstrously expensive queer in Paris." He jerked a thumb at a Cézanne over her bed. "How about replacing that with a Jules Feiffer cartoon?" He maintained a light tone, for neither of them took their recurring threats of divorce seriously. The symbiotic nature of their relationship, he assured himself during infrequent periods of calm, made their marriage stronger than had they always seen eye-to-eye. It was a question as to who would lose more in a divorce. True, Yvonne was no beauty and never was, but she wasn't afraid to speak her mind, which had always been first-class. Not many of his associates and so-called friends had the courage to tell him when they thought an idea of his was asinine, but with Yvonne, you got truth unfiltered. As time went on he had come to realize how much he relied upon her for giving him painful yet valuable assessments.

Yvonne didn't bother to respond to his threat. He watched her doing some arcane thing with her hair, then walked to the window, looking out on the distant spire of the Washington Monument, a lighted sword aimed at the dark sky. His knuckles tapped a tattoo against the glass as he reflected on what his next move should be.

Within days of Moody's decision to implement this Operation SUCCOR, Looey was reporting on it in detail. Of course, going back to what was it—World War II?—was comic strip nonsense, but since neither Moody nor Rodale was a fool, there might be something to it. One did not take chances when so much was at stake. The removal of General Armitage had not accomplished what he had hoped. Now the new man, this retired officer, must be eliminated. If that failed, then the plane—or *vehicle*, as Looey called it—stashed away somewhere in New Jersey must be found and destroyed. That would settle this thing once and for all. Then he could relax and wait for—his thoughts were interrupted by Yvonne.

"I hope you have sense enough not to try anything else," she said. "Let Moody go ahead with his ridiculous scheme. You said yourself it was a nuthouse idea with no chance of succeeding."

Pyle left the window and seated himself on the Louis XV brisée. Idly, he picked at the gilt, knowing that it annoyed her. "Oh, it might have one chance in a million. But even so, I can't risk it. That's why I had to lean on Armitage." He gazed into the depths of his snifter ruefully.

Yvonne swiped viciously at her face with cleansing cream. Pyle watched in the mirror as she removed the cleverly applied makeup that transformed an elderly, homely woman into appearing *soignée*, as the French put it.

In midpass, she suddenly stopped, the arm and hand holding the cotton pad frozen.

"What did you say?" Her eyes were round with horror. "This thing they're trying does have a chance? You mean there *is* a possibility of finding a cure for cancer?"

Startled by her vehemence, and conscious of having made an error, he nevertheless recovered quickly. "A very, very small chance," he assured her. "Infinitesimal. The whole wobbly structure is based on a dubious premise and a lot of inadequately tested technology."

"Then you're keeping your hands off."

"I didn't say that."

"You must, damnit!" Her eyes blazed. "Spencer Pyle, you can't stand in the way of what the world has been working and praying for so long."

"Now wait a minute." He cursed himself for getting into this mess. "If I thought it had a real chance, of course I'd lay off. What do you think I am, some kind of an ogre?"

She waited just long enough for the word to resonate, then said quietly, "You're not making sense and you know it."

He was on the defensive and angry about it. "Look," he said, "I'm probably doing Moody a favor. He's getting his hopes up over nothing—he's sending men out to die for nothing." Yvonne's expression was unchanging, hard. He tried again.

"Listen, my dear." He hated cajoling, but sometimes it was necessary. "I've been giving a lot of thought to this cancer thing. The incident rates keep going up faster than the cure rates. It's a nightmare. So I'm going to establish the Pyle Foundation for Cancer Research. I've already talked to my attorneys." He spoke more rapidly now. "Initial endowment—seventy-five million dollars. Annual funding—twenty million dollars. Bring in the best medical minds in the world. When I'm president, I'll lobby Congress for additional federal funds, I'll speak to the world, do the 'vision' thing George Bush always talked about. We'll lick cancer without going the mumbo-jumbo pulp fiction route."

He got up and placed the empty brandy glass on the mantel. Yvonne had gone back to her mirror. He hesitated, looking at the stiff back with the bony shoulder blades moving under the skin. Why couldn't she say something? What the hell, did she think he was kidding?

He closed the door behind him. A damn good idea, that cancer foundation. Great tax write-off. Maybe some day soon he'd get around to putting the thing together.

It had been quite a day, Kogan reflected as he checked the clock. It was ten o'clock—better make that 2200 hours and get used to military time again. They were all going to have to make adjustments, learn things. The last few days had been kindergarten for time travelers. Working in the small library where Kogan had first met the president, and which was, he discovered, called the Treaty Room, they had poked at maps, examined

diagrams of plane interiors, discussed history and alternate strat-
egies, and listened to Staff Sergeant Otis Hiraga joke about his
rank.

"Wonder what a staff sergeant's pay was in 1942?"

"About eighty dollars, I guess," Kogan said.

"A week?"

"A month," Kogan answered, chuckling. "If it would make
you feel any better, I could promote you to master sergeant, even
make you an officer."

Hiraga shook his head. "Support group recommended the
rank. And making me the crew chief gives me a low profile."

"Probably best, unless you can look Italian," Kogan said.
"There were damn few Japanese-Americans in the Pacific
Theater and most of them were interrogator-translators." He
glanced sharply at Hiraga. "You don't happen to speak Japanese,
do you?"

"Speak it? About enough to order sushi and find the can.
Should I?"

Kogan shook his head. "No. Not important. Just thinking that
if anyone back there asks, we might use it to justify having you
along."

"Well, as a kid I used to spend every summer with my grand-
parents in the San Joaquin Valley. Thanks to them, I'm a fluent
listener."

Kogan picked up a three-dimensional drawing of the T-ray
projector. "Okay, Sergeant, what does this damn thing do?"

"You really want to know?"

"Sure," Kogan replied. "Just keep it simple."

"Simple? But of course, *mon général.*" Hiraga chuckled, then
sobered quickly. "Tell you the truth, Joe, even those of us who
worked on the original project don't fully understand why it
happens. But it works when we do certain things, and for now,
that satisfies us."

"The key to it all," the physicist continued, "took place in
1973, when two physicists studying cosmic ray showers discovered something that just couldn't be, according to Newtonian

laws and Einsteinian theory. Their instruments, which recorded primary cosmic rays colliding with the atoms of the Earth's outer atmosphere before striking Earth, showed something scary. The cosmic rays traveling at about the speed of light were being beaten to the recording instruments. In essence, my friend, something was moving *faster* than light."

"Whoa," Kogan said. "According to Mr. Pendergast, who taught me eleventh grade physics at Somerville High, that isn't possible."

"Mr. Pendergast was right, but it happened. And perhaps you remember that he also taught you the greater the velocity of any object, the slower time moves, right up to the speed of light, when time stands still."

"So?" Kogan cocked his head to one side. "By implication, you're saying that if the speed of light is exceeded, time moves backward?"

"Precisely. Now you can understand the importance of these tachyons. That's what those speedsters are called. *Tachy* is Greek for 'accelerated'; *on* is from the French, meaning an elementary particle."

Hiraga warmed to his subject. "The initial problem," he said, "was that we physicists knew that no material object can *reach* the speed of light. Einstein's theory of relativity proved that. However—and this is fundamental to understanding the success of tachyon development—there is nothing in his theory that says objects can't go faster."

"Now, just a damn minute, Otis," Kogan said. "That doesn't make sense. If your Porsche can't reach the speed of light, no way is it going to go faster."

Hiraga nodded, his face a mix of amusement and frustration. "English is the most versatile and expressive language in the world, but it is a poor tool for understanding complex physical science. If I could write a few equations on this sheet of paper, you would understand what I'm talking about."

"Sure. About like I can paint the ceiling of the Sistine Chapel."

"Precisely," Hiraga said. "So let me jump quickly through this semantic thicket by quoting a colleague of mine. He described it as a 'kettle boiling before the heat's turned on.' In other words, things *can* move faster than light if they could reach the speed of light—"

"But—"

"Please." Hiraga frowned and extended one hand, palm outward, rather like an Indian chieftain asking for peace. "Let me go on. Supposing your rays *did not have to reach* the speed of light? Supposing they exceeded that speed from the instant of their creation or inception? Would Einstein's theory be violated? A rhetorical question, Joe, but I assure you it would not. Once we accept that, and once we have physical evidence of the existence of tachyons, there is no scientific reason to reject what at first seemed to be a physical impossibility."

"I'll take that on faith, Otis," Kogan said. "But you're talking theory. What I want to know is how you get that ugly piece of artillery you call the tachyon projector to send things back in time."

"It wasn't...hell, it *isn't* easy. The key to it lies in the fact that the tachyon is an elementary particle. That means it can be combined with the molecules of other elements. By using subatomics, we in essence could marry it to any common element, and by doing so could control it, even transport it, by a specialized beam technology developed through particle physics. Working that out drove some of us crazy. Okay. Once the tachyon beams strike an object, regardless of whether it's organic or not, and dependent upon the quantitative strength we give to the beam, the act of transcending temporal–spatial limitations is accomplished. The real fun part, scientifically speaking, is to get back to not only *when* we want, but *where* we want. That drove the *rest* of us crazy."

Hiraga folded his hands on the table and inclined his body forward. It was obvious that he was warming to his subject. On the other side of the table, though, Jake Longford's eyes glazed and he expelled a breath—of boredom and incomprehension, Kogan thought sympathetically. The physicist was doing his best to keep his explanation simple, but it was like describing a carburetor to a couple of Lhasa apsos.

"There are, however," Hiraga continued, "boundaries that we cannot cross. I think I mentioned earlier that with current tachyon technology we cannot retrogress more than fifty-five or sixty years. With further study and adequate funding, I'm sure we can push those limitations back. You see, Joe, the problem is—"

"Thank you, Otis," Kogan said, interrupting. He had something more pressing on his mind—a question that needed resolution right now. "I sincerely mean that. You've been very patient with us. If you say the projector works, fine, I believe you—especially since you're going along. All I can say is I'm glad I don't have to fieldstrip that sucker."

Kogan refilled his coffee cup. He felt somewhat shaky, because now he had to go beyond the academic lecture and get into real *terra incognita*, into places he didn't understand and could never comprehend, but where he—where they, all of them—absolutely had to go. If Hiraga said they couldn't, Kogan might as well walk into the Family Quarters, shake hands with the president, and apologize for taking up his time.

"Now, my friend," he said, easing into it, "let's get to the bad news. I remember you saying that we're going back through a middle-of-April window, correct?"

"April 17 to 19, 1942. Right."

"Why?"

"Let's see." Hiraga gave that some thought. "Armitage briefed us on that a few weeks ago. Well, as I recall, he said we had to wait until MacArthur had shifted his headquarters to Australia. That way we could issue fake orders in his name to General Wainwright on Corregidor." The physicist drew designs on a pad. "I'm not sure I understood that. Why not go earlier and issue fake orders from the War Department to MacArthur?"

"Because, my friend, MacArthur would have told the War Department to shove it. He followed orders only when they suited him."

Hiraga raised his eyebrows at that. "So," he said, "do we have a problem with the window?"

"We do, Otis. Middle of April won't do a thing for us. We've got to change it." Kogan watched him closely. "Can do?"

"Change the date?" Hiraga rolled his eyes heavenward. "Jesus, Joe, if you only knew how much work went into setting that up." He sighed heavily. "Okay, hit me with it."

"A very narrow window, my friend—April 29, 1942."

The physicist cocked his head at Kogan. "You *are* serious about this?".

"Dead serious. You see, there's only one day—one night, really—that we can get Babcock off Corregidor. April 29, 1942. We get there too early, we could get into trouble—the Japanese have an air base at Davao a few hours away, and if they spot us..." Kogan didn't finish the sentence. "If we get there too late—hell, don't even think about it, we'd never get Dr. Babcock off the Rock. So, do it. Get us in there as close to the evening of April 29 as you can. The only guideline I can give you is that if you have to err, get us in early rather than late. Let me put it this way—early isn't good, but late is fatal." Kogan rapped his knuckle on the big table and spoke slowly, with emphasis. "This, Otis, is all-important."

"All right, but I wasn't joking about needing mainframe time—a lot of it. There's more than a thousand lines of programming to be revised and rechecked."

"Will it keep us from leaving Pearl Harbor on time?"

Hiraga rested his head against one hand. "Maybe, maybe not, but I tell you one thing, the sooner I get to that VAX 8800 on the plane, the better chance we've got."

He turned to Longworth. "Can you get me a flight up there tonight?"

Longford reached for the phone. "Doctor, you've got it. I'll set up a chopper to get you out to Andrews. The White House

Military Office can order a special air force flight to New Jersey. It'll be waiting for you when you get there."

Hiraga stuffed papers into his briefcase and headed for the door. With his hand on the knob, he turned back to Kogan.

"You say I make eighty bucks a month?"

Kogan gave him a look of synthetic concern. "We'll throw in a quarter's allowance. That's another thirty-six dollars."

"Well, hell, that's very generous. See you in New Jersey."

"Otis, wait a minute." Kogan threw down his pen and leaned back in his chair. "Got one more question for you. You're married, aren't you? Got children?"

Hiraga's smooth-skinned hand toyed with the doorknob. "Yes. I have a wife and one child—an eight-year-old girl, Machiko." He looked uncomfortable.

"Why you? There are other scientists qualified to operate the equipment. Single men, without families, right?"

Hiraga nodded. Just for an instant, the impassivity of his face broke, then the stoic mask fell in place again. "I've talked it over with my wife. Told her only that it was an assignment with some danger. She said it was up to me. I should do whatever I thought was right."

"Otis, that's my question. Why are you going?"

"Let me give it to you straight, Joe. We couldn't get another scientist to volunteer. This is a long jump, the tachyon projector has been installed hastily on the carrier, and the computer tie-in can be tricky. In other words, because of the time element, R & D has been skimpy, almost nonexistent. I don't know what's going to happen after we get back there, but the time transition phase both going and coming could be tough."

"You still haven't answered my question. If those young, single hotshots are coming up short on guts, why the hell you?"

"Oh, I don't know." Hiraga sounded weary. "Maybe it's because I'm the only one around who was involved with the experiments back in 'seventy-eight."

"What's that got to do with it?"

Hiraga opened the door and started out as though the conversation was finished. Then he turned back. "Remember the video I showed you? I still have nights when I wake up staring into that poor woman's face. Maybe this will help." And he was gone.

After Hiraga left, Longford and Kogan continued to work, but it seemed only a short time before Charles stuck his head in and asked if they wanted supper. Kogan looked at the marble-and-malachite clock against the wall and saw with surprise that it was already five. They were hungry. And drinks, gentlemen? Definitely. Sipping a very old, satin-smooth scotch, Kogan eyed the littered table with distaste.

"Who's our administrator?"

"Administrator?" Longford shook his head dubiously.

"Yeah. The detail man, record keeper?" Kogan gestured at the pile of books and papers.

"General Armitage was going to do that himself, I guess. The guy had a fantastic memory. Prided himself on never forgetting anything."

Kogan felt an urge to point out that Armitage would have been a great sergeant major, but there was no point in criticizing the fallen. A sergeant major was really what they needed. His mind ranged a bit.

"Gotta make a phone call." He picked up the phone and asked for Passmore's office. "Let me ask you a question, Bill," he said to the security director. "You by any chance run a security check on Michael Witkowski at the National Archives?"

Passmore answered without hesitation. "All Archives personnel have background clearances."

"I'm not talking standard clearances. Did you do anything special on him?"

"I'm sorry, General Kogan, the law forbids me to give out that information."

Kogan's first reaction at being called "general" was shock. After the president's announcement, he'd pretty much forgotten it. Actually, the promotion was sort of meaningless—not like the real struggle through the ranks that took nearly a lifetime.

"Mr. Passmore," he said formally, "it seems to me the laws are being sort of bent around here already. Now, it's important that I talk to Witkowski about our little trip. You understand what I'm saying?" He waited. "So have you checked him out?" Kogan thought he heard the crash of another Secret Service scruple falling.

"Yes, sir." Passmore sighed. "When we worked the Mac-Arthur files. He's clean."

Kogan then made another phone call.

The clock struck a melodious eight. "How's the pie?"

Witkowski stuffed another bite of cream pie into his mouth and looked around the sumptuous furnishings of the Treaty Room. "Great, but I intended to vote for President Moody all along. Jesus, what a place. Never thought I'd get to the second deck of the White House." He scraped the remains of the pastry off the plate with the edge of his fork. "Which brings a question to mind. How is it that someone—like you, say—who isn't rich, famous, or particularly attractive—gets in here without a tour ticket?"

Kogan leaned forward, all seriousness. "I'm going to explain that. Then I'm going to ask you a question. If you answer no to the question, you absolutely must forget everything I've told you." He let that sink in. "I'm very sincere about this, Mike."

The plump archivist in his rumpled old Ivy League suit placed his plate carefully to one side and folded his hands in front of him. "All right, Joe, go ahead."

"Before I dump the big one on you, there are a couple of things to clear up. You know computer technology pretty well, don't you?"

"We talking about building or running them?"

"Suppose you had to load a lot of information into a computer from, oh, say, documents and books at the Archives."

"No problem."

"Quickly."

"No problem."

"Over a long distance. Say, from here in Washington to a plane flying over the Pacific?"

"No problem," Mike said. "We've got a couple hundred satellites, commercial and government, that could do it. As a matter of fact, the National Archives transmits data worldwide that way."

Kogan nodded in satisfaction. "Great. That's what I wanted to hear."

"I dunno," Mike said slowly. "You need a lot of clout and money to get transmission time over our net."

"We've got it, friend."

Mike gave a wry glance around the elegant room. "I can believe it." He shook his head. "Weird. Couple days ago you were bitching about needing new tires for your car. Now, all this. What the hell *is* going on?"

"Not yet. One last question. How's your love life?"

"Have mercy," the archivist protested.

Kogan's face sobered. "I'm not kidding, Mike. I know you're single, but is there someone out there you're real serious about?"

"No, not really. I date now and then—she's an instructor at Georgetown—but it's no big deal, if you know what I mean." He leaned forward, one hand extended beseechingly across the table. "Now, come on. What gives here?"

So Kogan told him.

He left nothing out, including his own doubts. When he finished, he gave Mike the bottom line. "So. I want you to become...oh, let's see...Master Sergeant Michael Witkowski, serial number 1425876, born about 1910, and enlisted in 1930 at the start of the Great Depression. You're an administrator—been a company clerk, first sergeant, and sergeant major. In March 1942 you were shipped out to Melbourne, Australia, where you're attached to MacArthur's headquarters. There you become administrative assistant to Major General Joseph Kogan." He took a deep breath. "At least, that's the sort of thing you might have to tell people back there."

Finished, Kogan leaned back and waited for Mike's reaction. All during the recital, the archivist had listened intently, his eyes on Kogan's face, his expression unchanging. Even the time travel had hardly caused the flicker of an eye. Would he blow up Kogan wondered. Call the whole scheme insanity, as he himself had first done? Stomp off, shouting with a cynical laugh that they'd have to find themselves another guinea pig?

"Well, Mike?"

"Born in 1910! Good god, I'd be eighty-four years old!"

"You've taken good care of yourself." Kogan tensed. The expedition really needed the archivist.

Mike's expression was thoughtful. "Jesus, Joe, when we land on Mindanao, what are we going to tell them? What's our cover story? Who are we? What are we supposed to be doing back there?"

Kogan couldn't restrain himself. He chuckled aloud. Pushing his chair back, he got up, walked to the fireplace, and braced himself against it with both hands, still amused. He felt good. Witkowski had accepted the bizarre, incredible story completely—had become so wrapped up in it that he was already anticipating the tough spots. Kogan looked into the ornate mirror. He wondered if old Ulysses Simpson Grant had ever stood here after a long day and examined *his* reflection. With the dark circles under his eyes and the stubble of beard, Kogan thought that tonight he looked about the general's age. But he felt good. He'd recruited a top-notch man.

Kogan checked his watch. Almost midnight. As the government sedan headed east on Independence, the lights of the dwindling traffic flashed in his face erratically with hypnotic effect. He slumped down in the back of the government sedan, closed his eyes, and tried to put his mind in neutral.

The intensified throb of the car's engine brought him to full consciousness. They were moving more swiftly now, crossing the bridge. Kogan heard his driver speak rapidly into a handheld radio.

"There's a tail on me," the driver said, then listened for a moment. Putting the radio down, he gripped the wheel firmly with both hands.

Looey yawned just as the radio beeped. About time, he thought. The two of them had sat for hours in the big black van a couple of miles east of the Anacostia River, and Cramer was not scintillating company.

"Yes?" he said into the transmitter. Tersely, a voice informed him that Kogan had left the White House riding in the backseat of a standard government sedan, a Chevrolet. Looey checked his watch.

"Finish your coffee," he spoke softly to the middle-aged ex-fighter who drove for him on those occasions when skill at the wheel could mean the difference between success and failure. Cramer might be a bit thick, but he handled a steering wheel like Bernstein plying his baton. The big thug took a quick, noisy gulp, recapped his thermos, and buckled his seat harness.

Careful study had picked this spot. Lathrop Street was low-scale residential, unlighted, with thick tree branches arcing over the pavement to intensify the darkness and shield the van from curious eyes. The street opened on busier Adams Avenue, just a couple of miles from Kogan's apartment. The plan was simple. Simplicity, Looey had found, was like money in the bank. He had found that since existence itself is complicated, it follows that doing something to someone who does not want it done to him can be extraordinarily perverse. Why, then, he rationalized, complicate things?

Seven blocks east, at the corner of another street much like the one on which the van was parked, a brick serpentine wall, one of those much beloved below the Mason–Dixon line, curved gracefully around the corner. At the precise point where the two roads met stood a mighty southern oak. The tree, Looey had pointed out to his assistant, was what he wished the government sedan to encounter at considerable speed. But should Kogan's car somehow manage to avoid the oak, the brick wall behind it would do the job very nicely.

"Gotcha," the old fighter had said.

The radio beeped again. Their prey was just two blocks away.

"Let's go," Looey said. With a well-tuned rumble, the van's motor turned over, the headlights came on, and the big vehicle moved smoothly onto Adams Avenue, sparsely traveled at this hour. As Cramer guided the van into the left lane, Looey craned his neck to spot the headlights of Kogan's sedan coming up behind him on the nearly empty road. He saw them and smiled. When the government car passed on the right, Cramer would hang back a ways, pacing the quarry until the big oak tree came in sight. A sudden acceleration, a twist of the wheel, and the heavy van would knock the lighter sedan across the road into the tree, or alternatively, the wall.

Reviewing the plans may have been why Looey missed a battered LTD station wagon and an old pickup entering the street from the south side. The station wagon pulled out in front of the van, while the smaller truck, loaded with house painting equipment, eased abreast in the right-hand lane.

"What the hell?" Cramer muttered, and blinked his headlights. The driver ignored the signal, seeming content to stay well within the speed limit. A faint warning flashed in Looey's mind.

"Pass him," he hissed.

Cramer looked across at the pickup to his right. "Sumbitch in my way."

"Well, move him out of the way, dammit!"

The old pug had just started to twist the wheel when an explosive sound came from the station wagon. A tire had mysteriously blown. The old LTD started to fishtail, the brake lights flashed on, and it screeched to a halt. Cramer, cursing, slammed on his brakes, but too late. With a crash of crumpled steel, the van hit the back of the station wagon, bouncing it forward a few feet. The pickup running in the right-hand lane skidded to a halt, backed quickly, and came up behind the van.

Looey and Cramer were shaken but unhurt. The driver of the station wagon—a short, stocky man in a flashy Hawaiian shirt— eased himself out and walked back to examine his crumpled bumper. At the same time, Looey saw the government sedan bearing Kogan pass.

"Back this thing up! Let's get out of here!" Looey's voice was frantic.

"Can't. Fuckin' pickup's behind us."

"Well, get that wagon out of the way!"

Cramer grunted, and filling the air with curses, hit the ground and started toward the other driver, now examining his blown tire. The man turned to face Cramer. In a split second, Looey knew that he had made a very serious mistake. This was not some Joe Citizen wearing a flashy shirt and driving a beat-up station wagon that had just been rear-ended. The man seemed not at all upset by the formidable Cramer.

Looey yelled frantically at his driver to back off, but the fighter had heard the bell and come off his stool, like old times. Nothing was going to stop him.

"Shorty," he snarled, "move that wreck or I'm gonna bounce you like a rubber ball."

The smile never left the small man's face. His right hand flashed, hitting Cramer alongside the head. The small automatic in his hand added considerably to the impact. Cramer fell against the van and hung there for an instant, defying gravity, before slumping to the ground.

As Looey started out his side of the van, the door handle jerked from his grasp. A large man in paint-spattered coveralls held a gun on him, gesturing an unmistakable invitation for him to get out.

• • •

In the glare of headlights, Kogan got a quick glimpse of a man in a sport shirt kneeling by a flat tire. He thought he recognized him. Leaning forward, he tapped the driver on one beefy shoulder. "Hey, friend, that looked like Passmore back there."

"Could be, sir."

"Let's stop. Looks like he's got trouble."

The driver shook his head. "He can handle it," he said, and kept on driving.

"Yes?" Her voice was drowsy.

"Hi," Kogan said, checking his watch. It was late. He had spent some time telephoning the White House after being dropped off. His call had evidently been expected, for the operator patched him into the radio security net and Passmore came on the line. In a short, rather disjointed conversation with the director, he'd found out that someone had been trying to take him out of the picture. The plot had been monitored and broken up, and four people were now in the federal slammer, at least temporarily. Since the culprits had not been caught in the act, their release tomorrow was expected. No further aggression was expected from them, the agent said, but the person behind it—and Kogan had the feeling that Passmore knew who it was—might launch another attempt soon. In the meantime, he could sleep soundly. A couple of agents posted outside his apartment would see to that. Kogan thanked Passmore, who wished him well on the forthcoming enterprise.

Fay was next. He gripped the phone in his hand tightly. He did not look forward to the call.

"Honey, I'm sorry as all hell to bother you this late, but I'm going out of town for a while."

She came awake instantly. "Where are you going?"

"Well," he said uncertainly, "I'm afraid I can't tell you. It's on . . . government business, classified. I don't like sounding mysterious, but my lips are sealed." He laughed, and the sound of it rang false in his ears. It was a lousy way to treat someone as good and generous and loving as she had been. He jacked up his cheer quotient to maximum brisk.

"Look, Fay, I won't be gone long. Be back in town before you know it. Give you a call as soon as I get here." He couldn't make it sound convincing.

For a few seconds, all he heard was the sound of deep breathing, as though she were trying to get control. "Joe, does this have anything to do with that snapshot?"

Suddenly, he was tired of giving her the runaround. He really wanted to say yes, it has a helluva lot to do with the snapshot, but he knew he couldn't—or shouldn't.

"Nope, not at all," he answered. "It's like I said, a little trip out of town."

She must have caught the make-believe. Her voice sounded lifeless. "All right, Joe, whatever you say." They both held silent phones. He probably shouldn't ask the question—he'd already made his decision—but he couldn't stop his mouth from forming the words.

"Uh . . . speaking of the photo," he said casually. "You have any idea where it was taken?"

"Yes, it was captioned. Mindanao. That's part of the Philippines, isn't it?"

"Yeah, right." Well, that was that. He had known it since seeing the locket, but he wanted to hear her say the words.

"So long," he finally said.

"Good luck," she answered, "and good-bye."

CHAPTER SEVEN

Planes being ferried to England in World War II had taken off from its broad runways. During Korea, several reserve squadrons had been activated and trained there. It had been closed down from 1955 to 1966, but the Vietnam War had brought it to life again as helicopters and attack bombers roared over the aging buildings and the flat New Jersey countryside. For more than two decades now it had been totally abandoned, the concrete of its runways succumbing gradually to sturdy weeds while the metal of its structures oxidized to a scabrous red-brown. Surrounded on all sides by pitch pine, scrub oak, and laurel, the old air force installation showed little more signs of life than the surface of the moon.

The hangar that sheltered the only plane on the base had a

haunted look. It was huge and neglected. Rubble cluttered its floor, old crates were stacked in corners, rusted thumbtacks held scraps on a bulletin board.

The vast interior amplified the sound of the men's footsteps as they slowly circled one hundred thousand pounds of Boeing 737. The big transport's hide was camouflaged circa early World War II.

"What the hell's that?" Kogan pointed to the nose of the plane. In letters two feet high, the name *Sucker One* appeared.

Longford gave a chagrined chuckle. "My fault. Hired a commercial paint company to put the camouflage on the plane. Told them it was for a movie. As sort of an afterthought, I remembered that most World War II planes had names, so I gave the guy a phone call and told him to paint *SUCCOR I* on it." The big pilot gestured. "This is how it came out. I'll get it changed at CINC-PAC."

They started to move away, but Kogan stopped and looked back at the name. "Leave it the way it is."

"Why?" Longford was surprised. "That name ain't exactly inspiring."

"Maybe not, but it's got a certain validity."

"I don't get it."

"We're going back telling the folks on Mindanao to cheer up. We tell them we're from MacArthur's headquarters in Australia, and we're going to get food, medicine, and ammo to them, and who knows, the marines may be on the way. Beautiful. One week after we leave the island, the roof falls in. They end up dead or POWs."

"I get it," Longford said. "Come on," he motioned. "I'll show you the interior."

Kogan interrupted, placing his hand on Jake's arm. The more he saw of the big fellow the better he liked him. Longford seemed easygoing and friendly, yet strong-minded, but there was a hint here and there—his eyes, the set of his mouth, a tenseness in his movements—that bothered Kogan. He needed to know more about his second in command, because this wasn't an ice cream social coming up. Longford could well end up commanding the operation.

Kogan leaned against an engine housing. "Jake, I'd like to know. What are you doing in this outfit?"

Longford's brows dropped into a frown. "Maybe we should talk about it later. The crew will be here any moment."

Kogan decided that it was time to find out if those two stars the president had pinned on him were made out of tin. "Let's get one thing straight. From now on, when I ask a question, I want an answer. I'm not just making conversation. I need to know, you understand?"

Understand? Yeah, he understood. A ghost of a smile touched Longford's lips. He figured sooner or later Kogan would make a move to pin down the reversal in their roles. He felt no resentment. He admired the guy for clearing up this command thing, and for his toughness. No operation this dangerous should be an exercise in democracy. It was too perilous, too fast-moving for decisions by committee. If Kogan wanted to know more about his exec, that was okay. But where the hell should he start? With his sick wife? Or with him standing at attention in front of General Crofter's desk in Omaha? Whichever, he wasn't going to enjoy talking about it.

"All right, General, here it is." He decided to see if he could get away with the abridged version of Jake's Perils. "Three months ago, I was assistant G-4 of SAC, in Omaha," he began. "The chief of staff, General Weldon Crofter, called me in one day and said he knew I had problems, that I wasn't too happy. He asked me if I'd be interested in a top secret job. I'd be flying, he said, and it was hazardous, but it paid quite a bit of extra money. He warned me not to ask him any questions about what I'd be doing, because he just damn well didn't know. I said I was interested, they cut me some orders, and I flew to Washington. There General Armitage interviewed me."

He sneaked a look at Kogan. The rough features of his face were unreadable, but it didn't look like the sanitized version of Jake's story was going to make it. "Well, Armitage thought I'd do, SUCCOR sounded a bit crazy but interesting, and here I am."

"That's it?"

"Yeah. That's it."

"Those problems General Crofter mentioned—what were they?"

Jake let out a deep breath. Now he had to say things he didn't even want to think about. Open the Pandora's box of memories. Recall the wonderful woman he'd married twelve years ago, her blazing intelligence that was so superior to his, and the pitiful thing she had become.

"Well, this is what happened." He'd go over it as quickly as possible, then put it back where he tried to keep it—in the little theater of the mind where attendance was mandatory, particularly about two in the morning.

He began at the beginning. He had been stationed in California, at Norton Air Force Base. One night he went alone to some long-forgotten party and met Vivian. She was teaching comparative literature at the University of California at Redlands and he had never met a woman who knew so many things about everything except the air force. She was warm and funny and of course damned bright, and for some reason that still escaped him, she was interested in him. It hadn't been a case of instant love. It was definitely not a case of common interests. But they liked each other and both were ready for something more than just casual sex or living together. Liking soon turned into loving, and they married. When Jake got transferred to San Antonio, Vivian quit her teaching job and followed him and that was the pattern for the next seven, eight years—happy, wonderful years. Then something happened.

He explained to Kogan that looking back, he realized there had been clues even earlier, but the first time he really noticed the change in Vivian had been at a reception for a new commanding general. Jake had been talking to another major's wife, a woman he hardly knew, not particularly attractive or witty, and the small talk was pretty slow going. Looking for an excuse to leave and find Vivian, he laughed excessively at something the woman said, then glanced across the room to see his wife staring at him. He smiled and raised his glass in a toast, but there had been no response, only a malignant glare that chilled him.

With that first small incident, he entered the very worst years of his life. Vivian's baseless jealousy intensified. She threw tantrums with increasing frequency, marked by fits of screaming that seemed to go on forever. At last there had been hospitalization. The diagnosis: schizophrenia. The treatments didn't work and she retreated into a vegetative state, barely and only infrequently recognizing him.

"Joe, *I* was going crazy, too. Seeing her just killed me. Staying away was worse. My job at SAC headquarters was a lousy paper-shuffling bore. I needed to fly, to do something that would save my own sanity." Longford looked up at the towering shape of the plane. "God knows, if anything can get a man's mind off his troubles, this is it."

Kogan reached out and gripped Longford's shoulder. Jake was amazed at the power in his hand. He started to say something, but his words were cut off by the rackety-rack of a helicopter dropping down to shatter the stillness of this deactivated air force base.

"Well, General," Longford said. "Sounds like the boys are here."

A bank of computer dials, keys, and digital readouts extended from just aft of the galley a dozen feet down the starboard side of the plane. Seats had been removed to accommodate the big VAX 8800 and a small office, which contained a desk and shelves holding reference works and manuals. Other seats had been removed to provide six Pullman-style bunks.

Kogan leaned against one of the seats near the computer bank, facing five men. Two of them, Jake Longford and Otis Hiraga, he of course knew. The other three he had just shaken hands with. Mike Witkowski was still in Washington, getting data organized for transmission to the plane's computer.

Kogan had explained the addition of Witkowski to the group and commented briefly and regretfully on the death of Armitage. Now it was time to get down to business.

"For the most part," he continued, "look on me as sort of a tour guide. I'll explain the local customs, point out places of interest, and try to keep us out of trouble. I pretty much know what's going to happen from hour to hour—"

"I doubt that, General." The interruption came in a clipped Boston accent. Kogan turned toward the speaker. Dr. Arthur Von Porten, world-class botanist and expedition physician, slumped negligently in his seat, watching him coolly, his agate blue eyes crowding a long, arrow-straight nose. His words had very little give in them.

"Mind explaining that?" Kogan asked, having a little trouble keeping his tone pleasant. *Christ, there's one in every outfit.*

"The history books are going to be changed—by us," Von Porten said. "Our presence on Mindanao in 1942 is an alien intrusion. People back there will react to that. What they do will inevitably change history, all because we are there." He took an empty pipe from his pocket and stuck it in his mouth, seeming to draw comfort from it. He smiled winningly at the group. "It's as simple as that. And, General," he added, "that is why you will not know what is about to happen."

Kogan had hoped this kind of transphysical thing wouldn't be brought up. The expedition's configuration was designed to make them as inconspicuous as possible. Their uniforms, their identities, the plane itself, had been chosen to give them the lowest of profiles, to fit unobtrusively into the war-torn world of late April 1942. He could answer the doctor, perhaps not to everyone's satisfaction, but adequately, he felt. Yet, coming into the organization late placed him at a disadvantage. He needed to give the crew a little time to accept him. It wasn't good leadership to preach to them in the first ten minutes. He passed to Hiraga.

"Otis," he said equably, "got an answer for Dr. Von Porten?"

Hiraga took the baton with grace. "Doctor," he said, "this is not the time for bullshit, so I won't even give it a try. I'll just say we're dealing with things that are outside human experience. Now, I'm a scientist, not a philosopher or psychic, and I think your logic is pretty solid. Things *will* be changed by our presence back there, and in ways, perhaps, that can't be foreseen. But if we go back on kitten's feet, slip in and out with no fuss or bother, history isn't going to be changed all that much. If we big-mouth it and make a lot of mistakes," he shrugged, "who knows?"

Von Porten's brows met in a frown. "That's just not satisfactory. The slightest impingement on the past could have incalculable effects on the future."

Kogan jumped in quickly. "You hit the nail on the head, Doctor. The effects *are* 'incalculable,' so let's not waste any more time speculating." He decided his words sounded harsh, so he softened his tone, adding a line he remembered from an old TV series. "Let's just be careful out there."

From his talks with Longford and the bios he'd been given, Kogan knew that Von Porten was a reluctant volunteer. A brilliant researcher specializing in tropical plants, he was also a medical doctor, though he had not practiced in some years. A perfect choice, on paper, he had only agreed to come along after a desperate and emotional plea from Dr. Sidney Eccles, an old friend and mentor. Von Porten might not be the best of team players, Longford had explained, but his expertise could be absolutely vital in obtaining B-juice.

Kogan turned to the fourth man, lean-framed, with a wrinkled, deeply tanned face far older than the rest of him, which was about thirty-five. "Betts, isn't it?" he asked.

"Yes, sir, Larry Betts."

"Aeronautical engineer with Boeing?" Kogan was just repeating what he already knew, but it was a way for him to get acquainted.

"Well, I was, but I'm about to become a first lieutenant in the U.S. Army Air Corps, which, considering that my highest previous rank in the service of my country was private first class, makes me mighty proud."

Betts, according to Longford, knew the aging 737 about as well as anyone on earth, and since they were going to be a long way from home, it would be up to the engineer to fix whatever went wrong. "When you see him, you won't believe he's in his thirties," Longford had said. "Looks ten, fifteen years older. Don't know if it's genes, losing his wife and son in a drowning accident, or the booze he used to drink."

Kogan asked Betts, "What part of the South you from?"

"Tennessee, sir." It came out *suh*. "Little place called Hanging Limb, about eighty miles east of Nashville."

"Helluva name."

"Helluva place. When I turned eighteen, I couldn't wait to get out of there. Didn't realize how far I'd leave it behind one of these days."

"Plane in good shape?"

"The best." Betts slapped the bulkhead with a proprietary air. "She ain't much to look at, General, but you pour the coal to her, and this old lady will make some eyes bug out back there."

"Okay, but just remember—and you, too, Jake." He eyed Longford. "We're not back there to show the wonders of Future World to the yokels. If we can lumber in and out of Del Monte at a hundred and seventy-five knots, so much the better. And speaking of that, how are we going to talk to these people? We got a radio that will net with theirs?"

Hiraga, sitting at the computer, grinned. "We've got a dandy, General. Support Group couldn't get the Smithsonian to let go of the old SCR-287 set they've got, so I had a couple friends of mine from the engineering department at MIT come down and look it over. In a week, they built a totally compatible radio one-tenth the size of the original."

"Do we know what frequencies they were using at Del Monte?"

"Doesn't make any difference," Hiraga said. "This little jewel not only can transmit and receive across the range from 200 to

12,500 kilocycles, but they built a scanner into it. Can pick up transmissions from Del Monte in half a second."

Kogan nodded approval and turned to the fifth man, handsome, dark-haired, with powerful shoulders and a lithe way of moving. He looked vaguely familiar, but Kogan couldn't place him.

"John Hortha," he said. "We met before?"

"No, sir, I'm sure we haven't."

"You did some flying in the service, didn't you?"

"Yes."

"And you're a test pilot for Boeing."

Hortha nodded. He definitely wasn't a motor mouth, Kogan decided. He would be copilot on the flight, and according to Longford, possessed an incredible knack with planes. "He's one of those guys born to fly," Jake had said, but admitted that Hortha's personal life was chaotic. He was movie-star handsome, but either didn't realize it or didn't care. No personal vanity. Quiet, and too nice for his own good. He had a lot of trouble saying no to anyone. His current wife, Lisa, had forged his name to a home improvement loan and used the money to buy herself a flaming red Mercedes 450 SEL that she had totaled before getting insurance. Now she was suing for divorce and everything Hortha owned, which wasn't much. Jake had chuckled, but he was at least half serious when he said that Hortha might be going on the flight to get away from his wife and her lawyer.

Kogan looked at his watch. "What time is the tanker due here, Jake?"

"Oh, in about twenty to twenty-five minutes."

"All right," Kogan said to the group. "Make yourselves comfortable. We've got just enough time to review the things we want to get done at CINCPAC—"

A buzzer, its sound halfway between a telephone and a doorbell, went off. Betts stepped quickly to a radiotelephone and answered. He listened, then glanced at Kogan. "For you, General." He handed the instrument over.

It was Passmore on the radio. "The fuel truck there?"

"No. Be here soon, though." Something in Passmore's voice made him wary. "Why?"

"Listen, General," Passmore's voice crackled with urgency. "Get that baby off the ground right now, before—I repeat, *before* —that truck arrives."

Kogan didn't need it spelled out. More trouble. Someone was after them like a pit bull with tunnel vision. He held the handset close enough so Passmore could hear what he was saying.

"Emergency, Jake." His voice was low. "Have we got enough fuel to get this thing in the air right now?"

Longford whirled and dashed for the cockpit, Hortha close behind. Kogan spoke into the mouthpiece. "Damnit, Passmore, you said you had security on this field."

"We have." The answer came quickly. "I've already contacted my people there, but they may not have enough muscle to stop whatever's coming. Can't chance it. You gotta get out of there fast."

Longford hurried back. Over his shoulder Kogan could see Hortha going through preflight. "Eighty-two hundred pounds is all we've got," the big pilot reported. "But as soon as the tanker gets here—"

"Forget the tanker. How far can we get on what we've got?"

"Oh, maybe Wright–Pat, but we'll need clearance to land there."

Kogan passed that on to Passmore. The Secret Service man assured him that the White House Military Office would get the clearance, wished them a quick good luck, and broke the connection.

"Let's move this baby out!" Kogan barked.

"Come on." Betts slapped Von Porten and Hiraga on the shoulder as he dashed for the open hatch. The three men hit the floor of the hangar with Kogan close behind. Betts jumped on a tractor hooked to the pulling lug of the 737. The others ran to open the hangar doors. A brand-new major general, a famed botanist, and a noted physicist strained mightily to open ancient, rusted doors. Behind them, Betts pulled *Sucker One* slowly toward the widening opening.

The door opened. Kogan, breathing hard, took a few steps outside and looked across the tarmac toward the main gate. Two government sedans, their tires screeching, sped from the old administration building toward the gate. The cars stopped, blocking the entrance and exit lanes to either side of the abandoned guardhouse. Four agents jumped out and with weapons at the ready, manned positions behind the sedans, peering down the old road running through the flat New Jersey meadows. In the distance, Kogan thought he could see the glint of a large vehicle moving along the highway toward the air base.

He jumped on the tractor. Hiraga and Von Porten hung on the other side.

"Move it!" Kogan yelled to Betts over the engine noise, and pointed at the oncoming tanker. They bumped over potholes for a couple hundred yards before Betts braked and disconnected the tow bar. The others ran for the plane. At the top of the still extruded ladder, Kogan looked over his shoulder. A half mile from the gate, a silvery tank truck coming at high speed bore down on the Secret Service sedans.

"Shoot, damnit," Kogan muttered through his teeth to the distant agents, then ran to the cockpit. The pilots were completing their checklist.

"Jake." Kogan pointed at the agents firing ineffectually at the truck thundering down upon them. "Get this thing rolling, quick!" Longford needed no urging. The engines accelerated with a shrill whine and *Sucker One* bumped across the crumbling asphalt toward the old, weed-eaten strip. Kogan stayed where he was, leaning forward between the pilots' seats, watching the oncoming truck.

The big tanker was only a couple hundred yards away from the gate and moving, Kogan estimated, at more than seventy miles an hour. The Secret Service men, frantically firing machine pistols, might as well have been throwing peanuts at a charging bull elephant. At the last second, the agents behind the sedan blocking the south lane jumped to either side. The juggernaut hit the car, disintegrating it, the bulk of the debris catching one agent in midair, throwing his broken body a hundred feet into a chain link fence. The other men kept up their futile fire as the tanker plunged through the gate, major parts of the sedan dangling from its massive bumper.

Longford pointed the plane's nose down the runway and advanced the throttles. "We're going downwind, Johnny. We got room to get her off?"

Without hesitation, Hortha answered, "No sweat. We're lighter'n a kite." He looked out his window. The tanker, about a thousand yards away, was speeding at a tangent across the field to intercept the jet. "We've got a little problem over here, though. That bastard's really moving."

Longford moved the throttles up to the fire wall. "Let's kick some sand in his face."

"Oh, shit!" Hortha exclaimed, still looking out the window.

"What's up?"

"Big, big trouble. They've got rocket launchers."

Kogan leaned forward to see. Two of the hatches on the huge silver fuel container had popped open. Men wearing stocking caps wriggled half out of the big vat, looking like tank captains in an open turret. They leveled launcher tubes at the plane.

"Jesus," he muttered.

Longford looked over his shoulder at Kogan. "What are we up against?"

Kogan squinted. "Misery. Those look like old Redeyes. They've got a range of nearly three miles."

Longford leaned forward, urging the plane on. Hortha, watching the dials, yelled "Rotate," and the big plane angled upward, leaving the runway, gaining speed.

"V2!" Hortha roared. "Maneuver speed!"

Sucker One fought for altitude. The tanker, still running at maximum speed, seemed to fall back. Kogan watched the men on the tanker put their weapons to their shoulders.

Longford shot a glance over his shoulder. "What the hell are they waiting for?" he asked Kogan.

"They're gonna shoot right up our pipes. Redeyes are infrared homing." Kogan bit his lip. "They'll probably wait until we're about a half mile out."

His words seemed to galvanize Hortha. "Jake, pick up some speed and level off. I'm dousing the engines."

"You crazy? We're only at sixteen hundred!"

Hortha seemed not to hear. He reached down, hooked his fingers in the fuel cutoff levers, and pulled. The roar of the engines quieted.

Longford grunted, then cursed. "Shit, I get it. Okay, now help me fly this thing." Both pilots grabbed the yokes. Longford's hand flew to the control panel. "Give the engines some flame retardant. Cool 'em down." Kogan heard the faint hiss of Freon splashing between engine cowlings and hot metal.

Above the whisper of air passing over the fuselage as the plane dropped lower, two muted explosions could be heard in the distance.

"Starboard her!" Longford jerked the wheel to the right. As the plane tipped, two rockets zoomed past. "Straighten out!" the pilot shouted. The wings tipped back to horizontal.

"Six hundred, Jake," Hortha called out. Longford held on to the wheel grimly.

"Four hundred!"

Kogan felt the sweat pour from his body as he watched the scrub trees come closer.

"Start engines!"

With a reluctant cough, the fuel ignited and the engines roared. "Ease into it!" Longford warned. The trees came closer, then stabilized. The big jets thundered triumphantly and the nose lifted.

The three men stared silently ahead as the New Jersey countryside swept beneath them, then slowly, Hortha leaned back and dropped his hands off the wheel. Kogan straightened and slapped both men's shoulders. "You guys always leave town this way?"

"Naw," Longford said. "Sometimes it gets real exciting."

"Sir," Looey said, "if I had been there, the whole matter would now be at an end. My subordinate somehow let the thing get out of hand." He sighed, then continued. "But you understand, sir, that I was incarcerated. Even now they are watching me closely."

"I know, Louis, and I appreciate your position," Pyle spoke into the scrambler phone, keeping his voice calm, winning by a very close margin over the urge to shriek obscenities. Only the knowledge that the four men in the tanker truck had been successfully picked up by helicopter and spirited away permitted him to exercise some control.

"What do you wish me to do now, sir?"

Cut your fucking throat, you feckless ass! The one thing that would have put a clean end to this whole operation had failed. So maybe it wasn't Louis's fault. After all, he hadn't been there. Nevertheless, a suspicion took form in his mind. Was Louis chronically inept—the Inspector Clouseau of operatives?

He stopped grinding his teeth long enough to check the calendar on his desk. "I want close surveillance of the situation at Pearl Harbor. But attempt nothing, do you understand? Nothing." Pyle paused for maximum effect. "If and when our friends return to Hawaii, I must be notified immediately."

"Sir?" The monosyllable suggested dissatisfaction.

"Yes? What is it?" Pyle's tone was impatient.

"Would it not be wiser to smash this endeavor before it gets into its final leg?"

"You mean while they outfit at Pearl Harbor?"

"Yes, sir." Looey waited.

It took a long time for Pyle to respond, and when he did, his words dripped with sarcastic anger. "I believe I've explained what I want you to do. You are not to question it. Remember, you are on probation. Fuck up again and you're through."

Pyle cut the connection and sat tapping his fingers on his desk. He hoped the behavioral reinforcement would improve Louis's future performance.

True, he had thought about a last effort at Pearl Harbor, but decided against it. The emphasis had suddenly shifted. Two abortive attempts, he realized, made a third too risky, too indicative, perhaps, of where the attacks came from. Besides, the security at CINCPAC would be impossible to penetrate. He could not risk having Louis or one of his agents captured. In the final analysis, Kogan and his people were headed into dangers that raised to astronomical numbers the odds against their ever returning.

Pyle's rapid breathing had abated and so had his temper. He even managed a small smile of confidence. Why take chances doing something that might not ever need to be done?

CHAPTER EIGHT

The office of the commander in chief, Pacific, was big, appropriate for the boss of the largest military command in the world. Its dimensions also fit the man who occupied it, Admiral Jefferson Edwards, U.S. Navy.

Huge, affable, and profane, the admiral had gotten much media attention in the last few years as he had climbed to the top operational command in the navy, the first African-American ever to hold it. There had been a lot of admiration voiced for his abilities, as well as some skepticism that his appointment had been politically motivated to capture minority votes for the president's party.

Kogan sipped the drink the admiral's steward served him, and on the basis of what he'd heard in the last few minutes, decided that Jefferson Edwards deserved his high post. Rising to the top ranks of any service demanded a mélange of qualifications— intelligence, drive, judgment—plus luck. Kogan knew well that for a black officer, the road was tougher, and the navy, hide-bound conservative in its selection of top officers, was toughest of all.

Standing well over six feet tall and maybe forty pounds heavier than when he'd been a stellar defensive back at the Naval Acad-emy, Edwards gave what Kogan guessed was the standard brief-ing for general officers coming through USCINCPAC. In a rumbling, mellifluous baritone, using language ranging between that of a professor of philosophy and a New York cabdriver on a bad day, Edwards spun a capsulated, precise rundown on the problems of the Pacific Rim. As Kogan listened, he guessed the commander in chief, Pacific, could be one extraordinary friend or one hell of an enemy.

At this moment, Kogan wasn't sure which it was going to be.

Underneath a surface cordiality, the big officer's words were edged, and Kogan sensed a bitterness verging on anger. He was pretty sure he knew why, and to some extent could appreciate it. Except for material and technical support, the president had cut CINCPAC out of Operation SUCCOR. Secrecy, to Moody, was paramount. The more people who knew about it, the more risk there was of public exposure. It was too dangerous. Yet to Jefferson Edwards, whose command stretched from the Cali-fornia coast across the Pacific, and through the Indian Ocean all the way to the east coast of Africa, it must seem a failure of presidential confidence in him.

"By the way, General." Edwards dropped his briefing tone. "I'm not sure what circles you move in back in Washington. You know the president?"

"I've met him," Kogan replied carefully.

"You heard he spent a few days out here not long ago?"

"Yes, sir." He left it at that.

"I didn't get a chance to speak with him. He wanted no so-cializing, no ceremonies." The admiral's face was guileless.

"Otherwise, I imagine he would have told me something about your project."

"Maybe, maybe not. It's his baby, but SUCCOR's got a very high security classification."

"Yeah." Edwards grunted. "I assumed you're not out here to visit the seven sacred pools."

Kogan could feel the anger building and tried to stop it. "I'd like to tell you more about what we're actually doing," he said, "but my hands are tied."

"Well, let me ask you something." Edwards's voice was ruminative and carefully casual, but Kogan stiffened for the storm he felt was coming. "What would you do if a bunch of strangers came swooping into your command area demanding a whole lot of this and that and not telling you a damn thing?"

Kogan saw that conciliation wasn't going to work with Edwards. He gave up trying. "Glad you asked, Admiral, because I'd bust my ass to make them happy, comfortable, and satisfied. Particularly if I knew my president was all wrapped up in what they were trying to do."

Edwards's chuckle was cold. "Well, you and I must have gone to different service schools,'cause I don't agree." His voice suddenly boomed. "When I took over this command, I assumed full responsibility for everything that happens in it—I mean everything. If something breaks, pulls loose, or turns sour, I'm not going back to CNO and say, 'Gee, sir, it was secret and I didn't know anything about it.' Uh-uh. This is my command, friend, and any secrets here belong to me. Lemme put it this way. If I have to have a bellyache, I'm sure as hell going to enjoy the ribs and pecan pie first. That clear?"

"Very clear."

"Okay, then. You've imposed a whole list of demands on me." Edwards waved the sheets of paper Kogan had given him. "Now you tell me more will be forthcoming, and I'm supposed to act like nothing more than a goddamn quartermaster sergeant."

"Admiral, we're grateful for your help." Kogan kept his voice deceptively mild.

"Listen." Edwards's voice clanged like an iron skillet slammed on a stove. "Demonstrating the social graces isn't going to cut it. You aren't just asking for some hot meals and clean sheets for a couple of days. You've taken over an entire wing of the BOQ for the seven of you and you want the rest of the building sealed off. You want a twenty-four-hour guard on that jet of yours. You want all air traffic suspended over a five-thousand-square-mile area of the Pacific for two nonconsecutive days to be designated." Edwards flipped a page and continued. "You've installed some damn mysterious thing on one of my carriers and sent it—along with escort vessels—charging off to WesPac." Edwards stopped reading and gave Kogan an outraged glare. "You want meteorological forecasts over the western Pacific beginning three days from now and continuing for the next ten days."

He slapped the document on his desk and leaned forward. His smile lacked humor. "General," he said with exaggerated courtesy, "have I missed anything? Would you like Maui? The seas to part?"

Kogan put his drink down and leaned forward in his turn. He didn't want to lock horns with Edwards, but they might as well have it out now. Arguing was wasting the one thing they didn't have—time.

"Admiral, let me explain something." Kogan's tone was calm. "I appreciate your feelings. This project is disruptive. Your fleet operating schedules are getting screwed up. But I'm telling you that Operation SUCCOR is important. I wish I could find a word that carries more meaning because what I need from you is wholehearted cooperation. And frankly, I don't see it forthcoming." Kogan pointed at the list on the admiral's desk. "You think that's all? Hell, that's just the big stuff. I've got little stuff that will drive you crazy—like exclusive use of a lease line to Washington with scrambler capabilities, and some fancy work in your machine shops. I want priority for all SUCCOR transmissions in and out to anywhere. The same for our housekeeping details: laundry, tailoring, messing, barbering, and medical."

As the words poured out, Kogan began to enjoy himself. As a lieutenant colonel, he would be standing at attention before Edwards's desk. As a major general, he was seriously outranked. But by God, he'd given up plenty to take on a job that didn't offer much chance for a protracted life, and no sailor, four stars or not, was going to give him a ration of shit. "In short, Admiral," he continued zestfully, "I'm gonna be a real pain in the ass to you."

Edwards sat quietly for a moment, intently examining one large black hand. Then he laughed—a short explosion of sound without humor.

Kogan, impatient, said, "I don't know what that means, but my bottom line is, do you support us all the way or not?"

"Let's suppose, General, that I give you one hour to pack your goddamn bags and get your bizarro troop out of here. Then what?"

Kogan's eyes narrowed at the challenge. He was having trouble controlling his temper. "I don't have time to play guessing games. Do we or do we not get everything we want exactly where, when, and how we specify?"

Edwards got up from his chair, walked to the liquor side table, and waved his glass at Kogan, who shook his head. "You know," he said, and all the pugnacity had left his voice, "I can tell when a man's bluffing, and Kogan, I don't think you are. To tell you the truth, I've got a feeling that if I ordered you out of here, I'd be heading for early retirement. And, man, there's nothing sadder than an old sailor with nothing to do but play golf every day." Edwards finished making his drink, but instead of returning to his chair, he walked to the huge wall map that defined his command. He rapped his knuckles on the map and spoke in a voice so low that Kogan had trouble hearing him.

"Friend, there's one thing I've gotten so far out of our talk." Edwards paused. "Whatever you're doing is damned big. Probably a helluva lot bigger than anything the Pacific Fleet is doing right now. If that's true, you need the best support you can get, and I'm the only one out here who can give it to you."

Admiral Edwards slumped down in his chair and sighed. "Here we are at each other's throats and we really want the same thing: for Operation SUCCOR, whatever the fuck that is, to succeed. But, Kogan, understand this. How well could I do my job out here if I didn't know my country's policy in the Pacific and the Far East? How do you expect me to help you if I don't know where the hell you're going and why? I'm nothing but a goddamn mule with a lot of muscle and no brains. Why settle for a mule when you can get a top-notch driver, besides?" The admiral's grin was broad.

Kogan nodded slowly, his mind whipsawing between Edwards's solid argument and the presidential order to keep a tight cap on this thing. Sure, the admiral would comply with orders to support them, but there were dozens of ways a commander could slow down jobs, and one was to let his people know how little enthusiasm he personally had for the task. Edwards was tough and smart, and if he wanted to, he had the power to make things hum. If he didn't, God knows when they'd get away. He was an asset SUCCOR needed.

Kogan made his decision.

"All right, Admiral. I'll recommend to the president that we open the project up to you. That's as far as I can go."

Edwards's face showed no sign of victory. It had a touch of sadness in it. "When you talk to him, tell him I'm sorry."

"Sorry about what?"

"His illness. Cancer, isn't it?"

Kogan hoped his face didn't show his dismay. "Come on, what are you talking about?"

Edwards snorted. "Look, my command provided the housekeeping, cooking, and area security for the so-called presidential party while it was in Kauai. I told my Intelligence people—and I'll match mine against any in the armed forces—that I wanted confirmation of the man's presence. It was easy enough to pick up a glass that he'd used. The fingerprints didn't match. I then had blow-ups made of all the recent news photos taken of the president. The last picture we could definitely identify as being of Simon Moody shows him badly underweight and aging. A week later another photo showed a purported president who had gained twenty pounds and was the picture of health. So, am I right?"

"I don't know what you're talking about." Kogan pointed to a red phone on the desk. "Will this get me the White House?"

"I've got an operator out there who'll get you God." Edwards stepped to the door. "I'll take a little walk." He pointed to the desk. "Hit that button when you're finished."

Six minutes later, Kogan replaced the phone and pressed the button. He felt better. The door opened and the admiral's big frame thrust itself partway into the room. "Well?" he asked.

Kogan nodded. "Admiral," he held up his glass, "for the price of another drink, I'll tell you the goddamnedest story you ever heard."

Briefing Room, CINCPAC

Four Days Later

"*Ten-shun!*"

Kogan cracked the command out as Admiral Edwards entered the room. The men of *Sucker One* scrambled to their feet and into a semblance of the position of attention. They were a damned unmilitary-looking bunch, Kogan noted, but they at least resembled the World War II soldiers they were supposed to be. The faded khaki shirts and trousers, web belts, shoes and socks, close haircuts, stem-wound wristwatches—even the underwear—were all as authentic as the support group could provide.

"At ease, please," Edwards called out, and the six men—Witkowski had joined them yesterday—sank down into the comfortable theater seats in the paneled briefing room. Kogan shook hands with the admiral.

"Glad to have you with us this morning, sir," Kogan said rather formally, in deference to the others present. He and Edwards were friends now, and the admiral considered himself one of the group, showing the keenest of interest in the details of the operation. "Look on me as your chief of staff, Joe," he had told Kogan. "All you gotta do is tell me what you want us to do here and you can damn well count on it getting done." And it had been. But even with the admiral's powerful backing, they had only just kept to schedule.

A new interior configuration gave Von Porten a small office in the rear; a plexidome had been installed for 360-degree observation; realistic plastic props had been constructed that could be blown off the nacelles if need be; special cantilever tires for short runways and heavy braking had been flown in from Seattle and put on by CINCPAC crews. Through it all, Otis Hiraga had labored mightily at revising the target window on the VAX 8800, sending his new lines of programming across the Pacific to the carrier *Theodore Roosevelt* for checking and installation.

Only late last night, pale and red-eyed, Hiraga had stumbled into Kogan's room at the BOQ and said that it was finished. Not only that, but the support group scientists aboard the carrier had put their approval on the changes.

"We get in on the twenty-ninth, then?" Kogan had asked. He thought the physicist was going to hit him before he staggered away toward his own room. Well, shit, it *was* a dumb question.

As the admiral sank into a seat this morning, Kogan shuddered to think of where they'd be had they not cut him in on Operation SUCCOR. The admiral had been a mountain of strength, and their clash of wills four days ago seemed like ancient history.

"Glad to be here, gentlemen," Edwards boomed. "Tell you the truth, this is the only excitement going on in the entire command." He grinned at the others and shifted his bulk, causing the chair to squeak in protest. "Let's hear how you're getting along."

Kogan leaned on the podium. He didn't have a lot to say, and much of his unease had vanished with Hiraga's announcement last night. All the others were pretty much up-to-date on problems and solutions. This meeting was more for Admiral Edwards's benefit—sort of a thank-you for his help.

"I had the pleasure of talking to President and Mrs. Moody earlier this morning," he began. "And, Admiral, I want to pass along their heartfelt appreciation for what you and your command have done for us. It goes without saying that we here join in that sentiment."

Edwards grinned broadly and nodded his thanks.

"We leave this afternoon and fly to Guam, refuel there, and then rendezvous with the *Theodore Roosevelt*—provided courtesy of the admiral here—for the jump back."

Edwards broke in. "I had a little talk with the carrier's skipper, Joe. He's a good man. He'll do his part." He chuckled. "He'd better. I told him if he screwed up, his next command would be the fleet garbage scow."

"That's comforting to know, Admiral. Well, once we're back there, we get hold of Dr. Roger Babcock and obtain the serum, or at least the formula for it. Dr. Von Porten," Kogan glanced at the botanist, "must be satisfied that he understands the ingredients, proportions, and dosage. Then we come back."

Edwards leaned forward, his eyes alight. "Joe, you said something about using flying boats to get this Babcock off Corregidor. I want to ask you something. They did have submarines going in and out almost to the very last, didn't they?"

"Yes, sir."

"Well, look," Edwards spoke persuasively. "Wouldn't it be safer to get him out on a sub?"

"Only if we controlled the submarine, Admiral. The problem is, of course, that we could get a vertical deviation on rematerialization of . . ." He looked at Hiraga. ". . . how much, Otis?"

"Can't say for certain, General. As much as five, ten thousand feet."

Kogan turned back to Edwards. "How'd you like to find yourself in a submarine ten thousand feet over the Pacific?"

The admiral shook his head. "Or *under* the surface. Boy, even a Los Angeles class sub would collapse like a tomato can. But what I was asking—"

"Yes, I know," Kogan interrupted. "Okay, why don't we get him on a submarine such as the old *Stingray,* or *Swordfish,* or the others who made trips in and out just before the surrender?" He had hoped a question like this would not be asked. It brought into uncertain focus the whole otherworldly nature of the project.

"All right," he continued. "Suppose we bring Babcock out in one of the subs they had back then. He'd end up in Australia or Pearl Harbor. That means that Babcock didn't die in a Japanese prison camp, he survived the war. That's changing the past. More important, he would probably have given the secret of B-juice to the world."

"Jesus, I see no problem with that," Admiral Edwards said.

Kogan smiled ruefully. "In the long run, you're probably right. But we have to take a shorter view." He stepped closer to Edwards. "Anyone in your family ever die of cancer?"

"Nooo...not that I can recall," the admiral said slowly. "Though my mother's first husband did, a couple years after they were married."

Kogan nodded. "And then your mother remarried."

"Yeah, the guy who turned out to be my father."

"Suppose a cancer cure had existed back then. You wouldn't be here today. Your last name wouldn't be Edwards. You might look something like you do, because of your mother, but you'd be someone else." He paused and reflected. "Maybe that person would hate the navy. There could be hundreds of thousands, maybe millions of cases like that. The world could be unrecognizable." Kogan stopped. He wanted to back off from the speculation and get back to cases. "You see, Admiral," he continued, "these Catalina flying boats left Corregidor and flew into Lake Lanao, on Mindanao. They're real; they're part of history. We'll be there to meet Babcock when he gets off. We can control the situation. And he'll end up in a POW camp just as history intended."

Von Porten's reedy voice broke in. "And what if the good

doctor doesn't want to end up in a POW camp? Suppose he wants to come back with us?"

"You know the answer to that one," Kogan growled.

"If he stays behind, he dies unpleasantly, right? That's a helluva reward for what he'd done."

"Von Porten," Kogan said carefully, "let's not let our brains turn to oatmeal. Dr. Babcock died. We can't, we won't, change that. But if it's any comfort to you, a lot of fine things are going to be written and spoken about Roger Babcock . . ." He glanced at his watch. ". . . if we can pull this thing off. In a real sense, he'll be immortalized. And that's about all we can do for him."

Then, surprised, he checked his watch again. It had stopped. "Hey, fellas." He held up his wrist. "Remember to keep winding these things, okay?"

Betts raised his hand. "One thing I don't understand is how General Armitage missed the flying boat possibility. You told us those crates flew all the way from Australia to Corregidor and back to pick up nurses. That's a long flight—hell, I guess you could call it an epic flight."

"I guess you could," Kogan agreed. "Because it was. Too bad it's forgotten. I think Armitage was just too overburdened to read all the literature. Look," he reached behind him and picked up a large, green-covered book. "This is *The Fall of the Philippines*. It's the official version of what happened out there, from the time the Japanese attacked until the islands fell. It was written by the late Professor Louis Morton of Dartmouth on an army contract and published by the Government Printing Office. It's a marvelous job of research—sort of the Bible on the campaign— yet Dr. Morton himself missed the flying boats. Scott Armitage used this book—"

"How did *you* run across the flights?" Longford asked.

"I had a lot more time on the job than General Armitage."

Admiral Edwards frowned and shifted in his chair. "There's something I don't like about this, Joe. You said the PBYs made that trip to pick up nurses? How are you going to get this Babcock aboard one?"

"Bump one of the nurses."

Edwards's scowl deepened. "Yeah, how?"

Oh-oh. What they planned to do was not really unjust, and every step had been programmed so as *not* to change the past in any fundamental way, but Kogan hesitated because no matter what kind of spin he put on it, the explanation was going to sound like self-serving crap.

"All right, Admiral. The night we arrive we send a radio to Corregidor on MacArthur's command frequency. General Wainwright will assume it comes from Australia and the great man himself. The message will tell Wainwright to bump a nurse and put Babcock on the plane."

"Just like that—no explanation?"

"No explanation, Admiral. Remember, this is MacArthur talking."

Edwards's big forefinger waggled in the air. "By God, whoever he was, if I had that command I'd tell him to fuck off."

"Admiral, I believe you. But Wainwright . . . old Skinny, as they called him, had a special feeling for MacArthur, sort of like a dog for his master. He worshiped him, even though he recognized his egotism, his distortion of reality. Wainwright wouldn't think of disobeying, or even questioning the order, no matter how much he disagreed with it."

"So you doom a woman to POW camp or death, and you get Babcock out." But even as Edwards spoke, his sense of outrage faded visibly. Kogan realized that the admiral's logical mind had taken over, balancing the cost against the gain.

"Yeah, okay," Edwards continued. "I guess it's worth it." His smile apologized. "Sorry I lost my cool."

"Let me clear that up a bit more because what we're doing is not all that bad," Kogan said. "You see, we have the names of the women on that flight. That and a lot of other stuff is in our computer data base now, courtesy of Master Sergeant Michael Witkowski, my administrative chief. And we also know that only about half the nurses ever made it to Australia. One of the flying boats busted its hull on Lake Lanao and the nurses it carried ended up stranded on Mindanao. They eventually became POWs. We bump one of those. The only difference is she'll be captured on Corregidor, rather than Mindanao. It won't change history, and it won't change her life...much." He turned to Witkowski. "Mike, what's the nurse's name?"

The archivist quickly opened a file and ran his finger down a list. "General, you said to pick her alphabetically. Her name is Crane—Captain Marie Crane, Army Nurse Corps."

"Did she survive?" Edwards asked.

"With all due respect, Admiral, that is something we don't want to know." Kogan hurried on. "Okay. Now, there's a couple of other items we need to cover—"

A phone in the back of the briefing room rang. Witkowski picked it up, then looked at Admiral Edwards. "It's for you, sir." Kogan waited while CINCPAC listened, muttered a question, then cursed fluently.

"Joe," he said, putting the phone down. "Rough weather moving toward your transfer area. Close to typhoon strength. My meteorologist says you can make your rendezvous ahead of it, providing you get out of here within the hour. Otherwise, you might have to hang around for three, four days."

Kogan glanced at Longford. "Plane ready?" he asked.

"Yes, sir." The answer was emphatic.

"Thank you for your help, Admiral," Kogan said, gathering up his papers. "We're hauling ass."

They had refueled at Guam, where a puzzled naval air station commander had carried out the orders he'd received from CINC-PAC. Having turned out his entire U.S. Marine complement to beef up security during the two hours this strange-looking craft was on the ground, he was more than pleased to see it leave without incident.

Now *Sucker One* sped westward across a cobalt panorama of

emptiness. The race to beat the storm had been close, but they had won. Far to the southeast, towering thunderheads and a black, churning sea marked the advance of the massive front.

Except for the muffled roar of the jets, the interior of the plane was quiet, the conversation minimal, in sharp contrast to the relaxed noisiness of the flight from Pearl Harbor. Within a very few minutes, they would arrive at the time transference point.

In the dinky cockpit, Longford and Hortha leaned forward, scanning the ocean surface ahead.

"See anything, Johnny?" Longford asked.

"Nope." Hortha sat back, ran his fingers through his jet black hair, and yawned. If he was nervous, he didn't show it.

Betts sat on the jump seat behind the two pilots, watching the instrumentation. Kogan leaned against the bulkhead just forward of the galley, overlooking the cockpit. Hiraga sat back in his chair, facing the massive board that controlled the timing, placement, and intensity of the tachyon ray. An amber light flashed.

"Four minutes to lock-on," Hiraga spoke over the intercom. There was nothing more for him to do at this point. Everything was programmed to take place when GPS determined that the plane was properly positioned over the carrier group. He had gone through this transition phase once before, back in the penultimate flight before the project was shut down. It wasn't a pleasant experience, although he didn't recall much pain. Bizarre and otherworldly, it was sort of what he imagined an endless fall might feel like. He wasn't looking forward to it. Glancing forward at the cockpit, he saw Kogan in profile. The sight gave him confidence. The strong lines of the general's face—Hiraga was amused as he realized how natural it was to use the new rank— showed unconcern. *Sucker One* might as well be coming in for a landing at LAX. If only he could be that calm. But what was coming depended entirely upon his knowledge and competency. Not an easy load to carry.

What he wasn't sure of was hitting the window right at April 29. God help him—and the operation—if they came in late.

What Hiraga hadn't told Kogan was that he'd calibrated the hit at the day before—Tuesday, April 28, not Wednesday, April 29. He had thought a lot about what Kogan had said: "Early isn't good, but late is fatal." The variables—and he had pumped hundreds into the electronic guts of the mainframe—were just too unpredictable over a transit jump of fifty-two years, and he couldn't explain them to Kogan, so he had made the decision on his own. A little unhappiness if they were early he could handle, but to have to take responsibility for total failure—no way. There was no point in sweating it now. He and the VAX 8800 had done their very best. Hiraga shifted in his seat and waited.

In the cockpit, Hortha pointed. "Task force at one o'clock." Kogan squinted at the barely visible specks ahead. The carrier *Theodore Roosevelt* had been on a circle course of thirty miles radius for nearly twelve hours, her ship's officers ignorant of why the ship and her escorts were there or the purpose of that strange, menacing projector squatting on the flight deck elevator. The captain in particular was not thrilled by his assignment, nor with the taciturn covey of scientists and technicians who handed him his instructions, among which was the directive to turn off the entire array of *Roosevelt's* radar.

Although he had been forcefully told by none other than CINCPAC himself that he must follow orders to the letter, the captain could not help protesting—his ship would be blinded, he told the scientists, against incoming aircraft and their missiles. "It's only for one hour," the senior scientist had said soothingly, adding unnecessarily, the captain thought, that the international situation was not that tense. And so at precisely 1424 hours, as Hiraga was giving his countdown, the ship straightened out her course and sailed serenely in a northeasterly direction, her officers unaware that *Sucker One*, a dun-colored, nearly invisible speck in the sky, approached at an altitude of twenty thousand feet from directly astern.

"Two minutes to lock-on!"

"All right," Longford's voice came over the speaker. "Everyone buckle up." Betts gave the instruments a last, concerned look and left the cockpit for the passenger compartment. Kogan squeezed the shoulder of each pilot and walked back to the first seat on the port side adjacent to the bank of time transition equipment. Witkowski took the seat behind him, strapped himself in, removed his glasses, and polished the lenses carefully before slipping them into a protective case. Across the aisle, Von Porten, his sandy hair newly cut, peered out a window port at the ocean below, fingers tapping nervously at his seat arm.

"How do we look, Otis?" Longford asked.

"Fine. Hold her as she goes."

"Switch off autopilot," Longford said. "I'll take her to lock-on."

"Autopilot off," Hortha droned.

"One minute to lock-on." Hiraga's voice was flat as his body angled slightly, his eyes shifting across the control board to the atomic clock with its spinning digitals marking tenths and hundreds of seconds. "Ten seconds, nine, eight, seven, six, five, four, three, two, one..."

"*Lock-on!*"

Simultaneously, the plane's course shifted a fractional degree to starboard and its altitude dropped a half dozen feet as its controls were taken over by a sister VAX 8800 aboard *Roosevelt*. Three separate entities were now tied together under the control of the computer: the steering gear and power train of the carrier, the sighting mechanism of the tachyon projector, and the flight controls of *Sucker One*. All was in readiness for a signal emitted from eleven thousand miles above, coming from four equispaced GPS satellites. When the alignment of the plane and the ship matched the figures programmed into the memory of the computer, the T-ray would be fired. From lock-on until the projector fired, human reflexes were too slow and crude to carry out the maneuvering requirements.

Hiraga had explained to Kogan that he estimated it would take less than forty seconds from lock-on until firing. He was wrong, but not by much. Fifty-two seconds passed—a period of time Kogan remembered as interminably long—and then the T-ray struck. For the briefest of instants, the body ceased being a coherent organism and regressed into nothing but its billions of atoms. Kogan felt no pain. He remembered only a dulling of consciousness, a relaxing of involuntary muscles, a feeling that his life force was about to drain away. Then it was over. He got his bladder under control in the nick of time.

Laboriously, he released his seat belt and made his way forward.

"Okay up here?"

Longford answered with a monosyllabic grunt. He and Hortha were busy scanning the ocean below. Kogan joined the search and three sets of eyes swept the Pacific. The carrier group was gone.

Longford flipped on his intercom. "Otis, see if you can pick up the satellite frequencies." He glanced over his shoulder at Kogan. "Quickest way to find out if we're still in 1994."

Hortha stared down at the waters far below. "Pacific hasn't changed a damned bit."

"No transmission from GPS," Hiraga responded.

Betts's voice came through the earphones. "I'm running through the frequency spectrum now to see what I can pick up. So far all I've got is just garbled music, coming in from the east. Might be Honolulu."

Kogan tapped Longford on the shoulder. "Jake, let's turn her around and see if we can spot Mindanao."

Longford disengaged the autopilot, maneuvering the plane into a long, flat turn to port. Halfway through the turn, the dark smudge of the big island could be seen on the horizon.

"Good," Kogan muttered. "How far?"

"About a hundred miles. Want to make our approach now?"

"Not yet—too much light. What time is it?"

Hortha looked at his watch, shook his head, then peered out the window at the sun. "Hard to say. I'd guess about four or five in the afternoon. Hiraga should know."

Of course, Hiraga *had* to know. "Otis," Kogan called, "did we make it?"

"Hold on," Hiraga answered tensely. Then he raised his voice jubilantly. "Wow! My instruments say we did. A 19,139.723 day jump." Then he spoke slowly, uttering an oath as though it were a prayer. "Jeezzuss!"

Kogan scrambled back to the physicist's station. "What's wrong?"

Hiraga sat in front of his instruments with his mouth open.

"Otis! What the hell is it?"

Hiraga turned toward Kogan. He was pale, and beads of moisture covered his forehead, but a small grin began to spread across his face. "A damn close thing, Joe," he said. "We hit the far side of the window, but we're in it. I figure it to be five thirty-five in the afternoon, April 29. That's . . . Wednesday."

"Perfect!" Kogan slapped him on the back. "You did it, my friend. A goddamn bull's-eye!"

"Yeah," Hiraga said, and let his hands fall limp into his lap. "A bull's-eye." Silently, he blessed the innate caution that had caused him to set the target up one day.

Kogan started toward the cockpit, then stopped. "Hey, this is what you aimed for, isn't it?"

Hiraga chuckled. "Approximately, dear general, approximately."

"You sure about the time of day?" Kogan eyed him speculatively.

"Absolutely," Hiraga said. "But I want to run the star scanner. That'll give our position, as well—I hope." And he bent to his task.

Kogan could hear his labored muttering as he made adjustments. "This thing . . . [grunt] . . . damn well better . . . [heavy breathing] . . . work . . . or we're gonna sure as hell be stuck in World War II."

The instrument, refined by MIT for Operation SUCCOR, was a trilens catadioptric telescope with an electronic mount hooked up to the VAX 8800. Each lens sought out a predesignated star—

Regulus in the constellation Leo, Sirius in Canis Major, and M76 in Cassiopeia, pinpointing by resection *Sucker One*'s position on Earth to within thirty feet, then feeding the data to the computer that calculated time, latitude, and longitude.

"We got it, Joe!" Hiraga sang out. "Confirmation on the time to less than two minutes." He paused. "And we're about one hundred and thirty-two kilometers east of Mindanao. Hey, I think this baby will get us home."

Kogan set his watch, then tapped Longford on the shoulder. "Jake, we can't go in until near dark. That's a couple of hours away. Fly north, then get us back to Del Monte about seven-thirty."

"Good," Longford said. "We'll burn off some fuel. Johnny, set a course to northeast—three hundred knots. Stay well away from Samar and Leyte. We'll turn 180 degrees at eighteen hundred hours."

CHAPTER NINE

Forty miles north of Mindanao, *Sucker One* droned southward at seventeen thousand feet, air speed down to a lumbering 210 knots. Longford was navigating on the highest point of a landmass that became more distinguishable with each passing moment.

"Christ," the pilot said, wiping sweaty palms on his shirt. "I'm getting the willies. I can't believe this. I tell you, we're gonna land here and find Corazon Aquino in charge."

"Yeah," Kogan agreed. Getting the operation on the road had kept him so busy that the implications of being in a long-past time had not yet caught up with him. He hoped they wouldn't. Keeping their masquerade going while getting to Babcock wasn't going to leave a lot of time for staring at the sights and saying ain't this wonderful.

He turned toward Betts's station. "Picking anything up?"

"Like a tomb, General. They're just not transmitting."

Kogan looked at the purple-hued island ahead. He tapped Longford on the shoulder. "Okay, Jake, see if you can raise them. Betts hasn't been able to get a thing."

The pilot keyed the switch on the modern replica of the old SCR-287. "Del Monte Field." Longford's voice was casual. "This is Army 7114. Request landing instructions." No answer. Longford started to repeat his call, then stopped. "Hell, we'll see if we can pick 'em up with the scanner." He flipped the scanner switch, but the speaker remained silent.

The black mass of the island of Camiguin, northern sentinel to Macajalar Bay, loomed ahead. As the plane swept on into the gathering night, Longford tried again. There was nothing but silence.

"What the hell's wrong down there?" he growled. "Their radio operator asleep?"

"This isn't Dulles International," Kogan replied dryly. "General Sharp's got no planes. General Wainwright's got no planes. And they're not expecting anything in from Australia. No reason to monitor their radios."

"What'll we do?"

"Keep going."

Sucker One swept over Camiguin and started across the bay. Fishing boats could be seen hurrying homeward across the dark waters, and lights from small villages flecked the south shore. The waters of the bay fell behind and the plane crossed the coast on a southeasterly heading, following a strip of highway climbing from the bay into foothills.

"Getting close, Jake," Kogan said. "When we get there, buzz 'em low and slow. That'll get their attention."

"There it is!" Hortha pointed. "On the plateau dead ahead."

Kogan strained his eyes and saw it. There were no lights, but a broad swath of lighter green stood out against the darker foliage of the jungle growth. A half dozen pyramidal tents formed an uneven line along the west side of the strip. Near one of them, dimly seen in the twilight, an air sock hung listlessly.

Longford held the jet to 175 knots as it crossed the field. Easing the throttles forward slightly, *Sucker One* roared along the plateau, then climbed up and over the foothills of the Bukidnon Mountains to the east.

The radio crackled, and with a grin, Hortha flipped the speaker on.

Filtered through a primitive radio transmitter, the voice still carried authority. "Unidentified aircraft, this is Mindanao Force Command. Identify yourself."

As the ground station started to repeat its message, Longford broke in. "Mindanao Force Command, this is Army 7114, request landing instructions."

Kogan could sense relief in the voice as the answer came. "Army 7114, welcome, whoever you are. Use the main runway, northeast approach, but get down quickly—we could have visitors."

Longford increased speed slightly as he brought the plane around. "Take over, Johnny," he muttered. "I'm gonna be busy with the radio."

As Hortha took the controls, Longford transmitted again. "Mindanao, do you have any field lights?"

The response took on a note of amusement. "Our regrets, Army 7114—no field lights. We will have a truck meet you at the end of the runway and lead you to a revetment near the control tower."

Kogan leaned forward. "Jake, I spotted a revetment at the south end of the runway. Tell him we'll park there." Longford nodded and transmitted the message.

The voice took on a sharper note. "Army 7114, for security reasons, you will park where assigned."

Longford glanced up at Kogan, who shook his head. The pilot spoke again into the radio. "Mindanao, we prefer the south revetment. Please keep all personnel away from that area."

The voice on the ground went crisp with authority. "Army 7114, this is Colonel Edmonds, deputy Mindanao force commander. You land your plane, we will handle field arrangements. Is *that* clear?"

Kogan took the mike. For the first time, he was going to pull rank—his new rank. "Colonel," he said, "this is Major General Kogan, U.S. Army. We don't want to add to your burdens, but we *will* park in the south revetment. Keep all personnel away from this plane's taxi area. Send a vehicle only when called for. Is *that* clear?"

The tone of the voice changed. "Yes, sir, Army 7114. I understand. We'll send a sedan when requested."

Sucker One made a last clumsy lurch and came to rest in the vast, tree-walled space carved out of the Philippine jungle. The big JT8D engines stopped, the diminuendo whine of the rotor blades sounding like a great, tired animal bedding down. Except for the soft beat of tropical rain, the dark revetment that hid the big jet was silent.

Inside the plane, lights flickered on and a minicelebration began, with even Von Porten joining in, his Back Bay reserve partially dissolved. Longford's booming voice rose above all the other "We made it!"'s. He ran to the pantry, yanked out a bottle of champagne, and threw his arm around Kogan's shoulders.

"Hey, Joe! I stashed this away. Let's have a quickie for old *Sucker One*." But something in Kogan's face brought Longford back to earth. He stood holding the champagne awkwardly, his expression changing to sheepish embarrassment. "Dumb of me—sorry." Tossing the bottle to Betts, he said, "Put this away, Larry."

Kogan leaned back against a seat, his arms folded across his chest. "Okay, listen up." He wasn't sure what he was going to say, but he had to squelch the euphoria and get them back on track. The tough part of their mission lay ahead.

"We've done what no men have ever done before," he said

quietly. "We've left our own time and entered another. You feel good about it, you're excited. All right. Now forget it—wipe this wonderful, unique thing out of your mind and consciousness completely. Because it's not true. And this is an order, a direct order, from me to you: You are not from the future. I repeat: *You are not from the future.* Right here and now is *not* the past, damnit. It's the present for all of us, you understand me?"

Heads slowly nodded.

"I don't want a bunch of starry-eyed tourists walking around like this was some damn museum full of wax images. It's April 29, 1942, and these people are real, and they're in trouble. They've been fighting a losing battle for the last five months. And we're in trouble, too, because we're all in the same army and the same air corps and the same war. So act like it. Don't go around grinning and backslapping and saying we're going to win this war, because that's something they don't know, and so we sure as hell don't know.

"Okay. We've had a long flight from Darwin and we're tired, but we're on a mission from the Great Man himself, Douglas MacArthur. This is serious business, and you are to conduct yourselves accordingly." He checked the circle of faces. From their expressions, he guessed he'd gotten to them.

"Any questions?"

"Joe," Witkowski glanced worriedly at his watch. "It's after seven. Maybe we ought to send Corregidor the message bumping the nurse."

Kogan checked his own watch. "Not until the last minute. Some wise asshole with a soft spot for nurses may decide to send an interrogatory."

"Jake?" He glanced at Longford.

"No, sir." The big pilot grinned and slapped Betts's shoulder. "Time to get the props attached."

"Right." Betts hurried to the rear of the passenger compartment and tugged at the dull black strips of Styrofoam. "Otis, Mike," he called out. "Give me a hand."

The three men shouldered the cumbersome but light burden.

Hortha pressed the hatch button and the door swung open, letting the sweet, warm smell of rain-drenched grassland waft into the cooler interior of the plane. The three men scrambled out, carrying the collapsible propellers fashioned in the machine shops of CINCPAC and realistically painted. They could be blown off the engine nacelles by a tiny explosive charge detonated from the cockpit.

The radio squawked. Longford picked it up in the cockpit, listened, then stuck his head out.

"General, they want to know if we're ready for transportation yet."

"Tell them to send it out in ten minutes."

The three men scrambled back into the plane.

Kogan grinned at Hiraga. "How is it out there?"

"Great," the scientist grinned back. "Soft, warm air. Smells good—sort of like Maui."

Kogan turned to Witkowski. "Mike, make up a watch list using everyone except Colonel Longford and myself. Someone *must* be on board at all times. No exceptions. I'll get Mindanao force to put twenty-four-hour perimeter security around us, but no one gets aboard."

"Now, one last thing. You all know we have an autodestruct system aboard, but I want Larry to go over it so there'll be no misunderstanding."

Betts reached out and pulled a handle set innocuously in the bulkhead above a window port. A hatch opened to expose a recessed socket painted to resemble a keyhole. Inside, secured by brackets, was a gold key. Betts snapped it out and held it up. Glowing softly in the reflected lights, it looked like a large latchkey.

"We're talking worst-case stuff now," Betts said, his weather-beaten face deadly serious. "We're talking not being able to get this plane back to our time, for whatever reason. If that happens, it's got to be atomized. I don't have to tell you what could happen if the technology we have aboard falls into the hands of the Japanese. So this baby is wired to send her to hell. There are over six hundred charges of C-4 circuited together, varying in size from a marble to a billiard ball. To give you some idea of their power—the smallest would destroy an automobile. If we blow 'em, old *Sucker One* becomes talcum powder."

Betts paused to let his words sink in. "Once I activate the system," he held the key aloft again, "only this key will keep the plane from destructing. Every three hours and fifty-five minutes a Klaxon horn goes off, and loud! We then have five minutes to use the key. If we don't, *ka-pow!*"

Von Porten spoke, his voice languid. "So we've got six hundred of those charges scattered around this plane. I wonder if the geniuses who dreamed that one up considered what a Japanese bullet might do."

Betts gave him a look of ill-concealed pain. "Doc, you must think our backup people are cretins. The only thing that kicks this stuff off is an electronically detonated cap. You can shoot it, pound it, or piss on it all day long and it won't blow."

"Jake," Kogan said, "got anything you want to say?"

"Yeah...I mean, yes, sir, General." He winked at the circle of faces. "That's what I've got to say. Except for *General* Kogan and me, you're all civilians and you've got habits hard to break. But until we pull out of here, you're soldiers of the U.S. Army on active duty in World War II. That means you act the part. When people are around, there'll be no 'Joe' when you speak to the general, here, and there'll be no 'Jake' when you speak to me. It's General Kogan and Colonel Longford. You got it?" He grinned again as five heads nodded. "Good. We can all become buddies again tomorrow, when we bust out of here."

Hortha leaned down and peered out of a starboard port. "Headlights coming our way."

Four men sat in what was to be the quarters of Major General Joseph Kogan—a substantial frame house with a large sleeping and eating room, a small kitchen, and a real basic bath—originally owned by the Philippine Packing Company.

"Place was used by Norris Sinclair," Colonel Edmonds explained. "He ran the PhilPak operation here—it's a subsidiary of Del Monte Food Packing Company—that's where the field got its name."

"Not putting him out, are we?" Kogan asked.

"No, sir. Sinclair is going to be heading for the hills with some other PhilPak people. They're trying to stay out of the Japs' way, maybe organize a guerrilla band. For civilians, they're showing a lot of spirit."

Kogan and Longford seated themselves facing Colonel Edmonds and Major Frederick Thomas, operations officer, Mindanao Force.

"Coffee or booze, General?" Colonel Kenneth Edmonds asked.

"It's been a long day, Colonel," Kogan said. "A little whiskey might help me get a good night's sleep." He felt light-headed, but elated. Here he sat, six years before he had been born, about to have a drink with two officers of a doomed garrison. Whoa! Stop that. This was the kind of gee-whiz thinking he'd warned the crew about.

"What's available?" Kogan asked.

"The house drink is still bourbon, sir," Colonel Edmonds said with a smile. He was about fifty, broad-shouldered but carrying some excess poundage around his middle. A fringe of iron-gray hair around a bald pate gave him the appearance of a benign cleric, but the level eyes belonged to a soldier.

"Bourbon's fine," Kogan said. "With a little water."

"You, Colonel?" Edmonds said to Longford.

Longford had been craning his neck, examining his surroundings curiously, looking out the open door into the night. "What?" he asked, then said, "Oh, vodka if you have it. And a squirt of tonic."

Kogan groaned inwardly.

"Vodka?" Edmonds seemed puzzled. "That's a Russian drink, isn't it?"

Jake's pink skin flamed as he realized his mistake. "Uh . . . yeah. That's okay, bourbon's fine for me."

Kogan managed a casual chuckle. "We've been getting a few bottles in from the Soviets since the war began. Sort of reverse Lend-Lease."

A middle-aged Filipino with a perpetual smile made the drinks. Edmonds raised his glass. "Here's to the . . . let's see." He picked up a copy of the orders Kogan had given him when they arrived. "Ah, yes, Operation SUCCOR—Special Mission to Resupply the Philippines. Mighty glad to see you folks. We need small arms ammo here at Del Monte, but things are real bad up north on Corregidor. They're hanging on by the skin of their teeth. They need food—medicine, particularly." Edmonds chuckled deprecatingly. "Oh, hell, General, you know all this."

"Sir," Major Thomas spoke up. "How do you intend to get supplies to Corregidor?" He wiped the sweat from his face with his sleeve and the gold of his West Point class ring gleamed in the dim light. Kogan couldn't see the date on it, but he guessed at about 1934 or 1935. Thomas was eager and probably a hard-charger. His thinning brown hair and all-American face gave him the look of a young Eisenhower.

Kogan glanced at his watch. He had planned for just enough time to make contact with these people and engage in a few pleasantries before the roof fell in, and Edmonds and Thomas would be called away. Then he'd be free to get back to the plane and radio the crucial message to Corregidor. What he *didn't* want was to get stuck with having to explain a resupply expedition that would never arrive.

"Well, Major," he said, "I expected General Sharp to be here for my briefing." *No, he didn't. Sharp was a hundred miles away on the coast, near Parang.*

Edmonds took a swallow of his drink and leaned forward. "Sir, General Sharp is inspecting one of our regiments at Parang. But we'd sure like to hear about what's coming in. And it would do a world of good if we could pass the news on to Corregidor."

Kogan picked up his own drink and sipped it leisurely. He checked his watch again—8:04. News of the Japanese landing should have arrived ten minutes ago. Could he be mistaken? He'd better check. He reached down and pulled a manila folder from his briefcase. "Well," he said slowly, taking his time, "let's check the shipping schedule, here." He ran his finger down the chronology he'd made up. There it was: "1956 hours April 29, 1942: Sharp's headquarters receives information of Japanese landing west coast Mindanao." What the hell was the holdup? Why hadn't the field telephone on the table rung? He couldn't stall any longer.

"Our schedule, Colonel Edmonds," he began, "has a supply ship leaving Pearl Harbor three days ago." *Sure, and the damn thing will be only halfway here when the command surrenders.*

Major Thomas had a pencil poised over a small notebook. "When will it arrive, General?" His voice was breathless.

Kogan downed the rest of his drink and set the glass carefully on the table. "Well—" he had begun when footsteps shook the boards of the porch and a heavy fist pounded on the door frame.

Major Thomas, with an annoyed expression, called out, "Come in."

A sweating private entered, saluted, and handed Thomas a radio message. Spotting the two stars on Kogan's shoulder straps, the soldier's position of attention became even more rigid.

"Jesus Christ!" Thomas exclaimed, scanning the message. "Goddamn Japs have landed south of Parang."

He handed the paper to Colonel Edmonds, who was on his feet. "Tell Operations I'm on my way," he ordered the messenger, who dashed out.

"General Kogan." Edmonds put on his old World War I helmet and strapped on a pistol. "There's nothing to be concerned about right now. The Japs are still a hundred miles away. Juan will help you get settled in. I'll notify you of any new developments." With a salute he was gone, Major Thomas following close behind.

As the sound of their footsteps faded in the distance, Longford picked up his glass of bourbon and examined it. "Christ, I hate this stuff. Gives me a sour stomach." His expression turned sheepish. "Sorry about the vodka business, Joe."

Kogan went to the door and stared into the darkness. He checked the time again. "Come on," he said. "We're cutting it pretty close. Let's get to the plane and radio. Babcock has got to be on that flight."

Corregidor, P.I.

Evening, April 29, 1942

Except for the waters of Manila Bay—light green around the Rock's narrow beaches, white-capped indigo as they deepened between the island and the looming dark bulk of Bataan—the world of Corregidor was brown. Tan khaki uniforms, light brown concrete portals leading into Malinta Tunnel, brown dust eddying in the evening offshore wind, brown debris geysering up when the big Jap 150s smashed against the Rock. The last vestiges of green—the grass, shrubs, and trees—had been blasted away, exposing the subsoil of Corregidor, dull brown, lifeless, matching the despair of the defenders.

In the dank air of a cubicle off the main tunnel, Captain Marie Crane got ready to make a dream a reality. She was getting off the Rock! Chief Nurse Maude Flanigan had approached her as she had come off duty an hour ago. White-haired, implacably calm as always, the fiftyish woman spoke quietly, without dramatics.

"You and some others are leaving tonight. You'll be flying out to Australia." Flanigan had put a cautionary hand on Marie's shoulder. "My dear, you are to say absolutely nothing to anyone of this." The chief nurse added a few words of instruction that came to Marie through a happy daze, then she was gone, as erect and unswerving as a general on parade.

Marie wanted to dance and to sing, but her happiness was flawed—the two small flying boats Maude had described couldn't take many to safety.

She glanced from the small suitcase lying open on the bunk to the three civilian dresses hanging from a wooden bar in the corner of the room. Shaking her head in amused frustration, she tossed the precious, hoarded gowns onto a chair. She picked up toilet items from a small chest of drawers and stowed them in the luggage. Some underthings went in next. Her expression changed as she picked up a small, silver-framed photo of a smiling, pleasant-faced army major. *Dear Harry,* she thought, *in the last few months I have almost forgotten you.* The endless stream of wounded, the hours of bloody work in surgery, and the physical and emotional strain of life under the muzzles of Jap artillery had pushed him aside, made even his picture that of someone she hardly knew. The wonderful few years they were together now seemed as remote and unreal as the Fred Astaire and Ginger Rogers musical they screened in the main tunnel last week. She placed the picture carefully in the suitcase.

"How ya doing, honey?" The words came from the doorway. Beatrice Falk, captain, Army Nurse Corps, folded her arms and leaned against the wall of the little room. Thickset, her stomach bulged below the web belt of her khaki trousers just a bit less prominently than her bosom above it. But her round face was kindly, and from behind thick glasses, brown eyes gleamed with intelligence. From one finger, she dangled an oval box garnished with shiny flowers.

"Heard you're leaving us," Beatrice said without preliminaries.

Marie looked up, startled. "How did you hear? It's supposed to be secret."

"Hell, a secret doesn't have a chance in this place. It's all over the Rock by now." A burly cockroach climbed the scabrous wall next to her shoulder. She stuck her tongue out at the insect, but made no move to dislodge it. "Hey, take a big, deep smell of that sweet air coming out of the blowers." Beatrice pantomimed vomiting. "Ain't you going to miss it?"

Marie picked up the whimsy. "Don't forget the tender steaks, fresh vegetables, and wonderful fruit desserts," she said, then her eyes went wide with chagrin and one hand covered her mouth. "Oh, Beatrice, I'm so sorry. That's really rubbing it in."

"Hey, kid, forget it. About the only thing I've got left is a sense of humor." Beatrice eyed the suitcase. "You about finished?"

Marie gestured helplessly at the dresses and other things of hers in the room. "Easiest job of packing I've ever done," she said. "Ten pounds is all we're allowed to carry on. You may not want the dresses, but anything else is yours." There weren't a lot of other things—a tennis racket that hadn't been used since December, riding boots beginning to mold along the soles, her dress blue cape with the crimson silk lining.

She had been stationed at Sternberg General in Manila when the Japanese had struck. On Christmas Eve MacArthur declared Manila an open city and she had been evacuated, along with everyone else, to Bataan. For some ridiculously overoptimistic reason, she had hauled a lot of her things along. At primitive Bataan General Number One, she watched the terrible casualties pour in, and for the first time, it struck her with an almost physical blow that this was one fight Americans weren't going to win. When Bataan fell, about everything else she owned stayed there. Why the boots, tennis racket, and cape? Sentiment, perhaps. Reminders of happier times, or tokens of an infinitely better future that now seemed beyond reach.

"Gawd, I'd love to be able to wear those dresses," Beatrice said, glancing at the taller woman's slender waist. She fingered a green silk frock. "This always looked great with your red hair. Remember the Thanksgiving dance? Boy, that was about the last good time I can remember." She added thoughtfully, "You know, we ought to burn these numbers. Otherwise, they'll probably end up in a Manila whorehouse."

"What!" Marie's laugh was half shocked. "Where'd you get such a wild idea?"

"It's logical. In a few days, some little slant-eye is gonna come charging through here looking for loot. He sticks a dress or two in his pack, gets back to Manila, and wins a free roll in the hay."

"Bea..." Marie's tone started out to be reproving, then she blinked back tears as she looked at her stocky friend. "Oh, Bea, I'm so torn up inside. I want to get off this damned Rock more than I've wanted anything in my life. I'm frightened, like everyone else, yet—"

"You feel guilty."

"Yes, wouldn't you? Nineteen of us chosen God knows how, a hundred staying behind. Why me and not you? I'll ask myself that for the rest of my life."

"Honey," it was Beatrice's eyes that now dampened. "Don't torture yourself with questions that have no answers. You go on and get out of here and have a good life. This damn war isn't going to last forever. One of these days, our boys will spring me from wherever the Japs put me—betcha it won't be in a whorehouse—and before you know it, we two will be serving together again." Her confidence seemed to ebb. Diffidently, she held up the garishly decorated box in her hand. "Will you do me a big favor? But only if you've got room."

Marie looked at the box dubiously. "I don't know, Bea, what is it?"

"Well," Beatrice fumbled with the ribbon, "let me show you." She lifted the cover off and held up a hat—a small, frivolous, jaunty hat with a wisp of veil. It was teal blue, made of satin and silk. "My mom sent this to me last Christmas. I never had a chance to even put it on. I'd like you to have it. When you get back home, wear it when you go to some nice place—maybe the Top of the Mark or the Fairmont, if you're in San Francisco, or..." Bea's round face went slack. "Oh, hell, forget it. I don't know why I'm doing this. I'm not going to bother you with the stupid thing."

Marie took the hat and turned it in her hands, examining it critically. "It's not stupid, it's just lovely, it really is. And it only weighs a few ounces." She laughed. "I may have to have it reshaped though, because I can't take the box." She started to put it down on her bunk.

"Try it on, will you, honey?"

"Of course." Marie picked it up, then shook her head. "No, Bea, I want to see you in it."

"Oh, come on." Bea gave an embarrassed little chuckle, but she took the hat and went to the mirror. She slanted the hat this way and that, trying to get it right. She patted her wispy hair into place while Marie fussed with the veil. Finally, both women were satisfied. Bea whirled around and struck a model's pose, arms flung wide, her smile exaggerated, her eyes fluttering dramatically.

"It's gorgeous," Marie exclaimed, her hands clasped.

Bea gave herself another look in the mirror. The little blue thing sat incongruously on her thin brown hair. She wiped her sweating face with a handkerchief and took her glasses off, leaning forward to peer at her reflection, twisting her head from side to side.

"It is kinda cute, isn't it?" She spoke wistfully, turning to Marie. The two women looked at each other for a long instant, their smiles slowly fading, the held-back emotions thrusting to the surface. "Oh, God, Bea," Marie wailed, and the tears came as they embraced.

They were wiping their eyes when a baritone voice came from the doorway. "Personally, Bea, I think the hat goes very well with your fatigues." A very large, tired-looking officer stood leaning against the door. He was Colonel Daniel Gross, now chief surgeon on Corregidor. Well-liked by all medical personnel, Gross seemed to have a special understanding of nursing problems. Marie smiled at him through reddened eyes.

"Oh, hi, Colonel," she said. "I guess you've heard. I was going to stop in and say good-bye."

Dr. Gross glanced down at a paper in his hand. Marie thought the distinguished lines of his face had eroded terribly in the last few months. He seemed unsure of what to say.

"Something wrong, sir?" Marie asked. She suddenly feared

the look on his face. It told her that what he held in his hand was bad—very bad.

"I'm sorry," Gross said, handing her the paper. "This radio message just came in."

She took it, her heart skipping because she knew the words were going to hurt her, and what could harm her the most? Getting bumped off the flight. Staying behind to fall into the hands of those terrible little men. Shivering with fear in this dirty, stinking place until they overran the island, killing, robbing, raping.

The short message blurred, then came into focus, and she read the Date-Time Group: 292012 April; the Originator: Commanding General, Southwest Pacific Area (that was MacArthur, she knew); the Addressee: Commanding General, U.S. Forces in Philippines (that was Wainwright); then she read the important part aloud.

> Captain Marie Crane, Army Nurse Corps, is to be replaced aboard the evacuating aircraft by Captain Roger Babcock, U.S. Army Medical Corps.

She was proud of the way she read it, her voice strong and clear. And then, as she looked at her friends, she found that it really didn't hurt all that much.

A wail filled the cubicle. "Oh, no, Colonel Gross!" Beatrice cried out. "This is cruel! Marie's due to leave in just two hours! Can't you do something?"

"I'm sorry," Gross said, and took Marie's hand in both of his. "I really am. But, my dear, there's absolutely nothing I can do. The orders come from MacArthur himself."

"That's all right, Colonel," Marie said, and her smile was real. "I couldn't stand to be parted from my boots, anyway." He smiled at her little joke, patted her shoulder, and left.

Marie watched as her friend carefully removed the hat from her head and put it back in the box. "Bea, I'm sorry, damnit. I wanted so much to wear it to some wonderful place and drink a toast to all the brave friends I left behind."

She lifted Harry's portrait from the luggage and returned it to the little stand beside her bunk. "You know, I don't feel guilty anymore."

A bomb exploded. From the muffled impact and the amount of concrete flaking off the ceiling, Marie guessed it must be one of the five-hundred-pounders. The two-hundred-watt bulbs over the operating table flickered briefly before going out. The operating team stood motionless, waiting for the generator to kick in, their white gowns a ghostly green in the light of the battle lantern on the wall.

"Where the hell's the power?"

The surgeon's growl was interrupted by the pop and roar of the generator as it cut in. The lights flared over the operating table and the team continued amputating the gangrenous left arm of a Filipino soldier. Two fans managed to move the rank air about, but did nothing to alleviate the thick heat in the room. A Filipino nurse trainee constantly wiped the sweat that poured from the surgeon's forehead. Marie took her eyes off the bloody, foul gore of the amputation and checked the big clock on the wall—10:40. The flight would be taking off about now, and Dr. Roger Babcock and eighteen excited nurses would wing their way to freedom. She reached down and swabbed blood away from a vessel, then handed a clamp to the surgeon.

She wondered where she'd be next week at this time. The word was that the Rock could only hold out for a few more days. Then she'd be left to—what was the phrase?—the tender mercies of the Japanese. Part of her, the thinking part, rejected the hideous stories of rape and sexual abuse circulating wildly through Malinta. It was exaggeration, hysteria, she told herself. Another part of her, the woman part, shuddered with horror, and wondered whether she could survive such brutality, or whether she even wanted to. There had been no man since

Harry. How long had it been since he had crashed on a night flight off the California coast—two years? No, nearly three. They'd been married six years, almost. It had been a good marriage, physically and emotionally. She missed it—missed him, sometimes desperately.

People asked her why she didn't remarry. With your looks, they told her, you must have men lining up. Oh, yes indeed, men did line up, but not for marriage. Just this last year, out here in what was called the lustful tropics, a couple of colonels, quite a few lieutenant colonels and majors, and even one brigadier had lined up. All had wives back in the States—dull, uninteresting wives—the officers were quick to point out, too fat or too skinny or too boring. *So give me a break, Marie, darling. God, you're swell-looking. I'll do anything for you—get a divorce, anything—just give me a break.* None of them got a break, not even the one major—she'd nearly forgotten about him—who was single. His approach had been hapless and hopeless. Probably, Marie guessed, because he was used to getting turned down. Overweight, with body odor, and sort of creepy, he placidly accepted her caustic refusal as his due.

Strangely enough, she recalled him with a touch of warmth. At least he hadn't lied to her. And a few weeks ago she'd seen his name on the casualty lists—killed in action on the San Vicente River line. Maybe she should have taken him to bed—once. He'd given his life—she could have given him a few moments of pleasure. Hadn't they both been the same kind of person—awkward and out of place? With her, the awkwardness was her age—thirty-three. The single officers out here were all mostly lieutenants and captains in their twenties. They admired her looks, and liked dancing and joking around with her, but when it came to serious dating, they looked for the daughters and younger sisters of other officers. That was okay with her. People snickered at older women going around with younger men.

The swollen, purplish arm came off and dropped into a bucket of waste with a grisly thump. The clock said 10:52. Twenty-eight minutes for an amputation. *Not bad,* she thought, but on the other hand, the surgeon had a lot of practice. The flying boats would probably be—*oh, damnit, get your mind off those planes.*

She gave a little shriek as a strong hand pulled her forcibly away from the operating table. Colonel Gross loomed over her, his face cast in urgent lines, yet with a suppressed excitement in his eyes. The surgeon noticed the interruption. He looked up, annoyed, then muttered an "Evening, sir," as he went back to work.

As Gross hustled her to the other side of the room, a thickset figure stepped into Marie's position at the table. Over a mask, Bea's glasses glittered as she gave her a big, knowing wink.

"Colonel," Marie stammered.

He slipped the mask down off her damp face. "Listen," he spoke rapidly. "We can't find Babcock. We've searched the entire Rock. You're going after all." He pushed her suitcase into her hand. "Bea threw some things in here, along with that damn hat of hers. There's a truck standing by outside the east entrance. Now, run!"

"But . . . sir." A warmth suffused her entire being. Suddenly she knew how much freedom and life meant to her. But it couldn't be. The colonel must be mistaken. The flight had already taken off.

"It's too late!" She pointed at the clock.

"It will be if you don't get a move on," he snapped. "They've been holding the plane for Babcock." He took her by both shoulders and shoved her toward the door. "Hurry, damnit! They gave me just fifteen minutes to get you down to the landing."

Gross was a very tall man so Marie had to stand on tiptoe to kiss his cheek. Then she ran as fast as her long legs could take her.

CHAPTER TEN

Sleep eluded Kogan. Across the room, he could hear Longford's deep, peaceful breathing. The big pilot wasn't letting a little thing like a trip back in time disturb him.

"You going to be able to sleep?" he had asked.

The pilot looked at him in surprise. He tested the mattress by pounding on it. "Pad's a little thin, but hell, I've had a long day." Yawning cavernously, he rearranged the mosquito bar and then looked up. "Hey, I don't know whether the air's cleaner back here or what, but it sure breathes good." He stretched out and within minutes was asleep. *Ah*, Kogan mused, *how wonderful to be second in command.*

Hours ago he had crawled between the cool, rough sheets. Since then he had tossed restlessly, his mind ranging back and forth between the events of the day and the all-critical meeting with Dr. Babcock tomorrow. He and Longford had gotten back to the plane and sent the canned message bumping the nurse— what was her name? Crane. Corregidor had receipted for it. The PBYs were on their way south. They would arrive tomorrow morning at Lake Lanao, sixty-five miles away from where he was now fighting his demons.

He forced his mind back to what had to be done tomorrow. Between the times the flying boats land and take off for Australia, he and Von Porten must find Dr. Babcock and get the formula for B-juice. Assuming that Von Porten understood everything the young savant had done, that should pose no problem. But one doubt kept nagging at his mind. The two PBYs would make it to Lake Lanao safely—that was a matter of history. And sure, their message had been received. But would Babcock be on the flight? Or had he refused to take away a nurse's chance for freedom?

The smell of coffee and cigarette smoke filled the officers' mess—a big room in one of the largest PhilPak bungalows. At one of the tables near a jalousied window, Colonel Edmonds hosted breakfast for Kogan, Longford, and a silent, obviously disgruntled Dr. Von Porten. A dozen or more officers ate at other tables, casting covert glances at the major general who had flown in last night. Most of them ate hurriedly, talking among themselves in short bursts before donning helmets and rushing away.

"Sorry, General," Edmonds said to Kogan. "Got a message last night that General Sharp is going to stay on to coordinate the beach defenses against the Japs. Won't be back today, at least."

"How's the thing going?" Kogan asked.

Edmonds shook his head. "I don't know. We've had only fragmentary reports."

"Can you hold?"

Edmonds gave Kogan a direct look. "I doubt it."

"Isn't that rather defeatist?" Kogan decided to play his role as a senior officer from MacArthur's headquarters might. Part of the game meant chewing on the deputy commander.

"I assumed you wanted an honest answer, General."

"Well, let me put it this way, Edmonds. If senior officers have no confidence in winning, what kind of attitude can the men have?"

Edmonds snubbed his half-smoked cigarette out roughly. Tiny beads of sweat appeared on his upper lip. "I presume you're familiar with the Twenty-sixth Cavalry, the Thirty-first and the Forty-third Infantry Regiments, the Eighty-sixth and the Eighty-eighth Field Artillery Regiments—"

"Yes, yes," Kogan interrupted curtly. "What's your point?" Oh, he knew the colonel's point, and it was a very good one. Kogan was prepared to lose this argument. He stole a look at his watch. The PBYs had landed. Dr. Babcock was finally within reach. Right now, all Kogan wanted was to get away from the pineapple rinds and stinking cigarette butts and head for Lake Lanao.

"My point, sir, is that those units were old line regular regiments of American soldiers. And under the leadership of Douglas MacArthur and Jonathan Wainwright, two pretty fair generals, they got their ass kicked good by the Japs on Luzon. Now we have the 104th Infantry Regiment defending Parang. The 104th didn't exist three months ago. It's filled with Filipino recruits who have fired only six practice rounds on the range— six, sir, because that's all the ammunition we could spare. We're asking these poor devils to beat some of the best soldiers in the world—Jap infantry that conquered Manchuria in 1931 and beat China in 1937. Their grandfathers defeated the Russians in 1904. Their great-grandfathers thirty times removed stopped Kublai Khan."

Edmonds picked up his cup with a hand that shook. "I don't know, General," he said quietly. "Maybe, if we'd had enough time, we could have gotten ready. But we didn't. Not nearly enough time. I don't think we have a chance. I'm sorry."

Kogan had leaned on him enough. The man knew the situation and he was giving him an honest report—something not always easy to get in the army. He nodded forgivingly, thinking what a sly bastard he'd become. "I appreciate your candor, Edmonds, and thank you."

An awkward silence replaced the tension. Edmonds spoke up, obviously searching for a new, less controversial subject. "Been meaning to ask you, General," he said, breaking open a pack of Lucky Strikes. "What kind of a plane have you got there? I'm not a flyer, but I don't think I've ever heard engines that sound like that."

Longford had been primed for this sort of question, so Kogan sipped his coffee and leaned back against the window, trying for a breath of fresh air in the smoke-filled room. Except for himself and Longford, every single officer in the mess was laying down a smoke screen. And SUCCOR had contributed. The support group had chivvied a couple of the big tobacco companies into producing a hundred cartons of cigarettes apiece, identical in packaging and composition to those manufactured during World War II.

"Ever hear of a turboprop, Colonel?" Longford was answering Edmonds's question.

"Yeah, guess I have, but aren't they a long way from production?"

"This is an experimental model we brought in."

Edmonds offered cigarettes to his guests. When they declined, he lighted his own and took a deep, grateful drag. He held up the green Lucky Strike package. "Sure appreciate you bringing these in. What few packs we have left have gone moldy."

A well-modulated voice spoke up. "Colonel, you wouldn't have an extra pack of those, would you?" Kogan looked up to see a plump man of about thirty shaking hands with Edmonds. His plastered-down brown hair was parted precisely in the middle above an intelligent, full-cheeked face, and he wore gray, knee-length shorts with a striped civilian shirt.

"General Kogan," Edmonds said, "this is Mr. Norris Sinclair.

Del Monte was part of his domain before MacArthur took it over for his B-17s."

"Glad to know you, sir," Sinclair said, shaking hands first with Kogan and then with the others. "Wish we had some of those Flying Forts still operating out of here." He took the cigarette the deputy commander offered and lit it, blowing the smoke gustily toward the ceiling.

"Here, Norris," Colonel Edmonds said, scrawling some words in a notebook. "Take this over to the canteen. They'll give you a couple cartons of fresh cigarettes. That's only fair, considering all the free pineapple we've eaten here."

"Appreciate it, Ken," Sinclair said, then turned to Kogan. "Heard you had come in, General. Does this mean we're getting troop reinforcements here?"

Kogan eyed him coolly, saying nothing. He rather liked this young man who was about to disappear into the hills and fight a guerrilla war, but his question was out of line. Sinclair realized it instantly.

"Oh, sorry, sir, didn't mean to pry." He glanced around self-consciously. "Guess I'll be running along. Next year, after we've run those little bastards out of here, I want you all to come back as my guests." He gave a lighthearted little salute to the table and was gone.

"Fine young gentleman," Edmonds said as he watched him leave. "Lots of guts." Kogan agreed, silently. But far too optimistic. Sinclair was going to discover that the "little bastards" were not to be chased out so easily. Part of Kogan's research had been conducted with the Del Monte Corporation in San Francisco, which had been very good about responding to his requests for information. Polite letters to Kogan had described in cool, corporate prose the courage of the men and women caught in the Japanese advance a half century before. Most had been captured, ending up in the infamous Santo Tomás internment camp in Manila. One young couple—Kogan thought he remembered that their name was White—hid in the hills. The wife, eight months pregnant, died giving birth to a son. The father, infant boy in his arms, fled, eluding the Japanese for three months. Capture finally came and the fugitive little family was sent to Santo Tomás. Had the baby survived? Again, Kogan wasn't sure.

As for Norris Sinclair—the young man who was hurrying in the direction of the canteen for his cigarettes—he had led a band of Filipino guerrillas in the hills until one day the Japanese had ambushed them. Try as he might, Kogan could not remember whether Sinclair had died in the fight or survived. Had he known he was going to bump into the Del Monte executive, he would definitely have paid more attention.

His preoccupation with these figures who had stepped out of his notes was interrupted by Edmonds's voice.

"By the way, Colonel Longford, I'd really like to take a look-see at that plane of yours, if you don't mind."

"Sorry, Edmonds," Kogan took over. He wanted no misunderstanding here. Not even the deputy force commander was going to approach *Sucker One*. "No one gets to inspect that aircraft. The less you know about it, the better." He smiled to lessen the harshness of his words. "I'm sure you understand."

He heard the muffled sound of marching men. On the dirt road running by the bungalow, a long double line of Filipino soldiers moved stoically toward the west, old Enfield rifles nearly as long as the men were tall slung over their thin shoulders. The battalion's American officers, mounted on diminutive Mindanaoan ponies, constantly exhorted the column to move faster. As Kogan mentally contrasted the boyish, bewildered troops with the stocky, well-equipped Japanese they were going up against, the harsh truth of Edmonds's words hit home.

Kogan checked the time and glanced out the open door. A battered LaSalle sedan, newly washed, awaited him. A fresh-faced lieutenant and a Filipino corporal stood by the car watching the bungalow anxiously. Time to go. He picked up his helmet and got to his feet. The others rose quickly.

"Better be on our way," he said.

Edmonds spoke up, his tone apologetic. "General, I don't want to sound like a broken record, but I really recommend that you not make this trip. I understand your wanting to know what's happening over there, but our Operations Center has a situation map that's pretty much up-to-date."

Kogan put on a thoughtful look, as if considering Edmonds's plea. If only the deputy commander could know how far they had come, how priceless the goal they sought, and how close it now was.

As he stepped out onto the porch, Kogan felt the tropical heat blanketing the land. The heavy green foliage was dusted from the passage of the Filipino battalion now disappearing down the road.

The lieutenant and the corporal, seeing the high-ranking officers, snapped stiffly to attention and saluted. Kogan tossed them a soft return and mouthed "At ease" before turning to Edmonds again.

"No situation map is as good as taking a look at the ground and talking to unit commanders," Kogan intoned pontifically, and found himself admiring his own performance. If they ever got out of this place, maybe he ought to take up acting as a career. "MacArthur will have a lot of questions when I get back to Melbourne." As if that disposed of any further objection, Kogan led the way to the car.

"General," Edmonds said, "this is Lieutenant William Burke." Kogan extended his hand and the tall young lieutenant stumbled over his own feet in his eagerness to shake it. "Willie knows the road. He'll be your driver and sort of aide-de-camp. Corporal Barretto, here, is a good man with that Enfield. Might come in handy."

Kogan put out his hand and the corporal, startled, quickly wiped his own on his shirt before taking it. Barretto was a different soldier from the thin youths Kogan had seen heading down the road—older, but erect as a ramrod, with a few white hairs showing among the black, and muscular, with a barrel chest above a slim waist. His collar insignia indicated that he was a Philippine Scout from the one regular Filipino unit in the islands. And he wasn't scared. His dark eyes glowed with pride and self-confidence.

"I assume, Colonel Edmonds," Kogan said with a smile, "that the corporal can protect me adequately against General Kawaguchi's force?" He snapped his mouth shut, but too late. *Ah yes, you dumb shit, you've done it now. Couldn't keep quiet, could you? Just had to make your stupid little joke.*

Edmonds picked it up immediately. "Kawaguchi? General, we've taken no prisoners—we have no reports of the identity of the Jap commander." Kogan could feel Longford's and Von Porten's eyes on him. Hell, they were all staring at him. *Okay, big mouth, start talking.*

"Of course, Edmonds," he said, "we're not absolutely positive that it's Kawaguchi." Kogan reached out casually and took Barretto's Enfield, pretending to look it over. "Just an assumption. Melbourne broke down an intercept a few days ago saying the Kawaguchi Brigade had been detached for southern operations. I meant to tell you about that." He handed the Enfield back and patted Barretto on the shoulder. "Well, gentlemen," he said brightly, "I think we'd better be on our way."

Burke got behind the wheel and Barretto sat on the passenger side, holding his rifle between his knees. Kogan and Von Porten got in the rear. Leaning out the window, Kogan spoke in a low voice.

"Jake, I want to be back here before dark. Keep everything and everybody ready to go on a moment's notice—got that?" Longford nodded, stepped back, and saluted. Burke revved up the engine and the car started to move forward.

"General, wait a minute!" It was Edmonds. He ran around to Kogan's window and leaned in. "I nearly forgot. There's a couple of PBYs scheduled to fly in from Corregidor today with a load of nurses and a few civilians. They're landing on Lake Lanao. If they make it, they should be in Dansalan—that's on the north shore of the lake—when you go through there."

Kogan hoped his face was on correct—mild interest, that's the ticket. "Glad to hear it." His tone was noncommittal. "Hope they get through all right."

"Yes, sir. Well, they're being flown out of hell and I guess if they make it, they'll be a bunch of pretty shaken-up women. I'd appreciate it if you'd stop by for a couple of minutes—find out if they're all right and extend General Sharp's compliments... and mine, too, sir."

Well, well, finally a small, lucky break. But don't seem too eager. Kogan pursed his lips in thought. "Of course, Edmonds," he said. "Glad to. If I have the time." *If* he had the time. Ha, ha. He touched Burke on the shoulder and the sedan lurched down the narrow road.

Burke drove very well, sitting up straight with both hands on the wheel—a deference to his high-ranking cargo, Kogan assumed—while skillfully maneuvering the car along the narrow road crowded with refugees pathetically unsure of the direction in which they should flee.

The exuberance of this young man reminded Kogan of himself at twenty-one, leading his infantry platoon in Vietnam. What would happen to Willie Burke, second lieutenant, U.S. Army? Within days, he would be killed or captured, that much was sure. If a POW, would he survive the war? The answers were all there, aboard *Sucker One*, available to anyone who tapped into the data base of the big computer. If Kogan ever got back to his own time, he might check on the officers he had met back here, but not now. Knowing another person's future was the worst kind of voyeurism.

Let's see, Kogan calculated, Burke was probably born about 1920. *He* had been—would be?—born in 1948. Bemused, he compared the unlined face in the rearview mirror with his own weather-beaten one. If Willie were still alive in the world of 1994, he would be in his midseventies. He raised his voice.

"How much longer to Lake Lanao, Lieutenant?"

"About another hour, sir, if this road doesn't get any worse." Burke grinned at him in the mirror.

Von Porten reached over and touched his arm to get his attention. "Something's been bothering me, General," he said in a low voice.

"That's pretty obvious, Doctor," Kogan said, his tone cold. This Boston Brahmin had irked him during breakfast, with his withdrawn demeanor and disinterested air. In the next few hours, success or failure of this operation would be up to Von Porten, so he damn well better drop the high-and-mighty attitude.

Von Porten shrugged. "Sorry, but going into a combat zone wasn't exactly what I signed up for. Sid Eccles never said anything about this."

"Look," Kogan was irritated, but Burke's presence in the driver's seat reminded him to keep his voice just above a whisper. "I don't know what Dr. Eccles told you, but we're not going into a combat zone. I didn't like handing Edmonds that garbage about visiting front-line units, but it was necessary. The Japanese are thirty, forty miles the other side of Dansalan on the lake, and Dansalan, my friend, is as far as we go. We'll find Babcock, get the stuff, and hightail it out of there. Nothing to be worried about." *Yeah, sure, then why were his nerves strumming like a banjo?*

Kogan looked out at the shallow canyon they were negotiating. He'd never been here, but he knew the topographical maps like the back of his hand. In another few miles, the twisting, descending road would bring them to the town of Cagayan and the sea. There the road turned west to follow the shoreline of the Mindanao Sea. Another hour's driving, and they would leave the coast to climb sharply into the highlands around Lake Lanao—a ride he would have relished, had he not been nagged by fear of what they would find in Dansalan. He turned to the doctor.

"I take it you didn't want this assignment."

"Let's just say I was ambivalent."

"Meaning what?"

Von Porten took his time answering. "Physics is not my field, but I have enough of a science background to know that the operation was an impossibility—at least I thought it was. I told Sid Eccles so, but he cajoled me, quite cleverly, into spending some time with Hiraga. I understood just enough of that presentation to realize that," he lowered his voice to a husky whisper, "traveling in time might be possible. I was both fascinated and repelled—I think I've made myself clear on that—but the bottom line was this B-juice thing. I simply could not convince myself that any such thing ever worked. So, even though the concept of the trip piqued my spirit of adventure, I told Eccles that I would not go."

"But you're here."

Von Porten wiped his forehead, rolled the window all the way down, and stuck one hand out. "Christ, it's hot out there." He leaned forward. "Lieutenant, how about...uh, forget it."

He leaned toward Kogan. "Damn near asked him to turn on the air-conditioning." There was amusement in his agate blue eyes. "Yes, I am here and enjoying it immensely."

Kogan grunted at the whimsy. "Why did you decide to come?"

"I don't like being manipulated."

"We're being sort of cryptic this morning, aren't we?"

"Okay, General. Short and sweet. Right in the middle of the hassle with Eccles, I got a fax from Amsterdam. A Dutch company offered me a contract to do research in Indonesia. Fifty thousand plus expenses for just one month, beginning in September. Wonderful, huh? But ambiguities in the contract and the size of the fee raised a lot of questions in my mind. I called the company and cross-examined the official responsible quite roughly. Turned out they had some kind of a make-work job any graduate student in botany could do blindfolded. He wouldn't tell me who was behind this, but I figured someone with money and power didn't want me on SUCCOR One."

Kogan chuckled, a short, cynical sound.

Von Porten looked at him sharply. "You know who was responsible?"

"I've been working on it. There have been other things designed to knock this operation off track—one directed at me personally. Let's see: who has unlimited money, and who would benefit most if we didn't bring a cure back for the president? Don't bother to answer that, Doctor." Kogan used a handkerchief to wipe the sweat off his neck. "So, back to you. The Dutch thing give you second thoughts about B-juice?"

"Right. Somebody big thinks it might work—enough to pay a lot of money to keep me out of it. That's good enough for me."

In the distance off to the right, the blue of Macajalar Bay sparkled in the sun. Far to the north, beyond Negros and Panay and Mindoro, the remnants of the army and navy held out on Corregidor, the last few days winding down before General Masaharu Homma's Fourteenth Army made its final assault on the Rock and overwhelmed them. Kogan recalled the photos he'd seen of General Wainwright sitting hatless and humbled before his conquerors, shock plainly visible on his honest old features. With a distinct wince, Kogan remembered the fake radio message he'd sent that had bumped the nurse Cain—or was it Crane? Well, like he'd told Admiral Edwards, she would have been captured on Mindanao anyway, so it wasn't all that bad. He jerked his thoughts back to the present. He glanced at his watch and remembered to wind it, then, with his skin prickling, he estimated that in less than an hour he'd be talking with the legendary doctor.

Von Porten left off watching the scenery and spoke again. "What's really bothering me now is this Roger Babcock." He lowered his voice even further. "In the original 1942—that's the only way I can describe it—why didn't a medical officer who makes one of the great discoveries of all time get the formula out of Corregidor, even if he couldn't get himself out?"

"Don't know," Kogan replied. He'd tangled with that one himself. "Could be a lot of things. Maybe he sent it out in an old

P-40 that crashed or was shot down. Maybe he waited too long. Maybe he sent it with this bunch of nurses we're going to meet."

"That, I don't get."

"One of these PBYs, remember, knocks a hole in its hull and has to leave its cargo of nurses behind on Mindanao. If Babcock gave B-juice to one of those gals, she and the formula ended up in a POW camp. Who knows what happened then. Maybe she died." Kogan shifted in his seat and dropped his too-tight cartridge belt with its holstered pistol to the floor of the car. "Anyway," he added, "we'll find out soon enough."

The talk didn't settle anything, but it pleased him, because he now felt that he understood Von Porten. Settling back, he watched the countryside go by. Along the road, the thick growth of coconut palms had given way to thin-foliaged trees with pods hanging from nearly naked limbs.

"What are those trees, Willie?" Kogan asked.

"Not sure, sir. I only arrived out here in December." Burke grinned. "Ugly, aren't they?"

"They're kapok trees," Von Porten spoke up. "The pods produce fiber for pillow and mattress stuffing and life preservers. It's a marginal crop, not very profitable. This is an exceptionally poor part of Mindanao—not enough reliable rainfall."

"You been here before, Doctor?" Burke asked in surprise.

"Not here in Lanao, but I've spent a lot of time in the next province over, Zamboanga."

"Tell you something, General." Burke seemed pleased to be included in the conversation again. "They may be poor around here, but they seem to have plenty of money for what goes on there." He pointed down the road to a large, open structure whose trilevel roof resembled stacked umbrellas made of rusted metal sheeting. Dozens of rude poles supported the building.

"What is it?"

"A cockpit, sir," Burke answered. "Just about every evening and weekends you can find a big crowd here. Attracts a very bad element, too."

"Plenty Moro," Corporal Barretto muttered.

A few rough-looking men watched the LaSalle pass the cockpit. Their attitude was vaguely menacing.

Burke spoke over his shoulder again. "I sure don't understand this Moro business, Doctor. Are they Filipinos?"

"Not ethnically," Von Porten said. "They're mostly Malayan. Most of them arrived before the Spanish conquered the islands."

"Well, if they're Malay, why do they call them Moros?"

"That's Spanish for 'Moors.' It's used mainly in a pejorative sense."

Willie twisted his neck around. "Come again?"

Von Porten smiled. "The Spanish didn't care for them either. These Malay immigrants had been converted to the Muslim religion hundreds of years ago, before they ever came here. They're a very reclusive people, with their own culture. They have a legal system based on the Koran, wear turbans and robes, carry bolo knives, and know how to use them."

"Some very bad men," Barretto muttered again.

"Oh, they have some very good men, too," Von Porten added. "The trouble is, they don't bend easily to any government other than their own."

Burke craned his neck, apparently looking for landmarks. "We're getting close to the Agus River, General," he said. "Another forty minutes and we'll be in Dansalan."

The car approached a sharp bend in the road obscured by a mixed clump of mango and banana trees. Burke braked. The car slowly negotiated the turn, then came to a dead halt. A large mound of palm fronds and branches covered the road.

Instantly, Corporal Barretto barked, "*Teniente!* Back up! Quickly!"

Burke reversed gears but it was too late. An earsplitting crash came from the left rear of the car. As Kogan jerked around, three men leaped from the brush and ran at the driver's side of the car. Pulling open the door, they dragged a furiously fighting Burke into the road. On the other side of the car, Barretto threw open his door and jumped out, his rifle bolt clicking home. Another bandit lunged from the brush, his dark face agleam with anticipation, his machete raised. The corporal slammed the butt of his rifle into the man's face, knocking him sprawling. With lightning speed and practiced movements, the scout leveled his rifle and fired across the hood of the car, his shot hitting one of the men assailing Burke, spinning the bandit around and dropping him groaning to the road.

Barretto slammed another round into the chamber and started around the front of the car. Behind him, a small man with almost negroid skin slipped from behind a tree. One skinny arm raised a heavy machete over his head, and the blade flashed down across the corporal's spine with the sound of a meat cleaver striking a side of beef. Barretto's arms flew out, the rifle clattered to the road, and he collapsed into the dirt, his legs jerking spasmodically. A choking sound vented from his throat as great gouts of blood stained the dust of the road.

Kogan gripped his .45 automatic. Now, as he jerked the slide back to load a round, he saw a half dozen men holding Burke. One was behind the lieutenant, jerking his head back by the hair while holding a long krislike knife at his throat. Others held Willie's arms. Kogan dropped the automatic back to the floor of the car between his feet. He couldn't use it now.

"Are they going to kill us?" Von Porten asked, his face ashen. Kogan said nothing, watching helplessly the bandits' abuse of Burke.

A second crash boomed against the rear of the car, and a man appeared at the door on Kogan's side. Dressed as the others, in cheap white cotton garments, he wore around his waist a broad sash of multicolored velvet holding a wide-blade, nickel-plated machete. A fez of dirty red felt sat on his thick, sweat-soaked hair. A heavy silver linked chain gleamed dully against the coffee-colored skin of his throat. From it, a medallion with the crescent and star of the Islamic religion dangled. In his hand he carried a thick wooden club with which he slammed the car, this time Kogan's door, a third time.

The man let go an incomprehensible torrent of language at

the other men and pointed to the fallen corporal. The small, dark man who had killed him pulled his machete from his belt and, bracing one foot on Barretto's back, slashed repeatedly at the junction between the neck and shoulders. He reached down, and grabbing the dead corporal's hair, jerked the head free of the body. Holding the dripping object aloft and grinning in triumph, he jammed it down over the LaSalle's hood ornament.

Von Porten gasped and clutched Kogan's forearm convulsively.

The leader peered into the open window of the car. "Oh-ho," he chortled, pointing to the grisly object on the hood. "You see? *Una decoración nueva*. You like?" He looked closer. "So! Mee-litary men. Why you have thees car? You steal it from PheelPak, no? Now I steal it from you."

"Let the lieutenant go," Kogan said.

"Eef you say so, *Capitan*," he said, roaring with laughter. He peered closely at the stars on Kogan's shirt straps, then jammed his club painfully against Kogan's shoulder.

"What ees thees? You are *coronel*, maybe?"

"I am a general," Kogan said, then regretted his words. This guy was dangerous enough without letting him know how valuable his prize was. "Let the lieutenant go," he repeated, knowing the man wouldn't, but stalling for time.

The bandit's red-rimmed eyes flashed bright with hashish and his bluish-lipped mouth grinned with deadly humor. A wrong move and they would all die. Hell, right move or not, these bandits intended to kill them.

Kogan felt physically sick. B-juice had been all but in their hands. A hot core of anger dissipated his nausea. If he was going to die, he was sure going to try to take this stinking son of a bitch with him.

"*General!*" The man straightened into a travesty of attention and saluted. "*El general tomará el mando!*" Then he lapsed into an incomprehensible stream of words that caused his men to mimic his actions. Burke slumped as they released him for their clowning. One of them struck him savagely in the pit of his stomach with the butt of an ancient rifle. A spew of vomit reddened with blood flew from Burke's mouth.

Turning his head slightly, Kogan muttered to Von Porten, "You know what the hell he's saying?" It wasn't Spanish and he didn't think it was Tagalog.

"He switches between Spanish and Tausog. I can make out a few words." Von Porten's voice was surprisingly firm.

The leader turned back to the car, breathing hard, with spittle clinging to his lips. "*General*, eef you pleeze to step out of the car now."

"*Amigo*," Kogan said, putting a worried note in his voice, which wasn't hard. "If we give you the car and our money, will you let us all *go*?"

The leader loosed another flood of Tausog to the men that caused them to roar with laughter, punctuated with vicious kicks at Burke.

The bandit turned back to Kogan. "Of course, *General*. We are kind, good men." He grinned, his lips twisting into a travesty of a smile.

"Not a chance," Von Porten whispered. "This guy's talking killing. Besides, he's high on drugs."

"Okay." Kogan's voice was a low growl. He'd seen men like this sweaty Moro before. There was a swing of moods between outward reason and savagery that built momentum as time went on. For this man, the quiet phase, the time when the cat toys playfully with its prey, had come to an end. His amusement with his helpless captives had run out. Kogan was sure that his next act, unless it could be stopped, would be to kill his captives.

He whispered to Von Porten, "Keep your eyes open."

Kogan turned to the bandit, playing the frightened officer to the hilt. "*Señor*, we have much money. Tell your men to release the lieutenant." As Kogan spoke, he pointed out the window toward the half conscious Burke. With his other hand he picked the automatic off the floorboards.

The bandit leader's eyes followed Kogan's gesture, and turned his head toward Burke's agony. Kogan's left hand grabbed the heavy silver chain around the leader's thick neck, and jerked with all his strength. The bandit's face hit the door flange with a sickening thud. His knees buckled until his chin, pulled tight against the door ledge by the chain, was all that kept him upright. Blood poured from a broken nose and stubs of teeth protruded through his mashed lips. Kogan stuck the barrel of the .45 cruelly into one nostril. The glassy eyes opened.

"*Amigo*," Kogan grated, "can you hear me?"

The bandit did not answer. Kogan jammed the .45 harder into his nose and tightened the chain.

"Can you hear me now?"

The bloody head nodded.

"Listen carefully. I do not like to repeat my words. Tell your men to release the lieutenant."

The bandit started to speak and failed. He swallowed blood and tried again, haltingly, "I tell my men...eef you no let me go *rápido*, they kill the lieutenant."

Kogan's lips pursed sorrowfully. "What do you use for brains, *compadre*—goat shit? When the lieutenant dies, you die."

The bandit's eyes shifted to a point over Kogan's shoulder. Von Porten yelled, "Watch out, Joe!" Kogan swung around and fired in the same motion. In the confines of the car, the roar of the big pistol was deafening. A mustached face in the car's right window hung there for an instant, a dark hole just above one bushy eyebrow. A mist formed of blood, flesh, and bone drifted down from the big exit hole in the back of the man's head. Then the face disappeared. A hand holding a bloody machete opened slowly and the weapon dropped to the floor of the car. Then the hand, too, disappeared.

Kogan swiveled back and his eyes were very close to the bandit's face. "Okay, lard ass. What's one lieutenant? Have your men kill him. Go ahead, damnit, tell them to shoot him. I want you to, because then you and I will play a little game." He shifted the automatic in his hand. "We're going to see if I can shoot your *cojones* off one by one. Then we'll finish up with some gut shooting. *Comprende* gut shooting?" He twisted the silver chain, and sweat and blood dripped off the bandit's chin, spotting the gray felt of the car's upholstery. "Keep up this bullshit, friend, and like they say where I come from, you're gonna make my day."

The bandit's eyes, bright with drugs, anger, and fear, rolled back in his head as he seemed to contemplate his future. Then he nodded vigorously. "Okay. I do eet."

"Tell your men to bring the lieutenant to the car, then put down their arms and clear that brush away from the road." Kogan gave the bandit leader a push that sent him sprawling to the ground. Then he got out of the car, his pistol aimed at the man.

Kogan drove the LaSalle, having some difficulty with the long gearshift rising from the floorboards. Von Porten shared the front seat with him, while Lieutenant Burke sprawled out in the backseat, beaten, dirty, and subdued. Occasionally, he would raise himself to give Kogan directions.

"Is he going to be okay, Art?" Kogan asked.

Von Porten had helped Burke into the car and looked him over. Now he said, "Yeah, but he's going to be sore for a few days. Lucky no ribs were broken."

He glanced at Kogan. "Good show back there, General. For a while I expected my skull would be bleaching in the sun."

Kogan grunted and reholstered his pistol. The old 1911 model .45 had come in handy. He had assured the crew when they were issued that the weapons were only part of the uniform, along with the World War I–style helmets. There's not going to be any shooting, he had said. No combat. They were going to be in and out of Del Monte long before the Japanese arrived. It goes to show you how hard it is to predict the future—or the past, in this case.

His combativeness had subsided but his anger had not. As he looked at the red smear of blood on the car's hood, he raged at the useless waste of the sturdy little corporal's life. While the roadblock was being cleared and Barretto's body laid under palm fronds, he had fought the urge to kill the bandit.

As he had debated what to do about them, a mounted patrol had clattered up, an American sergeant in charge of the dozen men.

"Christ!" he had exclaimed, sliding off his pony. "What the hell happened here?" Then he spotted Kogan's insignia and snapped to attention and saluted. "Uh...sorry, sir. We heard the shots and came running."

Kogan explained briefly what had happened and led him to where Barretto's body lay covered. The sergeant lifted the fronds. Von Porten had tried to place the head on the neck, but it had rolled an inch or two away. Barretto's eyes were closed and his mouth slack, showing big, red-stained teeth between the lips. Although it was unbruised, the face looked as though it had been beaten.

"Goddamn!" the sergeant muttered as he dropped the foliage back in place.

"Take care of him, Sergeant," Kogan said. "He was a brave soldier."

"Yes, sir." The sergeant called his men over, then nodded toward the bandits. "Sir, may we also take care of *these* men?"

Kogan nodded, knowing he had imposed a death sentence. He helped Burke into the car, and they had bumped on down the road again.

Now, twenty minutes later, they came to a small coastal village. Burke raised himself up and mumbled, "General, this is Iligan. There's a road junction up ahead. The left fork, sir, will take us to Dansalan."

At the intersection, Kogan pulled the car over to one side. He reached up and unfastened the two stars of his rank from his shirt.

"Willie," he said over his shoulder, "for reasons you do not have to understand, I don't want to be recognized as a general. From now until we return to Del Monte, you will refer to me as Colonel Kogan, is that clear?"

"Yes, sir," Burke said, his battered face surprised.

Kogan glanced at Von Porten and lowered his voice. "All hell will break loose if these people get to Darwin with stories about a strange major general on Mindanao."

═ CHAPTER ELEVEN ═

Under a blazing sun in a sky of unremitting blue, the main street of the tiny old resort town curved gently, paralleling the north shore of Lake Lanao. Several *Los Bares,* a *Botica Nueva,* a *Buklaklak* Store, the Varsity Fashion Beauty Parlor, plus a few sundries shops represented the commercial life of Dansalan. A Catholic church marked the town's southern boundary.

Dominating the street and the town was the Hotel Dansalan, a sprawling sixty-year-old structure, vaguely Victorian in architecture, that occupied a select position overlooking Lake Lanao.

Kogan pulled the LaSalle up short of the hotel. "Can you drive okay?" he asked Burke as he and Von Porten got out.

"Yes, sir."

"All right, Willie, get over to that military police unit sta-

tioned here. Have them fix up those cuts and bruises."
Kogan started to walk away, then stopped. "Oh, yes. Be back
here by fourteen hundred hours." Something in Burke's face
made him pause. "Is something wrong?"

"Uh . . . no, sir. I was just wondering how the general knew
we had a military police unit here."

He'd done it again, but hell, he was getting used to it. He
grinned. "Generals get paid to know things." He slapped Burke
on his uninjured shoulder, then turned toward the hotel.

The long wooden porch was noisy with feminine chatter.
About two dozen women, most of them nurses, sat at tables along
the veranda, their faces dazed and happy. A close eye, though,
could have detected that the hands holding drinks and cigarettes
were not entirely steady.

Kogan tried for calm, keeping his face expressionless as they
mounted to the veranda. He glanced hopefully at several male
officers sitting with the nurses, trying to figure out which one
was Babcock. He cursed silently—all the men were navy. He
and Von Porten stood awkwardly just outside the entrance to
the lobby, unsure as to how to proceed. A young army nurse
emerged from the lobby, nearly bumping into them.

"Excuse me, Lieutenant," Kogan said. "Have you seen
Dr. Roger Babcock?"

The woman shook her head. "Babcock? No. I don't believe I
know him."

"I'm sure he must have flown in with you." He said the words
automatically, for a cold chill had crept over him. Slowly but
surely, he began to suspect that something had gone wrong—
damn wrong.

"He might have, I guess," the nurse said. "He could have
come in on the other plane." She scanned the crowd quickly,
then pointed to a table. "Sir, there's Captain Marie Crane. She's
senior nurse. Ask her—she'd probably know."

He felt Von Porten's hand clutch convulsively at his arm. *The
world had become bitter, cruel, and unjust, for if Crane was here,
Babcock was not.*

"The message we sent, General," Von Porten whispered hoarsely. "Didn't Corregidor get it?"

"They got it," he mumbled in return. "God knows what happened."

"What do we do now?"

Kogan leaned against the wall. For the first time since he had caught that piece of steel in Vietnam, he felt faint. The sun-splashed veranda turned dark. He sensed Von Porten's hand under his elbow, easing him through the door into the lobby. The quiet coolness helped. Von Porten spoke rapidly in Spanish, and a Filipino waitress swiftly handed Kogan a drink. He gulped the raw liquor gratefully.

"You all right?"

"Yeah, sorry," Kogan muttered. His head was still muddled.

"Okay, it's understandable. You've been carrying a ton of stress for a long time now," Von Porten said. "And that big trouble on the road didn't help. Let me give you something."

"No, no. Gotta think. Gotta find out what happened."

Von Porten took the glass from Kogan's hand and set it down. "You remember what you said in the car coming over?"

Kogan's head was clearing. He felt better now. He didn't know what Von Porten was talking about, though. "What was that?" he asked.

"You said Babcock might have given the formula to a nurse to bring out." He gestured toward the veranda. "One of these nurses."

Kogan nodded. He remembered. He guessed it was possible, but he didn't really believe it. The kinds of things he'd run into today meant that what they were trying to do was never meant to be. You don't screw around with universal laws, you don't go back in time, you don't try to change the way things happened, no matter how carefully you plan. Even getting Babcock away from the Rock, now that he looked back, had been a long shot. Finding a nurse who could help ... well, he could imagine the conversation. *By the way, do you have the formula for B-juice? Why, yes, now that you mention it, I do. Right here in my purse.*

Sure, that's how it would be—a bunch of crap.

"Let's get the hell out of here," he growled at Von Porten. "We've run out our string." He started off the porch.

"No!" The hand on his arm was strong. Kogan turned to see the doctor's thin, intelligent face eager, even hopeful. "Come on, Joe, it's not over yet." He spoke quickly, his lips close to Kogan's ear. "These are nurses, trained professionals. Doctors have to have them. Hell, I assure you, some of them are *better* than doctors."

"What are you talking about?"

"Look, one of these nurses may have worked with Babcock. She may remember the formula. Jesus, even if she only remembers a few of the ingredients, think what that could mean."

"It won't help Moody."

"He's just one man. With a few clues and enough money, we could have a chance of beating cancer." Von Porten jostled Kogan, as if to wake him up. "Joe, come on, we can't just walk away. This is our last chance."

Kogan forced his shoulders back against the wall, fighting bone-deep weariness. Von Porten didn't understand. They were players—no, puppets—incapable of changing in the slightest way the events of the past. What the hell, old *Sucker One* making it back must have been a fluke. Or was it? Maybe the puppeteer pulling the strings let them through to watch their antics for his own amusement. Or maybe they'd been just lucky enough to plunge through a rip in the fabric of time.

"What do you say, General? Let's hit on one of these women."

Kogan pulled back from his musing. Von Porten had him by the shoulders, looking into his eyes, his expression—was it really pleading? Cold, cynical, bored Dr. Von Porten?

"Doc," he said, almost carelessly. "We can't change the past. All our clever little lies, all Hiraga's technology, aren't going to change things one damn bit back here. There's no Babcock, there's no B-juice, and I tell you, we're gonna be real lucky to get back where we came from."

"I think you're wrong," Von Porten said. "I think we can and will change history."

"You said that in New Jersey."

Von Porten grinned and slapped Kogan's shoulder lightly. "That drink seemed to have helped." His eyes narrowed. "So you think it's impossible for us to change anything back here, is that it? Is that why you're giving up?"

"Now, wait a minute—"

"No, *you* wait. Think. There's the headless corpse of a good man somewhere in the jungle. There's a bunch of Moro bandits out there probably just as dead, all because of us." His smile was lopsided and a trifle cynical. "I think we're changing the past pretty good for people who were going to come back on kitten's feet."

"So what's your point?"

"Maybe we can do some more changing, in a way that will help the world. What do you say we give it a try?"

Kogan tossed down the rest of his drink. He was *really* tired, discouraged and fed up. How the hell had he gotten here? One day he was an overage student leading the quiet life of academia, the next he was fighting his way through this episodic madhouse, being punished, apparently, by a Calvinistic God for unidentified sins. His grubby little apartment, the penny-pinching, the boring stacks of letters and journals that smelled of mildew and tragedy, all seemed infinitely appealing right now. And so did Fay Donello. For the first time since that late-night phone call, she entered his thoughts. His fatigue didn't hinder his recall of a few interesting images of their freestyle sexual antics. Making love to Fay had been like taking off your clothes and starring in a porno movie. He'd had a nice seductive life in Washington, all things considered—maybe too good for an old soldier. Too good to last, as it turned out. Would he ever see Fay again, and if he did, what would he say? That he had been out of town on government business? That was about as precise as saying Hitler had this little character flaw.

"Joe?" Von Porten jiggled his arm. "How about it? Let's see what we can find out."

He took a deep breath. Recess was over. It was time to stop the whining kid bit and act like a major general again. They might not win, but what the hell. "Okay," he said. "Let's give it a try. I just hope to God you're right."

Von Porten slapped him on the shoulder. "Glad to have you back. I was getting tired of being in command. Where do we start?"

Kogan blinked. His mind was clearing. Where *should* they start? He looked around. At the end of the veranda were the three nurses the young lieutenant had pointed out. He could see captain's bars glint in the sun. "I'll start with Crane over there. I feel like I almost know her."

"That's understandable, considering what you tried to do to her." Von Porten grinned.

Kogan managed a meager smile in return. He was feeling almost normal again. "Cute, Doctor," he said over his shoulder as he walked away. "Suppose you spread some of that devastating wit around. See what *you* can find out."

The red-haired captain did not look up as he approached. The other two nurses did. A second lieutenant smiled at him. She was young and had darker red, almost auburn hair—in her mid twenties, Kogan guessed, and quite lovely. An older first lieutenant, wearing glasses and with a touch of gray in her brown hair, glanced up, stubbed out her cigarette, and reached for another. The table was littered with ashtrays and glasses. Captain Crane—he guessed that's who the redhead was—seemed unaware of his presence, choosing to sip her drink while staring moodily down the street. Kogan noticed how white and slender the hand holding the glass was.

"Captain Crane?" he asked.

She glanced up without much interest. "Yes."

"I'm Joe Kogan." He hadn't planned what to say. "I wonder if I could speak with you?"

Her eyes swept over his shirt. He suddenly remembered that he wore no insignia of rank. "Are you a war correspondent, Mr. Kogan?" Her voice was cool. "Here to interview us poor women escaping from the jaws of death? Well, you can quote me as saying what a marvelous, uplifting experience serving on the Rock has been, and how we're going to miss it—"

"Captain—" he interrupted.

She interrupted back. "Let me finish, please. Also tell your readers back in America how grateful we all are for the shiploads of food, medicine, and ammunition that have just *poured* into Corregidor."

She seemed to have finished, but he waited to make sure. The silence appeared to disconcert her. Somewhat defensively, she glanced up again. "Well, sir?"

He fingered the empty shoulder straps on his shirt. "I'm afraid I dressed rather hurriedly this morning. I'm from General Sharp's headquarters at Del Monte."

The other two women moved uneasily, as if bracing themselves to stand. Kogan decided to take the initiative. He extended his hand to the rather masculine-looking first lieutenant. "I'm Colonel Kogan," he said, and looked questioningly at her.

"Lieutenant MacNeil, sir." She started to rise.

"No," he said firmly, "please don't get up." He turned to the young lieutenant. She smiled radiantly and placed a small hand in his. "Lieutenant Redmond, sir," she said.

Captain Crane, however, seemed unaffected by his overtures. "Excuse us all, Colonel, if we don't get up," she said. "I'm just too damned tired for military courtesy."

"I understand, Captain." And he did. Crane's sarcasm and bitterness were natural reactions to what seemed to be cruel abandonment by the government. He glanced at the two other women and tried a smile. "I wonder if . . ." He got that far and stopped. *Redmond? The auburn-haired beauty must be Juanita*

Redmond! He looked at her oval-shaped face, with dark circles of fatigue under large, intelligent eyes, and realized that *this woman* would not only make it to Australia, but all the way back to the States and to a reception on the White House lawn. And he knew something else about her—

"Colonel?" Lieutenant Redmond interrupted his thoughts about her. She looked concerned. "You were saying?"

"Yes, I'm sorry." He got a grip on himself. "I wonder," he repeated, "if Captain Crane and I could have a few words in private?" The nurses immediately got to their feet, but Captain Crane waved them down.

"Sir," she said, and he noticed the exhaustion that shadowed her wide-spaced blue eyes. "As you can see, we're having a private conversation. We're enjoying a few drinks. For the first time in months, we're not getting hit by Jap shells and bombs. We fly out of here tonight and we may make it or we may not." He heard the rising crescendo of emotion in her threaten to get out of control. She bit her lower lip and he wondered whether she was going to say more. Her angry eyes met his.

"So I ask you, Colonel," she continued, her voice tremulous, "could we not, for this little while, be left in peace?"

Brother, couldn't one goddamn thing go right today? Oh, he couldn't blame her for her hostility. He knew it wasn't personal. It probably had nothing to do with her own situation. His guess was that she was speaking for those still stuck on that miserable little island in Manila Bay. Well, no point in going on with what was threatening to become a scene. He'd back off and maybe try another nurse, or see what luck Von Porten was having.

"I'm sorry, Captain." He really was. Sorry and embarrassed, because this was the woman he'd ordered left behind on the Rock. So who's getting screwed now? It was poetic justice, he had to admit. "Excuse me for intruding."

He turned and walked away, threading his way through the tables, noticing Von Porten deep in conversation with a heavyset naval officer. Kogan entered the lobby, stopped briefly at the bar for a whiskey and water, and carried it out to the veranda fronting on the lake. He stood there, leaning against a railing, watching the green-blue water of Lake Lanao and wondering what he should do. Maybe he should use his rank, call them all together—

"Colonel?"

The voice was tentative, almost timid. He turned to see Marie Crane looking up at him, a hesitant smile curving over white teeth. "That was really inexcusable of me. I'd like to apologize."

Relief swept over him. And gratitude. Maybe things were finally going better. "No...I understand," he said, smiling back at her. "Sherman said it first—war is hell." She laughed, her voice a light soprano, then appeared embarrassed, looking down and scuffing her shoe at the wooden planks of the floor. How different she seemed, how young and pretty. She was tall, too. He hadn't realized that while she was sitting, but the top of her head reached well above his chin.

"Well, sir...you said you wanted to talk?"

There were several empty tables nearby. "Why don't we sit here," he said, holding a chair for her. He went to the lobby door and beckoned to the bartender. She gazed out over the lake, her eyes contemplative.

"It's so peaceful here. I guess the contrast with Corregidor did something to me, caused me to snap at you." A waitress appeared and Marie asked for a rum and Coke. Kogan ordered a refill. "Last night," she continued, "I was so happy—delighted—to get away from Corregidor, but here, after a nice long shower, a very good lunch, and a drink, I was sitting there listening to all the laughter and happy talk going on around me, and suddenly it all disappeared. Being here is a dream. Reality is back in those stinking catacombs of Malinta, waiting for the final assault and God knows what else. I have such good friends stuck back there."

He eyed her keenly. Her voice had risen and he thought for a moment he heard the thin edge of hysteria breaking through. But she controlled it, even managed a chuckle at some vagrant thought.

"Something amusing?" Maybe he could edge her off the emotional brink, back to calm.

"Oh, nothing really, but a wonderful woman I've known for years gave me something to bring out for her." Again her lips curved as she remembered. "You would never guess what it is." Her eyes invited him to join in the game.

He grinned and went along. He liked her in this mood. It might help him later with the really important questions. "Letters, maybe," he said. "Nope, that's wrong. Too obvious. Maybe a frilly hat—a pretty one for a party or something."

He picked up a bamboo swizzle stick and stirred his drink, waiting for her to laugh at his dumb guess. She didn't. She just sat there, looking at him. *Then, oh God, it hit him.* Somewhere, in that vast mass of papers he had gone through, there had been a letter telling about a silly woman's hat that had been brought off Corregidor. He even remembered the description—a tiny hat, dark-colored, with a veil. At the wrong time, when his guard was down, the image had come back.

"How did you know?" She asked the question quietly.

He took a gulp from his drink. "Easy," he said casually. "Captain Crane, what would be the last thing anyone would bother to take off the Rock? Answer—a foolish hat. Something for a garden party. I can even describe it. Kind of a pink color, with a broad brim and lots of roses or tulips decorating it."

She laughed then. "Not quite right, but an incredibly good guess. It is a hat and I *am* going to wear it on very special occasions. And when I do, I'll think of Bea and..." Her voice faded and she sat quietly.

Kogan knew where she was. *Don't push her—let her come back on her own,* he thought. And she did, with a deep sigh and a smile that apologized for her absence. "Anyway, Colonel, it's so wonderful to know that the Japs are five hundred miles away."

Oh, boy. She hadn't heard of the landings at Parang. This example of American womanhood—clear-eyed, clean-limbed, looking like an ad out of the *Saturday Evening Post* of the 1940s—had managed to keep her sanity through a hellish five months. But he wasn't sure how much more she could take. He'd find out, because she had to be told.

"Captain," he said, "you're going to hear this anyway, so I might as well give you the bad news. The Japs landed south of here last night."

She looked at him, her face suddenly white. "You wouldn't joke about that?"

He worked on what he hoped was a confident smile. "I'm not joking, but you don't have to worry. They're nearly fifty miles away."

"How long before they get here...here in Dansalan?"

He replied carefully. "We have enough men to hold them off for several days."

Marie looked directly into his eyes. "And you, Colonel? What will happen to you? Will you die fighting them, too?" Without waiting for his reply, she covered her eyes as though blocking out an intolerable vision. "The Japs are like some evil thing. They seem unstoppable, superhuman. How could we have scorned them so, laughed at them?" She looked at him and he could see tiny lines at the corners of her eyes. "Last year I read that one of our admirals said we could beat the Japanese fleet in the morning and be back in time for lunch." She laughed, a cynical, unhumorous sound. "Why, we haven't even seen an American war vessel in months!"

Without thinking, he laid his hand on hers. As if seeking safety, her slim fingers clutched at his. For a moment, he wanted to pull her close to him, to hold her in his arms, to protect her. *Hey, Kogan, what the hell is this? There's a job to do.* Suddenly, she dropped her eyes in embarrassment. They both pulled back.

"I'm sorry, sir, for sounding off like this." She glanced up at him, her cheeks red. "You wanted to talk to me, and I've done all the talking." She took another swallow of her drink and he signaled the waitress for refills. "Now," she said, "it's your turn. What can I do for you?"

What can you do for me, young lady? Well, just for starters, you can make me the happiest man in the world by reaching into your purse and bringing out the formula for B-juice. Then get ready to administer CPR to the man across the table who's been shocked into cardiac arrest. Nope, wrong thought. CPR's way down the road somewhere. As remote from this pretty redhead as this god-damn B-juice she probably never heard of and we are never going to get our hands on. Well, let's give it a try.

"Do you know a Dr. Babcock?" That seemed as good a way as any to begin.

"Roger Babcock?"

A very small spark of hope flared. "You know him?"

"Yes, of course. We served in the same hospital—General Number One, on Bataan."

The spark got brighter. Could it be that their luck had changed? Taking a deep breath, he plunged in, throwing caution to the winds. "We've heard that Babcock developed a cure for cancer. Know anything about it?"

Before she could answer, the waitress arrived with the drinks. Kogan sipped his, watching Marie closely, waiting for, yet dreading her words. Her forehead furrowed as if trying to recall something of no particular significance. "You know, Colonel, I'd almost forgotten about that."

God Almighty, she had *forgotten* it! How could that be! All the bombs in the world couldn't knock that out of someone's head.

She was speaking again. "A couple of months ago, I guess, a rumor circulated about Babcock coming up with a cure for cancer. We were all quite excited, but later we heard it had been a mistake—there was nothing to it."

He picked up his drink again. Throw some more alcohol in there and maybe the pain would go away. So this was the answer—this explained why no information on the miracle cure had gotten out. No miracle cure existed. B-juice had started with a bang and then fizzled out. Why hadn't anyone thought of that? Suddenly, he realized the hand holding his drink was shaking. He set it down quickly, but Marie noticed.

"Are you all right, sir?"

"Yes, a little tired, I guess."

She opened her purse and brought out a pack of cigarettes. "Maybe a cigarette would help."

"Uh, no thanks."

She took one and laid the pack on the table, a book of matches beside it, then looked at him expectantly, her unlighted cigarette between her fingers. Kogan continued to wrestle with shock. With a little frown, Marie picked up the matches and lit her own cigarette.

"That's strange, Captain," Kogan finally said, his lips stiff with disappointment. "We heard that there had been remissions. I recall one name in particular—a Captain Peter Moody. Did you know him?"

She blew smoke at the lake. "Oh, yes, I remember Peter well. A remarkable recovery—almost overnight. We released him from the hospital a few days later. And we had several more later on, very similar."

Kogan leaned forward, trying to control his breathing, both hands clutching his drink. "Well?"

"The cases were apparently some sort of pathological aberration. Temporary remissions. Later, they all died."

"That's not true, Captain," he said, trying to control his excitement. "Peter Moody lived on for a couple of—" He clamped his mouth shut just in time. "Our records indicate that Captain Moody was captured on Bataan and right now is a prisoner of war."

Her eyes narrowed. "Your records? You have no records of our personnel. You say he's a POW? Colonel, what is this? Am I hearing you right?"

Oh, this is pitiful. Get yourself out of this one.

"You're hearing me okay." His chuckle sounded more like a croak. "I'm afraid I'm not saying things right. What I meant was that Southwest Pacific Area has a POW list. Moody's name is on it. He couldn't have died of cancer."

At first she seemed to accept his explanation. Then she shook her head impatiently. "I didn't know there were such lists." He waited while she thought about it. "Well," she continued, "whatever lists they have must be in error. Moody and the others all died. We have a physician's certification as to that."

"You saw the bodies?"

"No, of course not. I told you we released them from the hospital."

Damn, but he must be getting thick. Something here eluded him. "Look, Captain—uh, could I call you Marie?"

She nodded.

"Okay, Marie, step by step. You say the patients got well. They were released from General Number One. Then they died and you saw a physician's certificate of death on them. Correct?"

"Yeesss." She dragged the word out uncertainly.

"But if they worsened, wouldn't they have returned to the hospital?"

"Well, that would be the normal procedure, sure." She bit her lip and stubbed out her cigarette. "It *was* strange, now that I think about it. Of course, the fighting was awfully fierce and we were getting heavy casualties, so we didn't have a lot of time to dwell on it." She shook her head in self-deprecation and chuckled briefly. "It really is hard to believe that they all died elsewhere, yet they did. A couple of them died at General Number Two, and I believe Peter Moody died at a front-line battalion aid station."

"And each one had a duly certified death certificate by a physician?"

"By one physician. I guess because of the strange nature of the cases—the remissions and all—Dr. Babcock signed all the death certificates."

Von Porten ordered a drink in the lobby and handed the bartender money. The man, heavyset with a pleasant, jowly face, was apologetic.

"Sir," he said, holding up the ten-dollar bill. "Would you have something smaller?"

Von Porten pulled out a small wad of bills. He hadn't really looked at what had been given them for pocket money. Not a lot of dough, he remembered. The support group had arranged for the Treasury Department to resurrect old plates from the thirties and run off enough so that each crew member had spending money. "Forty bucks!" he recalled Betts exclaiming as he had checked it over. "Jesus, I really don't feel safe with all this money on me." The officer had frowned, then proceeded to bore them all with a discourse on the effects of inflation.

"Well," Von Porten said to the bartender while riffling through the money. "I've got a couple of ones. That cover it?"

The bartender laughed, as at a joke. "Yes, *Capitan*, it will cover it," he said, taking one of the bills and putting down change. Von Porten left the silver on the bar and walked away with his drink. From behind him, he heard a fervent "*Muchas gracias, señor.*"

He seated himself at the only vacant table on the veranda, sipping his drink, wondering how to proceed. At the next table a thin blond woman—her well-cut slacks and silk blouse setting her apart as a civilian—glanced directly at him, her brows raised coquettishly. That surprised him. Somehow, he expected a woman of a half century ago to be less obvious.

A military truck pulled up in front of the hotel. A sweating, overweight lieutenant commander got out and climbed heavily to the veranda. Spotting Von Porten alone at his table, he walked over.

"Mind if I sit down?" Without waiting for a response, he tossed a clipboard on the table and slumped into a chair. He waved urgently to a waitress, then turned to Von Porten and shoved out a beefy hand. "Fitzgerald. Jack Fitzgerald." The waitress arrived. "Bourbon, baby," he said, a leer on his broad Irish face. "Double shot, Coke chaser." He looked at Von Porten's collar. "Doc, huh? Don't remember you gettin' aboard last night. You on my list?" He picked up the clipboard and perused it.

A surge of excitement swept Von Porten. That clipboard on the table might hold the answer to what happened to Babcock. *Stay cool, don't get grabby*, he thought.

"No," Von Porten answered calmly. "I'm Art Von Porten. From General Sharp's headquarters at Del Monte. You fly in with the nurses?" he asked.

Fitzgerald took off his cap and mopped his sweating face with a grimy handkerchief. "Yeah, my party. I flew number seven boat."

"Great show," Von Porten said. "Run into any Japs?"

"Hell, no." Fitzgerald grunted. "Wouldn't be here if we had. We couldn't run away from a sick sea gull." The waitress placed his drink on the table. He lifted the bourbon and sipped it delicately, then let go with an explosive sigh of satisfaction.

"You certainly made a lot of women happy." Von Porten gestured toward the other tables. *Enough chitchat*, he decided. *Let's find out what happened.* "Commander—"

Fitzgerald interrupted. "Jack's the name. Yeah, you spend a little time on that Rock and you'll see why these gals have got the giggles." He chuckled. "Man, you should've heard them last night when they got aboard. I thought I took on a load of geese. After we got to altitude we passed out three bottles of Vat 69. Finally quieted them down."

Von Porten made another attempt. "Jack, I wonder if—"

Fitzgerald was in a sending mode. His booming, South Philadelphia accent rolled serenely over his companion's words. "Tell you the truth, Doc, for a while, I thought we'd never make it off the water." He took another, less delicate sip of bourbon, wiped his mouth, and leaned forward. Von Porten sighed inwardly and leaned back, defeated. A story loomed ahead.

Fitzgerald tapped a thick forefinger on Von Porten's arm. "Lemme tell you what happened." The rest of the bourbon went down in a gulp and the waitress was again summoned. "Darker'n hell when we landed, I tell ya. Had to wait around on the water off Monkey Point longer than I wanted, but finally got everybody aboard. Easterly wind, so we had to take off directly toward Manila. Number one boat made it all right, then it was our turn. I had taken two extra people aboard, so I knew it was gonna be a long run, but I was pretty sure we could make it. Couple minutes later, I wasn't so sure. Couldn't get 'er up on the step.

With the spray and all, hard to see through the windshield even with the wipers goin' full blast, but I could see the lights of Manila coming closer—too damn close. Bob Ellis, my copilot, kept yelling at me to pour it to her. Hell, I already had those Pratt and Whitneys going all out. Tell ya, friend, we don't get this baby off soon, we're gonna end up on Dewey Boulevard."

The waitress brought more bourbon and another chaser, even though the first Coke remained untouched. Never taking his eyes off Von Porten, Fitzgerald's big hand crept along the table until contact with the glass was made. Half the bourbon disappeared. Smacking his lips, he continued.

"We got a problem. The damn boat is running tail heavy. Had to do something, and quick. I told Bob to get the women forward, on the double. He did it, damned if I know how. Guess he half scared 'em to death. Could hear them screaming as they jammed themselves against the forward bulkhead. Bob jumped back in the right-hand seat, took one look at the lights, and said, Oh, shit. But getting the women forward did it. Bob and me leaned back on the wheel and we went over the waterfront about ten feet above the docks." Fitzgerald grinned and tossed off the rest of the bourbon.

In spite of his impatience, Von Porten had listened with interest. "That's quite a story," he said truthfully.

"Hell, that ain't all." He played with the empty shot glass, looked for the waitress, but when she turned in his direction, he regretfully shook his head. "Rest of it ain't pretty. Anyway, we turned south, climbing slow because of the load, and keeping a lookout for number one boat. Found her when we got up to about five thousand. Set a course for Mindanao, cruising at a little over a hundred knots, and hoped we wouldn't run into any Japs. Got cold at that altitude, so I told my crew chief to break some blankets out of the storage bin in the tail and pass them around."

"Few minutes later, the chief came forward holding this blond guy by the neck. Fucking stowaway. That was what damned near got us cracked up. Hundred fifty pounds of shit. Funny thing, though, the guy kept grinning at me. No damned shame at all. Crew chief asked if he could throw him over the side. Would have, too, if I'd given the word. I told him to shove the prick back in the storage compartment—without a blanket."

Fitzgerald shook his head in disbelief. "Doc, I tell ya, I never ran into a son of a bitch like him. Know what he said to me? He said if I'd let him have a blanket, he'd let me keep it—*me keep it*—when we got in. Then he said something else. He told me someday I could give the blanket to my children and tell them that it once kept Roger Babcock's body warm."

Fitzgerald's big forefinger traced a design in the moisture on the table. "Well, I gotta get a couple of hours of shut-eye before we take off tonight. Nice talking to you, Doc."

He looked up, but his drinking buddy had disappeared.

". . . and right now, they've got him in the *cárcel*—the jail." Von Porten's face was flushed with excitement. "Joe, we've got it made. I'll go down there and get the stuff and we can be on our way."

Kogan shifted his gaze over the doctor's shoulder. Lake Lanao glittered in the afternoon sun. In the distance an outrigger plied the shallows, a fisherman standing in the bow, a crude spear poised to impale an unsuspecting fish. A providential vision, Kogan thought, the scene a metaphor for Operation SUCCOR, with fate in the guise of the native. Whether the barbed tip of a mythic spear would destroy their hopes posed a question that became more unanswerable as time went on. First there was a Babcock, then there was no Babcock, then he miraculously appears, but in a form far different from what they had expected.

Marie sat by herself at the little table halfway down the veranda, out of earshot and a bit puzzled, he could see by her expression. Understandably so. Moments ago, Von Porten had rushed up and seized Kogan's arm, pulling him away without so much as an apology. Now the two men leaned against the low railing of the balcony, and Kogan's initial euphoria at Von Porten's news had evaporated. While he listened to the doctor's excited account, Marie Crane's story had sunk in, leaving him with a clear impression that the estimable Dr. Babcock was a liar and self-serving bastard. Kogan's face must have reflected his doubts.

"What's wrong?" Von Porten asked. "Where's the happiness?"

"My friend, we've got a real problem. I'm afraid we're dealing with a grade A, number one asshole." Then, with a glance over his shoulder at Marie, he quickly repeated what he'd learned. "This guy isn't going to be easy."

Von Porten nodded slowly as he listened, then his face brightened. "Let me handle him. No point in both of us dealing with this slime. He may be a little reluctant, but doctor to doctor. . . ." He smiled confidently and Kogan could see a bit of the old Von Porten ego flare up. "I think I can convince him."

Von Porten left, and as Kogan started back to the table, Marie got to her feet. "Colonel—"

"Joe," he said.

"Okay, Joe, I really have to leave." She held out her hand. He took it and held it longer than he had intended. He had also sat longer than he had intended, but no harm was done. He liked Marie Crane. He liked her a lot. How much of it was a genuine attraction between a man and woman, or just fascination because she was from another world, he couldn't say, nor did he much care. He did care that their afternoon was ending, because that meant that he would never see her again.

"Couldn't you stay for another drink?" He had a feeling the answer would be no. He flipped through his money and handed a bill to the waitress.

Marie looked at her watch, and for a moment he thought she might stay longer, but she looked up with what he thought was genuine regret in her eyes. "I'd love to, but we've arranged to have a picture taken of our group. I'm senior nurse, so I have to be there."

The waitress placed a tray with his change on the table. Kogan left a couple of dollar bills on the tray and put the rest in his pocket. He reached out to take Marie's elbow, but she stood still, looking down at the table, her face shocked.

"What are you doing?"

"What's wrong?"

"All that money you left."

He shrugged. "Little tip, that's all."

"Two dollars!" Her voice was indignant. *Oh, oh, he finally got it.* Marie picked up the money and thrust it at him. "For heaven's sake, our bill for four drinks was only a dollar." She extracted a coin from her purse and laid it on the tray. "There," she said, and marched off, Kogan trudging disconsolately behind her, glad the episode hadn't been witnessed by the crew of *Sucker One.*

Nurses milled around on the veranda. A fat Filipino with an imperfect command of English was trying to get them into position for a group picture. Out in the street, a large box camera sat on a tripod, a black hood hanging down. Marie shook her head in dismay.

"I think I'm needed here," she said. "Bye, Joe." And she was gone. Kogan turned and wandered back through the nearly deserted lobby, wondering how Von Porten was getting along with Babcock. Maybe he should get down to the jail, but he didn't want to blunder in, ruining delicate negotiations. He ordered a drink he didn't want and stood at the bar, listening to the giggles and noisy raillery coming from the photo session. As soon as it was over, the nurses would be on their way down to the lake where the two PBYs were hidden. Then they'd fly to Australia— that is, one plane load would. The other would be dumped here.

He snapped erect. Marie Crane would be on the damaged boat, stuck here and doomed to spend the next four years in a POW camp, perhaps never getting out, perhaps dying from malnutrition or disease.

Then he slumped over his drink again. There was nothing he could do about it. They were not to interfere with history.

Suddenly his drink looked good. He took a big gulp. "Can I get you another, *señor?*" The bartender waited, a fresh glass poised. Kogan shook his head. But supposing Marie *had not* gotten on the boat that stove in its bottom, and instead went on to Australia? What really would be changed if he persuaded her to get on the other PBY? She would live, she might marry, and she might have a child. Unless the kid became another Hitler, or started a new world religion, where the hell was the harm? By saving Marie, he would only be dropping a small pebble into a vast ocean. There would be a tiny splash, a few ripples that would quickly disappear, and all would be the same.

He drained his glass and headed for the veranda. At the last moment he saw that the picture was about to be taken, but too late, his momentum had carried him to the edge of the veranda. Two rows of nurses stood on the steps in front of him, and the photographer had disappeared under the black hood. Kogan quickly turned away, but not before the powder flared and popped. The women, who had been quiet for the first time since arriving in Dansalan, burst into talk and laughter and began to stream across the street toward two personnel carriers.

Kogan spotted Marie's hair gleaming in the sun, and trotted after her. "Marie," he said, as she supervised the loading of the nurses.

"Oh, hi, Colonel," she said over her shoulder. "Something more I can do for you?"

He suddenly felt embarrassed standing there, the only male among so many women, some of whom were looking at him and whispering. "Wonder if I could...just have a word with you before you leave?"

"Just a minute." She walked back to check the second truck. "All right, girls," she called out, "you all have your luggage?" She walked to the lead truck. "Be right with you," she told the driver, and turned to Kogan.

"I really can't tell you any more than I already have," she said. "I feel so stupid about not learning more about B-juice, but we were so busy—"

"No," he broke in hurriedly. "It's not that. I want to ask you to do something. It may sound crazy, but please do it."

She glanced at her watch and gave him a quizzical look. "Well, yes, I will if I can. What is it?"

"Get on number seven boat for the flight."

"Number seven? I didn't know they had numbers."

"They do. You'll see it on the tail. Remember, number seven."

She gave him a long look. "I don't understand. Is there something you're not telling me?"

Well, yes, as a matter of fact. He'd left out just about everything under the sun, and what he *had* told her were mainly lies, so one more wouldn't hurt. "Well," he pretended to be reluctant, "I happen to know that Jack Fitzgerald is about the best PBY pilot in the navy. He's flying number seven boat. So," he smiled, "will you promise?"

Marie smiled back and stepped closer to him. Behind him, he could hear voices encouraging her. "That's awfully sweet of you, Joe." She lifted her face and kissed him lightly on the lips. The voices from the trucks got louder. The noise stopped as their lips met, and for Kogan, there was just the two of them, looking into each other's eyes on a dusty street in a small town. He cupped her face with his hands and kissed her again, a kiss that lasted longer than he had intended. He stepped back and the sound came on again—the girls were really whooping it up.

He watched as the personnel carriers rolled down the road, raising clouds of dust that obscured the blue of the lake. Then he realized someone was speaking to him.

"Gen...Colonel," Willie Burke said. "Military police here are going to escort us back tomorrow morning. After what happened today, Del Monte is worried about the Moros."

Kogan frowned. As soon as Von Porten got what he wanted from Babcock, they were leaving. "Tell them to forget it, Willie. We've got to get back tonight."

"They've got their orders, sir." Absolute sincerity showed on Willie's battered face, and a determination that made him argue with a major general. "Besides, I don't think we'd make it through without an escort, especially at night. After what happened today, I've got a feeling other chieftains are out there waiting to jump us."

═ CHAPTER TWELVE ═

The day had started off well, with lots of sun, low humidity, and just enough of a breeze to freshen the air. But September in the power capital of the world is fickle. By midafternoon, the lacy, brilliant white clouds had darkened, the breeze had become a tugging wind, and a gray curtain of rain had moved from the Appalachian slopes down across the tidewaters of the lower Potomac.

Thunder rattled the window of Rodale's office, and though it was only three o'clock the lights were on. He eyed Passmore, standing in front of his desk.

"You sure about this, Bill?" he asked. It was a dumb question. The agent didn't make mistakes—not with matters of this magnitude.

The agent nodded, his short, thick arms akimbo. "My contact in Pyle's office says the letter has already gone out to the cabinet."

"Damnit." Rodale frowned, recalling the talk with Pyle in the Family Quarters. "The vice president promised the president and Mrs. Moody he wouldn't do anything until the cabinet made the decision. Crooked bastard." His eyes wandered over the walls of his office as if he could find the answer there. "I knew we couldn't trust him."

"Anything I can do, sir?"

Ah, Passmore the solid, the reliable, the one stable element in this screwed-up world. Without changing his expression, Rodale answered, "Yeah, damn right. Find Pyle and kill the son of a bitch."

"Sir!" Passmore took a second to get it. Then the ghost of a smile touched his lips. "Put that in writing and he's dog meat."

Rodale turned grim again. His fist slammed down on his desk. "I can't believe it. Simon's the president of the United States, and there's not a goddamn person out there who will help him."

"I dunno, Chief. There are a lot of people who love the guy and would like to help." Passmore walked to the door and turned. "Trouble is," he said, "they don't know the problem and we can't tell them." He left, closing the door gently.

The buzzer sounded. "Mr. Rodale, the secretary of state is on the line." He picked up the phone.

"Yes, Mr. Secretary."

"Afternoon, Martin," Talbott's dry voice came over the line. "I wonder if you and the president are aware of a certain letter that's circulating."

"Just heard about it, sir. Quite a surprise. Could you tell me more?"

There was a pause at the other end. "Not over the phone. It's my impression that you will be apprised of the document by the originator—and quite soon, I believe. I'm sorry, and Simon knows my feelings, I'm sure." The secretary cleared his throat. "This particular amendment—you know what I'm speaking of—

has never been used, so precisely what the mechanics of it are remain to be seen. Uh, Martin . . . if I can be of any help, please call on me."

"Thank you, Mr. Secretary."

"Good day, Martin."

Rodale put down the phone and slumped in his chair. Passmore was right, as usual. He thought about what the agent had said. Desperate times call for desperate measures. They already had their back to the wall. Maybe help was out there somewhere. Of course, the thing could backfire. But what the hell, right now they had damn little to lose.

Passmore led the vice president along the broad corridor, the chandeliers lit against the autumn gloom. Pyle glanced at the well-barbered back of Passmore's neck and said, "Why the escort? Think I'll steal the White House silver?"

The agent plodded along as though considering the question. He waited just long enough for the point to be made. "No, sir." He knocked on the door of the Family Quarters. Charles appeared and bowed slightly when he saw Pyle.

"Good evening, Mr. Vice President. Mrs. Moody will be along shortly."

Pyle entered and looked around the empty room. "How about a scotch and water while I'm waiting?"

"Yes, sir, right away." Charles turned away, but before he could open the anteroom door, the First Lady entered.

"How nice to see you, Mr. Pyle." Lillian, wearing a cream-colored silk suit with a taupe blouse, walked forward and took his hand. Smiling brilliantly, she indicated a chair, then seated herself opposite him. "Would you like something to drink?"

"I've ordered a scotch," Pyle said, glancing at Lillian's legs. The First Lady pressed her knees firmly together. "Well," he said. "What's this all about? Rodale said the president wanted to see me."

"Yes, we'll go into the sitting room in a moment. We have several guests this evening and Simon thought it would be nice if you could join us."

A slight narrowing of his eyes was Pyle's only sign of surprise. "Guests?" he asked. "Is that wise... considering the circumstances?" He started to say something else, but Charles appeared with his drink. Pyle sipped it. "Who's here?"

Lillian got to her feet. "People you know, Mr. Pyle," she said. "Senator Moser, Congressman Collines, and the chief justice of the Supreme Court." She smiled. "And, oh yes, the secretary of state."

"What?" This time he couldn't conceal his shock. "I don't understand—"

"Let's join them, shall we?" She started toward the sitting room.

"Wait a minute," he said, reaching out for her arm. Almost imperceptibly, Lillian drew away from his touch. "We—the cabinet and I—were sworn to secrecy, specifically with reference to Congress. Now you've got the leaders here. What gives?"

"Things change," she replied, and led the way out of the room.

As Lillian entered the large, comfortable room, followed by Pyle, Rodale excused himself to the other guests and walked over to shake hands with the vice president.

Jesus, he'd be glad when this affair was over. And so would Lillian, he guessed. She was as beautiful as ever, but even her expert makeup couldn't hide the pallor of her skin. She must have warned Pyle about the others being here, but if that had surprised him, he didn't show it. He had his tough, board-meeting face on, his eyes glittering specks under brows that formed a solid line over his nose.

"Nice to see you, Mr. Vice President," Rodale said, winking at Lillian over Pyle's sparse growth of hair. It would be even nicer if the little bastard were suddenly transported to Neptune's third moon. "I see you've got a drink. Come over and join the others."

"Where's the president?" Pyle asked.

"Be along shortly."

The four other guests managed formal, cool smiles as Pyle approached—Senator Newton Moser, his septuagenarian face as crisscrossed with canyons and ridges as the Rockies his state was famous for; Congressman Gould Collines, in his late forties, his black hair unruly. The dark suit hanging on his lean, tall frame made him seem Lincolnesque—an artful ploy, his political foes claimed, since he represented Illinois. The third man, Chief Justice John Brown Mullins, balanced a martini as adroitly as he avoided identification with either broad or strict constructionism. In spite of the rumpled suit and heavily lidded eyes that gave him the look of having just awakened from a long snooze on a park bench, Mullins of Louisiana was deemed the first really intellectual chief justice since the 1940s.

Secretary of State Quentin Talbott, as usual, stood slightly back from the others, preferring to look into the depths of his soda water while listening carefully.

"Gentlemen," Rodale said, "the president will be with us in a moment." No one said anything. The expressions on the guests' faces were uniformly noncommittal, but Rodale noticed Senator Moser glance quizzically and significantly at Gould Collines.

Lillian came to the rescue. Her radiant smile was all-inclusive as she wondered about their drinks. "Chief Justice," she said, her southern accent broadening for his benefit, "for gracious sakes, let's get you a fresh martini." As she motioned to Charles, Rodale caught her eye and inclined his head.

"Excuse me, please," she said, and slipped away from the circle. Rodale eased out, too, leaving the five men to make small talk.

On the other side of the room, touching up an arrangement of fresh flowers that was already perfect, Lillian spoke in a low voice.

"What is it, Marty?"

"Where the hell is Simon?"

"He's . . . well, he's in bad shape. He nearly fainted this afternoon. Eccles is with him now. He's given him something."

"Me and my great ideas."

"It *was*, it *is*, a great idea. Don't crucify yourself. We really have no choice, do we?"

They turned as the large double doors on the opposite wall opened. Beth Diego maneuvered the president's wheelchair in, then left. The wheelchair was a new development, an admission of Moody's weakness dealt them by the hand of fate with excruciatingly bad timing. Night before last, the president had weakened to the point where he could no longer walk. Yet, when just this afternoon Rodale suggested making a clean breast of his condition to the three most important men in government, Moody considered it only for a moment before approving.

"Wonderful, Marty," he had said enthusiastically. "I like it. It will be great to be able to tell the truth to somebody besides my cabinet . . . and my vice president. I suddenly feel good, really good. It's a rush of adrenaline."

"It could backfire, Simon," Rodale had warned. "You could find yourself out of office very quickly." That was true. The three officials were good men, but they were conscientious public servants who took their responsibilities seriously. Moody's condition would come as a shock to them—one that might very well catapult Pyle into the White House almost overnight.

"And if we can't hold off Pyle and his letter, how long will I stay in office?"

Rodale answered bleakly. "About the same amount of time." He had a thought. "Listen, you can still stand. Why not position yourself by this chair when they arrive? You shake hands and sit down. That eliminates the wheelchair." He turned to Lillian. "What do you think?"

She and the president exchanged dubious glances. "No," Simon said. "We've had too much deceit. Let's tell them the whole truth—except the details of SUCCOR. But you know," he added, "I feel good enough right now that I might even be able to walk in."

He hadn't made it. He hadn't even come close. Rodale could see in Moody's strangely immobile face what Lillian meant—the president was in bad shape, hurting deep inside and exhausted.

The effort to get dressed, shaved, and groomed for this confrontation—even with Charles's help—must have been enormous. Rodale's heart ached as he walked over, placed his hand briefly on Moody's shoulder, and pushed the wheelchair across the room.

"Good evening, gentlemen," the president said, and Rodale wondered from what source he drew the strength to smile and deepen his voice to that magisterial baritone. "Please," he continued, motioning, "sit down."

Senator Moser leaned forward, scowling at him. "Mr. President, what the hell's happened?" Rodale watched carefully. If Moody's strength held out, he might be able to field all their questions. If not, Rodale himself might have to step in.

Moody chose not to respond directly to the senator's question. "I appreciate your coming here tonight," he said. "And I'm very sorry to spring my physical condition on you like this. So let me be candid with you. Four months ago," Moody said, "this thing hit me. At the time, there seemed to be a chance I could beat the disease, but when it began to metastasize—"

Moser broke in. "You mean, all this time you've been lying to us?"

"Not to all of us, Newton." Talbott's quiet voice sounded in the room. "The president has confided his condition to his cabinet and to his vice president from the beginning."

"That's fine, Quent, but what about us?"

Moody's head went high and two red spots appeared on his cheeks. "I'm sorry, Senator. I wish there had been another way."

"That doesn't answer my question."

"Yes," Lillian's clear voice took over. "We have lied, but only a few people have been harmed."

"And who, Mrs. Moody," Chief Justice Mullins asked, "are they?"

"Simon, principally, and me. And the others who have known about it." Lillian held herself rigidly erect, her chin up. *God, she is one helluva woman*, Rodale thought. No one would have faulted her had she stayed in her room and let the men fight this thing out.

Lillian continued. "All our lives we have been honest and forthright people, Simon and I. What we've done has been unbelievably hard . . . it's contrary to our nature. We did so only to give Simon a chance to achieve the thing he promised the American people and the world—the beginning of genuine nuclear disarmament."

Hey, hey, Rodale applauded silently. *But that's not quite all, though, is it, Lillian? What you really mean is we don't want that turd of a vice president to take over.*

"Isn't that a trifle specious, Mrs. Moody?" Congressman Collines drawled the question. "You're saying deceit only harms the deceiver. It would be difficult for us to judge that without knowing—"

"Gentlemen," Rodale broke in quickly. *Time for show-and-tell*, he decided. "It should be no secret to you that Simon Moody and his vice president differ profoundly in their ideological approach to national security and defense spending." He stole a glance at Spencer Pyle, whose face might as well have been carved from stone. "Every president since Eisenhower has been a virtual captive of the Pentagon—even Jimmy Carter, in the last years of his administration, got into the spirit of the thing. Every move by the Russians to bilaterally disarm has consistently been met with suspicion and sullen rejection—"

"Wait a minute, Marty," Pyle broke in. "You're going too far. You make a lot of patriotic Americans who care very deeply for their country sound like paranoids. It's the arsenal we've built in the last forty years that has kept the peace, and just because a bunch of Slavs cry uncle is no reason to tear it down."

Rodale turned to the group and spread his hands. "You see, gentlemen? Next month the leaders of twenty-two countries meet in Brussels to begin the DOE talks. The hopes of all reasonable men and women for the denuclearization of Europe hover over the delegates." He looked at Pyle. "Yet, if I am not mistaken, should Spencer Pyle lead our team, the talks will produce nothing. Am I correct in that, Mr. Vice President?"

Pyle seemed not at all abashed. "Maybe, but that's our system.

I won't go unless...well, unless I'm president. What happens then at Brussels will be my business, and just because I think the denuclearization of Europe is stupid and dangerous doesn't mean I'm a right-wing ideologue. And I don't think that 'all reasonable men and women' are on your side on this issue. There are a lot of people who think the way I do."

"Are you referring to the Czech cabal?" Collines interjected.

"I don't know where that stupid name came from." Pyle made an impatient gesture. "But if you mean European officials who don't want their countries to be stripped of their nuclear umbrella, yes." He turned to Simon. "And, Mr. President, they're not alone. Bedford Shaw, your own secretary of defense, is against it."

Rodale spoke up again. "Bedford's a reincarnation of Cap Weinberger—he never met a weapon system he didn't love."

"It's not an unreasonable position, damnit. The Middle East is like a beehive that's been hit with a stick. You can hear and feel the fury building. One of these days, unless we and Europe keep our guard up, that place is going to explode and take western civilization with it."

"That's precisely my point, Spence," the president said. "If we are going to stop nuclear proliferation in the Middle East, we must take the first step—set an example. Then, through the UN, we'll pressure the Arabs and the Israelis to do the same. Otherwise, the march to Armageddon—and I don't think the allusion is excessive —will quicken into a mad rush. But we must act quickly. Time is running out."

Senator Moser tossed off the remainder of his drink and wiped his lips with the back of his hand. "I've been hearing a lot of this in the Foreign Relations committee, but I don't think that's why we're here tonight. The subject, as I understand it, is your health, Simon, or lack of it." Pyle stirred, with the obvious intent of getting the floor back, but the chief justice's lazy voice intervened before he could. "I agree with the senator, Mr. President. What exactly is your purpose in bringing us here tonight?"

Moody turned to his vice president. "I think I'll give Spencer a chance to answer that."

Pyle seemed disconcerted by the reversed fields. "What are you talking about, Mr. President? You invited them, not me."

"But *why* did we invite them? That's the question." Moody's eyes never left Pyle's face. "Why would we do it, Spencer—or are you keeping it as a surprise?"

Pyle met the challenge. "All right," he said, moving as if to distance himself from the group. "You're going to find out very soon now, anyway. I have initiated a letter to implement the Twenty-fifth Amendment."

"Wait a minute. The Twenty-fifth is only used if the president is unable to carry out his duties," Collines said.

"Simon can no longer even walk," Pyle replied, as though that settled it. Rodale kept his face straight, but he wanted to laugh. That was the first dumb thing he'd ever heard Pyle say.

Moser snorted. "For twelve years, and from a wheelchair," he said emphatically, "Franklin Delano Roosevelt ran the country and most of the free world."

Pyle didn't back down. "Senator," he said, "we're not talking about the same thing." His eyes swept the group. "Let me answer Congressman Collines's question candidly, because I believe the security of our nation demands it. Yes, it is my *opinion* that Simon Moody can no longer carry out the functions of his office."

For a brief stretch of time, no one said anything. Then Chief Justice Mullins said, "Does the cabinet go along with you on this matter?"

"The majority does. Look, I really have no choice." Pyle turned to the president. "Simon, I'm sorry, but I have to do what I think is best for the country." As he spoke, Pyle's hard face seemed to soften. *Great job of acting*, Rodale thought. One might almost believe the vice president *did* have regrets.

"I don't believe my question was ever fully answered," the chief justice said, his soft voice edged. "Again, Mr. President, what *is* the purpose of our being here tonight?"

"To ask your pardon for the subterfuge we have practiced, and to explain why we did it," the president said. "And most important, Mr. Chief Justice, to ask for time. You see, there is a chance, and I believe a good one, that I can be cured. All I need is a few more days."

"I don't understand," Collines said. "You must have had the best care modern medicine can provide. Yet your condition, according to you, has worsened. What in God's name is this cure, and where has it been hiding?"

"Gould," Rodale spoke up. "We can't tell you the entire story. Just believe me when I say that it has required all the power of the presidency to get as close to this thing as we have, and that right now we are very close to success or—let's admit it, failure." Looking at their faces was like trying to judge what a jury would decide in a very close case. He wouldn't have bet on it one way or the other. Maybe he shouldn't have pushed for this showdown, but even now, with the issue in doubt, he felt relief that the ghastly charade was coming to an end.

"Please realize what it is we're trying to do," Lillian said, and Rodale could see her eyes fill with the wonder of her vision. "This is not just a cure for Simon. It could be a miracle for all the world, for all peoples everywhere. Give us, we beg you, the time we need."

"How much *do* you need, my dear?" Senator Moser asked.

Rodale watched Lillian turn to her husband for an answer, for she didn't know, nor did anybody. Late that afternoon, from Pearl Harbor, they had received a classified dispatch sent by CINCPAC, but the signature line bore the name Kogan. It was very brief, stating that SUCCOR's ETD would be in three days. But what was the date of return? The message didn't say. And even if SUCCOR was successful, there were so many things they didn't know. Like even if the serum worked, how long would it be before B-juice cured Simon? Rodale waited tensely for the boss to reply.

Licking his dry lips, the president answered, "Seven days,

Newt, that's all. We'll either have it then . . . or we won't." Rodale let his breath out slowly. Were they asking for too many days? Would they get any time at all?

"Hell, that's not much." Moser grunted. "What's the damn difference? I say we give Simon the time he wants. If the cure works—and I'm sorry to sound cold-blooded—it'll save the trouble of changing administrations." He looked around. "Y'all agree?"

Heads nodded. All except the vice president.

"Absolutely not," Pyle said, his thin lips compressing into a hard line. "How many of you really expect this cure to materialize? Oh, sure, we can all hope, but miracles don't appear just because they're needed. That means I've got to get ready for Brussels, and that means a helluva lot of work and not much time to do it in. But aside from that, Simon Moody, in his present condition, is unable to carry out the duties of his office."

"Mr. Vice President." Lillian's voice had the sound of shards of breaking glass. "He's doing very well and you know it! What has been left undone? We haven't gone to war, we're not in a recession, the terrorists are lying low, and we're on our way to taking nuclear arms out of Europe. Name just one goddamn thing that's been left undone!"

If ever Rodale saw pure fury on a human face, it was on Lillian's. Her lovely features had disappeared, replaced by a snarl that would have done credit to a she-wolf protecting her cubs. The president, startled, reached his hand out to his wife.

"Lillian, my dear, please . . ."

At his touch, the heightened color fled the First Lady's face. She backed up to stand quietly beside her husband, her posture suddenly submissive. Her eyes, though, still glared at Pyle. Remarkably enough, the only person in the room who seemed unaffected by the outburst was the man at whom it was directed. Pyle shot a glance at the First Lady and then continued on, his voice as smooth and modulated as if the tirade had never happened.

"What I'm talking about is a crisis that would require the president to put in sixteen hours of concentrated work, day after day, as John Kennedy did during the Cuban crisis. Could we depend upon Simon for the critical analysis and split-second decisions we would need to meet that challenge? The answer to that is quite obvious."

The vice president turned to look at Moody, as if to point up the pitiful condition of the president. At just that moment, Moody passed a shaking hand over his waxy face. Rodale groaned deep inside. He wondered if any president in history had had to undergo such humiliation in his own living quarters.

Secretary Talbott didn't seem impressed by the vice president's suggestions. "Anyone can create nightmares, Mr. Pyle. Be realistic, and please, have some faith in my department."

"All right, Mr. Secretary," Pyle shot back, "let's be realistic. Even if the cure materializes and proves to be effective, how long will it take for the president to regain his health? Months, perhaps a year or more. Crises don't send calling cards. They arrive unannounced. We can't take a chance on world troubles waiting around until the president is well."

The chief justice looked at Moody. "He's got a point, Simon. What do you say to that?"

"Uh..." Moody seemed to have difficulty collecting his thoughts. "We have indications that the recovery period is remarkably short. How short, we really don't know. Gentlemen, I'm asking for just a week. If the cure isn't obtained by that time, I...well, then the question may become moot, anyway."

"All right." The chief justice slapped his knees in an impatient gesture. "Let's give Simon his seven days. Mr. Vice President, we ask you to hold off on that letter for that period of time."

"I'm sorry," Pyle said, and this time his expression said otherwise. "I have a constitutional duty to perform."

"Bullshit!" The curse ricocheted around the room as Moser came to his feet. "There's something wrong here when a vice president is so damn anxious to take over." With a baleful look at Pyle, he stomped up and down the room, his big body graceless, but in spite of his years, still powerful. Heavy breathing and lip-smacking indignation told the rest that he intended to hold the floor. He stopped beside Lillian's chair. "Now, I admit," he rumbled, "I don't approve of Simon's covering up and all, but I guess he had his reasons. As long as I've known him, he's been a good man." He laid a hand lightly on Lillian's shoulder. "And he's got a good woman. Okay. So Gould, here, and the chief justice and me, are willing to give Simon his week. And it's pretty obvious that Secretary Talbott will go along. But the vice president won't. Well... I guess that's his decision to make." Moser faced Pyle.

"But I just want to tell you, Mr. Vice President, what the facts of the matter are. You write your letter throwing Simon out of the White House and every editor and news commentator and all the men and women in the street are gonna peg you for a grasping, power-hungry jerk. Wouldn't be surprised if word of what went on here tonight leaked out. Tell you another thing. New presidents usually have a honeymoon with Congress. You keep on like this, and the only part of the honeymoon you'll get is the screwing, you understand me?"

Without waiting for an answer, Moser walked over to stand beside the president's wheelchair. He looked back at Pyle. "Now, if Simon agrees, here's the deal. You hold off on that letter for a week. If the cure doesn't materialize by that time, President Moody will publicly ask you to take over and save the republic. You'll be a goddamn hero."

The old senator leaned down and peered into Moody's face. "That okay by you, Simon?"

Eagerly, the president nodded.

"Well, Mr. Vice President," Moser said. "How about it?"

Rodale knew it must have taken all of Pyle's self-control to beat a graceful retreat. With a faint smile and an air of nonchalance, he nodded. "All right, I see no problem with that." But as the others emitted a collective sigh of relief, his voice harshened. "Let's be clear on this. Mr. President, the cure you speak of must arrive within one week."

CHAPTER THIRTEEN

Kogan waited until the military police sergeant left the cell, then turned to Babcock, who was meticulously combing his hair in front of a cracked mirror. At first, Kogan had pegged him as handsome, and then, when he decided he wasn't, he wondered if it was because the doctor had turned out to be such an asshole. He was somewhere in his late twenties, perhaps, with a straight, almost classical nose, and blond hair worn a bit long for the military. But the doctor's eyes were cold gray-blue under vague eyebrows, and his mouth formed a perpetual pout. above an inadequate chin. He had trouble making eye contact, seeming to prefer examining the second button of Kogan's shirt.

Von Porten, slumped on a three-legged stool against the cell wall, eyed Babcock as though he were some weird botanical

specimen. In a guarded telephone call to the hotel, he had con-
fessed to Kogan that he could make no headway in getting the
formula for B-juice from Babcock. "I tell you, Joe," Von Porten
had said, "this guy is really stonewalling. B-juice was a flop,
according to him, and he's going to prefer court-martial charges
against us if he doesn't get on that flight to Australia."

So Kogan had come down to the *cárcel*. "You're in a lot of
trouble, Doctor," he said.

"You think so?" Babcock replied. "Wait until General
MacArthur finds out that I'm not on this flight out. Then we'll
see who's in trouble."

"What the hell are you talking about?" But Kogan had already
guessed the answer. Some of the nurses on the flight south must
have told him about the fake orders bumping Marie. From that,
Babcock had drawn the inevitable conclusion.

The doctor turned away from the mirror. "You know what I'm
talking about. MacArthur sent orders for me to be evacuated
from the Rock. Then some officious cunt decided to get on the
plane in my place. When I—"

Kogan grabbed a handful of Babcock's shirt and lifted him so
that just the toes of his shoes made contact with the floor. The
physical act felt good—better even than shoving a gun up a
Moro's nose. On any scale of morality, this guy, with his abject
cowardliness, lies, and foul mouth, was in a class by himself.

"Two things you got to do, buddy boy." Kogan spat the words
into the doctor's face. "Or you're gonna have to comb that pretty
hair all over again. One is quit pretending you came out with
orders. You stowed away. We got witnesses, statements. The
other thing is you clean up your mouth." Maybe there was a
better way of handling a guy like Babcock, but this scumbag was
getting to be a real trial.

Babcock struggled briefly to break Kogan's grip, found it useless, and whined a threat. "Let me go, damnit. I'm under the
protection of MacArthur's headquarters. You'll pay for assaulting an officer."

Kogan grinned over his shoulder at Von Porten. "Hear that,

Art? He's got protection." He released Babcock's shirt and leaned against the cell door. "I've got some bad news for you, Doc. MacArthur sets high standards for his officers. You've made him very unhappy." Kogan ticked the offenses off on his fingers. "You deserted your post, sneaked aboard an overloaded PBY, and almost got a couple dozen people killed. Matter of fact, your case is going to be handled right here on Mindanao."

The nonchalant grin on Babcock's face vanished. His head lowered between hunched shoulders, his lips drew back, exposing his teeth with feral savagery, and he took a menacing step toward Kogan.

"Why, you son of a bitch! You have any idea what you're meddling with? This rinky-dink outfit won't last a week against the Japs. I can't be taken prisoner. I've got to get on those boats, y'understand?"

Kogan clucked his tongue in dismay. "Really, Doctor," he said reprovingly, "your charge sheet is filling up. Insolence to a superior officer constitutes another specification under Article Ninety-six."

Babcock whirled and banged his fist on the wall, then rested his forehead on the rough planks. When he turned back, he had himself under control. "Sorry, Colonel. I lost my head there for a moment. Look, I'm no fool. Orders were written getting me off the Rock, and you know it. Now, somebody must have wanted me down here pretty bad, and I can figure out why—it's to get B-juice from me. Von Porten here has as much as said so. Okay. Let's make it a quid pro quo. I'll write out all the information you need to reproduce the medicine. All you have to do is get me aboard one of those flying boats for Australia." Babcock arranged his face in what he must have believed was a frank, open, ingratiating smile.

Kogan turned and called for the MP sergeant. His stomach curdled at what lay before them. Talk about pushing a big rock up a mountain. Hell, the Greeks didn't know what trouble was. First of all, Babcock wouldn't give them what they wanted—it would be stupid to believe he would. Even if he wrote something out, it would be a damn lie. And no matter what he did, they *couldn't* put him on one of those flying boats.

"Yes, sir?" the sergeant said.

"This officer will remain here tonight." Behind him, Kogan heard a muffled curse from Babcock. "Tomorrow morning he will be sent under guard to Del Monte Field."

As the cell door closed behind him and Von Porten, Kogan turned to the sergeant. "I want this cell placed under special security. Dr. Babcock is not to be released without a written order from me, do you understand?"

The church bells of the old cathedral tolled sonorously as the little convoy made its way down the main street of Dansalan. A small personnel carrier filled with Philippine Scouts led the way, followed at a good distance—to avoid the dust—by the LaSalle, and bringing up the rear was a second personnel carrier carrying an unhappy Babcock guarded by four more scouts.

Kogan checked his watch. It had stopped. "What time have you got, Art?"

Von Porten looked at his wrist, held the watch to his ear, and shook his head. "Mine's stopped, too."

"Nearly eight, sir," Willie's voice sang out. "We'll be back at headquarters by eleven." He glanced back at them, concerned. "Something wrong with your watches?"

They drove on through air still cool but heavy with the scent of wood fires mixed with the spicy fragrance of the flowering narras trees. By contrast, the sounds of war had begun at dawn. Behind them, from the south, came the distant bark of artillery.

"Golly, sir," Willie spoke again. "Japs are getting closer."

Von Porten glanced at Kogan. "General, what do you think? Is that American or Japanese artillery we're hearing?"

"Hard to tell, Doctor."

"Might be the Sixty-first Infantry." Willie got into the conversation again. "They've got a couple of mountain guns attached. Sixty-first is commanded by Colonel Eugene Mitchell,

General. Maybe you know him. Helluva fine officer. Betcha he stops the Japs."

Von Porten answered Burke. "Let's hope so, Willie." Then he looked at Kogan again, his eyebrows raised. Joe put his hand up to cover his mouth.

"The firing we hear," he muttered, "is probably coming from Kawaguchi's light tanks. They're moving up from Malabang. Be here late tomorrow."

Von Porten whispered back. "The nurses got out just in time."

Kogan nodded. "Some of them did. Not all. Remember, one of the flying boats busted its hull and couldn't take off."

"Japs capture them here at Dansalan, then?"

"Nope. Early tomorrow morning, the army will put the nurses on trucks and bring them to Del Monte." In spite of having violated a basic dictum of the operation, he felt only a small guilty flush thinking of what he had done for Marie Crane. Changing the past as he had done was specifically forbidden, and last night, lying awake in his room in the Dansalan Hotel, he had wrestled with that knowledge. But no matter how he cut it, he could see no wrong in it, no possible adverse effects on the future. At the least he had saved her years of hell in a prison camp. At the most, he might have saved her life. He wasn't going to wear a hair shirt over that.

The car bumped over a pothole. "Sorry, General," Willie called out.

During the whispered conversation between him and Von Porten, Kogan had noted with amusement the way Burke's head had angled toward the rear seat, trying to hear what was said. He imagined the shock the young officer would have gotten had he been able to hear everything.

Von Porten touched his arm and asked why Kogan didn't have Babcock ride with them. "Granted he's a real shithead," he said. "We just might be able to establish some kind of rapport with him."

"No way," Kogan said. "It would give him too many opportunities to dig information out of us. He's sharp." He watched the last buildings of Dansalan slide by. "I still haven't figured out how to deal with the guy."

They had been on the road about ten minutes when the harsh sound of a motor being driven at high speed caused Willie Burke to look in the rearview mirror. "Army bike coming up, sir," he said to Kogan. "Looks like he's got something for us." He honked to stop the lead carrier, then eased over to the side of the road. An American corporal dismounted, saluted, and gave an envelope to Burke. The lieutenant glanced at it and handed it to Kogan.

"It's for you, sir—a radio dispatch from Del Monte."

Kogan opened it.

> JAPANESE HAVE SPOTTED YOUR PLANE. FIGHTER PA-
> TROLLING OVER DEL MONTE FIELD. COLONEL LONG-
> FORD SUGGESTS YOU EXPEDITE YOUR RETURN.
>
> EDMONDS

He resisted an impulse to smash his fist into something solid. Instead, as the LaSalle moved out again, he passed the message to Von Porten. "Jesus," the doctor muttered. "We'd better tell Willie to step on it."

Kogan shook his head. "No point in it. Half an hour one way or another won't make any difference. Besides, we can't take off with a Zero looking down our throats."

It was an effort for him to speak casually. He turned his face away, pretending an interest in the scenery, so that Burke and Von Porten couldn't read his expression. This was the kind of ultimate disaster he'd been afraid of—Japanese fighters discovering their presence. Right now, *Sucker One* might be nothing but smoking junk. He unfolded the radio message again. "... Longford suggests you expedite your return." What the hell did that mean? Was it bureaucratese for "The Japs are about to blow your plane sky-high?" "Hurry back and join the we-are-about-to-become-POWs club?" He forced himself to settle back against the upholstery of the old LaSalle and try to think about something else during the next two hours. Red hair and a beautiful smile came to mind again. By this time, Captain Marie Crane must be halfway to Australia.

Flight Warrant Officer Jichiro Shengo's Zero cruised in large, shallow circles over Del Monte Field, maintaining precisely his assigned altitude of five thousand feet. It was a matter of pride to Shengo that he not vary from his assigned height, an ingrained philosophy of obedience that cut through the anger and frustration he felt. As the most skilled pilot in the Third Air Flotilla, based at Davao City, he really should not have been given this routine patrol. His twelve kills against the best pilots that China could send aloft over Chungking—although he admitted they were not very good—and five victories here in the Philippines over Americans flying their cumbersome P-40s, would have excused any of the other commissioned pilots of the flotilla from this dull task. But he understood why he caught these details. It was his warrant officer status—higher than an enlisted man, but not really a commissioned officer—that kept him at the top of the patrol assignment list. That and—yes, he might as well confess it— his peasant background and scanty education that had ended in his third year of middle school. He would have spent his life in the rice paddies of his family's small plot of land near the bay of Habata had not the war begun in China five years before. The thought gave him momentary ease. Still—and his lean, dark-hued face set stubbornly—caste discrimination was not supposed to exist in the military, according to his flight instructors at Kasumigaura, but it did, in subtle and not so subtle ways.

He sighed and affectionately patted the cowling of the plane. Oh, well. How much better it was to be flying his magnificent Zerosen than staring all day at the rubbery asshole of a water buffalo.

To some extent, it was his own sharp eyes that had led him into this boring task. Yesterday, on a routine reconnaissance of Del Monte, he had spotted a camouflaged plane—a transport— near the south end of the airstrip. He had radioed flotilla headquarters, describing the plane and requesting permission to destroy it. To his consternation, his request was denied. Only after returning to his base had he learned that the new island commander, Major General Kiyotake Kawaguchi, wanted the American craft as a replacement for his aging personal monoplane. A special infantry unit was being dispatched to capture it, and until that could be accomplished, a Zero would mount patrol over the field, keeping the transport from taking off.

Shengo glanced down at the scene nearly a mile below. The Bukidnon area of the Mindanaoan highlands was as beautiful as the hills of Japan. The verdant green of the unused pineapple fields alternated with darker strips of forest, and in the distance, the deep blue of Macajalar Bay rimmed the Cagayan coast. The main Del Monte airfield itself was a single, mile-long stretch of heavy grass changing color as the wind tossed the blades to and fro.

In his mind's eye, Shengo could visualize the big plane below lumbering out of its revetment and taking off. He smiled as he mentally enacted the scene. Lazily, he would push the control stick forward and, keeping the throttle back, virtually glide down upon the unwitting transport.

Perhaps he might play a little game, much as he had a few weeks ago with the pilot of a P-40 attempting to get from Corregidor to Mindanao. Admittedly, the plane was old and patched up, but had it been new, the outcome would have been the same. He had overtaken it easily, surprising the pilot, and had pulled alongside, barely fifty feet away. He remembered the startled face of the American, the light brown of his eyebrows, the round O of his mouth, and sensed—although the pilot did not show it—the man's fear, for by this time the superiority of the Zero over the plodding P-40s was well-known to both sides. Shengo had smiled archly and used both of his hands to simulate a dog fight. Without warning, the American wrenched his plane around, attempting to get off a burst at close range. But Shengo was prepared. He turned well inside the slower, less maneuverable P-40, and before 180 degrees had been traversed, had the tail of the other plane in his gun sights.

He did not fire, watching with amusement the P-40's frantic

efforts to elude its pursuer. It attempted Immelmanns, loops, even rolls, but Shengo stuck like glue, never more than a couple of hundred feet behind. The American was skilled, there was no doubt of that, and Shengo wished the man had been flying one of the vaunted British Spitfires he had heard so much about. That would have made the engagement memorable. But in the clumsy P-40? It was no contest. In extremis, the American pointed the nose of the heavier P-40 down toward the dark waters of the Sulu Sea and gave it full throttle, trying to outrun the devil stuck to his tail. But the Zero, with its speed advantage, closed to less than a hundred feet.

The game had gone on long enough, Shengo decided, and flipped the firing button of his 20-mm cannons to on. No, he wouldn't use them. The big shells were expensive. The flotilla commander himself had warned his pilots against extravagant, unnecessary firing. He turned the cannons off, then shifted his hand slightly and pressed the firing button of his two 7.7-mm machine guns. He could hardly miss. Bits and pieces of the P-40 floated back, chewed off by the machine gun bullets. Varying his bursts for maximum effect, he continued to fire and the P-40 continued to flee, veering wildly from right to left and back, trying ineffectually to escape the fusillade tearing it apart. Shengo was amazed. By now he had fired five or six hundred rounds and the big fighter still continued to fly.

He drew up alongside the P-40, their wingtips almost touching. The other plane's wings and tail were in tatters. Patches had been blown off the fuselage, leaving gaping holes, and black smoke was beginning to trail back from the engine. The American, a stream of blood running from his mouth, was hunched over his controls. Shengo banged his wing to get his attention. The pilot looked up and Shengo could see that he was not young, as he had at first thought. Sweat ran down his face and mixed with the blood on his big chin. A gold oak leaf on his shoulder flashed in the sun. What rank was he? Shengo remembered the charts of American insignia they had to memorize. Ah, yes, a major. Well, perhaps he should salute, and mockingly, he did. The major's pallid face creased as his bleeding mouth shouted unheard curses. He extended his hand toward Shengo, the middle finger vertical. The American plane suddenly lurched at the Zero in an effort to ram, but Shengo had foreseen that. He pulled away easily, fell back to a firing position, fingered the 20-mm cannon switch to on and blew the P-40 up in a short burst. As he watched the flaming wreckage fall toward the sea, he felt a twinge of regret. The American had been brave and a good pilot. But then, what did that signify? They were both soldiers in the service of their countries. One had to die, and the American had died well.

Shengo pulled himself back to the present, and noted by his wristwatch that he had less than an hour to go before being relieved on station. He yawned and looked down on the field. The huge camouflage net covering the transport stood out from the natural foliage. It was strange, he mused, how once camouflage is penetrated, the object it is designed to conceal becomes so plainly visible.

Halfway up the highway that led from Cagayan to Del Monte Field, Kogan stopped the vehicles and got out, searching the sky in the distance over the airstrip. It was still too far away. He could see nothing.

"Willie," he said, "see if you can spot a plane over Del Monte."

The lieutenant climbed to the running board and squinted in the sun that was nearly overhead. He nodded his head vigorously. "Yes, sir. Just a speck, but I see it."

Kogan drew a deep breath. The plane was still patrolling overhead and there was no sign of smoke. *Sucker One* must still be intact. "Let's go," he said.

The crew sat in the shade of one wing eating a lunch of sandwiches and beer.

"I don't understand, Joe," Longford said. "This Babcock

wants to make a deal? We get B-juice if we get him to Australia? Hell, we can't do that."

"I didn't say we could," Kogan said. "But right now I'm wondering how we explain to this jerk why we can't without giving everything away." He took another bite of his sandwich, washed it down with beer, and tossed the remainder disdainfully into a paper bag.

Von Porten took a bite and chewed tentatively. "What do they call this stuff?" he asked.

"Horse cock," Kogan answered.

Von Porten looked around hastily for a place to get rid of his mouthful.

"Figure of speech, Doc," Betts volunteered.

"So," Kogan said, "anyone got an idea?"

"He may not know it, but he's got us over a barrel," Hiraga said thoughtfully. "I don't suppose you could appeal to his better instincts."

"Wait until you meet him," Von Porten said.

"Well, what are we looking for—this B-juice, or the formula for it?" John Hortha asked.

"Either," Von Porten said. "But we've searched his personal effects at Dansalan. Nothing—no B-juice, no formula. He must be carrying it in his head."

A field telephone rang insistently. Witkowski stepped over to where it leaned against one huge wheel and answered, "*SUCCOR One.*" He listened, frowning. "All right, I'll tell him." He shoved the telephone back in its leather case and looked at Kogan. "General Sharp is back. He's scheduled a briefing in his command post in one hour, if it's all right with you."

Witkowski looked at Kogan, worry in his face. "Joe, I think you should cancel it. We should be getting the hell out of here."

Hortha jerked a thumb at the sky. The persistent, nasal drone of the Zero's engine came through clearly. "We ain't going anywhere, Mike, as long as that guy's up there."

Longford turned to Kogan. "According to the Fifth Air Base

guys here, the Japs don't fly after dark. We could leave tonight, or tomorrow morning before dawn. I'll ask Edmonds to set out fire pots at the north end of the strip."

"We've got things we've got to do, Jake," Kogan said. "I've got to see Sharp—keep up the pretense that our mission is important—and we have to get the dope from Babcock." He looked at his watch. The damn thing must have a weak spring. "Who's got the time?"

"One fifteen, General," Witkowski said.

"Okay," he said, setting his watch, "that gives us about six hours before dark. If we can break Babcock by tonight, we take off."

"And if we can't?" Von Porten said.

"We'll stay another day."

"Excuse me," Witkowski intervened again. "But we had planned to get out of here yesterday. By tomorrow, we're two days overdue. I really think we're pushing our luck if we don't leave tonight."

Kogan realized what Witkowski was saying, even though he hadn't spelled it out in detail. The archivist knew the history of the Mindanao campaign almost as well as he did, and a time and date banged around in both their minds—1600 hours, May 3, just fifty-one hours from now. Stay over until tomorrow and that left just twenty-seven hours until the Japanese swept across Del Monte Airfield. Kogan smiled with a confidence he didn't feel.

"Plenty of time, Mike," he said.

He stood up and stretched. "All right, guys, I'm on my way to spread a little more bullshit. I don't like it, but we've got to keep up a front. Johnny," he said to Hortha, "come along and give me a hand with the charts, will you? Jake, check with Edmonds on the fire pots. The rest of you stay close. Things may just break our way. If they do, we could be hightailing it out of here real soon." He gave his little speech with a lot more conviction than he felt. Sharp wouldn't be much of a problem, but Babcock—ah, now there was a *problem*.

CHAPTER FOURTEEN

Slow, heavy footsteps dragged across the porch of Kogan's bungalow. Colonel Edmonds stood in the doorway, his face etched with fatigue and worry.

"Sorry about that Jap plane, General," he said. "I didn't think they'd penetrate the camouflage."

"Neither did I, Edmonds. We can count ourselves lucky our transport isn't a pile of scrap."

The deputy commander wiped his brow with a damp handkerchief. "Pretty obvious they hope to capture your plane if and when they get here."

"Yeah," Kogan said. Although they still had a fair margin of time, there wasn't an awful lot of give in it. It bothered him. "I want to take off either tonight or early tomorrow morning." He was having trouble keeping his mind focused. Babcock, damn him, kept eating away at his concentration.

Edmonds continued. "I understand your trip to Dansalan got a bit exciting."

"A man my age shouldn't have to go through that sort of thing," Kogan growled.

"From what I hear, you did very well for any age."

Kogan grunted and held up his glass. "Drink? We've got time before the briefing, haven't we?"

Edmonds mopped his face again and checked his watch. "Oh, I guess one won't hurt." Juan quickly poured bourbon. Then the Filipino disappeared into the rear of the house and busied himself in the tiny kitchen.

"He working out all right, General?"

"Who? Oh, Juan. Yes, he's doing fine." A thought struck him. "Not very talkative, though. He apparently doesn't have much English." There was a purpose behind his remark. There were some things he had to say to his crew that he didn't want going beyond the walls of this bungalow.

"No, sorry about that, but we're short-handed here. Anyway, if you talk slow and do some gesturing, he should be able to handle your basic needs.

"Well, sir," Edmonds continued. "I suppose you heard about the one PBY bashing in its hull. No one was hurt, but we had to bring the women here to Del Monte. They just arrived and they're pretty depressed."

Kogan's head jerked up. "You say they're here now?" That couldn't be right. According to the historical record, the nurses in the banged-up PBY hadn't arrived until May 2—that was tomorrow.

"Yes, sir," Edmonds said. "Japs are moving pretty fast. Thought we'd better get the women out of Dansalan as soon as possible." He looked at Kogan hesitantly. "You seem surprised, General. You don't think we should have left the women at Lake Lanao, do you?"

Kogan was still wrestling with this new information. "What? Oh, no, not at all. Better to get them out of the way."

"Well," Edmonds said slowly, "if that damn Jap fighter stays away long enough for you to get off the ground, it would be an act of real kindness if you could take the women back to Australia with you."

Kogan tried to hide his shock. The support group had run through a lot of possible scenarios, but the combination of *Sucker One* getting off late and the nurses arriving early had eluded them. History wasn't supposed to change.

He pretended to think about it. "I don't believe that's practical, Edmonds," he said. "That Zero has pretty well got us nailed down. We can give it a try ourselves, but I sure wouldn't want to risk these poor women's lives in the attempt."

Edmonds's face was crestfallen. He took a gulp of his drink. "Boy, oh boy!" he groaned.

"You got a problem with that, Colonel?" Kogan asked sternly.

"Uh . . . well, I was so sure that you had room—you see, there's only ten of them, General—that I sort of promised the head gal that you'd take them."

"You should have checked with me before making a commitment like that," Kogan replied. He had to shut this development off real quick. "I simply will not place these women's lives in jeopardy."

Edmonds set his glass down deliberately and faced Kogan, his eyes cold. "May I remind you, sir, that these women could be facing a future in which death might be a welcome alternative."

So fifty years ago they really did talk like that. A fate worse than death. And maybe the women *would* prefer death to what fate had in store for them—locked up in grim Santo Tomás for more than three years. Some would never get out. Some would die from malnutrition and disease, and some from what a future generation would call depression. He thought of Marie Crane. By getting her on number 7 boat, she at least wouldn't have to go through that hell. But this was all beside the point. If *Sucker One* was really going to Australia and not to a world so far off and strange that it could hardly be imagined, much less believed, he would have taken them. He pitied the women and he pitied Edmonds, but he had to get off the hook.

"I understand what you're saying, Colonel, but I will not do it."

Edmonds started a retort, then sighed and picked up his helmet. "All right, General, I'll tell them." He stood in the doorway, his shoulders slumping. "I guess I can put it off until after the briefing."

Kogan watched Edmonds's sweat-stained back retreat down the porch, an old man with too many problems. Well, maybe he could ease his burden a little. "Ken, wait a minute. Would it help if *we* explained the situation to the nurses?"

Edmonds's face was that of a man taken off death row. "I'd really appreciate it, General," he said gratefully, and hurried off.

The dark speck of the Zero circled over the 737. Kogan watched it for a moment.

"Johnny," he said to Hortha. "I've got to get over to the command post. Uh . . . I wonder if you'd mind talking to the women."

Hortha didn't look happy. "Don't you have some Moro bandits I can tangle with?" He handed Kogan the charts under his arm. "I'll do my best."

"I'm mentioning you in dispatches, my friend. Oh, yeah. Tell the women we're radioing MacArthur's headquarters, asking for a bomber to come pick them up. That'll make it a little easier."

Hortha stopped on the porch steps. For the first time since he'd known him, the pilot's eyes were downright chilly. "I hope, General, that's the truth."

"That's the truth. I swear it, Johnny. Melbourne will send an old B-24. But like just about everything else that happened here, it'll arrive too late." He slapped Hortha on his shoulder. "I tell you, fate gave these ladies a royal screwing."

The pilot's handsome face clouded. "Hard times," he said as he stepped off the porch. "Damn, I never read anything like this in the history books."

• • •

General Sharp's command post was built into the side of a hill a few hundred yards from the airstrip, accessed along a narrow path through palms, banyan, and monkeypod trees. Beyond the cleverly concealed entrance, overhead lights illuminated a cavelike room. An operator manned a portable field telephone switchboard set against one wall. Map boards covered with acetate sat on easels around the room, and two large fans stirred the dank, sultry air. A long, narrow wooden table sat in the center of the room.

It was right out of World War I, Kogan noted. From his research, he knew that Sharp had had this anachronism built because of his trench line experience in France.

"Glad to finally get to meet you, General Kogan," Sharp said as they shook hands. It hadn't been difficult to pick out the commander, Mindanaoan Force. The tallest and oldest man in the dugout, Bill Sharp with his lean, studious face and thick glasses could have been a schoolteacher. Nearly sixty, he was a bird colonel when the Japs had struck. MacArthur had promoted him to brigadier general and given him a mission so impossible as to be ridiculous—to hold Mindanao and the vast stretch of the Visayan island chain with poorly trained Filipinos. The strain of the losing battle he was fighting showed in Sharp's stooped shoulders and drawn face.

"I think you've met Fred, here," Sharp said, inclining his head toward Major Thomas. "And if you don't mind, I'll have him give the briefing. He's up-to-date on the latest developments from all fronts."

Major Thomas stepped forward. His earlier self-confidence had fallen away and he, like his commander, seemed tired and uncertain.

"General Kogan," he said quietly, "the Japs are coming at us from two sides. We think there will be an assault from a third direction very shortly."

Thomas pointed to the map with a walking stick. "The enemy

landed two days ago at Parang. They ran into strong opposition from Filipino regulars under Colonel Calixto Duque, but eventually outflanked the regiment and took Cotabato and Malabang. That left only Colonel Mitchell's Sixty-first Infantry between the Japs and Lake Lanao. An hour ago, he sent us a radio saying he could no longer hold. That means the enemy is pretty much free to take Dansalan and the Lake Lanao district.

"Another enemy force," he continued, "is heading toward us along the southern end of the Sayre highway. Right now Brigadier General Vachon's forces are holding well, but we're not sure for how long. Even more serious, our coast watchers to the north report a possible landing at any time through Macajalar Bay at Cagayan de Oro. Once the Japs have landed there, our encirclement will be complete." Major Thomas eyed the map as if looking for something favorable. Absently, he put a cigarette between his lips, then hastily got rid of it.

"Uh . . . do you have any questions, General?" he asked.

The game had grown old and dreary. Kogan had no desire to repeat his role as the asshole from headquarters. What he desperately needed to do was to leave this cavern as quickly as possible, get Babcock to talk, and fly away from this doomed Philippines island.

But he had to say something. "I presume," he said, "that you have a reserve force you can commit."

"Yes, sir," Thomas said. "General Sharp is holding back the Sixty-second and Ninety-third Infantry Regiments, but their state of readiness isn't good. We'll probably have to throw them into the line very soon now. It's doubtful that they'll be able to delay the Jap advance much more than a day."

"I see," Kogan said, then turned to General Sharp. "Is there any way Mindanao can be held?"

"Give me a full American infantry division tomorrow," Sharp answered quickly, "and this can become a base for stopping the Japs everywhere in the Pacific."

Kogan nodded. Sharp was asking for the impossible, and he

knew it, but the sincerity in his voice was unmistakable. He believed in what he had just said.

Sharp took off his glasses and cleaned them carefully. Deep lines arcing from his long nose to his chin enclosed his mouth. "General Kogan," he said slowly, "we appreciate your coming here, but any relief efforts for us, I fear, have been overtaken by events. You may, though, be able to help those poor devils on Corregidor." He replaced his glasses and stared intently at Kogan. "I just don't know how much longer they can hold out."

I can tell you, General—six days. Old "Skinny" Wainwright will surrender in six days. And now, let's get this goddamn miserable briefing over with.

"Maybe we can help," Kogan said. With Major Thomas assisting, he unrolled a map on the table and secured the corners with wooden blocks. Red lines stretched across it from the California coast to Hawaii and then on to Mindanao. Kogan leaned over the map.

"The plan, General," he said, "was to get the supplies in here, either into Macajalar or Gingoon Bay, and then transship by smaller boats on to Corregidor. I agree with you, however, that in view of the Jap advances in the last two days, we must rethink the entire effort. Do you have any suggestions?"

"For what it is worth," Sharp said, his finger tracing a route on the map, "I recommend you send the ship directly into Manila Bay and off-load at Corregidor."

Yeah, sure, Kogan thought. *Ask the navy to risk a ship and crew and see how far you get.*

"The problem with that, General," he said, "is that the Japs have their big guns sited on Bataan, within five miles of Corregidor. No ship would have a chance."

"Let them pull into South Dock then, on the opposite side of Corregidor. The Japs won't be able to lay direct fire on the ship while it's there."

"What about their bombers? The ship would be blown up the day it arrived."

"It can be done, General Kogan," Sharp said, his face set in stubborn lines. "Have the ship lie off Manila Bay, say, thirty miles over the horizon, until dark. It can then make a high-speed run without lights to South Dock. Have it start unloading at ten that night and continue on until four in the morning. Six hours. The ship pulls out before dawn, lies over the horizon during the day, comes back that night, and repeats the performance until the unloading is completed."

Not bad, Kogan mused, not bad at all. It might work, at least until the Japanese caught on. "Too dangerous, General," he said. "The ship might run into Jap destroyers, or a submarine might discover it."

Sharp made no attempt to respond. He sat quietly, his eyes fixed on his clasped hands. The group of staff officers gathered around the briefing table watched their commander and shifted their feet uneasily. Kogan groaned inwardly. He's thinking I'm a dumb, obstructionist, headquarters son of a bitch. *Please let this be over soon.*

"General Kogan." Sharp finally lifted his head and spoke. "Are we serious about getting supplies to Wainwright?"

"That's our goal." God, it hurt to say that.

"Then let the ship pull into South Dock after dark. Let the unloading go on through the night and into the next day until the Japs discover it. By then, hundreds of tons of supplies will have been off-loaded. Pull the crew off and let the Japs bomb the ship. Even after she's sunk at the dock, Wainwright's people could still salvage a great deal."

"You mean, sacrifice the ship?"

Why was he arguing with Sharp? Why continue to debate this thing? Hadn't he played the cretinous major general long enough? The answer, to his surprise, was that Sharp's ideas really interested him. If Washington or Melbourne had used half the imagination this old man displayed, Corregidor's garrison might have been spared some of the hell it had to suffer.

"Exactly, General Kogan." Sharp's eyes peered owlishly through his glasses. "Sacrifice the ship."

Kogan shook his head slowly. "I don't think the navy will go for that. The admirals are going to consider that a very expensive way to deliver a few tons of supplies."

"May I ask you a question?" Sharp's tone was brusque. "How do *you* feel about it? What is your personal opinion? You think the loss of a ship is too much to pay for 'a few tons of supplies,' as you call it? Are not the people on Corregidor who have sacrificed everything for their country worth one ship?"

Out of the corner of his eye, Kogan saw Major Thomas nudge a captain standing next to him. The officers of Sharp's staff were watching the two generals and listening to their words intently, silently cheering their general on. Fine. If it gave them pleasure, let the poor devils enjoy the visiting general's discomfiture. God knows there's little enough left for them to feel good about in their embattled and forgotten world.

He considered Sharp's very pointed query. "That's a loaded question, General. I'm only trying to be practical. Whatever plan we devise must meet the approval of the navy."

"That's quite amusing," Sharp said. "The president has told the navy to help. Roosevelt's words, as they were passed to us, said that 'the navy must do all in its power' to get supplies to the Philippines." He gave a short, bitter laugh. "Two weeks ago," he continued, "we heard that Tokyo had been bombed by sixteen B-25s. From where, General Kogan? The president says Shangri-la. Does that mean China? I think not. Chiang Kai-shek won't permit us air bases in North China for fear of Jap retaliation. Russia? The Russians are not at war with Japan and don't want to be. Alaska? Too far."

A long forefinger thumped the table. "Could it be, General," Sharp continued, "that a carrier was used? And if so, why couldn't carriers be used to fly a few bombers to Del Monte?"

The field telephone buzzed. An Operations sergeant answered. "General Sharp, sir, it's for you." Without taking his eyes from Kogan, Sharp impatiently waved down the interruption. The sergeant spoke softly into the phone and replaced it.

"You see, General Kogan, we haven't received a single plane

since the war began. Not one. How many hundreds of planes has the U.S. sent to England? To Russia? To the defense of the Dutch in Java?

"Now, let's talk about ships," Sharp continued. "Day after day we hear broadcasts from KGEI in San Francisco telling about ship sinkings in the Atlantic. Forty percent of some convoys going to England and to Russia have been lost—hundreds of ships, sir, *hundreds of ships.*" Sharp sat back and eyed the map, letting his last phrase hang in the air. His forefinger beat another tattoo. "Which brings me to my final question. If this country is willing to lose that many ships delivering war material to the Soviets and the British, why can't America risk one ship for Americans in the Philippines? Why, sir? What is the answer?"

Thank God the staff officers had the good grace not to cheer. But Kogan felt like it, for in the half century since this debacle, the American public had never really known how their government had abandoned their military men in the Philippines. Sharp had just put it all in fine perspective.

Kogan had no answer for the old man. Not that it made much difference. General Sharp not only had the questions, he knew the answers. All Americans, from Luzon to Mindanao, were doomed, expendable, their lives not worth the wasting of valuable ships and planes to save. Sharp was simply venting some of his indignation, for behind those icy blue eyes was a very realistic appraisal of the future.

But Kogan knew even more of the future.

He could lean across the table and say to the old man, *Yes, General Sharp, you are right. Your country has abandoned you. Now listen to me, you tired old hero, for here is what is going to happen. In less than a week, the Japanese will take Corregidor and order Wainwright to surrender all troops in the Philippines. Old Skinny will then have to tell you to surrender your forces. You will refuse, ordering your men to fight on in the hills as guerrillas. Only after the Japanese threaten to execute the captives on Corregidor will you knuckle under. You are one tough cookie, Bill*

Sharp, and you're going to need all your toughness because very soon now they're going to lock you up in a POW camp. You'll be there for most of the rest of your life. Oh, you will survive, but the struggle will take too much out of that leathery old body of yours. A few months after you come home, you will die.

He was glad he didn't have to say these things. He was sorry he had lied to this honest old soldier. And yet he had to lie once more.

He got to his feet and extended his hand. "General Sharp, thank you. I'll pass your recommendations along."

Marie Crane felt depression settle over the women like cold mist. The major from MacArthur's headquarters—an extraordinarily handsome officer—had seemed like the answer to their prayers. He started off by saying he had come about their evacuation. All of them had heard about the plane hidden in the jungle, the plane they just knew would take them quickly and safely to freedom. But after Major—Hortha, that was his name—had spoken his first few apologetic words, the truth struck home. The plane wouldn't take them out.

Jap fighters...too much danger...General Kogan doesn't want to risk your lives. Oh, don't worry, ladies, there's hope. We're sending Melbourne a radio message asking for a bomber to get you out of here.

Major Hortha asked if there were any questions, and waited awkwardly. No one could think of anything to say. Marie got to her feet and tried to smile.

"Thank you so much, Major," she said, "for taking the time to talk to us." The major smiled shyly in return and bowed, a quick, clumsy inclination of his body. For such a handsome man, she thought, he seemed terribly ill at ease. Men with his looks were usually at their best with a group of women.

He seemed anxious to get away, and eased toward the porch, but several women approached him, smiling brightly and now full of questions. Marie walked out on the porch, lit a cigarette, and leaned against the railing. She wondered whether the others were feeling, as she did, that a vengeful fate had brought them this far only to toss them sadistically back into the hands of the Japs.

That was funny, what the major had said about Joe Kogan—he called him general. A mistake, probably. She had thought about Joe a lot since they parted in Dansalan. Nice man. Not handsome like the major, but not ordinary, either. Not ordinary at all.

Come to think of it, she'd sensed a strangeness about him while they had had that drink and long talk on the hotel veranda. She couldn't put her finger on it, but there was something about his eyes as he looked at her—so much kindness, such understanding of what she ... of what all of them had been through.

Above all, though, there was the warmth she felt in him. She had the feeling—even now she shivered when she thought about it—that he wanted to put his arms around her. Nothing sexy—well, perhaps a little—but mainly to shield her from things she couldn't see but he could. And something else. That kiss—it was just a friendly touch of the lips as they stood by the truck, but it had struck fire. Something inside her had melted, at least a little bit—that cold chunk of ice that had frozen there when Harry had been killed. Half embarrassed at her thoughts, she took a final drag on the cigarette and flipped it over the railing.

Her thoughts were interrupted by a woman's high-pitched voice.

"They're showing a movie at the enlisted mess tonight."

The voice was familiar. It was Claudia Roberts, the daughter of the president of a large insurance firm and one of the richest Americans in Manila. Blakely Roberts was also a close friend of President Manuel Quezon and most of the senior American military officers. Marie could guess how it was that the young woman had gotten aboard the flight.

She had met Claudia a number of times at the Polo Club, and her gleaming blond hair could be spotted at nearly all of the big parties hosted by the officers' clubs. She was stylish, always beautifully dressed, and although her face was too angular for prettiness, she never seemed short of escorts. If rumor could be believed, it was not for her intellect, which was not overpowering. Claudia's reputation was just plain bad. A remarkably large number of officers in Manila referred to her as the punchboard.

Claudia outflanked Major Hortha and stood between him and the porch steps, her head tilted back teasingly. She moved closer, flaunting her body as Hortha attempted to sidestep around her.

"How about you and me going?" Claudia asked Hortha.

"Well, uh, I really can't," Hortha replied.

"What's the matter, don't you like movies?" Her voice was plaintive, seductive.

"Oh, sure, but you see, we've got work to do tonight." Hortha had managed to edge around her. He placed one foot on the steps.

"Hey, listen," Claudia giggled a little and placed a hand on his shoulder. "You know, you look a lot like Robert Taylor."

"That so?" Hortha's voice was polite. "Some friend of yours?"

"Who you kidding?" she said in a tone of disbelief. "Taylor's the biggest thing in pictures!"

Marie got to her feet. This had gone far enough. "Excuse me, Miss Roberts, but I need to talk to Major Hortha." Marie's voice was cold. The blonde angrily stood her ground, hands on her hips, then, her face hard, she flounced away.

"Ah, Captain Crane." Hortha smiled gratefully.

He did look like Robert Taylor, Marie decided. "You mentioned *General* Kogan?" she asked. "Was he recently promoted? He was a colonel yesterday in Dansalan."

Hortha looked uncertain. "Uh . . . the general preferred being incognito that close to the Jap advance."

Marie frowned at the explanation. The Japs shot everyone, colonels as well as generals. "Well," she said, "when you see him, tell him that I didn't . . . I guess I couldn't, take his advice."

Hortha looked puzzled. "Advice about what?"

"Just tell him," she said. "He'll understand."

Kogan stepped outside General Sharp's command post, closed the door, and breathed deeply.

Something was going wrong, damned wrong.

Before leaving, he had nodded to the group of staff officers, shaken hands with Major Thomas, and stepped to the door of the dugout, General Sharp accompanying him. The command post once more became a beehive of activity.

General Sharp extended his hand. "I hope you don't take my remarks as being critical of General MacArthur, sir," he said, his eyes worried.

Kogan smiled. "Not at all. I thought they were very much to the point." His eyes strayed over Sharp's shoulder and his smile froze. The operations sergeant was entering new enemy positions on the map acetate. He had just drawn a red arrow circling around the left of the American defenses—an arrow that, if extended, would point right at Del Monte.

Sharp looked over his shoulder. "Something wrong, General?"

Kogan pointed to the map. "That Jap thrust around your left flank. Is that correct?"

Sharp nodded. "The message came in from the 101st just before you arrived. A flanking movement. Small unit. We're watching it."

"But there shouldn't..." Kogan caught himself. He knew the Japanese movements like the back of his hand. He had a clear mental picture of the after-action tactical reports and there had been no flanking movement to the left. This was either a mistaken report, or—

"Shouldn't be what, General Kogan?" Sharp asked. "Would you like to see the message?"

"No...that's all right. Well, I'd better be getting along."

He'd beaten a graceless retreat out of the dugout.

As he stumbled down the footpath, Hortha fell into step beside him.

"Everything okay, General?" he asked. Kogan still wrestled with that strange red arrow on the acetate. Was it a Jap unit heading directly for Del Monte? Was it coming after *Sucker One?* Sure, he assumed they expected to capture the plane once the offensive had swept over Del Monte; otherwise, the Zero would have destroyed it by now. But send a special force cutting through the jungle? That changed the whole goddamn picture.

He was conscious of Hortha eyeing him. "Oh, sorry," he said. "Uh, how'd it go with the nurses?"

Hortha gave an agonized groan. "Not good. No fun telling those women they're stuck here. Wish I could have done a better job."

"Don't worry about it. There are some things that just can't be done well." They trudged down the path in silence.

"How'd *your* briefing go?" Hortha asked.

"What?" He couldn't get that aberrant unit out of his mind. If it *was* after the plane, they sure as hell had better start planning to get away quick. "Oh, about the same as yours, I guess. Wish *I* could have done a better job."

They had arrived at the dirt road that snaked beneath the palms, paralleling the airstrip. Kogan's bungalow was close by. A couple of enlisted men approached, saw the two officers, and saluted with precision.

Kogan looked around. "Tell you what. Colonel Edmonds is delivering Babcock to my bungalow under guard. Find Von Porten and tell him to get over here."

Hortha saluted and left.

Juan greeted him on the porch, perfect teeth agleam in his walnut-colored face. Would the *general* care for a drink?

Yeah, he wanted one, but he needed a clear head more. He sipped an iced lemonade as he wandered around the living room with its Spartan furniture. Their time could be running out faster than expected. *Babcock, Babcock.* Why had he turned out to be such a prick?

The wind, blowing from the west, brought with it the distant rumble of artillery fire. The Japanese were, Kogan estimated, not more than forty miles away, this side of Dansalan by now, plunging along the coast and pulverizing the undermanned, untrained regiments standing in their way. But the main assault didn't worry him nearly so much as that red arrow on the map pointed directly at Del Monte.

Von Porten and Babcock arrived at about the same time, exchanging glares as Juan served drinks. Babcock took the drink, scowling, and drained half the icy liquid in a single gulp. He squinted at the stars on Kogan's shoulders.

"We're getting promoted awfully fast, aren't we?" Babcock said. "What are you, colonel or general?"

"General," Kogan said tersely. "Now, let's get something cleared up right now. This B-juice of yours works. We have proof of it."

Babcock shrugged. "You're damn tootin' it does. I want to know how you people found out about it."

"Back on Bataan, Dr. Winfield Ritter wrote a letter, describing its effects," Kogan answered. That wasn't quite true, but now was not the time to get picky.

"Ritter, huh?" Babcock drained his glass and held it out to Juan. Kogan nodded and the Filipino delivered another. "Should have known the old fart couldn't keep his mouth shut." He looked at them both, his eyes calculating. "Well, like I said, I'm willing to share the formula with you. Just get me out of here."

"Doctor," Kogan said quietly, "we have a little problem. There's no way we can get you off this island. Now, this is not a negotiating ploy, it's a simple statement of fact. You can't leave this island with us. But all right. Here's what we *can* do for you.

Turn over the formula to us and I'll see that all charges against you are dropped. Also, you have my word that you, Roger Babcock, will get full credit for the discovery of this cure. Your name will go into all the medical journals—"

"Hey, wait a minute," Babcock interjected. "You sound like I was dead or something, and damnit, I will be if you don't get me to Australia. You don't have to worry about getting my name up in lights—I'll take care of that. You want this stuff, you gotta do just one thing." He mimicked Kogan's phrasing. "Get me to hell out of this place."

Babcock kept going. "Don't tell me you can't do it. Think I spent my time in that brig counting cockroaches? No, sir, old democratic Doc Babcock played up to the guards. A little noblesse oblige, y'know. So I found out all about you guys. You're from Melbourne, right? And you're going back to Melbourne, right?" His loud cackle of a laugh was humorless. "So let's can the shit about me not getting off this island. Just give me a seat in the back—doesn't have to be by the window. And you get the formula—after I'm on the plane."

Kogan got to his feet and motioned to Von Porten. "We'll be back," he said to Babcock, and led the botanist to the porch. "Over here," Kogan said, walking to the far end. He put a foot up on the railing and watched a guard detail march by.

"Art, I think you're right."

Von Porten eyed him curiously. "Right about what?"

"Changing history." And he told him about what he'd seen in the command dugout. "If that Japanese unit is really coming directly at us, it could get here by . . . oh, noon tomorrow."

"And you thought we had tomorrow to work on Babcock."

Kogan nodded. The sun was low in the west and its rays slanted in, striking the porch. The day was nearly over. "We may *have* to get out of here tonight. Now, let's just suppose this asshole does give us the formula," he lowered his voice. "Any way you can tell whether it's valid or not?"

Von Porten thought about it. "I don't think so. This is not some dimwit we're dealing with. If he decides to fake it, he'll probably be quite clever about it. I might not catch it unless he puts in something really idiosyncratic. If he gave us a sample—which he won't—we could take it back with us and do a qualitative analysis to identify the organic components, but that isn't going to happen." He shook his head decisively. "No. Uh-uh. Without testing controls, I won't be able to make a determination."

"You got any ideas?"

"If only we had anticipated this, I'd have brought stuff along that would make him sing like a bird." A shaft of the fading sun struck Von Porten's face and he held up a hand to shade his eyes. "I'll tell you something, Joe, if he finds out he's due to die in a Jap POW camp, you can forget about leaving him behind."

CHAPTER FIFTEEN

He knew Von Porten was right. Babcock would fight like a cornered rat to escape his fate. Could it be done? Was it possible for him to avoid death in a Japanese POW camp? All Kogan knew was that he wasn't supposed to. Whatever had happened to Babcock must still happen. Whatever's a matter of historical record must take place. So if the old War Department files show that a Dr. Roger Babcock died in an American bombing raid on Shizuoka Prison Camp in 1945, that, by God, is the way it's got to be. Sure. But that nice pat thesis was getting weaker all the time. Now it was downgraded to a maybe, a dubious one at that. Too many things—like the rapid advance of that Japanese unit— were getting out of whack.

"Come on, let's get back in there," Kogan said to Von Porten. "We can't give up."

Juan was pouring Babcock another drink. Kogan pulled a chair close and straddled it.

"You hear that plane?" He jerked a thumb skyward. The drone of the fighter's engine had become a constant background. "That's a Zero, just waiting for us to take off. It's the fastest, most dangerous fighter in the world. We've got an unarmed, slow transport. You'd be crazy to take that chance."

Babcock took his time answering. He examined his glass closely, sniffed it, and took a sizable gulp. "Do me a favor, will you, General? Stop insulting my intelligence. The safest person to be around in a war is a guy with stars on his shoulders. Generals never get killed. You fly, I fly. Besides," he grinned wickedly, "the brig guard told me they're already setting up a fire pot for a night takeoff."

The thing had been kicking around in Kogan's mind. Which actually was worse—breaking the rules or losing the whole ball of wax? Suppose they did get back without the serum—just walked into the White House empty-handed, and reported to the First Lady, her tragedy-soaked eyes questioning. Why, yes ma'am, we had a chance to get B-juice, but ha, ha, we had our guidelines, y'know. Horseshit. One way or another, even if he had to bend the instructions into spaghetti, he was getting that stuff back.

"Okay, Doc, let's get back to basics," Kogan said, hoping he sounded more on top of the situation than he felt. "You can't get off this island."

Babcock rattled the ice in his glass and said casually, "I don't believe you." His expression turned stern. "You know, I'm really disappointed. I've always thought generals were upright guys who got their stars by playing it square. But you've lied to me." He put on a mock face of sadness. "My faith in the army has been destroyed."

Kogan nodded. "I'm glad you've got a sense of humor, Babcock, because you're going to need it. We've lied to you, and for good reason, but from now on, we're telling the truth. Count on it." He was conscious of Von Porten's eyes on him, concerned and questioning.

"Let me repeat—you can't come with us. We're not going to Australia."

Babcock held up his empty glass and jiggled it, the ice making musical sounds. Juan refilled it. "Okay," he said, "I'm not fussy. Hawaii's just fine."

"We're going to Hawaii, but not the Hawaii you know."

Von Porten shifted uncomfortably in his chair. He reached out and laid a hand on Kogan's arm. "Joe..." he cautioned.

Shaking the hand off, Kogan continued, "You see, Dr. Babcock, we don't belong here. We're from another time."

Babcock cocked his head as though he hadn't heard correctly. "Another time, you say?" He rolled his eyes heavenward. "Oh, brother," he chortled. "You must really be desperate. I thought I'd heard everything. I'll bet you're from another planet, too. Jupiter, maybe. Lemme borrow your copy of *Astounding Stories*, will you?" Still laughing, he looked from one to the other. Kogan and Von Porten watched him coldly, saying nothing.

"Well, come on, you two," Babcock said. "The joke stinks. It ain't funny."

"No, it's not funny," Von Porten chimed in, joining the action with alacrity. "But the general is right. We *are* from the future. Now do you understand why you can't travel with us?"

Kogan tried to assess what was going on in Babcock's mind. The doctor was an intelligent man being told that the impossible had happened. He himself was a trickster—a con man who cheated and lied and expected others to do the same to him. He already distrusted them, considered them frauds. Convincing him, no matter how hard they tried, just wasn't in the cards. That insolent smirk on his face was there to stay.

Babcock's eyes swiveled from one to the other, his mood plainly changing for the worse. His pouting lips thinned and his light-colored eyes turned as cold as the ice in his glass. "All right," he growled. "You keep screwing me around and you'll never get your hands on that stuff. From now on, you guys level with me or go pound sand."

There was no point in continuing, Kogan realized. They had run into a brick wall. He turned to Von Porten. "Hear that, Art? He wants us to level with him."

He reached for the field telephone and twisted the crank. Babcock started to say something, but raised his glass and drained it, never taking his eyes off Kogan.

Witkowski answered on the other end.

"Put Jake on."

"Yeah, Joe," the pilot responded almost immediately.

"Who's got the plane watch?" Kogan asked.

"Uh...Betts."

"Good. Move everyone else out of there." Kogan looked at his watch. "Get them down to my bungalow. I'll tell Juan to bring over dinners from the mess. Don't let anyone wander off."

"All right," Longford agreed. Kogan could sense the question coming. "Everything going okay?"

"I'm bringing Babcock aboard and showing him around."

There was silence on the other end. Then, "Oh, boy." Longford's voice registered shock. "It's that bad, huh?"

"Yes." Kogan rang off.

They made the ten-minute walk along the edge of the airstrip in silence. Two guards stepped forward and challenged them, then, recognizing Kogan, saluted and resumed their patrol. Another fifty yards brought them to the plane.

Babcock stood stock-still, his eyes sweeping the jet beneath its camouflage net. The revetment had turned into a huge, gently lighted room with jungle walls glowing luminously green from the filtered rays of the sun now just above the horizon. The forest formed three sides of a room whose ceiling was the camouflage net soaring high over the giant tail. In this quiet greenhouse-like setting, the jet's mottled bulk seemed overpoweringly large.

"What kind of a plane is that?" Babcock asked, his nonchalance not quite coming off.

"A commercial transport from . . . where we come from. It's a Boeing 737," Kogan answered cryptically.

"What the hell's that?"

"We'll show you."

Larry Betts was sitting in the hatchway. As they approached, the stentorian blast of a Klaxon horn sounded from the interior. Betts glanced at his wristwatch, waved at them, and disappeared inside.

Kogan led the way through the hatch. As the three men stood just inside the plane, Betts hurried forward.

"Afternoon, General," he said. "Just turned the key to get us through another four hours."

"Larry," Kogan said. "This is Dr. Babcock, whom you've heard of. We're giving him a little indoctrination tour."

Betts eyed Babcock with distaste. Neither man offered to shake hands.

"Little warm in here, isn't it?" Kogan said. "Why don't you turn on the air-conditioning for a few minutes?" He turned to Babcock. "You know what air-conditioning is, don't you?"

"You think I'm a dummy?" Babcock said scornfully. "You condition the air by regulating its humidity and temperature. Air is usually blown through humidifiers, water-soaked material."

"Well, I guess your 1942 term for what you're about to experience would be *refrigeration*. This plane is refrigerated. Show him, Larry." Betts toggled a switch on the instrument panel, and a muted whine came from the auxiliary power unit in the tail. Cool air swept through the plane. Babcock looked around in amazement.

"Now point out an item on the control panel that differs from a World War II plane."

"That's easy, General." Betts grinned. "This speed indicator is calibrated to mach point nine five." Glancing at Babcock, he said, "You know what that means?"

Babcock shook his head.

"This plane will fly at ninety-five percent of the speed of sound."

Babcock sneered. "That's crap. That would be . . . over six hundred, maybe seven hundred miles an hour. Hell, our pursuit planes can only do about three hundred." His voice grew louder. "Besides, this thing's got only two engines. A C-54 has four."

"These are jet engines, Babcock," Betts said. "Extremely powerful, thousands of horsepower. The Germans will use them late in the war. No propellers. The ones on our engine nacelles are plastic fakes."

"Yeah, sure." Babcock's tone of disbelief seemed weaker.

Kogan moved back to the entrance, motioning Babcock to follow. He pointed to a TV surveillance screen above the hatch. It showed the jungle area to the port side of the plane. "See this?" Kogan asked. "With the hatch closed we can see anyone approaching."

"That's just a picture," Babcock said.

Betts reached up and pressed the rewind, then the play button. The recording rolled. Kogan, Babcock, and Von Porten, their movements jerky from the timed tape, approached the plane.

"What the . . ." Babcock pointed. "Hey, that's me." He licked his lips nervously. "This is some kind of trick," he muttered unconvincingly.

Kogan nudged him. "Back here," he said, and walked to the console of the auxiliary computer used for their data base. He pointed to the blank CRT. "See this?"

Babcock peered at it. "What is it?"

"A computer. Very important in our time, very necessary. You couldn't go to medical school without one."

"*Your time!* You keep saying that. What is this crap, your time?"

"A half century in the future." Kogan kept his voice calm and reasonable, as though he were lecturing a slow student on the Hoover administration. "Now, take this computer. It's got thousands of uses. It can write books, manage businesses, fly this plane, navigate ships, land men on the moon—"

"Men on the moon? Now you've gone too far. You expect me to believe that?"

"How old are you, Babcock?"

"Twenty-eight," he answered truculently. "Why?"

Kogan did a quick math problem. "Along about your fifty-fifth birthday, you could watch an American by the name of Neil Armstrong land on the moon." He waited, then added, "While you're sitting in your living room watching TV."

"Jesus! You guys are crazy." He looked puzzled. "What's TV?"

"Television," Von Porten said. "You've heard of it."

"Television? Yeah, I saw something about it in *Popular Mechanics*. Years away from being practical, though."

Von Porten looked at Betts and both men laughed. "We should have brought a *TV Guide* along," Betts said.

Kogan flipped the computer on and the monitor glowed. "You see, Babcock," he said, "the great thing about computers is the amount of information you can store in one, and the speed with which you can get it out."

The steady whine of the auxiliary generator stopped. The computer screen flickered as it went to battery power. The cool air flow in the cabin ceased. Betts muttered a curse and hurried aft toward the tail section.

Kogan started back up the aisle in the direction of the galley. "Okay, now I want to show you something else." Babcock continued to look at the luminescent screen. Kogan stopped, annoyed. "Come on."

"Wait a minute." Babcock leaned forward and examined the keyboard. "This looks like a typewriter."

"Yeah, a glorified typewriter."

"What's that blinking thing?"

"It's called a cursor. Tells you where you are on the screen." Babcock seemed fascinated. "Okay if I hit a key?"

Kogan walked back and winked at Von Porten. "Go ahead."

Babcock placed his hands on the keyboard and slowly typed his name. A small, intense smile spread across his face as he saw the letters appear on the screen. "Jesus," he exclaimed. "Look at that!" He typed a comma, *M*, and an *E*.

"Oh-oh." He peered anxiously down at the keyboard. "Made a mistake. That should have been *MD*."

"Press this key." Kogan pointed to the left arrow.

As the offending letter disappeared, Babcock typed *D*, and chortled as the correction appeared on the screen. "Goddamn," he said, never taking his eyes away. "Hey, what else does this thing do?"

Von Porten grinned at Kogan and held up his circled thumb and forefinger. The battle lines had moved somewhat in their favor.

"It tells you just about anything you want to know about the Philippines during the first five months of 1942," Von Porten said.

"Yeah? How does it do that?"

"Easy," Von Porten answered. "You type—"

"Art!" A warning note sounded in Kogan's voice. In a different tone, he continued. "Let's get a breath of fresh air while Betts fixes the auxiliary unit." He looked at Babcock. "Coming, Doctor?"

"Naw," Babcock said, peering at the screen. "I'll stay here and play with this thing."

"Type *Date* and press the key marked *Return* and watch what happens, then do the same with *Time*." Kogan shepherded Von Porten down the ladder, while Babcock pecked at the keyboard.

"That'll keep him amused for a while," Kogan said as they stood under the wing. "He's going to want to go back with us just so he can play with that damn computer."

Von Porten chuckled. "A genuine hacker, born fifty years too soon."

"Okay, we've got to get our act together. He's got to be convinced that the future is not for him."

"And that he's not going to die if we leave him behind."

"That doesn't leave us a lot of wriggle room," Kogan said. They heard the auxiliary power unit kick on.

"Well," the doctor said, "I'll give him a blast on the horrors of 1994—the pollution, congestion, crime, and all that." He looked up at Kogan. "All you have to do, it seems to me, is tell him he survived POW camp."

"Is that all?" Kogan's voice dripped with sarcasm. "I tell you, I've had it up to here with lying to these people." He kicked some turf. "It won't work with him, anyway. He's not going to buy three years as a POW."

"Tell him the war will only last a year—eighteen months."

Kogan shook his head. "There's got to be a better way." He started up the ladder. "I just wish I knew what it is."

Babcock still sat at the computer. Betts stood behind him, pointing at the screen. "This is called a menu," he said. "It lists directories and subdirectories. To access any of them, just press the number. That opens it up like a file folder. Some of the subjects have thousands of pages."

Babcock stared fixedly at the screen, chewing a fingernail vigorously. "How do you find what you're looking for? Does it have an index?"

"You don't need one," Betts replied. "Just type a word, or several words. The computer will find it in seconds, wherever it is." He pointed to the menu. "See, number seven is *Japanese Forces*, now—"

"All right, Babcock," Kogan broke in. He didn't want this to go too far. "Time to go."

"I don't give a shit how you got back here, but you guys have got to be from the future. You've convinced me." The three men sat around the table in the bungalow. In the twilit gloom of the living room, Juan served them coffee. Babcock grinned expansively as he continued. "Now all you've got to do to get B-juice is to take me back with you."

"For chrissakes, Babcock, don't you understand?" Kogan spoke heatedly. "We have direct orders from the president of the United States not to bring anyone back."

"That," Von Porten chimed in, "may not impress the hell out of you, but consider what kind of a life you'd have. You think you speak our language? You think you're a pretty smart guy and you know just about everything worth knowing? Wait until you run into people talking about fax, VCRs, ICBMs, CDs, RVs, satellite dishes, laptops, the Beatles, Elvis Presley, Michael Jackson, Bill Cosby, Martin Luther King..."

He stopped for breath and turned to Kogan. "Joe?"

Kogan got into the spirit of the thing. He rattled words off. "For starters, try Truman, Eisenhower, Kennedy, and the rest of them. The Korean War, Vietnam, NATO, the Warsaw Pact, the Defense Department, Trident subs, Aegis cruisers, Hondas, Mitsubishis, Sony, BMWs, yuppies, pro-lifers, Rambo—"

"You call yourself a doctor?" Von Porten picked it up again. "Hell, they wouldn't let you empty bedpans around a modern hospital. Ever hear of AIDS? Or CAT scans, chemotherapy, radiation therapy, ICUs, steroids, Alzheimer's, Parkinson's, beta blockers, angioplasty, positron emission tomography, auto-immune therapy, high cholesterol, and good and bad lipoproteins?"

They both stopped, temporarily out of breath and ideas.

Babcock grinned at them. "I'm a quick study. For all that advanced medical shit you're shoveling at me, you don't have anything to beat cancer. Now, look. You've never seen anything like B-juice. I still don't understand the chemistry of it, but the stuff's absolute magic. Got it from an old Negrito. You want it? Just get me out of here."

Before either could answer, they heard footsteps on the porch, then a knock.

"Come," Kogan called out, and a very thin first lieutenant entered. Saluting Kogan, he extended the clipboard in his hand.

"General Kogan, I'm Lieutenant Chapin, the comm officer. Sir, the deputy commander would like your signature on this request for a bomber to take the nurses out."

Well, well, Kogan thought as he pretended to give the message a judicious look. Poor old brain dead Joe and Art. Neither had hit on this thing now presented to them on a platter. Although Babcock said nothing, Kogan could sense his intense interest in what the comm officer had said.

Shaking his head, Kogan returned the clipboard to the lieutenant. "Thank Colonel Edmonds for me, but since the nurses are attached temporarily to General Sharp's command, I believe he should sign the release authorization."

Lieutenant Chapin saluted and had started out the door when Kogan called him back. "Oh, Lieutenant," he said. "Ask Colonel Edmonds to expedite this message, please. We don't want to keep these women waiting." A little additional bait for Babcock.

Both Von Porten and Kogan stared at Babcock, saying nothing, waiting. It didn't take long. "Okay, General," Babcock said. "You told me you'd drop all charges, right? Now, how about getting me on that bomber with those nurses?"

"What do you think, Art?"

Von Porten played his part well. "All right with me," he answered thoughtfully. Then, turning to Babcock, he said firmly, "Providing you give me everything—absolutely everything, you understand?—that I need to reconstruct the formula for B-juice."

"You got it, Doc," Babcock said, and extended his hand. Von Porten hesitated, then shook it briefly.

Witkowski took his chicken dinner out of the microwave, removed the plastic cover, and picked at the applesauce while standing up in the galley. Longford had told him this was their last night at Del Monte. Takeoff would be just before dawn tomorrow. He picked up a chicken leg and dropped it with distaste. He wondered what the others at Kogan's bungalow were having for their last dinner in 1942. Ah, well, so he'd miss a little celebration. The point was that they were getting B-juice, or at least what they needed to duplicate it. By dawn tomorrow, before the Zero got back on station, old *Sucker One* would be heading for the TTP, and if Hiraga could find it, they'd all be heroes, and quite well-to-do ones in the bargain. Get out of that crummy apartment, put a big down payment on one of those nice condos out in the countryside. Maybe he'd get a seven-series BMW, or at least a five-series, show up in front of that Georgetown address, and say to Frances, hey, my lovely, how about a spin—

"Hallo the plane!" The shouted words came to his ears faintly.

Witkowski stepped to the open hatch. A sentry stood at the edge of the revetment—that was their limit for approaching the plane—with an officer standing beside him. The man was blond and held his wallet in his hand.

"Yes, sentry," Witkowski said. "What is it?"

"Sir, this officer would like to come aboard." The sentry angled the billfold in the officer's hand so that he could read from it. "He's Captain Roger S. Babcock, Medical Corps."

So this was Babcock. Witkowski saw that he wore a most amiable expression. He was quite a nice-looking chap. From what he'd heard about him, he'd expected someone pretty grotesque.

"What can I do for you, Doctor?"

"Nothing really, Mike," Babcock said. "You are Mike Witkowski, are you not? General Kogan said you had the watch. I guess he told you I was aboard this afternoon, but we had to cut my visit short." His smile was really quite pleasant. "You know that we reached an agreement."

"Yes. I heard."

"Well, would it be possible for me to come back aboard, have you show me around a bit more?" Babcock glanced at the sentry and then winked at Witkowski, sharing their common knowledge. "You have a fascinating plane, there."

Witkowski shook his head dubiously. "I don't really see any harm in it, but I have my orders. Sorry."

Babcock laughed. "General Kogan knows you pretty well, Mike. He thought you'd say that." He pulled a folded paper from his pocket and held it up. "So he gave me written permission."

"All right, Doctor, as long as the general has okayed it. Tell you what, just hold on." He picked up the EE-8 field telephone installed just inside the plane's hatch, then stuck his head out again, holding up the heavy receiver for Babcock to see. "I'm sure there's no problem, but just let me double-check with General Kogan."

"Quite all right, Mike." Babcock grinned cheerfully. "I understand."

Witkowski turned the crank to power the signal through the wire. There was no resistance. He stuck his head out of the plane. "Wire's down. You know anything about this, sentry?"

The guard shook his head. "No, sir, but the wire's always gettin' cut by vehicles or some damn thing."

Babcock stood there waiting. Witkowski thought about it. Where was the harm in it? The guy had already seen about all they had to offer.

"Oh, hell, Doc," he said, "come on up." He nodded assent to the sentry. While Babcock climbed the ladder, Witkowski went back to the galley and picked up the chicken leg. He was gnawing on it when the doctor appeared in the hatch. He was not quite so impressive, close up, but his expression was pleasant. Babcock extended his hand. Witkowski declined, holding up the greasy chicken leg.

"Like something to eat, Doc?" he asked. "I've got a Hungry Man in the freezer."

Babcock looked startled. "A . . . what?"

Witkowski chuckled. "Frozen dinner."

"Oh, I see." Babcock still looked puzzled. "Uh . . . no thank you." He turned to go aft. "All right if I look around?"

"Sure, go ahead." He put down the chicken and wiped his hands. "Just let me take a look at General Kogan's note."

Babcock turned and fished the paper from his pocket. "Of course," he said. "Here it is."

He reached out, but the note slipped from his hand and fell to the deck. "Sorry," he said.

As Witkowski bent over to retrieve it, the lights went out—for him.

The single bulb hanging from the ceiling of the bungalow flickered as the old gasoline generator coughed, then kicked in again. An ancient black fan in the corner groaned briefly and began to stir the air.

Otis Hiraga held up his coffee cup and Juan, his face sulky, moved slowly to refill it. "Who the hell does he think I am, Yamamoto?" Hiraga said in mock anger, winking at the other four men lingering over the dinner table. Von Porten sat across the room, studying a small notebook.

"I'm telling you guys it feels good to know we're finally bailing out of here," Longford said. "That business with the Jap unit scares the hell out of me."

"Yeah," Kogan replied absently, his eyes straying to Von Porten. The others followed his gaze. The silence around the table became uncomfortable.

"Hey," Betts said, forcing a grin. "This is supposed to be a celebration. Juan," he said, holding up his glass. "Any wine left?"

"*Sí, señor.*"

Tight-lipped, Kogan tried to restrain his impatience. The old PhilPak bungalow, with its big living room in deep shadow, was not a festive place. True, things had finally seemed to come together with the handshake between Von Porten and Babcock, but the hour the two had spent together at this very table had at times gotten downright nasty. Kogan had found refuge on the porch, but he could hear the voices even when he couldn't make out the words. Babcock apparently used botanical terms Von Porten was unfamiliar with, and clarification did not come easily to these prickly personalities. Several times, Kogan had resisted the temptation to step in and bump heads together.

About an hour ago, the two doctors had come to a surly agreement and Babcock had said he was going for a walk. Kogan had hesitated, but Von Porten had said to let him go, he didn't think he needed to ask more questions. It wasn't as though Babcock was going to run away. That bomber ride he'd been promised would keep him close.

Now Kogan could no longer stand the suspense. He called out to Von Porten. "Art, how's it going?"

"I don't know." Von Porten shook his head. "Some of this doesn't make sense."

"Damnit," Kogan muttered. In a louder voice he asked, "What's wrong?"

Von Porten got up, slapped his notebook shut, and headed for the door. "That guy used a lot of what he said were aboriginal names for the plants involved. I've got a couple of reference works aboard the plane that might help."

"Doc," Longford exclaimed. "You think the guy is trying to screw us?"

Von Porten gave Longford a pained look. "Babcock? That prince among men? He wouldn't."

"It's funny," Hiraga grimaced. "Remember before we left, how we almost revered his name? Hell, I would have voted for canonization."

Von Porten nodded. "Saint Roger turns out to be damn close to a borderline sociopath. His world consists of one person—himself." He sighed heavily. "In answer to your question, Jake, and to the one you haven't asked, Joe—you're damn right he could be diddling us."

He whirled around as pounding feet hit the porch and the screen door slammed open. Babcock plunged into the room, standing spraddle-legged, his fingers clenching as his sweating face swiveled from man to man, and finally settled on Kogan.

"You son of a bitch!" He looked as though he was about to leap on Joe.

Hortha swept up a glass from the table and threw its contents into Babcock's face. Grabbing him by his shoulder, he pushed him back against the wall, holding him there. But when he spoke, his voice was soothing.

"Easy, now, Doc. That kind of talk can get you in big trouble."

"Let him go, Johnny," Kogan said. He didn't know what the problem was, but he sensed that it was bad. Babcock epitomized trouble. He was like some evil presence, casting a shadow over everything he came near, operating completely out of sync with normal human beings.

"Okay, spit it out," he said wearily.

Babcock leaned over the table, his eyes bloodshot, angry. "When will this fucking war be over?"

"September 2, 1945."

"Ain't that great. I spend three years in a goddamn Jap prison camp, then just before the war's over, I'm killed by some stupid navy flyboy." Babcock stalked to the liquor stand in the corner and splashed bourbon into a glass. He gulped it down and glared again at Kogan.

"And don't try to deny it."

"How'd you find out?"

Babcock pointed the drink at him. "I'll tell you, *General*! You set me up to fly out of here on that bomber, remember? Wonderful. Then I got to thinking. If I made it to Australia with B-juice, what the hell are you doing back here looking for it?" He filled his glass again. "I didn't make it, damnit! You never intended for me to get on that bomber. That whole business with the comm officer was a setup."

"No, Babcock, it wasn't." Kogan was tired, emotionally and mentally. Worn out. Getting through the time here at Del Monte was like running a footrace through waist-deep water. But cutting through the fatigue came a warning alarm that made his skin prickle—something Babcock had said.

He was talking again. "I told you not to lie to me." He looked at Von Porten and chuckled. "Having a little trouble with the recipe, Doc?"

Von Porten's eyes were cold as he faced Babcock. "You were

going to let us leave here with nothing, Babcock?" He took a step toward him. "You're filth."

Babcock glowered back. "Look who's talking."

Kogan jumped to his feet. His suspicion had grown to frightening proportions. "Damn you, Babcock, answer me! How did you find out about the POW camp?"

"Simple. I got it out of your computer. No problem. Great machine. I'm gonna get me one first thing when we get back to where you're going."

"Witkowski wouldn't let you touch that computer." He whirled to Longford. "Call the plane, quick!"

Longford cranked the field telephone. He looked up, his face pale. "I'm not getting through, Joe."

Babcock's expression turned to mock horror. "How awful. I wouldn't be surprised if someone cut the telephone line." He laughed. "Doesn't matter. I think the Polack may be taking a little snooze, anyway."

"Oh, my God!" Betts groaned. "Look at the time! The thing's gonna blow! Gotta get to the plane!" Knocking over a chair, he ran to the door and dived into the darkness.

Kogan checked his watch. It was 7:54—less than six minutes until *Sucker One* went sky-high. "Everyone out of here," he yelled. "Scatter. Grab the first vehicle you see and get to the plane!" He raced for the door.

"We'll play hell getting wheels, Joe," Longford yelled after him. "They're all in the motor pool on the other side of camp."

═ CHAPTER SIXTEEN ═

It was semidark when his eyes blinked open. Inches away, he could see a dust devil and a pencil. The splayed foot of a screw-down seat leg pressed against his cheek. Weird. Why in hell was he taking a nap on the deck with his face in some stickiness that gummed up his right eye? A little pool of the stuff seeped out from under his cheek. He dipped his finger in it. It was dark red—blood, by God. Yeah, now he remembered—Smiling Jack. *That goddamn Babcock! Gotta get up, quick. No telling what that son of a bitch will do. Come on, make the legs move, raise the head, brace the arms.*

Wish the clanging would stop. Every blare is a knife in the skull. Clanging? It's the alarm! The plane's gonna blow! Gotta stop it. Gotta get to the key. Pull the legs up, one at a time. Roll over,

that's it, up on the knees. Come on, move your butt! Almost there.
Don't stumble. Ooohh, someone stabbed my skull with an ice pick.
Light's going out again.

Betts ran without pacing himself, full-out, arms pumping, his
eyes adjusting to the darkness of the jungle-shrouded road. The
rutted trail was a bad choice—he was ankle-deep in dust that
sapped his strength. Through the trees off to one side, he could
see the airstrip. He turned toward it, forcing his way through
the brush to get to firmer footing.

Faintly now, in the distance, he heard the rhythmic clamor of
the alarm system. He tried to pick up his speed, running with
his mouth open, gasping for air. He checked the luminescent
dial of his watch. The minute hand was almost straight up.
Maybe two minutes left, maybe less. Try as he might to force
his legs to go faster, his muscles said forget it. Jesus! The plane
wasn't that far off now, maybe a quarter mile. Why hadn't he
gone on a fitness program—jogging, bicycling, anything? Not
old smart-ass Betts, laughing at the fitness nuts. Booorrrring, he
sneered. So was a Jap POW camp. So was Hanging Limb, Tennessee, but he wished to God he was back there now.

The tall grass of the strip lashed at his legs, putting more strain
on his quivering muscles. A root grabbed his toe and sent him
sprawling. He lay in the grass, tasting the thick cotton in his
mouth, wanting to stay there forever. The clanging was louder.
He could see the light pouring from the plane hatch of the 737,
a technological wonder about to fertilize the soil of Del Monte
with tiny, metallic fragments and Witkowski's blood—old Larry
Betts's, too, if he ever made it to the plane. Struggling to his
feet, he lunged on, afraid now to look at his watch. The revetment
was very close, the sound of the alarm a terrifying, pulsating
thing.

His last, staggering steps brought him to the clearing. Just a
few more yards and he'd be at the ladder and shit!—no way his
legs were going to carry him up those steps into the plane.

"*Hold it, buddy.*" A rifle pushed hard against his chest. A second sentry shouldered up beside the first, his jaw jutting belligerently.

"Gotta . . . get to . . . the plane," Betts panted, his chest heaving. He tried to edge by them.

"No, you don't," the sentry said sternly. "Lemme see some identification."

"The . . . fucking plane . . . is . . . gonna blow up! You understand?" Betts's hands searched his pockets as he looked into their unyielding faces. "Please, I left my ID in the bungalow!" Fear turned to anger. "Don't you understand, you dumb shits? What do you think that noise is all about?"

Pounding footsteps came up behind him. A voice out of the darkness said, "Hold 'em, Larry!"

Hortha plunged by at full speed. His captors shouted at him to stop, raising their rifles.

Extending both arms, Betts leaped on the sentries, taking them to the ground with him. They struggled, cursing, trying to throw him off. Lights flashed agonizingly as a fist hit the side of his head. He grabbed a pack strap in each hand, holding the thrashing bodies down. He managed to catch a glimpse of the plane. Hortha was leaping up the ladder two steps at a time.

He gasped at the men, "Keep your goddamn heads down," then ducked his own.

The clamor stopped.

The pile of bodies untangled itself. A sentry broke the silence with an angry stream of curses. Betts held out his hand placatingly. "Okay, it's over. It's all right now, guys, it's all right." Muttering to themselves, the guards stomped off.

Hortha appeared in the hatchway grinning, his chest heaving. "How ya doin', sport?"

Betts got to his knees and looked up at him. He could barely talk. "Glad you came along, you goddamn fitness freak." He stumbled toward the plane. "How's Mike?"

"Running cold water on his head. Then he's going to kill Babcock."

• • •

Marie turned away from the jalousied window to look around the smoke-filled room. Food had been brought over from the officers' mess and the tables were still cluttered. Some of the nurses had pushed the dishes to one side and were playing cards, several were writing letters, and the rest, like Marie, were listening to the music coming from the radio, engrossed in their own thoughts.

Dreary thoughts, if they were like hers. The message had gone to Australia asking for a plane, but the enemy was coming at them frighteningly fast. All the waiting at Corregidor and on the long flight to Lake Lanao could be futile now. They had enjoyed a few hours of freedom in Dansalan, but the damned Japs were on their trail again. It seemed unreal, and so unfair.

She again thought of Joe Kogan. Why was he popping up so constantly in her mind? It didn't make sense, yet her body grew warm thinking about it. Closing her eyes, she leaned back against the wall. Vagrant thoughts flashed and shimmered in her head. Images that had for years been locked safely away taunted her. Her body seemed to come alive with a hunger she thought had passed her by forever. She pressed her hands against suddenly flaming cheeks and scolded herself. Stop these outrageous thoughts!

Pushing away from the wall, Marie walked to the door, opened it, and stood on the steps, seeking a breeze that would cool her down. This Joe wasn't all that great. Had she met him a year ago in the Manila Polo Club, would she feel this way? Absolutely not—particularly if he gave her the standard BOQ line about his marriage being loveless, his wife cold and uncaring. No, it was the war, the presence of death, and the uncertainty of the future, that had made her just too vulnerable. Besides, the interest she thought she'd seen in his eyes was an illusion. He'd probably forgotten her or he would at least have sent a message of some kind. Major Hortha must have told him about her. If Joe was interested, where was he?

• • •

Just moments ago, a Signal Corps sergeant had finished stringing new wire to their field telephone.

Kogan completed his call to the plane and slipped the telephone back into its leather case. "Von Porten says Mike is okay. He has a mild concussion, but he can function. They'll stay on the plane."

He sat down and moved the pineapple around on his plate. It would be a long time before he would eat the stuff again in any form. There was nothing wrong with it, but from now on, pineapple would always remind him of Babcock, and that made him a little sick. But what the hell, unless things got better, he might never eat again anyway.

"Okay," he said with finality. "We're all agreed. We take Babcock back."

The four men—Longford, Hortha, Hiraga, and Betts—all found other things to look at. They'd picked at the subject one way and another until Kogan had finally slammed his hand on the table.

"Now, listen to me. We were sent here to bring back the cure—"

Hiraga broke in. "But we also were told what we could do and what we couldn't. We were given guidelines—"

"Screw the guidelines," Kogan snapped back quickly. "Because that's all they were. A bunch of guys with no more brains than we came up with crap like you're going back to World War II to get this terribly important thing and it would be nice if this happened or that didn't happen. Okay. It's like telling a regimental commander to take a hill and it would be nice if you didn't lose any men while doing it. So the regimental commander doesn't take the hill because he might lose some men. Helluva way to run a war."

He glared around the table. "There are three things you gotta keep in mind when you're given a job to do—the mission, the mission, the mission. Everything else is shit. We nearly lost the whole ball game tonight, and tomorrow isn't gonna be a walk in the park. So I say we take back a little souvenir of our three glorious days at Del Monte."

Hiraga quietly clapped his hands. "Right on. Very honest appraisal, Joe." He gave a little groan. "I just wish we could go back with a neater package."

Kogan felt his truculence ebb away. "Otis, I'm with you there." He held up his wineglass and Juan jumped to fill it. "Okay, then, here's what we do. Willie Burke picks up Babcock from the *cárcel* and delivers him to the plane at four—an hour before dawn. Shortly after, we all load aboard. Fifth Air Base Group lights the beacon at the north end of the strip and we roll at oh-four-thirty. Now, remember," he tapped on the table for emphasis. "Leave nothing behind, not a scrap. I'd take our tire tracks if I could. Make it look like we've never been here."

"Joe." Betts, still bedraggled from his night run, leaned forward and put his elbows on the table. "Why not get the hell out of here right now? This place gives me the willies. Why wait until morning?"

Kogan raised his eyebrows at Hiraga.

"Simple enough, Larry," Hiraga said. "Our group aboard the carrier has two blocks of time in each twenty-four-hour period to shoot off the tachyon ray. They'll execute on schedule for the next six...no, five days. I do the calculations on this end to establish a coincidence of times for our arrival at the transit point. If we take off much before dawn tomorrow, we won't have the fuel to keep us aloft that long."

"Anything else?" Kogan asked. No one said anything.

Chairs scraped as the crew rose to return to the plane. They stood awkwardly, no one seeming to want to make the first move. Then, for some reason, each man stepped forward to shake hands with Kogan.

Betts looked around. "Where the hell's my flashlight?" Hiraga discovered it on a chair and tossed it to the engineer. The four men trooped out, down the steps, and, guided by the thin beam of light, headed back toward the plane.

Longford watched them disappear, then stretched and glanced at his watch. "Nearly ten, Joe. Have to be up by three. We ought to hit the sack."

Kogan grunted. He leaned against the porch railing, looking out on the tropical night. He felt keyed up. Sleep wasn't going to come easy. Maybe the operation was winding down, maybe they'd get away all right, but a knife blade of doubt stabbed at him. How could he sleep—even relax? He should remain alert, watching out for the unexpected, the unknown and unseen that could destroy them.

He heard footsteps. Hortha emerged from the darkness, looking apologetic. "General," he said. "Nearly forgot. While I was over talking to the women, that chief nurse, Captain Crane, said to tell you she couldn't take your advice. Don't know what she was talking about—"

Kogan took two quick steps toward Hortha and groaned audibly. "What the hell! You say Marie Crane is here...at Del Monte?"

"Why, yes, sir." Hortha was startled by Kogan's vehemence.

"Oh, my God!" Kogan slammed his hand thunderously against the door frame. Longford, arranging his mosquito bar, whirled in alarm.

Kogan walked to the edge of the porch, where Hortha stood looking up with his mouth open. "That's okay, Johnny," Kogan said, getting himself under control. "Go on back to the plane."

Hortha turned away, then stopped. "Golly, dumb of me to forget. I'm really sorry."

"No...those things happen. It really doesn't matter." He watched Hortha vanish into the darkness. It did matter. He thought he had saved her, but maybe that just wasn't possible. His thoughts switched gears. So she's here, a couple of hundred yards away. Red hair, white skin, and those blue eyes that had seen too much pain and suffering. Eyes that at Dansalan had softened when they had looked into his, or at least he thought so. He wanted to see her again. He considered it, then rejected it. He'd already fooled around with the past too much. The good-byes had been said—why make it tougher by dragging it out? Unhappy but resolute, Kogan turned toward his cot.

From the porch, Marie looked back into the bungalow. She was tired, really all in, but she doubted that sleep would come easy. A few of the women had already disappeared into the three bedrooms set up with cots. Most, though, were still up, writing letters or just listening to the victrola one of the officers had sent over. Someone put on a new record. A caressing male voice drifted out to the darkened porch. That young singer, Sinatra—what a nice voice. The words to "I'll Never Smile Again" were just too appropriate.

In spite of her fatigue, she really wanted to get away from the bungalow for a little while, to stroll in the night's soft darkness. But they had been warned that marauding bands of Moros, emboldened by the closeness of the Japanese army, were beginning to infiltrate the Del Monte area.

Of course, if Joe Kogan had only come by, they could have taken that walk, side by side, under the moon, their hands occasionally touching, Joe's arm, perhaps, around her waist. *Now, stop that!* she thought.

Shivering suddenly, she crossed her arms over her breasts and squeezed until she was breathless. This was ridiculous. Besides, he was a general, with so many responsibilities, and of course, married. She'd never met a general who wasn't. And he had probably forgotten her by now. Ha! She attempted a light laugh. No "probably" about it. The whole thing was an aberration—a brief moment in which two people caught up in the madness of war had reached out and touched each other tenderly. Neither was to blame for being human. In a few months, it would be a dim memory.

"What do you think our chances are?" a voice spoke at her elbow.

Marie jumped, then caught herself. "Oh, hi, Sylvia," she said, wondering how much of her thoughts her face revealed.

"A bit nervous, aren't we?" Sylvia Kruloff smiled and grabbed Marie's elbow playfully. "What's the matter—can't stand all the quiet after the Rock? Maybe we should ask Colonel Edmonds to fire some big guns in our direction to lull us to sleep."

"Oh, no...I was just thinking." Marie liked Sylvia, a first lieutenant a few years younger than herself. Attractive, with honey blond hair, regular features, and a puckish sense of humor, she was also a very competent nurse.

"Yes." Sylvia looked back at the quiet figures in the living room. "There's a lot of thinking going on right now. And most of it is pretty morbid. Well?" she asked. "How about it?"

"How about what?"

"Our chances, for heaven's sakes. You think MacArthur will send another plane?"

Marie started a peevish answer. How would she know? She hadn't packed her Ouija board. All they had to go on was what Major Hortha had said. She caught herself. As senior nurse, she had responsibilities. The others were depressed enough, without her adding to the gloom. "I'm sure he will," Marie said with a confidence she didn't feel. "The other flying boat must have gotten there by now." She chuckled. "There's some pretty strong-minded gals in that bunch. They'll raise hell until something comes back to pick us up."

"Oh, God." Sylvia's voice was plaintive. "I hope so. We were so close..." Her words trailed off. "Well, whining isn't going to help. Got a cigarette?"

"No, just finished my pack, but there's a couple of cartons left of those Colonel Edmonds sent over."

Sylvia started to go inside, but Marie called out. "I've got an idea. It's so lovely out tonight. Let's take a walk. Maybe that will help us sleep."

Sylvia hesitated, then shook her head. "Uh-uh. And don't you go. It's too dark out there." She disappeared into the bungalow.

·　　·　　·

At first Marie walked in the night with some trepidation. Then, as her eyes grew accustomed to the darkness, her fears left, replaced by wry amusement. If the entire 14th Japanese Army hadn't been able to kill her, this quiet backwater of the war should hold no threats. She thought about her answer to Sylvia's dejected query. It hadn't been honest, for she had no idea whether a rescue plane would be sent or not, yet it seemed to her that the law of averages was in their favor. In the last four months, the gods of fortune had dumped one darned bad thing after another on them. Wasn't it reasonable to believe that at long last something good would happen?

As if in response, the half-moon slipped out from behind a cloud, casting enough light to form shadows on the jungle floor. Through the trees she could see the lighter grass of the landing field, and beyond it, the darker mass where the forest began again. She walked to the edge of the airstrip and leaned against a mahogany tree, its smooth bark cool against her shoulder. She reached for a cigarette, then realized she'd come away without any.

A sound broke the quiet. Something, somebody, was moving close by. Marie tensed and eased carefully back into the shadows. A figure moved out of the tree line and walked along the edge of the landing strip. She relaxed. It was a man, too tall for a Filipino, and moving in too casual a fashion to pose harm. Hands thrust deep in his pants pockets, he walked head down, kicking his feet idly through the knee-high grass. She watched as he came closer, then felt her breath catch in her throat. She knew him—she recognized the broad shoulders and the dimly seen features.

It was Joe Kogan. A smile spread across her face. Maybe something good *had* happened. He didn't suspect she was there. Now was the time to step out in front of him and say something clever.

"Hi."

Even in her own ears her voice sounded weak and shrill, like an adolescent girl's.

Startled, Kogan stopped and peered at her. "Well, I'll be damned," he said. "Marie Crane. They put you on guard duty?"

They found a fallen nipa palm and Kogan straddled the bole while Marie sat back, hugging her trousered legs.

"I tried to get aboard the right plane, I really did, but it didn't work out," Marie said, half embarrassed. "Juanita Redmond and I were together, waiting on the dock, when I asked Jack Fitzgerald if we could ride number seven boat, and he said there would be no problem, but I don't think he even heard me. He was running around with his roster, shouting, getting things organized and too busy, I guess, to listen. Then the pilots yelled from the planes, everyone jumped into the nearest skiff, and we got aboard whatever plane they took us to. Juanita and I were separated and she got aboard the other PBY." Her hands clasped, a little shudder ran through her body. "It's such a long, dangerous trip to Australia, flying over all that Jap-held territory. Joe . . ." She put her hand on his arm. "Could you radio Darwin? Find out if they made it? Juanita was such a good friend."

"Sure, glad to," Kogan said. "But I'm positive they made it."

"How can you be so sure?"

"Uh . . . well, they'd be overdue by now. Darwin would have sent an interrogatory. They haven't." He would have liked to have told her more—how her friend Lieutenant Redmond had not only survived the long flight, but written a book about her experiences, eventually become chief of the Air Force Nurse Corps, and—he suppressed a smile—married a general.

And by all rights Marie, too, should be in Australia. He'd tried to make sure that's where she had ended up and it hadn't worked out. Now, if she was to have any life at all, this lovely woman must make it through the hell of a Japanese internment camp. And maybe she won't make it. Great future.

"It's a beautiful night," she said, looking up at the cobalt sky through the palm fronds. "A cool breeze, the smell of the grass . . ." She laid her hand on his arm and pointed. "Just look at the moon. How wonderful. It's so peaceful here, and it won't be much longer. I wonder if this damn war will ever be over."

"Believe me," he said. "Nothing lasts forever."

Her hand stayed on his arm, then found his hand. Her fingers, long, slender, and cool, entwined with his.

Oh, boy. Why hadn't he stayed in bed, tossing and turning? Why hadn't he taken a couple slugs of whiskey to beat the insomnia? Maybe if they didn't touch they could keep this thing on an even keel. Gently, he pulled his hand from hers. That seemed to startle her. He could sense her eyes on his averted face.

"You're leaving tomorrow morning, aren't you?"

He nodded. "Yeah, real early."

"Joe, could I ask you a question?" Marie said, her voice low. "I know so little about you. Do you want to guess what my first question is?"

He was pretty sure he knew, but it was better to pretend ignorance. He shook his head.

"You're married, aren't you?"

Maybe he should say he was—that would cool things. He decided she had been lied to enough. "No, I'm a widower."

"I'm sorry. For long?"

"Almost three years." His answer was terse. "She was killed in a car accident."

"I'm so sorry. Is it still painful?"

He smiled ruefully. "At times, yeah. But you go on, and it eases off." He glanced at her. "How about you? Are you married?"

"I was, for six years. Harry was an army flyer. He died. His plane crashed in a training exercise." She sat up briskly as though to put the subject away, and asked, "Could I have a cigarette, please?"

He went through a charade of patting his pockets. "Sorry, I don't have any with me."

"You don't smoke, do you?" she asked.

He shook his head. "I've got my share of bad habits, though."

"You consider smoking a bad habit?" She seemed surprised. "You sound like an old fuddy-duddy. I suppose you think if a girl smokes, she's . . . fast."

Kogan laughed. "I meant physically bad, not morally."

"Except for a little morning cough, smoking doesn't hurt you," she said.

He opened his mouth to argue, then shut it. *No, dummy, you can't lecture her on a habit that won't be declared bad for another twenty years.*

"I dunno," he said. "That cough could get worse."

"Oh, you," she laughed, and leaned forward in a playful gesture, her hand moving to his shoulder. Without volition, his hand moved to cover hers, and he turned his head to look into her eyes, dark against the whiteness of her face. Gently, he laid his cheek against hers, then felt her mouth seeking his. She twisted in his arms, pressing hard against his chest, her arms pulling his head down to hers. They were breathing hard when the kiss ended.

Christ, he thought, *this can't go any further.*

He pulled away and got to his feet. He could see her eyes widen with surprise and hurt, then she dropped her head, speaking in a voice so low he could hardly hear her words.

"Harry was the only man in my life. I want you to know that, Joe." He had a feeling that her fair skin was pink with embarrassment.

"I have never wanted another man until . . ." She lifted her head. Her face beseeched him to understand. "Until you. Oh, Joe," Marie went to him, pressing herself close.

Kogan couldn't help himself. He gathered her slender body close and kissed her. Her lips opened and her body moved, slowly, then insistently, against his. With a muttered curse, he pulled himself free of her arms.

"What's wrong?" Her voice broke.

What's wrong? Why nothing, Captain Marie Crane, Army Nurse Corps, soon to become a POW. Except that you're talking to a fake general from a fake headquarters flying a fake plane on a fake mission. For some reason, Marie Crane, you seem to have fallen for this phony who's done nothing but lie to you from the moment you met and will fly out of your life and your world in another few hours.

But let's assume that you survive the next few years and someday you wonder what happened to General Joseph Kogan. You write a letter to the adjutant general and get a nice formal reply that there is no record of any General Kogan ever being in the army and you'll wonder who the impostor was who almost made love to you a few nights before the Japs took control of your destiny.

That's a small taste of what's wrong, Captain Crane. Now, what I really urgently want is to leave you with as little memory of me as possible.

What he said was taken right out of an old black-and-white movie. "Marie, listen. Tomorrow I'll be gone. We may never see each other again. I think too much of you to do something we could be sorry for later."

"But," she murmured, pushing closer, "I can't help but believe we'll be together again. Maybe when we both get to Australia; maybe when this damn war's over. I don't know, but I feel it." She looked up into his eyes and put her hand on her left breast. "I feel it here."

What the hell could he say? He'd run out of words. His idea well had gone dry. He couldn't even look at her, but he knew her eyes were on his face, waiting for him to tell her he cared for her. Maybe he did, or would—if he could let himself. But he couldn't. He had to get out of there.

He pretended to look at his watch. "I have to leave."

Her face was stricken. "You mean, this is all? This is goodbye? Joe, this could be our last night!"

"I'm sorry," he said quietly. "I'm sorrier than you'll ever know." He took her elbow and turned her back in the direction of the quarters. "But it has to be this way."

Her eyes suddenly clouded with doubt. Her voice dulled, became lifeless. "This *is* our last night, isn't it? I'll never see you again, will I?"

She touched his arm, turning him to face her. He couldn't answer. Words formed, but the sounds wouldn't come. He shook his head helplessly.

"Marie, I . . ." He couldn't go on.

"Am I going too fast for you? Do I bore you?"

He groaned. "Oh, God, no."

"Maybe you really are married, or have girlfriends scattered around Australia."

"No, that's not it." He tried again. "It's just the uncertainty."

"No, not uncertainty, just the opposite. You know. You know too much. And it frightens me. How do you know?" She looked up at him, her voice pleading. "Please don't do this to me."

He fumbled for words. "Come on. I'm as much in the dark as you. But how can we plan for tomorrow in the middle of a war that we're losing? Marie, I don't want to make glib promises."

"Really, General?" He could feel her anger flare. "People trapped in a war live on promises. That's all we have left to hold on to." She was quiet for a moment, trying, he sensed, to get control of her emotions.

She began speaking, slowly at first. "There are some things, strange things, about you . . . and your crew and plane, that I don't understand. One day you're a colonel, and the next you're a general. The only explanation I heard was just plain stupid.

"You don't seem to care about the war. You don't even seem to be very angry at the Japs. Doesn't their sneak attack at Pearl Harbor infuriate you?" She didn't wait for his answer. "Look, I won't ask you—I have no right to—but there's talk that you even have a Jap as part of your crew."

"Let me explain—"

"No, Joe, the who and why of your crew is no business of mine." She seemed to lose her train of thought, then self-consciously weakened her disclaimer. "I just think it's funny, that's all. Anyway, you certainly don't have a bunch of party people with you. Everyone's talking about how you keep to yourselves. Half my nurses went to Happy Hour—" She shook her head in a bemused way. "Happy Hour! Good God! No one in United States Forces Far East has had a happy *minute* since the Japs hit. What was I saying? Oh, yes. The girls went to that makeshift O'Club here looking for Major Hortha. They're all in love with him. But not a single one of your crew was there. They were all back at that weird plane, or somewhere. And another thing, the major doesn't know he looks like Robert Taylor." She eyed him closely. "Don't you think he does?"

Who the hell was Robert Taylor? His mind, twisting and turning like a cornered rat, finally connected the name—a movie actor from long ago, back in the thirties and forties. "Oh, yeah, sure," he said hastily. "Close resemblance. Matter of fact, I noticed it when I first met Johnny." That was the truth, almost. Hortha *had* reminded him of someone. Now he knew who it was.

She looked at him, her eyes narrowed as though she were about to press him. "Well, there's something funny there. He acted like he was from another planet, another world."

God, she was getting close. He'd better break this up quickly. But she spoke again. "Sylvia Kruloff talked to one of the Fifth Air Base guys. He says he worked in design for Martin Aircraft before the war and knows all the new developments. He says he's never seen anything like your plane. He says the propellers are too small for it to ever get off the ground."

"Marie," Kogan began, but she cut him off.

"No," she said, "let me finish. Back at the lake, when I was telling you about Corregidor, I had the strangest feeling that you knew all about it, that you knew even more than I did." She shook her head. "And yet you've never been there."

"Marie, that's ridiculous. You were just overtired."

She didn't seem to hear him. "What I'm trying to say is that I think that somehow you have a gift of—extrasensory perception, or abnormal insight, or something."

He had to put a stop to this. "Hey, come on," he said, trying for a light tone. "The moon's getting to you. No one can predict the future. If you're talking about that business with the PBY, I explained that to you. Fitzgerald is a damn good pilot."

"He just happened to be in the right plane and it got off okay. Our plane ran into submerged rocks. It was as though you knew it wouldn't make it and that's why you didn't want me on it." She tried, in the gloom, to see his eyes. "Joe, I'm suddenly scared. Tell me this isn't happening."

They had reached the nurses' billet. They stood on the steps of the porch and Marie lowered her voice. "I wish I could hate you, General Kogan, I truly do, but I can't." For a moment she rested her head against his shoulder like a little girl. "You know how I feel about you. I can't help it, even if you don't feel that way about me—even if you aren't telling me the truth. I think you're a decent, honest man who hates lying. Yet I have the strangest feeling that you and your friends and that plane hidden at the end of the runway are lies."

He reached out, wanting to comfort her, but with a stifled sob, she evaded his arms and ran up the steps to the porch.

In the darkness, Kogan cracked his shins on a chair. With a curse, he sent it flying across the room.

"What the—" A flashlight beam shined in his face. Jake Longford struggled out from under his mosquito bar. "Joe!" he said. "What's wrong?"

Kogan staggered across the room and sat down, head spinning and thoughts jumbled by his anger.

"Get me a drink," he growled. Jake grabbed a bottle and poured bourbon into a glass.

"Problems?" he asked.

Kogan nodded, gulped his drink, and in a rush of words, told Longford what had happened. He turned off the flashlight and the two men sat silent in the darkness.

Longford spoke. "That's sad, real sad." He sighed. "But there's not a damn thing we can do about it. Joe, it's not long to takeoff. Don't you think you ought to get some sleep?"

"I can't get Marie out of my mind."

Longford nodded sympathetically. "It's tough." He hesitated, then added, "I wonder how many of those gals are going to die in the POW camps?"

Kogan looked at him sharply. Longford hurried on. "I'm sorry. I didn't mean to be cruel, but it seems to me that the women who don't make it ought to have the same chance we're giving Babcock."

For a moment Kogan seemed not to have heard. Then he reached out slowly and placed his hand on Longford's arm.

"By God, Jake," he said, his voice thick. "You're right. We made an exception with Babcock." He punched Longford's shoulder. "And we can damn well do it for the women of the Army Nurse Corps!"

He jumped to his feet. "Get out to the plane and have Witkowski stand by. I'll get a list of the nurses' names from Marie and we'll run them through the computer. Those who died are going back with us." In the dark, Kogan's face split into a wide grin. Marie was either going to survive POW camp or she was going with them. Either way, she had a chance to live.

Her eyes were wide and questioning as she came to him quickly, her hand clutching the front of the light robe she wore over her pajamas. He took her by the arm and pulled her down the steps.

"Marie," he said in a whisper. "We may be able to take a few nurses, but I need a list."

"Oh, that's wonderful! But how many of us can you take? And why do you need a roster?" She rubbed her eyes with the back of her hand. He had a feeling that she had been crying.

"Well, uh . . . we're working on the load limitations now so I really don't know how many we can handle," he said, improvising desperately. "If we can take just a few, then we'll need to pull some names from a hat."

She quickly got a list for him, asking how soon they would know who was going. "Not long," he said, and turned to go back to the plane.

•   •   •

Witkowski, his head bandaged, carefully smoothed the roster of names on the desk beside the computer. Kogan and Longford stood behind him as he booted up the mini. Von Porten, a Styrofoam container of coffee in his hand, joined them.

Kogan motioned to the two men. "Come on, let's go outside. I can't watch this."

They stood in the shadows behind the forward hatch of the 737. "If we find that Marie made it through POW camp okay, would you still take her back with us?" Longford asked.

Kogan looked at him in amazement. "For chrissakes, Jake, do you think I'd risk her life transiting her into the future if she has a life to live in this world? All I can do is wish her well. But I tell you, buddy, if I find out she dies as a POW, I'll get her aboard." He added softly, to himself, "Some way."

"Joe." Witkowski stood in the hatchway, a sheet of paper in his hand.

"Okay, let's have it," Kogan said, his heart thumping.

"Six of the ten survived," Witkowski said. "I used September 1, 1945, as a status date."

Kogan licked his lips. "What about Marie Crane?"

Witkowski looked down at the paper. "No, sir. She was one of the four who died."

He had trouble making his lips move. "You're sure?"

"Yes, sir. She was a POW as of May 10, 1942, but she's not on the list of repatriates after the war."

CHAPTER SEVENTEEN

Gould Collines smiled distractedly as Senator Moser's secretary handed him a tall glass of milk. This, and the coffee he had unwisely consumed, would be his breakfast. A nervous stomach, the legacy of past courtroom battles and current struggles on the floor of the House, bedeviled him—particularly when trouble loomed.

In the office lavatory, he could hear Newt Moser making toothbrushing sounds. The senator's office was spacious, as befitted the majority leader, the furniture leather-covered and expensive, a burnished, wide-planked wood floor bordering a muted gold and red Persian rug. On the walls, the coffee table, the mahogany sideboard, and his desk were the icons of thirty years of public service—warmly autographed presidential photos, certificates, plaques, silver cups, and regional sculptures.

The senator emerged, wiped his hands, and tossed the towel over his shoulder carelessly. He did not seem happy. Grunting to acknowledge Collines's presence, he muttered into his intercom, "Maggie, hold the phone calls." He kicked his chair into position, sank into it heavily, and contemplated his folded hands.

"Guess you know our problem."

Collines did. The week of grace given President Moody had expired. There was little doubt but that the vice president had also circled the date on his calendar.

Moser continued. "Got a call from Lillian Moody last night. Simon's bad off."

"And the cure?"

"Nothing. She didn't even want to discuss it." Moser offered coffee from a silver pot. Collines shook his head, drained the last of his milk, and set the glass down.

Then he asked, "What do you think we should do?"

"Dunno. I was hoping you could come up with something."

Collines leaned back. His stomach felt better, but considering the day's agenda, it wouldn't last. He really should go back to Rockford, Illinois, and that nice little law practice he once had.

"No, I haven't—well, at least nothing brilliant. We could call Pyle and ask for a couple more days. I feel morbid saying this, but with Moody so close to death, what difference does it make?"

"Shouldn't make any," Moser said. "That's what makes this pushiness of his look all the funnier."

"Why?"

"Well, it ain't natural. Be a lot easier if he'd relax and let nature take its course, wouldn't it?" Moser answered his own question. "'Course it would. There's only one explanation. He's afraid of the cure—whatever and wherever it is. I hate to say this, but Pyle doesn't give a shit about Simon Moody. All he wants is to be president."

They sat in frustrated silence, the sounds of Washington at midmorning muted by the thick walls of the office.

"Tell you what," Moser finally said. "Let's get to him before he gets to us." He reached for the intercom just as his secretary's voice announced, "Sir, Vice President Pyle is here."

Moser looked at Collines. "Ah, hell," he said disgustedly. Then he got up and went to the door.

"So, gentlemen, in accordance with our agreement, and in conformance with the Twenty-fifth Amendment to the Constitution, I present to you this letter." Pyle leaned forward and placed the sheet of paper on Moser's desk. "It states, as you well know, that President Simon Moody is no longer capable of executing the duties of his office."

Moser looked at the letter and passed it to Collines, who ran his eyes down the sheet and handed it back. "I see that only nine cabinet heads signed this."

"I believe that's more than adequate," Pyle said. "Inasmuch as eight constitutes a majority."

"Just curious, that's all," Collines replied. "Why didn't all of them sign?"

"Is that important?"

Moser spoke gruffly. "If we ask, it's important. From here on out, it's in our hands."

Pyle narrowed his eyes and seemed about to argue the point. Then he shrugged. "True," he said mildly. "Well, only Secretary of State Talbott and I have been able to see Moody in the last few weeks, so the cabinet members were forced to rely upon what we told them. Some used that as an excuse not to sign."

"No one said anything about loyalty?" Moser asked.

"It may have been mentioned."

"Strange, Mr. Vice President," Collines said, "that Talbott's signature isn't on here."

"Congressman, don't be naïve. Talbott is a confirmed dove. He wants to go to Brussels, with or without Moody. If I become president, that won't happen and the secretary knows it. The team *I* head won't be so anxious to trash our nuclear arsenal." Pyle shifted impatiently in his chair. "Gentlemen," he pointed to the letter, "what about that?"

Moser looked at the letter like it was toxic waste. "Sorry to have to say this to such a patriot, but the agreement, as I recall it, was that the president would voluntarily step down if the cure had not appeared in one week. For this letter, that's sine qua non."

"But the cure isn't here."

"Nor is the one week up. Not until nine o'clock tonight."

"You're quibbling over twelve hours?"

"Where the presidency of this country is concerned, yes, we quibble."

Pyle's jaw muscles tightened, making his ears twitch slightly, Collines noted with some amusement. The vice president had a temper and could use it, but he was outgunned. He managed to speak with some calm. "I'll be back here at nine tonight," he said. He picked the letter off Moser's desk. "I'll see you then."

"Afraid not," the senator said. "I'm an old man. Can't put in eighteen-hour days like I used to. This office closes at five-thirty."

September 29, 1994

8:14 P.M.

There was a light knock on the bedroom door.

"Yes?" Lillian laid aside her hairbrush. Roberta, her personal maid, opened the door.

"Telephone, ma'am. Congressman Collines."

She walked across the room to the phone. She hesitated before picking it up, getting her breathing under control, knowing that he was going to ask how Simon was and if they had the cure yet. These were the same questions she had asked herself for too many long, frightening days and nights.

"Hello, Gould."

"Evening, Lillian. How are you?"

"Hanging on, thank you. And you?"

"A bit embarrassed to be calling on the telephone. I really meant to be over there in person tonight, but there's a committee report that just has to . . . well, never mind. Again, I'm sorry." She could feel the discomfort on the other end of the line.

"I understand," she said. "I was pretty sure that I'd hear from you or Senator Moser about the matter that concerns us."

"Yes." He said only that and she knew he was hurting. Everyone was hurting. Maybe she could at least cut his suffering short.

"I'm afraid I have nothing to report—nothing favorable, that is."

"I see."

"It's overdue, Gould. It's coming, I'm sure of it, but something is holding it up." And it might be held up for eternity, a possibility that Simon foresaw as the cancer ate deeper into his body, sapping his strength, his courage, his very will to live. "We sent them on a wild-goose chase, my dear," he had said only this morning, the dawn of what might be his last secure day in the presidency. His voice barely a whisper he had tried to put a whimsical twist on it. "Make that," he had said, "a tiger hunt, with all the advantages going to the tiger. I shouldn't have done it. I shouldn't have thrown away the lives of those good men." There was no point arguing with him. She no longer had the strength left even to attempt it.

Collines's flat drawl came over the line again. "Would you like me to come over? I could be there in twenty minutes. Maybe it would help if I spoke with the president."

"Thank you, Gould, but I don't think it would do any good. I just wish..." Her voice faded. Wishes were all they had left.

"Lillian," he said. "The letter has been written. It has enough signatures. I saw it today."

The letter. Pyle had gone ahead and done what they suspected he would. Well, it was hardly a surprise. But oh, God, how she hated to have to tell Simon. "You have it?" she asked. "He's given it to you officially?"

"No. It will be delivered to us tomorrow."

She was barely able to hang on to the phone, to realize that the conversation had not ended.

"You still there?"

"Uh, yes."

Some of her dejection must have gone through the wires, for she could sense his compassion.

"Is what you're hoping for definitely not going to materialize? Have you given up on this?"

Suddenly, she was angry. Not at Collines, or anyone else. Just angry. She gripped the phone tightly. "No, damnit," she nearly shouted. "I haven't. It's coming, I just know it is."

"Good." She thought she heard a quiet chuckle on the other end. "Would another day or so help?"

She was breathless. "You mean it, Gould? Could you do it?"

"We can try," he said.

"All right. The letter has been delivered in accordance with the law of the land. I therefore consider myself acting president of the United States as of..." Pyle glanced up at the wall clock. "...ten o'clock, September 30, 1994."

He waited for them to respond. When the majority leader and the Speaker did not, he added, somewhat lamely, "I trust you agree."

Moser answered, "No, we do not."

Pyle stared at Moser. "I don't understand, Senator. I lived up to the terms of the agreement and even beyond. This is the eighth day. There is no cure—"

"How do you know that?"

For a moment Pyle seemed disconcerted, then replied, "Don't you think my office would have been the first to be notified if it had come?" Without waiting, he galloped on, anxious now. "Let me refresh your memories." Then he began, speaking in the cadences of a graduate student taking his orals. "In the case of a sick president, section four of the Twenty-fifth Amendment poses certain requirements, among which is that a majority of the cabinet sign a letter stating the president is unable to discharge the duties of his office. Once that is done and the letter is delivered to the Congress, the vice president shall immediately—I repeat—*shall immediately* become acting president."

Pyle stopped for a breath. "Now, gentlemen, how can you say that I am not now acting president?"

Moser pointed a blunt finger at the vice president. "Mr. Pyle, you're a novice in government. Let me explain something. You come running into my office and say here's a letter, so now I'm president. Whoa, now. Just back up a minute. You think you can call up the secretary of defense and start issuing orders? Call in Third World ambassadors and give them hell? Go on the evening news and tell the American people they've suddenly got a new president? Uh-uh. Ain't that easy."

"What do you mean? The amendment says I take over immediately."

"*Immediately* in government means 'pretty soon.' Sure, all you have to do is get the letter to us, but we—the Congress—have to make sure the president is disabled."

"Why?" Pyle pointed to the letter. "That contains my signature and those of a majority of the cabinet. What more affirmation do you need?"

Collines smiled and spoke up. "It's time for you to put away *your* naïveté, Mr. Pyle. The section you refer to is a virtual invitation to a conspiracy or a palace putsch to take over the presidency."

Pyle whirled on Collines. "Are you suggesting—"

Still smiling, the congressman held up both hands defensively. "I'm suggesting only that the Congress has to take reasonable steps to guarantee against such an event. And that takes a little time." He glanced at Moser, who nodded imperceptibly.

"Okay," Collines continued. "Today's Friday. Monday evening, say about nine, when everyone's available, you show up at the White House. Both Newt and I will be there. I'll call Quent Talbott about cabinet members. Chief Justice Mullins can bring another justice or two. That way, the three branches of government will be adequately represented."

Pyle's slitted eyes darted from one to the other. His cheeks flushed. "Listen, you two—"

Collines overrode his words. "We think that arrangement would be fair and equitable enough to satisfy everyone, especially the American people. Now, how about it?"

Pyle's eyes were cold. "I see no necessity whatever for such a charade. You've seen Moody, you know his condition." He stood. "As far as I'm concerned, I am now the president of the United States."

Moser leaned back in his chair with a look of disgust on his face. "Pyle, the only reason we're doing this, damnit, is to let Moody leave this earth with some dignity. Sure, we know his condition. He probably won't make it through the weekend." The majority leader picked the letter up and held it delicately between his fingers. "And we intend to let him go out as president of the United States."

He tore a tiny rip in the letter. "I'm going to tear this letter up. Gould and I will swear we never saw any such document, and by the time you get those signatures together again, Moody will be gone." The rip grew larger. Moser's voice boomed with menace. "Now, we're not asking you, we're telling you—that's the way it's gonna be. See you Monday." Moser's broad, mottled face looked implacable.

"Then, and not before," he added, "we'll call you Mr. President." With a shirring sound, the letter divided into two parts and sank into the senator's wastebasket.

Flight Warrant Officer Jichiro Shengo lifted his fighter off the Davao strip and tapped his rudder, banking the plane to the right. As he advanced the throttle, the 950 horses of his Nakajima Sakae engine responded instantly, raising the blunt nose of the Zero toward the notch in the mountains to the north of the Davaoan plain. The towering peak of Mount Apo fell behind him as the Zero reached cruising altitude and roared over the deeply clefted Mindanaoan highlands. To the east, across the blackness of the Pacific, a thin glow edged the horizon as the sun started a new day.

Twenty minutes away to the north, Del Monte Field awaited, along with its enigmatic plane.

The plane filled Shengo's thoughts. If by some unlikely chance he found it in the air and shot it down, his military reputation would be enhanced and perhaps Captain Onishi Ozawa, the Air Flotilla commander, would look with favor upon the peasant boy with the sharp eyes and lightning reflexes. It was true, of course, that he had orders to keep the plane on the ground until the infantry could seize it. He did not like these orders, but this conflict between his personal desires and his duty posed no problem for Shengo. The alchemy of ingrained military discipline left him no recourse but to do what he was told. But he could still dream.

He looked at his watch. It was 0433.

•   •   •

"The rest of the women are unhappy about not being able to pull names out of the hat for themselves," Marie said to Kogan as they stood watching the nurses stumble out of the billet. "And much as I want to go, promise me that my name was chosen honestly and not because of our...friendship. That would be disgraceful. I would be most unhappy about it."

"These are unhappy times," he responded curtly, watching the women flutter excitedly around an old PhilPak Dodge sedan that would take them to the plane. "But I assure you, Marie, that I did not choose you to go. I'm not a saint, but I do have some integrity." Well, he hadn't actually chosen her. The computer had done it. As far as having integrity, somewhere there might be a shred of it left.

Von Porten stood close by, his physician's bag in his hand. He had volunteered to come along against the possibility that some of the women, overwrought by their ordeal on Corregidor, the reappearance of the Japanese, and the upcoming flight, might need help. "If ever I saw a situation that calls for Valium, Joe," he had said, "this is it."

Kogan had agreed. "Hey," he had said, "save a pill for me."

The nurses were saying sleepy and tearful farewells. Kogan glanced at his watch. They were already behind schedule; takeoff was just thirty minutes away. They were cutting it close.

He heard the sound of a car. The LaSalle came down the narrow road toward them, moving too fast in the dark for safety. *Must be Burke with Babcock*, he thought.

The big sedan screeched to a halt. Willie jumped out and ran toward Kogan. His face was white and sweating.

"General..." he gasped. "Babcock's gone!"

Kogan grabbed him by the shoulders. "What the hell are you talking about?"

Words tumbled from Burke's mouth. "I'm not sure what happened, sir." His face was agonized. "The Filipino guard had passed out. There was an empty rum bottle and two glasses on the table in the shack. I think Babcock got him drunk."

"Where he is now?" Kogan tried to keep his voice calm.

"No idea, sir."

Sylvia Kruloff had joined them, tucking strands of hair under her cap. She looked at them, her expression curious. "What's happened?"

Kogan ignored the question and looked at Marie. "This doesn't make sense. Babcock knows we're taking off at four-thirty. I don't think there's anything in the world that could keep him away from that plane." Even as he spoke the words, he remembered Von Porten's analysis of Babcock—borderline sociopath, monumental ego, completely confident that the plane was there only for his personal use.

Sylvia laughed at his words. "Roger Babcock? There's only one thing I can think of that would keep him away, and it serves him right. He deserves to miss the plane."

Marie grabbed his arm. "Oh, Joe," she said quickly. "Let's get another nurse to go in his place."

The truth was coming closer. There was no way to avoid it now. "Sorry." Kogan didn't have time to explain. "I'm under orders to get Babcock out of here. He's all-important. We can't leave without him." Her shocked face told him she didn't understand.

Kogan whirled toward Sylvia. "Look," he rasped. "You said you knew what he might be up to. For God's sake, where is he?"

Her smile had disappeared. "I don't know, General. But I've worked with him, and my guess is he's with a woman. He had the worst reputation in Manila. He's supposed to be... well, insatiable."

Kogan looked at his watch. It was 4:17. He pulled out the tiny radio and flipped it open. "Jake, you read me?" he intoned. The women's eyes widened at the small instrument.

Longford's voice came back clearly. "Joe, what's up? We're running close to the wire."

"Is Babcock there?" Kogan asked, knowing the answer and dreading it.

"Ooooh, shit!" Longford's groan came over the radio. "Don't tell me he's missing."

"Yeah. We've got to start hunting, right now."

"Sunrise soon. You need us to help?"

"No!" Kogan's voice was rough. "Stay on the plane. I don't want people scattered. We're about to send the nurses to the plane. Let me know if Babcock shows up there."

"If he does, I'm going to . . ." Longford didn't finish his threat. "Before you sign off, Joe, I've got more bad news. Larry's been monitoring the tactical net here. There's a report that Jap troops are moving in from the south, not too far away."

That stunned Kogan. What the hell was going on? He had checked the map. The red arrow on the acetate couldn't—*wouldn't* get to Del Monte before noon. "What do you mean, not too far away?" he barked at Longford.

"Dunno, and I don't want to hang around to find out."

Kogan snapped the radio cover shut and jammed it in his pocket. The only possible way any unit could have covered that much jungle terrain would be not to stop or to sleep—and that must be the answer. If ordered to, Jap infantry could outmarch a Roman legion.

He tried to think calmly. Time was running out. Maybe it *had* run out. That damned Zero would be here at first light. Japanese ground troops were closing in. He had screwed up, no doubt about it. He had relied too heavily on the history books. He hadn't realized what a job old *Sucker One* could do on history.

Marie was looking at him, her eyes questioning. Off to one side, he saw Von Porten with Sylvia Kruloff. They were carrying on a conversation in low tones. With a part of his mind, Kogan noted that they made a good-looking pair. He was tall and slim, with precise features, and she was pretty. Sure, dumbo, up to your ass in crocodiles and thinking what a cute couple. He shook his head to clear it.

"Where's Colonel Edmonds?" he asked Burke.

"At the command post, sir."

"Get over there and tell him I want an immediate search of all buildings in this compound. Tell him to have his men look for Dr. Roger Babcock."

The lieutenant headed for the car, then stopped. From far away came the faint drone of an aircraft engine. Willie squinted into the darkened sky. "Jeeze, General," he said. "He's getting here early today."

Shengo cut the power to his engine and slowly spiraled down to examine the dark field below. In accordance with the new orders, he was on station thirty minutes early, and as he had expected, even his sharp eyes could not distinguish the position of the camouflaged plane. There were some small lights in the buildings to the west of the airstrip, however. Flashlights, he surmised, and a small thrill went through him. Perhaps the Americans were preparing for a predawn takeoff! He turned at the north end of the strip and flew back over the plane's position, but he could see no activity. He continued on, across the grass plains of the plateau, toward the Katanglad Mountains, increasing power to climb in a wide circle back to await the dawn.

Now the anger and frustration he had felt yesterday disappeared. He was in his element. Sitting at the controls of his beloved Zero was akin to being in the arms of a responsive and lovely woman. The plane was gentle and sensitive, with a great heart that throbbed at his touch. Understanding and intelligent, it responded to the suggestive pressures of his hands, ever forgiving of the few mistakes he made. His Zero was the very best plane in the world, Shengo was convinced.

He looked down over the edge of his cockpit at the field. Some details were visible. Soon it would be light.

Colonel Edmonds's eyes were red-rimmed and his cheeks gray-stubbled. The last three days had added years to his age.

"General," he said as he saluted. "I've got the provost marshal looking for Babcock." He jerked a thumb in the direction of the sky. "Well, you can't take off anyway. Our friend from Davao is here."

Kogan nodded, but he felt fear creep over him. Things could go from bad to irretrievable, depending upon how Edmonds answered his next question. "You got any reports that the Japs are getting close to Del Monte?"

"Afraid so," Edmonds replied. "Estimated company-sized unit is coming in from the south."

Oh, boy, that was it. Enemy above and enemy below. The swamp waters were beginning to rise. "Colonel," Kogan said. "That fighter up there means we're not going to be able to take off until tonight. It's absolutely imperative you hold the Japs off for that long."

Edmonds's heavy chin jutted out and he bit off his words. "General, that's exactly what we've been trying to do ever since they landed."

It *was* a stupid thing for him to say. He suspected that Edmonds believed Kogan's sudden concern with stopping the Japs was to save his own skin.

"Let me explain," Kogan said hastily. "Our ship is an experimental model. It can't be captured by the Japs. It would damage the entire war effort."

Edmonds seemed to accept that. "Well, we have a battalion of the Sixty-second Infantry in reserve. They're fairly close. I'll see if General Sharp will release them to cover approaches from the south." He looked at his watch. "If so, we could have them in place soon—maybe by eight. If the Jap unit is only company size, we might be able to hold them off."

"Good," Kogan said, relief sweeping over him. If the Japanese could be stalled through the daylight hours, things might work out. He added, "And please keep your people looking for Babcock."

Edmonds turned to leave, but stopped as a weapons carrier came bouncing down the road. Major Thomas jumped out and saluted. He spoke, his words running together. "Colonel Edmonds, Japs-less-than-a-mile-away-crossing-Mangima-Canyon-heading-toward-the-strip."

"Have they crossed yet?"

"No, sir." Major Thomas exhaled. "They're still on the other side."

Kogan grabbed Edmonds's shoulder. "What's that mean? How soon will they be here?"

"The canyon's a tough piece of terrain. Take them an hour to cross, another thirty minutes to get here. Hour and a half, maybe more."

Kogan checked his watch. "You're saying the Japs could be here by six-thirty. You've got to get that battalion here on the double."

Major Thomas's head snapped up. "What battalion is that, sir?"

"Third Battalion, Sixty-second, damnit," Edmonds answered. "Our Force reserve."

"We have no Force reserve, Colonel," Thomas said slowly. "Twenty minutes ago, General Sharp committed the battalion along the road to Cagayan. They've already left."

That did it. SUCCOR had tumbled around his ears. It wasn't a question of Babcock, or B-juice, or a dying president any longer. Very soon, events would decide whether they got back to their own time, or would have to destroy the plane and spend the next three and a half years working in a Jap POW camp. The smart money had to be on digging coal.

Kogan had used his radio to notify Longford. "Jake," he spoke into the little instrument, "in a little while we either take off or we blow the plane up."

"What the hell—?"

"Listen to me. The Japs are getting real close. Ken Edmonds asn't anything to stop them. In an hour, maybe a little more, they could be here."

"What're we gonna do? That goddamn Zero's got us pinned down."

"Talk to the crew. Explain it to them. See what they want to do."

"Hey, Joe, for chrissakes, this is your command."

Kogan took a deep breath and kept his voice even. "Thanks for reminding me. All I want is some input from you people. It's your lives, too. You understand me?"

Longford's answer came slowly. "Yeah, sure. Sorry. Anything else?"

"Have Hortha at the nurses' bungalow in ten minutes. Whatever happens, we can't chance taking the nurses aboard. I may not be here, I don't know. But someone's going to have to explain that to them."

It was 0515 when Hortha showed up and they walked into the bungalow. As they entered, Von Porten was sitting in the corner of the living room with Sylvia. He got to his feet and placed a hand gently on her shoulder, then walked over to join Kogan.

"Nurses not going, are they?" Von Porten let his eyes drift back toward Sylvia as he asked the question. Kogan shook his head.

The women sat obediently around the room, some on the rattan chairs, others at the table. Except for Marie and the other three chosen to go, the rest were still in their pajamas and robes. Some of them were wrapping handkerchiefs around their pinned-up hair.

Marie Crane peered around at the group, her lips moving as she counted. "We're missing someone," she said. "Anyone know who?"

"Claudia's not here," Betty MacNeil said. "She's probably in the latrine."

Marie turned and nodded readiness at Kogan.

"Ladies," he began, stealing a glance at his watch. "Maybe you've heard. The Japs are moving into the Del Monte area."

He stopped to let that sink in. Reactions varied. Some of the women went pale; one or two affected nonchalance; there was a notable increase in the puffing of cigarettes. "If you listen closely," he continued, "you will hear the sound of the Zero that has been patrolling over this airfield for the past few days. Unfortunately, it arrived this morning earlier than usual. I'm sorry to say that makes it virtually impossible for us to leave without being shot down."

Marie Crane spoke. "Joe—" She caught herself. "Sir, can General Sharp's troops stop the Japs?"

He might as well be honest. It was going to happen very soon. "No," Kogan said, "the Japs can't be stopped."

She clenched her hands together. He could see strain clouding her blue eyes. "If the Japs are that close, then the bomber coming from Melbourne won't be able to land, will it?"

Jesus, he'd forgotten the bomber. "No, Captain Crane, I'm afraid it won't. I'm real sorry about that. Things have moved just too fast."

A slight woman with close-cropped hair that made her look like a handsome boy stabbed her cigarette out so viciously the brass ashtray slid off the table. The clatter was the only sound in the room.

A stout nurse sitting at the end of the table raised her hand. "Sir, we heard that your plane was an experimental model. We thought . . . we hoped that maybe it might be able to get away from the Jap."

Kogan didn't answer her directly. He turned to Hortha. "Major, would you care to reply to that?"

There was a little stir among the nurses as Hortha came forward. His hair was mussed and he was unshaven, but if his male looks suffered from it, the women didn't seem to notice. "It's true," he began. "Our plane *is* an experimental model and it will fly faster than the transport planes now in service. But the pilot of the Zero will be watching us closely. The moment we start moving down the runway, he'll be on us like a hawk on a chicken."

"Are you saying, Major," Sylvia Kruloff said, "that you won't be able to take off at all?"

Hortha hesitated, then glanced at Kogan for help.

"Well," Kogan began. *Oh, boy, this is the tough one. This is the one I wish I had the answer to.* "I doubt it. We—that is, the crew—will get aboard and see what happens. If the Jap goes off station, or..." He couldn't think of another possibility. "...or something else develops, we might give it a try."

"Couldn't we go aboard with you?" It was Sylvia again.

"No," he said firmly. To be wishy-washy would only invite debate. Besides, he had thought it over. It was true that the four doomed women would die sometime within the next three years in Santo Tomás, but considering what *Sucker One* faced in the air over Del Monte, they would die this morning if he took them aboard. Maybe giving up one's life one way was better than another, but it wasn't his decision to make. Another three years of living, even under the unspeakable conditions of internment, was what fate had decreed for these women. Were he to present the facts to them right now, he believed that's what they would choose. Maybe—he let his mind range as he considered it—the nurses, using their professional training, might save other people's lives in Santo Tomás.

He decided to give the nurse named Sylvia more detail. "You see, we must keep the plane from falling into the hands of the Japs. If a chance appears, no matter how marginal, we'll go for broke."

He saw instant confusion on their faces. "I mean we'll gamble on taking off," he amended, and hurried on. "Even if the odds are...well, not good. You wouldn't want to be along."

"You mean," Marie spoke up, her tone accusatory, "you'll take off even if it's suicidal."

Kogan glanced at his watch. He wondered about that Jap ground unit. It would be struggling across the canyon about now. Better start breaking this thing up.

"Oh, no." He tried for a cheerful smile. "We're as anxious to keep on living as you are. Now, ladies—"

"I have one more question, General," the stout nurse interrupted. "As I see it, you're offering us a choice between a very dangerous, life-threatening flight out of here or an indefinite period in a POW camp. My question is this: as a general officer, how long do *you* think this war will last? We've heard a year or even less. Do you agree?"

He guessed he'd have to lean on her or they could chat this thing up indefinitely. "You haven't been listening, Lieutenant," he said, his tone stern, taking himself out as the kindly, avuncular figure. "You don't have a choice. You're not going aboard that plane. We won't risk your lives. As to your question about the war..." For an instant he was tempted to say yes, it will be over soon, but to hell with that. "I can't say how long you'll be captive." He'd leave it there.

"Well," a voice from one side of the room said wistfully. "I certainly don't like being a prisoner, but if it's only for a few months..."

═══ CHAPTER EIGHTEEN ═══

Rodale replaced the phone. "That was Congressman Collines," he said to Passmore. "They got Pyle to hold off until Monday, then the roof falls in." He watched the security director's shoulders slump as he turned toward the window, where in the distance beyond the Tidal Basin, the white dome of the Jefferson Memorial pressed gently against the sky. He didn't see any of the scenery, Rodale knew, for the view from that particular window had long ago ceased to charm either of them.

Passmore swung around. "Does the president know?"

"Yeah. Collines said Senator Moser spoke to Moody a few minutes ago."

"Damnit, Chief, why haven't we heard from CINCPAC?" Then he threw his hand out in disgust at his own question.

"Forget it," he said, walking to the door. "But okay, what *has* happened to SUCCOR? I thought they were supposed to be back before now."

"That's what we hoped." Rodale sighed. "But it was a long shot to begin with. Who knows? They either didn't get back there, or if they did, something bad happened. Maybe the technology screwed up somewhere along the line."

Passmore started to open the door, but Rodale held up his hand. "Wait a minute, Bill." He tapped a pencil on his desk, getting his thoughts in order.

"Let's just assume that right now we get word SUCCOR's back and B-juice is on its way here. Suppose certain people try to stop it. Have you got a contingency plan for that?"

The agent smiled. It seemed to Rodale that for the first time in a long while, Passmore looked happy.

"Yes, sir," he said cheerfully. "From Pearl to here, it's up to Admiral Jefferson Edwards, and he won't drop the ball. From Andrews Air Force Base to the White House, it's up to me."

"Well? You think they'll make a move?"

Passmore's smile grew into a wide grin. "I know they will." He winked at the chief of staff and left.

Del Monte Field, Philippines

May 2, 1942, 0552 Hours

Von Porten and John Hortha had returned to the plane.

Kogan and Marie stood in front of the bungalow. The LaSalle drove up, throwing dust still heavy with the morning dew high in the air. Willie Burke jumped out and saluted Kogan.

"I'm sorry, sir," he said, his young face worried. "We haven't been able to find Dr. Babcock."

"Keep looking, Lieutenant," Kogan said. "Tell Edmonds to put every man he can spare on the job."

After the LaSalle disappeared down the road, Marie put her hand on Kogan's arm. "It's that B-juice, isn't it?"

"What?" He was distracted. "Oh . . . yeah, it is." Babcock suddenly didn't seem very important. He wanted to open the radio and call Longford, although he was pretty sure that he knew what the crew would decide—or maybe he didn't. But he damn well knew what *he* wanted—to take a chance, get the hell out of 1942 and back home, or die trying.

Whichever, the next hour would decide.

Marie seemed to read his thoughts. "If you can't take off, what difference does it make whether you find Babcock?"

"I don't know. But if there's any way for us to get out of here, we'd better have him along." He turned her to face him. "I guess, Marie, it's time to say good-bye."

To his surprise, she pulled away from him, though her wistful smile stayed in place. She edged toward the Dodge pickup Edmonds had left behind. "Let me go to the plane with you? Please?"

He paused, thinking, trying to balance crises and possibilities. Last night things had seemed simple—put Babcock and the women on the plane and get out of here. Now, just getting out—even for the plane and crew—was becoming more improbable every minute. There were Japs in the air, and Japs on the ground. Why not spend a few last minutes with Marie?

He put his arm around her shoulders and squeezed. "Okay, sure." They got into the old truck. After some trouble getting the gearshift into low, he drove slowly toward the south end of the runway. A hundred yards down the road, he braked to a stop in front of his quarters. Forgetting to use the clutch, he killed the engine.

"Why are you stopping here?"

"Gotta pick something up." His briefcase was there, containing all the fake letters and orders. He didn't dare leave them behind.

Jumping out, he climbed the stairs to the porch and walked into the big living room.

Babcock was there.

Nude, he stood bent-kneed behind a naked woman braced against the bed for his thrusts. Neither saw Kogan standing in the door. The woman's head was down between her arms, her blond, tousled hair hanging over her face, her small breasts swaying. Babcock took a gulp from a bottle of rum without varying the rhythm of his sexual jabs. Kogan must have made a noise, but he wasn't conscious of it. Babcock turned his head. He grinned and raised the bottle in a drunken salute, then looked down at the woman.

"Hey, honey," he said, his words slurred. "We got company— a general. Ain't that nice?"

The woman's startled face peered through her hair at Kogan, then with a shriek, she lunged forward onto the bed, grabbed a pillow, and covered her head. Babcock stood gaping boozily at her, his erection going flaccid, then he extended the bottle toward Kogan.

"Have a drink, General."

Kogan's face was impassive as he approached Babcock, wrenched the rum bottle from the doctor's hand, and smashed it against the wall. His open hand came from the vicinity of his hip with all the power he could muster, lashing across the doctor's face with a crack like that of a handgun. Babcock whirled across the room, crashed through a chair and table, and fell crumpled into a corner, barely conscious, scrabbling around on the floor like a white crab. In a blind fury, Kogan grabbed his pistol hanging on the wall and levered a round into the chamber. So *Sucker One* gets blown away and the crew killed or captured because this son of a bitch had to hump a slut. He drew a bead on Babcock's head and saw a look of terror wash the drunken expression away. He squeezed the trigger ever so gently and the hammer arced slowly back. Just a little more pressure and it would slam forward to strike the firing pin. Babcock screamed incoherently.

Kogan snickered in contempt. He thumbed the hammer back to its safety position. God, seeing that expression of terror on

Babcock's face had been good therapy. He thrust the pistol into his waistband. Picking up a pair of trousers in one hand, he tossed a pitcher of water directly into Babcock's face, then threw the clothing at him. "Okay, asshole," he grated. "Ten seconds, then I start kicking your butt from here to the plane."

Blood running down his chin, Babcock jammed his legs into the trousers. Her head still covered, the woman sobbed on the bed.

Longford pulled out his checklist. "Let's get with it," he said.

"You're not planning to take off with that guy overhead, are you?" Hortha jerked his thumb at the sky.

"Maybe not, but we'd better be ready for anything."

Longford had told Von Porten and Witkowski to keep an eye open on the port and starboard sides. Betts and Hiraga were standing by the hatchway. Hortha flipped on the 287. Immediately a flood of Japanese came through the pilots' earphones.

"Otis," Longford called. "We may have the Zero on the radio. Set your frequency to . . . 798 kilocycles."

Hiraga put on earphones and listened for a moment. "You're right. He's talking to his base."

"Can you understand him?" Longford asked.

"Some of it . . . most of it. He's talking fast. I have to pick up on his intonation and rhythm."

"Hang in there," Longford said. "It's important I know what he says." He and Hortha went to work again. By the time they had completed their check-off, Longford yelled back at Hiraga. "What do you think?" he asked. "Any clue as to what he intends to do?"

Hiraga came up to the cockpit and shook his head. "Not yet— the transmissions are kind of cryptic. I've got the feeling, though, that the Zero's not out to gun us down. They want this plane intact."

The cockpit was silent. Hortha suddenly began to thump his fist on his knee, the beat increasing with every blow.

"What the hell's wrong with you?" Longford asked.

Hortha spoke softly, almost as if to himself. "Orders to take the plane would come from the top—probably some general."

"Kawaguchi—a major general," Longford said. "I remember Joe mentioning his name."

"If the general wants the plane," Hortha continued in his monotone, "and you're a Zero pilot patrolling overhead, what are you going to do if, say, the plane moves into position to take off?"

Longford thought about it, then nodded his head. "Yeah. You're not going to blast it—at least, not right away. You definitely want to keep the general happy, so you're gonna try to discourage the plane from taking off." He grinned at Hortha. "Might work."

"I don't get it," Hiraga said.

"Don't worry," Longford said, his hands going to the controls. "Stay on that radio. I want to know everything the guy says."

Wide-eyed, Marie watched Kogan manhandle Babcock out of the hut. The doctor landed in the back of the pickup with a thump and a groan. Kogan got in and settled back in the seat with a sigh.

"Was he with Claudia?" Marie asked.

Kogan nodded, his jaw muscles corded as he bottled up a stream of curses that would have shocked this 1940s woman. He stepped on the starter and the engine roared to life. His hand grasped the gearshift, maneuvered it about, then stopped. He draped his arms over the wheel and leaned forward, his chin resting on his forearms, contemplating the narrow dirt road paralleling the runway.

"Marie, maybe you'd better get out here. There's no point in coming all the way down to the plane. You'd just have to drive this damn clunker back."

There was a banging on the cab window. Babcock's angry voice reached them. "Come on," he snarled, "let's get to the goddamn plane."

Kogan stuck his head out the door. "One more word out of you, and I'll run your ass all the way there." He turned back to Marie. "Well?"

"Don't worry about me and this old clunker, as you call it. I can drive it better than you can." She reached out and clutched his arm with both hands. Her expression was pleading. "Please, Joe, I want to say something to you. Drive slow—we can talk on the way." She withdrew her hands and placed them on her knees, examining them intently. "I'm going to have to swallow my pride again."

He finally got the truck in gear and they bounced down the road. "That seems all I've been doing since I met you. I've told you how I feel about you. You've told me—not in so many words, perhaps—that you don't feel the same way. You don't return my, well . . . you know."

"Marie—"

"No, let me talk, please." She kept her face down as though she couldn't bear looking at him. "I'm not riding along with you for these extra few moments." Her chuckle had a forlorn sound. "Although they may be the last we ever spend together. I'm begging you, Joe, not to fly against that Zero. I watched your face in the bungalow. You don't have a chance of getting away from that plane, yet I know as surely as I love you that you're going to try it."

He reached out and took her hand. Her fingers clasped his fiercely. "Listen." He tried to make his tone light. "I don't know that myself. Like I said back there, we're not suicidal. If we can't make it, we won't go."

"Yes, you will, Joe. In your mind and heart, you know you will. There's something pushing you, a strange and powerful something I don't understand. But don't, please don't, give in to it. Stay on the ground. Save your life and the lives of your crew. Surrender to the Japs. Become a POW—it will only be for a few months. Who knows? Maybe after this is all over we can have some time together."

He started to answer, but the radio squawked. Longford's voice came through sharply.

"Joe, listen to me. There are Japs all around us."

Kogan pulled the truck over and cut the engine. That was it. The operation was over. He stared at the tiny set in his hand, noting the black matte finish, the luminescent glow of the battery power light—late-twentieth-century technology, like the big plane sitting out there. And a helluva lot of good either was doing them now. Maybe this was all a goddamn nightmare. If so, he wanted to wake up real quick.

But maybe Jake had made a mistake.

"You sure they're not Filipino troops?" He sensed Marie leaning closer for Longford's response.

"Listen, Joe, I've seen too many World War II movies not to recognize those little suckers—"

"Okay, okay," Kogan cut him off before Marie could hear more. "All right," he said wearily. "Have Betts set the destruct system for ten minutes, then come out of the plane with your hands up."

"No, wait, damnit," Longford spoke fiercely. "We can see them moving around in the trees, about fifty, sixty yards away. They seem to be sizing up the situation. Listen, maybe we can get you aboard."

"Yeah, sure." The monosyllable reflected what he thought of that. "Jake, why prolong it? Even if I get aboard, we don't have a chance of putting that baby into the air."

"But we do, old buddy," Longford hissed the words through the transmitter. "We really do. We've picked up the Zero's frequency. Otis is listening to him. Hortha's got a plan that just might get us home!" He stopped transmitting and waited.

"Joe?"

Kogan was thinking—not only of Sucker One, its crew, and the president of the United States, but of Marie. If what Jake said had any validity, maybe she *wouldn't* have to die in that damned camp.

"Yeah, Jake, I hear you." He checked his watch. For once it was running. "In exactly two minutes, I'm getting under way and I'll be coming fast."

"We'll be watching for you. Out."

Kogan flipped his transmitter cover shut.

Marie moved on the seat beside him. "Joe, please . . . can't you see it's too late? Don't try to take off."

"You heard him. We've got a chance. And you've got a chance. What do you say?"

She gasped a wordless sound of disbelief. "Joe, I love you, but I don't want to die with you. That plane of yours doesn't have a chance. I watched the Zeros sweep our fighters right out of the sky over Bataan. You don't know how fast and quick they are."

"I've got something to tell you." He didn't know what he was going to say, but whatever it was, he had to say it fast. "Remember your feeling that I know the future? Well, I do. Believe that. Every American here will be either killed or taken prisoner. Every nurse will be interned in camps on Luzon. Some will survive, and others . . . won't." He stopped speaking, unsure of what to say next.

She laughed, a thin, almost hysterical sound. "I think this is a cheap trick to get me on board that plane. But why, Joe? If you have any feelings at all for me, you wouldn't want to risk my life. Look, I'm sorry I said you could foretell the future. I know that's impossible. But don't try to get me to go with you."

His mouth set in a grim line. "I do care for you, Marie, far more than you know. But there's a reason why I couldn't tell you. So listen carefully, here's more future. This war is going to last nearly another four years, but America will win. In 1950 there will be another, called the Korean War. Almost twenty years later we'll be in another war in Vietnam." He shot a look at her. "In *that* war, I'll be a very young lieutenant."

There was silence beside him. He glanced at her white face,

her eyes bewildered and filling with tears. He knew she was trying to comprehend his senseless words, the impossible dates and meaningless events. And there was no way she could—it was too much, too illogical for any sane person to grasp. Either he was crazy, or she was.

He couldn't delay any longer. He started the engine.

She choked out a question. "What in God's name are you saying?"

"You know why I can't use the damned shift on this truck? I've never used one before. It's an antique where I come from. Hell, it's older than I am. I was . . . will be . . . born May 10, 1948."

"Oh—" She buried her face in her lap.

Babcock pounded on the window. "Come on, you two, stop all the damn talk and let's get to the plane!" Marie began to cry, muffled, desperate sobs.

Kogan depressed the accelerator and the truck lurched down the road. "Listen to me!" he shouted over the noise of the engine. "I said some of you will survive POW camp." He stopped, dreading having to say the words, but knowing he had to. "You won't."

He looked down at her bent head. "Did you hear me?" he yelled. "I said, you won't."

The red curls gave a meager nod.

Kogan fought the old Dodge's wheels in the deep ruts of the road. They were almost there. She could stay or she could go with them. He didn't see that there was much difference now. The odds might be about equal.

"I'm not making this up. I don't have that kind of imagination. So listen to me, Marie Crane. It's true that everyone on that plane may be dead very soon. But that plane can fly a lot faster than the Zero, so there *is* a chance. You understand me?"

Again she nodded, wordlessly.

"All right. If you don't want to come, I'll stop right here and let you out."

Marie raised her head and wiped her damp cheeks with the back of her hand. She kept her eyes fixed on the narrow, rutted road. "I don't understand . . . God help me, I just don't understand."

Time was getting short. "Well?" His voice was brutal.

"Keep going," she said.

It had been a busy field, Shengo recalled, in the early weeks of the war—the B-17s hastily fleeing Luzon for the safety of Australia, the remnants of P-40 squadrons shuttling in and out, and even a few civilian planes ferrying supplies to Corregidor. Then it was possible to chalk up a victory almost weekly. Now, as he looked at the empty field in dim, predawn light, he realized sadly that glory had passed him by.

He cast another glance downward and his bored expression changed to galvanized attention. Less acute eyesight might not have noticed a pattern of traffic to the west side of the airstrip. Every few moments, vehicles would roll along the jungle trails like ants, converging on one place near a small hillock heavily covered with vegetation.

Shengo dipped one wing and took his Zero-sen down in a shallow dive for a better look. As he flew low over the area he could see the dim trace of a footpath through the trees, and in the few seconds it took for him to flash by, a pale face glanced up at him before quickly vanishing through a dark opening.

Shengo grinned in satisfaction. He was positive that he had discovered the American general's command post! At the proper time he would report the information to his headquarters, thus adding worth to the name of Shengo.

He looked at his watch. It was nearly five. Another few hours and he would return to Davao. He would spend some time with his crew chief fine-tuning the Zero and preparing it for their next leap into the sky. He glanced down at the field. He could see the camouflaged plane almost as clearly as if the covering net were not there.

A few hundred yards north of the plane, figures scurried up

and down the trail leading to the hidden command post. The Americans were panicking.

A vehicle moving at high speed caught his eye—a truck racing through the forest toward the plane! It could mean that an attempted takeoff was imminent. This should be reported to headquarters.

He flipped his radio transmitter button. Using the call letters KD for Headquarters, Naval Air Kokutai, Davao, he spoke: "KD, this is Senki three-two." *Senki,* meaning "War Spirit," was his squadron's proud name.

The response was immediate. "Senki three-two, transmit."

"Passengers may be loading aboard transport plane. Takeoff could commence at any time."

There was a short delay. "Has the plane moved to takeoff position?"

"KD, negative."

"Continue to carry out your mission. Keep us informed." Davao signed off.

Shengo pushed the stick forward and went down for a closer look, flying low over the transport plane. There was no one on the ground near it and the hatches were closed. He could even see the propellers—they seemed too small for those strange, huge nacelles—standing motionless. As he zoomed over the end of the strip, he saw a thin file of brown-clad soldiers moving cautiously through the trees toward the west side of the airstrip.

Japanese infantry! General Kawaguchi was going to get this fine transport plane for his own.

He circled and flew back over the field. The vehicle might arrive at the plane before the troops did; he was not certain on that point. He could strafe the truck, but why should he do it? He was a warrior of the sky, and indiscriminate killing did not please him. Besides, if the vehicle carried passengers, their trip to the plane was futile. He would keep the transport plane on the ground until the troops arrived. His instructions were clear on that point. He began to fly tight circles, observing the scene below him closely.

• • •

"Damnit." Longford squirmed irritably in his seat. "Where is Kogan? He said he'd be here in two minutes."

From the passenger compartment a hoarse voice yelled, "Japs outside!"

Witkowski dashed forward and confirmed the warning. "That's right, Skipper. They're in the edge of the trees on the port side."

Longford looked quickly to his left. He could see mustard-colored uniforms moving among the trees and the dull glint of rifle barrels.

"Okay, you and Betts stand by to open the hatch." He grabbed the radio transmitter.

"Joe," he called. "You hear me?"

After a second's hesitation, Kogan's voice came over the radio. "Yeah, we're nearly there and we've got Babcock."

"Great." Longford's tone indicated that there were higher priorities now. "Now, listen to me. Japs moving in closer, but you may still be able to make it. When we spot you coming we'll get the ladder down, but hit the ground running and get aboard fast. They may try to take the plane while the hatch is open."

Kogan, driving furiously, yelled out the window of the Dodge. "Babcock! When we get to the plane, Marie goes up the ladder first, then you. Get ready to jump when we get there." Then he got back on the radio to Longford.

"Almost there, Jake. Tell the boys to keep their goddamn pistols in their holsters, you understand me? Don't try any heroics or you'll get us all killed."

Accelerating dangerously over the dirt road, the truck bounced and weaved as it sped closer to the revetment. Kogan yelled to Marie, without taking his eyes from the road. "Get your door open when we round the tail of the plane. When I say *jump*, I want to see you fly."

He fought with the wheel as the truck turned off the road and plunged under the green canopy of netting. The vehicle skidded past the tail and slowed as it approached the forward hatch. The ladder hit the ground simultaneously. Betts and Witkowski stood in the open hatchway, their arms reaching out as if to pull the latecomers up the ladder by sheer force of will.

From the other side of the clearing, a dozen soldiers burst out of the trees and dashed at the plane, shouting torrents of Japanese.

"Jump!" Kogan yelled. Marie, her feet already on the running board, leaped to the ground and started up the ladder. At the same moment, Babcock launched himself from the back of the truck and struck her with shocking force. Marie went to her knees, one hand clutching at the chain futilely, then slipped backwards off the ladder to fall heavily to the ground. Mouth slack with terror, Babcock scrambled up the steps to the hatchway.

Kogan catapulted himself from the truck toward her, conscious of the rushing footsteps of the pursuing Japanese so close behind that he could hear their labored breathing. As he lifted Marie with one arm, a Japanese soldier grabbed her and yanked her struggling figure from his grasp. Kogan lunged at the man as another soldier jumped on his back. Reaching back, Kogan grabbed the man's helmet and threw him crashing against the side of the plane. Turning, he smashed his fist into the face of the soldier dragging Marie away, and as the man fell, grabbed Marie and frantically leaped for the ladder. He reached it, but too late. A rifle butt hit him between his shoulder blades with stunning force. He fell to his knees. Two Japanese again pulled Marie, crying and fighting furiously, from his weakened grasp. Roaring with frustration, Kogan got to his feet and staggered toward Marie and her captors, his right arm outstretched, while his left hand fumbled for the pistol in his waistband.

It was a futile, dangerous gesture, one that he'd warned Longford against, but he'd used the last of his strength. All he had left was bitter anger that it was ending like this. Kogan waved the gun defiantly above his head.

From behind him, a Japanese officer shouted a war cry as he raised his sword and swung it down at Joe's head. Marie screamed and, breaking away, threw herself against Kogan, knocking him to one side as the shining sword swished downward. The blade struck Kogan's outstretched left arm a few inches below the shoulder, sweeping through skin, sinew, and bone without slackening its speed. The arm, with the hand still clutching the pistol, thumped heavily to the ground.

For a moment there was quiet, with even the soldiers' jabbering silenced. Then Marie pulled desperately at the web belt to her trousers, her racking sobs breaking the silence.

In the hatchway, Witkowski and Betts stood, their mouths agape, their faces shocked. With a wordless shout, Witkowski started down the ladder. Betts grabbed him from behind, locking his arm around Witkowski's neck, and wrestled him back to the hatchway. A soldier leveled his rifle at the struggling men, but an officer struck down the weapon and slapped the man across the face.

Kogan sank to his knees, his face ashen with shock. He held the stump of his left arm in his right hand, and as the blood spurted through his fingers, screamed hoarsely at the plane. "Get out of here, damn you! Take off!" Then he fell forward, senseless.

Betts, his face white, stumbled into the cockpit. "Jake, they got the nurse and Joe. He's sliced up bad."

Longford had seen most of it, watching from the cockpit window, his body moving as if watching a prizefight. He was helpless, the crew was helpless, and the stakes were too high for dumb heroics. They had lost Joe Kogan, but Babcock was aboard—that son of a bitch would talk now if he had to twist his fucking head off, but it wasn't going to do them a lot of good unless Hortha's plan worked. He peered through the cockpit window, looking for the Zero.

Witkowski stuck his head in. "The Japs have dragged them into the trees, Jake."

A small spark of hope flared. Kogan might still be alive. He might still be rescued. "Larry, get on the command frequency.

Tell them what's happened." Longford's hands moved rapidly over the instruments as he spoke. "We need some troops over here, pronto. Tell them General Kogan's life depends on it."

Hiraga came into the cockpit. "What are we going to do? Won't be long before the Japs storm the plane." Longford noticed again how naturally Otis used the word *Japs*.

Hiraga started away, then turned back. "You really think you can get us out of here?"

"We're going to give it a shot. This is gonna be a long, hard day," Longford answered.

He wasn't used to being in command of this operation, and God, how he wished Joe could have gotten aboard. It was hard to think of such a vital guy lying there in the bushes, his blood seeping into the earth of another world, losing his life there. Well, there was no guarantee that within minutes that Zero wouldn't scatter *their* bodies all over the surface of this weird place. They'd find out soon enough.

Hortha peered out the starboard window. "Jesus, they're screwing around with our propellers!" Both pilots watched in fascination as sweating troops draped the props with thick jungle vines. The soldiers finished their task and stood in front of their work, grinning triumphantly.

"Go ahead, Jake." Witkowski stuck his head in. "Blow those props off right in their faces."

Longford leaned forward to get a better glimpse. "Nope. Let 'em think they've got us stopped. I don't want them to get other ideas, like cutting our tires."

"Kokutai Davao, this is Senki three-two. Our troops have surrounded the transport plane."

"Senki three-two. Excellent. Has the plane crew surrendered?"

"From my position it is difficult to tell, but I do not believe so."

"Very well, Senki three-two. We suggest you make a low pass to remind the personnel of the transport plane that you are still there."

Good, Jichiro Shengo told himself, he would enjoy this. He turned his plane and flew north before turning back to line up with the long axis of the airstrip. He dipped the Zero's nose toward the ground and increased power, thrilling to the sensation of speed as the ground raced to meet him. He leveled off close above the fallow green fields of Del Monte, feeling the strain as gravity tugged on his body, then raced in toward the airstrip, coming lower. His spirit exulted as the trees rushed by, their tops above his line of flight. He glanced at his speed indicator—315 knots, close to his maximum. The ground was a blur as he swept proudly by, showing those Americans the speed and skill and daring arrayed against them. A quick glance at the transport as he passed was all he had, but it was enough to make him laugh as he climbed vertically back to his patrol station.

What a clever officer that infantry captain was! Shengo's brief glimpse had shown him troops draping jungle vines over the propellers of the transport. Shengo was familiar with these vines, which grew as thick and tough as rope. The plane commander would not dare to start his engines. That finished it. The crew of the plane had no choice but to surrender. And Jichiro Shengo's job was finished.

He looked at his watch. It was 0610.

The shrill whine of the Zero coming down the strip reached them, roaring to a crescendo, then diminishing as the fighter flashed by them.

"He's hotdogging it, giving us a little warning," Longford said. He turned impatiently in his seat. "Larry, you got an answer on those troops?"

Betts put down his earphones. "Sharp's pulling back that battalion he committed, plus a company of Philippine Scouts. He's gonna make a fight for Del Monte. That should take care of the Jap company moving on the strip. Be more than an hour before the battalion is here, though."

That wrapped it up for *Sucker One*, Longford realized. That hour would probably stretch to two or three. Long before that, the Japs would be prying the hatch open. Enough horsing around.

He spoke into the intercom. "Doc, Mike, get buckled up." He remembered Babcock. "Hey, you guys. Take care of our resident horse's ass." He called to Hiraga. "Otis, you listening to the Zero? I want to know everything he says." Hiraga gave Longford a thumbs-up.

He gave a last look around the clearing. There was no sign of Joe or Marie. He scanned the sky for the fighter plane.

"Ready, Johnny?"

"Whatever you say, Skipper."

Longford took a deep breath. "If this doesn't work, that guy's gonna be on us like flies on garbage. You got any idea how much time we need to outrun him?"

Hortha's hands flew over the controls. "We're breaking new ground here, Jake. But if we really pump it to her we can reach three hundred fifty knots in under four minutes." He grinned at Longford. "Problem is getting that much time," he said reflectively. "Hey, that's not bad. If I ever write a story about this I'll call it *Four Minutes to Freedom*."

"Hope it isn't four minutes to hell." Longford found it wasn't too hard to manage a grin. "So. Since we don't have much else on for today, let's give it a shot."

Hortha grinned back. "Hey, I'm ready whenever you are."

"Auxiliary power on," Longford commanded.

"Auxiliary power on."

"Blow the propellers!"

Hortha pushed a button. There were two loud explosions and the propellers, vines attached, sailed out from the engine nacelles and crashed to the ground. Hortha slid his window back and roared, "You're gonna lose this war, goddamn you!"

"Start engines," Longford said.

"Engines started."

The turbines whined for a few seconds, then the engines ignited with a muffled roar. "Keep them at idle," Longford said. "Then we'll move the nose out onto the strip, see what our friend upstairs does."

Running at minimum power, the exhaust from the two engines was still formidable. Japanese soldiers could be seen scrambling frantically from behind the plane.

"How do the engines look, Larry?" Longford asked Betts.

"Good, Skipper, but rev them up a little higher."

"Okay, Johnny, let's move her out, not too far." The engines' noise increased and the jet, for the first time in three days, rolled slowly forward until the nose and forepart of the plane extended out from under the netting. The filtered sunlight in the pilots' compartment changed to a bright glare.

"Let's hold it right here, and see what happens. Keep the engines at sixty percent RPM."

Hiraga yelled, "He's spotted us. He's reporting to Davao."

Casually, Shengo glanced down at the beleaguered transport nearly a mile below, then his eyes widened. The plane had moved! That was impossible. Had the crew started the engines, the vines would have bound the propellers, overheated the engines and destroyed them! But the plane was definitely out from beneath the netting. He had to act, and quickly.

"KD, this is Senki three-two. The transport has moved to a position preparatory to takeoff!"

"Senki three-two, keep the transport on the ground until the troops can take it. This is imperative!"

"KD, I am commencing my dive." Shengo pressed the firing button to test his two 7.7-mm machine guns. The staccato reply satisfied him and he pushed the stick forward. The Zero nosed over and started its dive, gaining speed gradually. Shengo needed accuracy for his shots—the rounds must trace a pattern directly in front of the plane. He sighted through the reticle in his windshield and held down the firing button.

He grinned as he saw the dirt and grass convulse under the impact of hundreds of machine gun bullets. They were exactly where he had aimed them, chewing a rectangle of churned earth right in front of the plane! He released the firing button and pulled back on the stick at the same time. The Zero pulled out nimbly and swung back into the skies overhead.

"KD, dive completed. Warning shots fired." Shengo looked back down at the plane. It had not moved. "The transport remains in position. I do not believe it will attempt to take off." The last phrase was a masterful understatement for which Shengo congratulated himself. Why, after such a warning, would the crew of an unarmed, slow-flying transport commit suicide?

But something troubled him. Could it have been a trick of his imagination or an optical illusion? As he pulled out of his dive he caught a glimpse of the plane's engine nacelles. They held no shreds of hanging vines, but what disturbed him most was that he could see no propellers! It was true that when engines ran fast and the light was poor, propeller blades sometimes were invisible, but these engines must be turning at idle and the propellers were in direct sunlight. Could it be that his eyesight was going bad? He shook his head to clear it. He was not that old— barely twenty-eight—and in excellent physical shape. Except for...well, he would speak to the Kokutai physician about the effects of prolonged celibacy on eyesight.

The turf in front of the 737 was torn and ragged.

"Pretty good shooting, I'd say," Hortha commented dryly. Longford didn't answer. He peered through the windshield, searching the sky for the Jap, weighing the odds. For Hortha's plan to have any chance, they had to draw the Zero down again. Would he come? And if he did, would it be to pound them into the ground with his cannons? Even if they got in the air, could they make it? The Japanese pilot was damn good, a helluva marksman, and he flew the best fighter plane of its time. Longford had studied its capabilities. The Zero could fly 350 MPH in level flight at 15,000 feet, and dive in excess of 450 MPH.

"Jake," Hiraga called out. "Our friend upstairs thinks he's got us stopped."

"How you think we should handle this, Johnny?" Longford asked.

"Timing, Jake—it's all in the timing. We've got to suck him down one more time, then go for it while he's on the deck. Let's hope he doesn't look back." He pointed to the throttle. "Let's move her all the way onto the runway." A wry smile wreathed Hortha's lean face. "And may I make another small suggestion? Keep 'er at right angles to the runway, like we haven't made up our minds."

Longford eased the throttles forward and the big plane lurched onto the runway, but still headed across it. Hortha's idea made sense.

"Otis," Longford called to Hiraga. "Remember, fella, we don't have a reverse gear on this baby. No way we can back up. If he's going to blast us, we've got no choice. We'll have to go for it. So listen good." It would be a suicide move, he had no doubt of that, but to die trying would be better than to sit waiting to be blown away.

Shengo's mind was unsettled as he pointed his plane's nose at a fleecy cloud lighted by the rising sun. The 7.7-mm barrage had certainly convinced the crew of the plane of the futility of taking off, but by doing his job efficiently he had eliminated his chance of shooting an American plane down, unless—he grasped at the thought—the American command at Corregidor had somehow repaired a P-40 or two to fly cover while the transport took off! How marvelous that would be! He scanned the skies hopefully. They were empty. Disappointed, he glanced down at the airfield.

A moment before, only the nose of the plane had edged from

beneath the camouflage. Now, in amazement, he saw the full outline of the transport sitting on the strip. It had moved completely out from beneath the camouflage net!

"Kokutai Davao," he shouted into the transmitter. "The plane has moved onto the airstrip!"

"Senki three-two, is the plane preparing to take off?"

"It is not positioned properly for a takeoff. It is at right angles to the airstrip."

After a moment's delay, Kokutai Davao transmitted again. "Senki three-two, we leave this to your discretion, but with one warning. The plane is not to be destroyed while it is still on the ground."

"KD, I will warn it one last time. This time I will use my cannon. I believe that will keep it on the ground."

"Senki three-two, let us hope so." Davao signed off.

Was that a rebuke? Shengo's ears were sensitive to any slight shading of words that might indicate criticism of his military abilities. He wished that this particular staff officer were here to witness the shooting exhibition that Shengo was about to give. Lying in dark, well-oiled steel cells in the wings of the Zero were hundreds of rounds of 20-mm point-detonating, explosive shells possessing power that could not be denied.

As he nosed the Zero over in a second dive toward the airstrip, Shengo was determined that this powerful fusillade would hit so close to the transport plane that the crew would flee the ship and run panic-stricken into the jungle.

Hiraga listened intently, his hands pressing his earphones tightly to his head. "He's talking, Skipper—*yeooowee*!" Hiraga's voice was triumphant. "He's giving us one last warning! Here he comes!"

"Stomp on those brakes, buddy boy!" Longford yelled to Hortha as he increased power. "Soon's he goes by, we make our move!"

Torn between the opposing pressures of brakes and engine

power, the 737 clutched the ground like a huge, tethered bird. The thunder of its jet engines reverberated across the Bukidnon Plateau, slammed against the mountains beyond, and raised startled heads as far away as Cagayan de Oro. Small trees strained frantically at their roots, the underbrush leaned horizontally, and dust rose a hundred feet in the air as the back blast from thousands of horsepower drove rearward.

Both pilots went rigid in their seats, their feet clamped to the brakes, their faces showing the strain. Longford fought the bucking wheel with one hand, while the other gripped the throttles, advanced to 80 percent power.

Suddenly, twenty feet in front of the plane's nose, the ground erupted as cannon shells plowed into the dirt. In an instant the Zero swept by, then, with a jubilant half roll, pointed its nose at the heavens.

"Kick 'er in the ass!" Longford roared. Releasing the brakes and swinging the plane in a half circle, he pushed the throttles to full power. The big transport jumped, moving so fast that clumps of dirt from the cannon shells fell on its nose. Engines screaming, the plane straightened and thundered down Del Monte field, throwing grass and clumps of mud high in its wake.

CHAPTER NINETEEN

The power of his plane's great engine pressed Shengo's spine against the back of the cockpit as he was once again borne to his station high over the airfield. The smooth growl of the Sakae seemed to congratulate him on his marksmanship, for the fusillade of 20-mm shells had hit very close to the nose of the transport, precisely where he had aimed. One instant's lack of concentration, one quiver of his iron hand on the control stick, and a barrage of shells could have blown up the plane, to the eternal disgrace of the navy air corps, and worse, of Shengo himself. But his aim had been true. The explosive shells, concentrated a few feet in front of the plane, produced an eruption of dirt like that of a small bomb, yet the plane was left undamaged. The scalpel cut of a skilled surgeon could not have been more precise. Shengo was pleased with his analogy.

As the Zero climbed swiftly again toward patrol position, he was confident that his mission had been accomplished. The Americans in the plane must now be stampeding for the exits, mad with fear.

With an easy skill borne of long practice, he rolled the plane through one-half of an outside loop and was on station again. He glanced down at the field and stared again, stunned.

The plane was gone! No, there it was, he saw it now, moving down the runway! And swiftly! He could not believe his eyes—those suicidal Americans were taking off! In the minute it took for Shengo to reach his station, the plane had moved a third of the way down the strip.

Quickly, he flipped his transmitter switch.

"KD, the plane is taking off!"

The seconds seemed interminable before the voice squawked in his ear, "Senki three-two. Destroy it!"

Ah, those words that he had waited so long to hear! The old, detested patrol mission was finished; one more suited to his talents was beginning. He was happy. The unarmed transport plane lying below him, struggling to get into the air, would be his first kill in too long a time.

Lazily, Shengo hit his left rudder and eased over on his stick. Although he did not enjoy killing for the sake of killing, it had been weeks since he had a plane in his gun sights, and he intended to be comfortable with it, perhaps even use the encounter to sharpen his air-to-air marksmanship.

That is how it was that Jichiro Shengo made a serious error in judgment, one that, later in the morning, he remembered with regret. Yet, even his stern conscience admitted it was not one for which he could be harshly faulted, for it was impossible for him to have known the true nature of the plane he pursued.

He descended in wide spirals, dropping slowly, giving the transport time to become airborne, picking in his mind's eye a spot midway between Del Monte and Macajalar Bay for the fatal meeting to occur. He was over the south end of the field, turning north to make his leisurely run, when he saw that the transport—that slow, lumbering aircraft—was off the field!

To his credit, he recognized very quickly that something out of the ordinary was taking place. Among his flotilla mates, the acuteness of his eyesight was legendary; otherwise, he could not have seen from that distance the remarkable speed the transport was making. Even as he watched, the big plane changed direction slightly and headed directly for the sea, its shadow on the jungle below matching the speed of the huge bulk above. No more dallying.

Shengo flipped the Zero into a tight turn, aimed for the transport, and pushed his throttle to a setting that would bring his speed to nearly 250 MPH, but no faster. He did not want to overshoot the transport.

The grass-covered airstrip was smooth enough for a 1940s plane traveling at propeller speeds, but fifty tons of jet bouncing along at full power would have brought screams from even seasoned travelers a half century in the future. Babcock had collapsed, semiconscious from fright and alcohol, held in his seat by his harness.

"You spot the Jap?" Longford asked Betts through the intercom.

"Yeah." In the plexidome, Betts grunted, holding to the braces with a death grip as the plane bounced and swayed. "He's coming down, but not full bore. Seems to be taking his time."

"Get her off at a hundred-ten," Longford yelled to Hortha over the noise of the engines. "We could blow a tire on this stuff."

"One hundred, one-oh-five, one-ten! Rotate!" Hortha yelled back. The jet's big JT8D engines, running at maximum power, roared their defiance across the plateau as the plane leaped into the air.

Longford ordered gear up. "We'll stay low and pour the coal to her," he said. "Move 'er out faster that way." So far, they'd been lucky. The fighter pilot could have looked down, seen them hightailing, and caught them before they got to the end of the runway. But he hadn't. They were still alive and gaining speed with every second.

The plane roared over the end of the strip at 140 knots and flew level, heading for the bay. The ground dropped away as the land sloped to the beaches at Macajalar. Beyond, the waters of the Sulu Sea were turning from cobalt to azure as the sky lightened. Directly below *Sucker One*, on a footpath, a farmer leading a bullock with a mountainous load of firewood turned his startled face up as the howling monster passed just overhead.

"He's gaining," Betts called out.

"Oh, shit," Longford muttered. "Give us a couple more minutes." He pushed at throttles already against the stops.

Hortha pointed toward the glittering waters of the bay a few miles ahead. "Let's fly down the slope, Jake—we can wring a few more knots out of her."

"Engines redlining," Longford warned.

"They run good when they're hot," Hortha said.

The plane streaked across the sandy beaches with less than a hundred feet to spare. Frightened fishermen ducked and watched in awe as the big plane flashed across the bay at a speed they couldn't imagine.

"He's gaining," Betts called out.

"Give us a little more time, just a little more," Longford pleaded.

"Only a mile and a half back."

"Jake!" Hortha said. "We're making it. Look at our speed!"

The air speed indicator was above three hundred knots, and the figures were spinning by. The waters of the bay passed faster and faster under the speeding jet.

"Move your ass, sweetheart!" Jake yelled, pounding one fist on the instrument panel. "Come on, baby, you can do it!"

Shengo's pursuing Zero passed over the north end of the airstrip at two thousand feet, two miles behind the fleeing transport.

The big plane was staying low, he saw, which was a wise decision on the part of the pilot. But he was puzzled—he should be closer than this. Shengo looked at his speed indicator—250 knots exactly. A transport plane in a takeoff run should not, at this point, be exceeding 100 knots, yet the one ahead must be going twice that! Incredible! At this rate, he would not overtake it before it reached the bay. He advanced his throttle. His speed inched up and the distance between the two planes narrowed.

But not fast enough. The plane was swift beyond belief. No transport in the world could fly that fast. They passed over the beaches and flew above the blue waters of the bay. His Zero was closing in, slowly but surely, and soon the prey would be within range of the 20-mm cannon.

Suddenly, Shengo had a desire to finish the task—to get within range and give the plane a burst that would send it into the sea, then return in victory to Davao. He estimated the distance at three thousand yards—much too far for accurate shooting. Ammunition was expensive and should not be wasted. He increased his power and the great radial engine responded beautifully. Shengo fingered the firing button and sighted the plane in his firing reticle. The image shocked him! The transport looked no larger! He had reduced the distance, but not enough. Unbelievable! He looked at his speed indicator. It read 310 knots.

There was a fury within him now. That plane—that lumbering, defenseless plane that was to take him to glory—was running even with his wonderful fighter plane. He would not have it! He threw the throttle all the way forward. The Zero responded, but the shrillness of the engine indicated that it had reached its limits. Slowly, ever so slowly, the transport grew larger in his sights. He estimated it as two thousand yards distant; he would fire at fifteen hundred—an extreme range.

But by the whiskers of Musashi, with his Zero streaking across the waters at its best speed, the distance began to widen! What manner of plane was this that hurled its enormous bulk through the air as fast as his Zero-sen? Faster, even, for he was falling farther behind. If he were ever to shoot it down, it must be now.

He pressed the firing button, aiming at the broad back of the whalelike body. The rounds fell short. Sudden panic gripped him—his prey was escaping!

What sneers and disbelief he would have to face from those jealous of him in flotilla headquarters. He could hear the words now—Shengo's ineptitude permitted a slow-flying transport to escape! Sweat flowed from his body at the thought, and he wiped the moisture from his face. He must shoot the plane down! Abandoning the reticle sighting, he lifted the nose of his plane to give his cannon optimum trajectory. The firing would be guesswork, success or failure depending only on the whims of his Shinto gods. He threw himself upon their mercy.

Camiguin Island passed by in a blur and the 737 raced north toward the open sea.

"He's damn close now, Jake," Betts called.

"We just passed three hundred fifty knots," Hortha said. "He can't keep up with us now."

"When he finds that out," Longford growled, "we could be in big trouble. He'll try to blast us with those cannon."

"He's falling back," Betts called out triumphantly. Then, in a different voice, "Jesus! He's shooting at us!" Silence, then gleefully, "The son of a bitch missed." Another pause. "Oh-oh!"

The plane shuddered from earsplitting explosions. A crash came from the passenger compartment. In the copilot's seat, Hortha grunted heavily. The wheel in Longford's hand jerked violently forward.

"What the hell!" he exclaimed, turning toward Hortha. His copilot slumped against the wheel, his face turned toward Longford, the chiseled features white and blank, his entire upper back a mangled mess. Blood from ruptured arteries spurted like fountains. For a few seconds, Hortha's eyelids fluttered, then quieted as the light left his sightless eyes.

Longford roared wordlessly for help, pulling back on the wheel made heavy by the weight of Hortha's body.

Hiraga stuck his head in the cockpit. "We got hit back here..." He saw Hortha. "Oh, my God!"

"Get him out of that seat, Otis," Longford spoke tight-lipped, struggling to remain calm. "I'm having trouble flying this thing." Hiraga pulled Hortha's body back, then struggled with the seat harness, his hands as red as a butcher's from the copilot's blood.

"Mike," he yelled toward the compartment. "Give me a hand."

Witkowski rushed forward. At the sight, he groaned wordlessly, then helped Hiraga ease Johnny's body back down the aisle into the passenger compartment. Hurrying back to the cockpit with towels in his hand, he swabbed the blood from the copilot's seat, then pressed Longford's slumped shoulder.

"Christ, Jake, I... I'm sorry." He wiped spattered blood from the pilot's shirt. "You hit?"

Longford shook his head. He was okay, but the gorge rose uncontrollably in his throat. "Get me a bag," he muttered. Mike got it to him just in time. Wiping the bitterness from his mouth, Longford tried to put aside what he'd just seen. Johnny was one of the finest men he'd ever known. He shouldn't have been shot in the back in a war that was over before he was born. The trouble was, Longford couldn't do anything about it. He wanted desperately to somehow even the score, but he had to keep his cool—fly the plane, stay in command. He glanced up at Witkowski.

"Everyone okay back there?"

Witkowski hesitated. He shook his head.

"Well?" Longford demanded.

"Jake, we've got big trouble—I mean *big*. Babcock got hit, too. It's all over. We lost the ball game."

In a daze, Longford muttered, "Babcock. Dead?"

"Yeah, piece of shell tore his throat out." With the towel, Witkowski continued to wipe the blood and shattered flesh from the copilot's seat. "If it's any satisfaction, we've outrun the Jap. He's a couple of miles back now."

Longford eased up on the throttles and the whine of the laboring engines dropped.

Betts came forward and spread a blanket over the copilot's

seat. "We've got four holes, Jake," he said, "close to midpoint, right along the back, and two more just forward of the wings. The radio transmission element is a bunch of junk, but we can still receive."

"What about the star scanner?" He tensed for the answer. With that gone, 1942 would be their permanent home.

"Otis is looking it over now. It seems okay."

"How about repairs?"

"Negative on the radio, but the fuselage holes are no problem as long as we stay under fifteen thousand feet. I'll patch 'em up before we get to the TTP. It will take about twenty minutes."

Longford continued to stare ahead at the sea lightening with the sun's first rays. Betts watched him, perplexed.

"Well..." he said uncertainly. "Guess I'll get to work."

"No." Longford's negative was firm. He looked up at Betts. "Not yet. You're checked out on this plane, aren't you?"

"Yeah," Betts answered, his tone dubious. "Got some hours in back in New Jersey."

"Take over." Longford got up abruptly and left the cockpit. He took Hiraga's place on the plexidome ladder and watched the pursuing Zero. After a moment he leaned down and called to Betts, "Change heading to one hundred and twenty true." He watched the Zero for a moment more, then came back to the cockpit. He sat there, staring out the window, letting Betts fly the plane. The anger in him smoldered. It was 1942 and they were getting the shit beat out of them. Having lost everything, they were running like scared rabbits.

Of course, the cool thing to do was to keep running, get back to their own time. And then what? Sorry, Mr. President, no B-juice. The man who could have saved you got killed by a little old plane that didn't weigh as much as one of our wings. Shot the hell out of us; shot the hell out of your hopes.

Bullshit! He tightened his grip on the wheel until his fingers ached.

They flew on for a few minutes, the Zero falling farther behind.

Betts looked at Longford. "You're not thinking what I think you're thinking, are you?"

"I'm thinking about Kogan and Marie, and Hortha getting blown to hell," he said finally. "I even feel sorry for that dumb bastard Babcock."

"So?"

"You realize that the president's body might just as well be lying back there, too."

"Yeah," Betts said slowly. "Guess you're right."

Longford pointed his finger in Betts's face. "World War II ain't the fuck over yet."

Betts's grin was weak and he spoke seriously. "Come on, Jake. That Zero's as quick as a cat and those cannon are murder. Besides, I don't recall seeing any Sidewinders mounted on this crate. What are you gonna do, give him the finger?"

Longford continued to stare ahead, then he glowered at Betts. "I'd have loved to get the son of a bitch," he mumbled, "I really would have."

His shoulders slumped. He realized he'd put the idea of revenge behind him. Big, dumb asshole, he berated himself. Good thing he had come to his senses. Jesus! Risking five lives for one lousy Jap. But how he hated to turn tail and run.

He took the wheel from Betts. "Ask Otis to give me a course for the TTP." He advanced the throttles.

Shengo's eyes narrowed in wonder as the distance widened. Then his earphones flooded with words.

"Senki three-two, this is KD. Have you destroyed the American transport? Report."

"I have damaged it, KD, but the aircraft still flies."

Shengo winced as he visualized the reaction of headquarters to this information. It came quickly.

"Senki three-two. Repeat."

He repeated his message.

"Explain why the enemy plane has not been destroyed."

What could he say that would be believed? The truth? No, was his first thought. But yes, it must be told, nevertheless. And well it should, so that headquarters might share the burden of comprehending that which he, Shengo, could not.

"KD. I have been unable to overtake the transport."

There was no immediate response. He could imagine the dumbfounded looks being exchanged at flotilla headquarters. Finally, the radio squealed.

"Senki three-two. Are you experiencing engine trouble? Have your guns jammed?" New outpourings of sweat coursed down Shengo's face. The day had begun so well. Now, moments after sunrise, his mouth was filled with ashes.

"Negative, KD."

"Very well. You will cease your cat-and-mouse game. Shoot the transport out of the skies immediately. This is a direct order from the flotilla commander. That is all." His earphones went silent.

He was once again a scrawny schoolboy in Fukuoka Prefecture in deep obeisance as his Third Form instructor, in front of the entire class, castigated him for his clumsy characters.

Kokutai headquarters would never believe what he himself, though seeing it, scarcely believed. He could imagine himself standing before Captain Ozawa, bowing low as he told of the transport plane that took off under the very guns of his Zero and escaped! He could see the sneer on Ozawa's lips and the disbelief in his eyes. He could hear the laughter in the pilots' mess as Shengo described a transport plane that flew faster than his fighter. He visualized the laughter turning to whispers about his courage, his judgment, even his sanity. He saw his beloved Zero-sen taken away from him and given to someone not subject to fits of cowardice and irrationality. He would be assigned perhaps to an assistant adjutant's duties, filling out personnel forms, or to the supply section, counting replacement parts.

In a flash of inspiration, he understood now what he must do. The answer was so clear. It would solve everything and would please his ancestors as well as himself. He pressed the button on his radio transmitter.

"KD," he said, his voice clear and firm. "The transport plane has escaped me. I accept full responsibility for this failure. In partial redemption, and for the greater glory of His Imperial Highness, I fly now to destroy the headquarters of the American commander on Mindanao, which I have recently discovered. This is my last transmission. It is my requiem."

Shengo turned his fighter toward the blue mountains of Mindanao, forty miles across the sea.

Hiraga rushed into the cockpit, his earphones around his neck. Witkowski was close behind. "Jake." The scientist's voice was harsh with urgency. "The guy's gonna do a kamikaze on Sharp's command post!"

Longford turned to Betts. "Call the control tower. We've got to warn them, quick."

Betts started out of his seat, then stopped. "What do I use, semaphore? The goddamn radio's in pieces."

The four men exchanged stares, gauging the implications. Hiraga spoke first. "Can we stop him?" he asked Longford.

Betts leaned forward, his face tense. "I think we'd better give it a try, Jake. There are a dozen or more people in that command post."

"It's not just the lives, Skipper," Witkowski chimed in. "We're getting into a real, quantitative change of history if they die."

"What the hell do you mean?" Longford said. "Sharp will surrender his command in another week anyway." He was trying hard to sort things out in his own mind, to balance the risks against the gains. His anger had long gone and he once more had to be a commander, but he needed input.

Witkowski spoke rapidly. "This is May 1942. The Battle of Midway takes place next month—historians call it the turning point of the war. By hanging on, General Sharp can tie up the air flotilla here for another week. Once he and his staff are gone, another hundred Jap planes can be released to take part in the big battle. They win that and who knows how long the war will last." The archivist started to say more, but Longford held up a hand.

"Okay, Mike, I got it." Longford jerked his thumb back over his shoulder. "Has he turned back toward the island?"

Hiraga rushed to the plexidome, then yelled back, "Yeah, Jake, he's just a speck."

"We've got some flying to do, Larry," Longford said, then spoke over the loudspeaker. "Everybody in their seats and buckle up, quick!" He started a sharp turn to port.

Hiraga came down from the plexidome and negotiated the narrow aisle, struggling for balance against the turn. He extended one arm in front of Longford's face. Tapping his wristwatch, he said, "I don't want to add to the stress, Jake, but we haven't got too much time to waste on this guy."

A white line of surf separated the dark green of the eastern cliffs from the blue of the sea. He would pass over the coast in five minutes, Shengo estimated. Soon he would be over the American airfield. He was already planning his final descent. At an altitude of two thousand meters—an excellent distance— he would push the nose of his Zero-sen over and scream down upon the command post, pushing the firing button of his cannon, emptying the armory in his wings. And then it would be over. He smiled in complete satisfaction. What a marvelous way to die! What a glorious day it will be for the humble Shengo family when an officer of the navy presents them with a box bearing the symbolic ashes of their war hero son!

A small frown furrowed his brow. Was he leaving something undone? This terrifying, unbelievable aircraft that had sped away from him—did it represent a new and dangerous technology that his superiors should know about? Perhaps he should try, before his last dive, to communicate what he had seen. No, he decided. He had already felt their derision—why suffer more? Yet.... He was debating his course of action when a faint thrumming—a strange, external sound, as from an engine more powerful than his Sakae 12—caused him to cock his head.

"What're you gonna do when we catch him, Jake?"

Longford leaned forward in his seat, as if to help the plane to greater speeds. The Zero was growing larger in the windshield. He estimated that he had more than three hundred knots' advantage in running up on it, and thank God for that. Hiraga and his warning about the time had just added to his worries.

He didn't answer Betts, but he had already made his plans. They were simplicity itself. The ponderous undernose of the 737 would brush against the Zero's tail as it passed, crumpling the frail structure like a child's toy made of balsa.

The plane was less than two miles away; another few seconds and it would be over. A thousand yards—he pulled back a fraction of an inch on the wheel; he didn't want the fighter splattered over *Sucker One*'s nose like a bug on a windshield.

Five hundred—he could see the red ball on the wings. *Now!*

The sound behind him became a roar. Shengo shifted in his seat and looked back. Even before his eyes fully registered the huge object rushing at him like some prehistoric flying beast, his hands and feet flashed over the controls with lightning rapidity.

"Son of a bitch!"

The Zero had been there, yards in front of them, and then it was gone, flashing down and to one side.

Longford pounded the console. "Damnit! How'd he get away?"

"Watch it, Jake," Betts yelled, his voice taut with alarm. "He can hurt us."

The words were scarcely out of his mouth when a cannon shot

exploded through the port wing, and another tore a piece of the engine housing loose.

Longford flipped the plane violently to starboard and the crash of loose dishes and thump of unsecured tools intermingled. Another shell came through the lower fuselage, passed through the decking, and pounded against the ceiling before dropping heavily onto the galley floor.

For an instant, it seemed that the firing was over. Then one final burst struck the port engine, silencing it. Longford hit the fire suppressant.

"Larry, check number one!"

Betts eased out of his seat. He peered out the port window at the massive engine, then turned back to check the instrumentation. "Could be the fuel controller's knocked out, Jake." The labored thunder of the starboard engine told of its increased load.

"Oh, Jesus." Longford looked up at Betts. "We're a ruptured duck now."

Betts nodded thoughtfully. "Afraid so. I've got a spare in the emergency pack, but I sure ain't gonna crawl out on the wing to fix it." He walked back and climbed to the plexidome. After a moment, he said, "Zero's a long way back, but he's hanging in there."

Longford wiped the sweat from his face. They were in trouble. That pilot, whoever he was, could fly. He'd whipped that Zero out of the way, somehow reversed its course, and fired his cannon fast and straight before *Sucker One*, traveling hundreds of knots faster, could get beyond range. Now he had cut them down to size. With just one engine, they probably couldn't outrun the fighter.

Hiraga came forward to the galley and poured himself a soft drink. Fragments from the fusillade had struck him and blood dripped from gashes in his forehead and his cheek. Von Porten started to bandage him, but Hiraga pushed by and walked to the cockpit.

"Is he still after us?" Hiraga asked while Von Porten stemmed the blood.

"How is he, Art?" Longford asked, nodding toward the physicist.

"Nothing to worry about," Von Porten muttered as he taped gauze to Hiraga's cheek. Scowling, he glanced over his shoulder. "Gentlemen, may I suggest we get the hell out of here?"

"We can't," Longford said. He nodded toward the port engine. "He can stay with us, now."

Betts came back from the plexidome and buckled up again. "What're we gonna do, Jake?"

"Maybe he's about out of fuel," Von Porten said. "If we can just stay ahead of him long enough—"

Longford shook his head. "That's another thing that made this Mitsubishi crate numero uno. It could fly all fucking day on a tank of gas." He eased back on the throttle and the noise of the engine diminished.

"Skipper." Hiraga's voice was worried. "We've *got* to get to the TTP."

Longford gave no sign that he had heard, but his teeth clamped down on his lower lip until blood ran. He cursed as he wiped it off. He felt the same sense of frustration he knew the day he took Vivian to the ward where she would probably stay until she died. His mind had run down alley after blind alley, searching frantically for a solution that would keep his world from coming to an end. There had been none.

Now, with demonic force, he gripped the wheel, trying to clear his mind, to find some way in which not only he but the others could live. To continue on would be suicidal—the 737 would be torn apart like a wounded stag set upon by wolves. They could not run, and they could not fight. What was left...?

"Okay. Everyone buckle up." His voice was stronger than his convictions.

"You want me to watch the Jap?" Hiraga asked.

Longford shook his head. The two men left the cockpit slowly, looking back over their shoulders. Giving them time to get into their seats, Longford's big hands worked the controls.

The plane arced up and back in a long, 180-degree parabola, bringing them back on a reverse heading. As the jet leveled off, the two pilots squinted into the distance, looking for the Zero.

"There." Betts pointed. Nearly five miles away, the fighter had begun to close the gap.

"Hang on," Longford said, and flew directly toward the Japanese plane.

Betts looked toward Longford, his face worried. "Hey, what are you going to do?"

The pilot didn't answer. His face intense, he gripped the controls with both hands. The distance between the two planes dwindled with incredible rapidity.

Shengo still trembled. The huge plane had nearly destroyed him. When he reflected upon how close disaster had come, he could only thank his Shinto gods for intervening. His great Zero had stoutly persevered under the pressure of that sudden dive. It had survived the gut-wrenching maneuver that had enabled him to fire his cannon at the fleeing transport. And the rounds had found their target—one engine seemed badly damaged, although the enemy plane soon was too far away to see accurately.

Once again he had forced his Zero to its utmost, trying to keep within range, but his dive and change of direction had cost him most of his speed.

One last fusillade from his 20-mms fell short, and a faint clatter from the wing ammunition wells told him that he had exhausted his supply of shells. Not that it mattered. The strange, alien plane had outdistanced him again. He flew on, disconsolate.

But no—it seemed to him that though miles separated them, he was holding his own, even closing on the transport. His rounds may have caused more damage than he had suspected. With all his heart and mind and body, he urged his fighter on to greater speed.

He jerked upright. Were his eyes deceiving him? He stared at the distant shape. By all the Gods, it had grown larger—could it be coming directly toward him? His eyes burned as he strained to see. He pressed an eye against the firing reticle. Yes, he could now see the bulbous nose, the knifelike wings, the strangely placed engine pods. Ah, yes, he now saw what had happened. With their last deadly coughs, his cannon had done their job!

In seconds he divined the transport pilot's intention—to destroy Shengo's plane by crashing into it! But this was strange. It was not the American way to give one's life deliberately for the glory of one's country. It was unheard of. But he had no time to dwell on this. The big craft was closing at an incredible speed!

Joyously, he leaned forward, keeping his aim directly on the center point of the huge fuselage lunging at him. His thumb fingered the firing button, but ah!—his cannon were useless. This way was far better, though, and surer—he and his plane would become as a guided three-ton artillery shell, striking the enemy with devastating force.

Only a few seconds more.

Betts stiffened. "Jake, you aren't gonna . . ."

He stopped as the faint outline became larger terrifyingly fast. His voice grated with intensity. "You know this guy isn't going to chicken out."

Longford didn't answer. He was counting on it—that the Japanese pilot wouldn't chicken out, that he would keep that fighter coming at him, straight and hot. His hands gripped the wheel tightly—too tightly. He willed himself to loosen his fingers. Everything depended upon his reflexes. Taut muscles were slow, and he had goddamn better be quicker than he'd ever been in his life. If only Hortha, with his marvelous touch, was sitting in the right-hand seat. *Johnny, wherever you are, old buddy, help me!* Longford blinked his eyes, clearing them.

Betts reached for the wheel. "Break off, for chrissakes!" With a muttered curse, Longford knocked his hands away.

The Zero rocketed at them!

Now!

He spun the wheel. The big 737 flipped on its side, one massive wing slashing like a knife through the frail wing of the Zero. There was a faint bump, a sound as from a distant car crash, and it was over.

The sky, a marvelous early morning cerulean, was to his right and the ocean, a warm cobalt blue, was to his left, and the world was wonderful and they were alive.

He brought the plane around slowly and watched the Japanese plane cartwheel lazily toward the sea below.

⟻ CHAPTER TWENTY ⟻

Witkowski brought coffee for the two pilots. "Enriched it a bit," he said. "Careful," he added as he eased the Styrofoam container into Jake's trembling hand. The brandy tasted good. By the time the coffee was gone, so were the shakes—almost.

"Otis," Longford said as *Sucker One* flew east, away from Mindanao. "How much time have we got?" He tried for a casual note in his voice, but he didn't quite make it. The answer was too important. He hadn't told the physicist about *all* the trouble they faced.

Hiraga leaned forward in the jump seat and glanced worriedly at his watch. "About twenty . . . three minutes."

Longford's heart thumped. He hadn't fully calculated it yet, but he had a feeling that they might as well be flying for Mars.

Betts's mouth dropped open. Looking at the physicist, he groaned. "That goddamn close? Why the hell wasn't there more leeway built into this thing?"

"There is," Hiraga nodded. "But we're already using it up. There's a thirty-minute window for our coincidence with the beam, but the task force started shooting it seven minutes ago. They'll continue on for another..." He checked his watch again. "...now it's twenty-two minutes. How far do we have to go, Skipper?"

Better give Hiraga the real bad news now, Longford thought. He glanced at Betts's seamed, worried face. The engineer, he was pretty sure, already knew the problem.

"It's not how *far,* it's how *high.* Just how much give is there in that twenty thousand feet?" Longford looked up at Hiraga. "We don't have to hit exactly, do we?" *Let him say, "Oh, hell no, Jake—fifteen, sixteen thousand will do it."*

"Give?" Hiraga asked as though he'd never heard the word. "Jake, there's no give. Oh, maybe thirty, forty feet, but no more. We don't make it to that altitude, we don't make it back at all. The beam just won't touch us."

Betts gave Jake a sidelong glance that spoke volumes, then both pilots checked the altimeter. It read 14,300 feet with the needle moving up slowly—too slowly. The thunder from the single engine indicated the load it was carrying.

"How much strain will number two take?" He looked over at Betts.

"Don't worry about it. Go ahead and lean on it if you have to." Betts's eyes riveted on the altimeter. "Are you giving it everything?"

"Yeah." Longford squeezed the monosyllable out. He checked the instrument panel clock. "We just aren't gonna make it this way."

"Can't we dump some fuel?" Hiraga asked. Longford noticed that the physicist's face had lost its healthy tan.

"No way," Betts answered. "Seven thirty-sevens don't have the capability."

"Okay, Larry, open the rear hatch." Longford raised his voice. "Start throwing out everything that's not fastened down. Put everyone to work."

Betts started aft, then stopped. "It's really bad, eh, Jake?"

Longford nodded.

"Seats weigh a lot. How about getting rid of them? I've got a chain saw with metal bits down below in the emergency kit."

"Do it. Tear the place up."

Heavy pantry gear thumped and banged as the men hauled microwave ovens, storage shelves, frozen food to the rear hatch. Longford saw that the freezer was too large to get between the seats, but Larry was solving that. A horrendous new noise came from the passenger compartment. Betts was using the power saw on the seat legs. Hiraga loaded up with reference works and threw them out the open hatch. Witkowski dragged a pile of computer paper boxes across the aisle and kicked them into the wind stream. Von Porten was out of sight behind the curtain that hid the bodies.

Longford checked the starboard EGT. The temperature was rising on number two. Engine had to work harder the higher it got. Better news on the altimeter, though. Sixteen-five, but that was still not fast enough. Jesus, he wanted to get back there and start throwing things himself.

He shifted in his seat to check the passenger compartment. Betts, with his screeching saw, had done a real demolition job. The galley was virtually destroyed—everything was gone, down to the eating utensils, coffee maker, dishes, and dinner mints. They were throwing the last of the seats out the hatch. Witkowski was tearing the carpet away from the floor.

Betts hustled up to the cockpit. "See anything we've missed?"

Longford looked back. The interior had an empty, torn-up, drug-bust look to it.

"Got rid of everything?"

Betts gave a brief nod. "Just about."

"What's that mean?"

"Burial at sea."

Jake glanced at his watch. Little more than five minutes to go. He had to think about it. It wouldn't be a burial—they'd just toss Hortha and Babcock's bodies out with as much ceremony as they had given the dishes. Still, if it would get them over the hump. . . .

"Jake!" Hiraga yelled from the star scanner where he was making adjustments. As Longford turned, the physicist pantomimed gasping for air.

What the hell!

Longford whirled back to his instruments, suddenly conscious of being short of breath himself. He checked the altimeter—*Nineteen four*! Close the damn hatch and he'd bet old number two would boost them home.

He pointed aft. "Button her up, Larry," he rasped. The engineer clapped him joyfully on the shoulder and loped through the empty passenger compartment. On his way, he picked up the chain saw, and with a mighty heave, sent it spinning into the Pacific. Witkowski joined him and the two men struggled with the hatch.

Longford checked the time. Three and a half minutes to go. "Otis, I'm handing the autopilot over to you."

Hiraga did a thumbs-up and prepared to marry the star scanner to the plane's controls. As the rear hatch crashed shut and the interior quieted, Longford started pressurization.

Von Porten stuck his head in the cockpit. His face had a strained look, as though he were struggling to suppress an inner excitement. "Are we going to make it, Jake? It's goddamn important that we do."

Longford watched the controls and thought that was a weird thing for Doc to say—of course it's important. He shot a look at Von Porten and saw the intense, almost fervid way he waited for the answer.

"I'll go along with you on that, Art," he said. "We're almost there. If the star scanner works, we might just be home."

A smile that radiated excitement crossed Von Porten's face. He punched Longford's arm in gratitude and hurried aft. Longford watched over his shoulder as the doctor disappeared behind the screen in the rear. It was strange behavior, not like the Bostonian—too much feeling.

The altitude gauge climbed steadily. Longford eased the power slightly back on the laboring engine and held it at twenty thousand. They'd made it, with a minute or so to spare. Now, if that star scanner came through, they just might see their own world again.

He took several deep breaths, trying to relax.

"Stand by!" Hiraga called out. Betts came forward and eased into the copilot's seat, buckling his harness and giving Longford a thumbs-up.

Then the plane was bathed in luminescence, and all detail faded.

The strange falling-apart sensation had come and gone with far less impact the second time around. Now, squawking incoming radio transmissions filled the plane.

Both pilots spotted the four ships of the task group simultaneously. Far below, on a sea that looked black, they could see the carrier and its supporting craft start a wide turn to the east, leaving long curved paths of white foam in their wake. Betts rapped Longford on the shoulder and nodded congratulations, but his face was grim. Longford understood. They were home, but there would be no victory celebration. They had lost too much and accomplished nothing.

The incoming radio traffic turned plaintive, asking for the acknowledgment *Sucker One* couldn't give. Hiraga's voice came over the intercom.

"Jake, we've got to get word to these people on the carrier, explain what happened to our radio."

"All right," he said wearily. "Mike, help me draft a message. Larry, rig some kind of drop package."

Von Porten touched his shoulder. "When you write the message, Jake, tell them we got what we went for."

•   •   •

Admiral Jefferson Edwards checked his watch, then looked west, searching for the speck that would be *Sucker One*. He stood alone, just off the runway of Barbers Point Naval Air Station, an auxiliary, little-used facility eight helicopter-minutes away from his headquarters at Pearl Harbor. The place looked like a scene from that old movie—he'd forgotten the name—about the world after a nuclear holocaust. The runways were empty except for a scrap of paper fluttering in the breeze, no one could be seen in the control tower, no cars moved, no people were visible except CINCPAC himself, standing alone for once, without hovering aides or staff officers.

But four-star admirals do not wander off alone, or show up at an auxiliary facility without purpose. A beefed-up platoon of military police patrolled the station perimeter. A trusted chief petty officer sat in the control tower, a microphone in his hand, watching the radar screen before him. An ambulance with sophisticated life support systems was parked beside the administration building. The admiral's personal helicopter sat close by with communication equipment that could be instantly netted around the world. An additional helicopter stood by to carry the crew of *Sucker One* back to the hospital for checkups.

Extending from just behind a hangar was the needle snout of a museum piece, but still one of the fastest planes in the world— a SR-71 Blackbird, a Mach-3 strategic reconnaissance craft.

Of the hundreds of messages coming in to CINCPAC headquarters in the last few hours, two had gripped Edwards's attention.

At 0420 hours, the command duty officer had awakened him with an EYES ONLY top priority message from the commanding officer of the carrier *Theodore Roosevelt*. It said that the aircraft code-named *Sucker One* had experienced radio failure and had dropped a message for further transmittal to CINCPAC. Edwards had blinked the sleep from his eyes and read the communication.

FOR: CINCPAC
FROM: SUCKER ONE

PROCEEDING GUAM TO REFUEL. ETA PEARL 02/
114415OCT. CASUALTIES: TWO DEAD. DAMAGE TO AIR-
CRAFT REPAIRABLE. LIMITED AMT B-JUICE OBTAINED.
PASS TO INTERESTED PARTIES.

LONGFORD

The admiral had immediately issued the initial orders to ready
Barbers Point. That didn't take long. When he finished, he
pushed a button on his wristwatch, saw it was 0950 hours in
Washington, and placed a call to the White House, asking the
red phone operator for the chief of staff.

"You got something for us, Jeff?" Rodale's words came in an
excited rush.

"Good news, I think. Our friends are coming in this afternoon.
They're bringing in some of the stuff you ordered—a limited
amount, they say."

"Okaaay." Rodale dragged the word out and paused. Edwards
could imagine the thoughts whirling through the chief's mind.
"All right. I hate to say this, but it may be too late, if you get
my meaning. Jeff, I can't tell you how important it is that the
shipment reach here absolutely as soon as possible."

"Don't worry," Edwards had responded. "I'll have a plane
standing by. You should have it real early tomorrow morning—
before dawn."

The phone was silent. "Admiral," Rodale began again. There
was a different tone to his voice. This was the White House chief
staff officer speaking *for* the commander in chief. "Every hour
is important. I mean that sincerely."

Edwards understood what he was saying. Rodale was telling
him B-juice could arrive too late. His commander expected him
to do better, to use all the vast apparatus at his disposal and to
solve the problem. He took a second to think about it.

"I could request SAC at Omaha to loan me a Blackbird. The

planes were phased out of service four or five years ago, but I understand they still keep a couple of them tuned up. That way, your package would get there before midnight—perhaps as early as eight or nine." Edwards reviewed that plan and could see difficulties. Not too long ago, he and the present SAC commander had exchanged sharp words at a National War College seminar. They hadn't been exactly lovey-dovey since. "Tell you the truth, sir, it'll go a lot better if you get on the horn and *order* them to send me one."

"You mean it could be at Pearl when the shipment arrives?"

"Yes, sir. Trust me. Those hummers can move."

"All right, will do. And Jeff, back here we can't thank you enough for all you've done."

"I appreciate that, but I've got a cold, nasty feeling this business hasn't come cheap."

"What do you mean?"

"The message. Joe Kogan didn't send it—Colonel Longford did."

The plane rolled to a stop, the engine rotor blades seeming to sigh with terminal fatigue before dwindling into silence. Witkowski swung the hatch open and saw commander in chief, Pacific, with his hands cupped to his mouth, yelling at him.

"Get the package out here, quick," he roared. In a moment, Von Porten came bounding down the ladder, a brown paper bag clutched carefully in both hands.

Without formality, Edwards pushed him toward his helicopter. "See my pilot, Doc," he said. "He'll patch you in to the White House. They're anxious to talk to you."

Longford came down the ladder next, placing his feet as though each carried lead weights. Admiral Edwards watched him, wondering what god-awful experiences had carved the long, sad lines in that good-natured face. They shook hands as the stretcher bearers raced up the ladder. With Longford following, Edwards moved around the nose of the battered plane, looking up at the gaping holes and the scarred paint. Finally, he stopped and faced the pilot.

"Okay, let me have it. I suppose the two dead mentioned in your message included Joe Kogan."

"No, sir. He never got aboard. The Japs got him as we were loading."

"Damnit, I suspected it was something bad." Edwards laid a sympathetic hand on Longford's shoulder. "What happened?"

"The Japs—Japanese attacked as we were loading aboard. Joe was trying to get up the ladder, when an officer whacked his arm off with his sword."

Edwards shook his head. "Jesus, that's just plain incredible. What a way to go." He scowled at Longford. "But if . . . well, who are the two dead you brought back?"

"John Hortha, for one. Killed by a twenty-millimeter shell from a Zero fighter."

Edwards shook his head in disbelief. "Christ! What a damn shame. Hortha was one helluva guy." He looked south across the glittering waters of Mamala Bay, a thoughtful, puzzled scowl on his features. "You know, Jake, I guess I never really believed all this time travel business. Oh, sure, I was convinced up here." He pointed to his temple. "But down here," he thumped his fist into his gut, "no way. Now I look at this big old bird sitting here and I see the holes, and Hortha's dead from some damn Zero, and you tell me Kogan got his from a samurai sword. Well." He expelled his breath. "Friend, I'm a believer now. You people came out of the Pacific just now, but it sure as hell wasn't the Pacific I know. You've been in a world that's been gone fifty years. You've been fighting World War II. I don't understand how it all happened, and I'm not sure I ever want to." He poked a finger into Longford's chest. "But, think about it. You're the only person on active duty today who's got the right to wear the old Asiatic–Pacific Campaign ribbon." He sighed. "Absolutely un-fucking-believable."

The admiral took Longford's arm and steered him toward his helicopter. "Come on, we've got a set of VIP quarters fixed up for you guys." He jerked to a halt. "Wait a minute. Who was the other casualty?"

"Babcock, Admiral. Dr. Roger Babcock. Killed by the same Zero that got Hortha."

Edwards put his big hands on his hips and leaned forward. "Dr. Babcock? The guy who was supposed to have died in a Japanese prison camp? What in the hell were you bringing him back for?"

"Admiral," Longford said wearily, "it's a long story and I'm just too damn tired to go into it now." He looked back at the plane. The cargo door was open and a group of ground handlers were lifting stretchers out of the storage compartment. They placed them on the concrete while they secured the door. The two officers watched.

"That them?" Edwards asked. Longford nodded.

Von Porten jumped into the copilot's seat of the helicopter and adjusted the earphones. While he waited for the pilot to make the connection, he watched the crew chief spread a square of four-inch-thick foam rubber on the floor of the helicopter, carefully take the glass vial from the sack, slip a heavy plastic bag around it, seal it, and place it in a Styrofoam-lined steel box. He held it up for Von Porten's inspection, then headed for the SR-71 parked a few hundred feet away.

The pilot nodded to Von Porten. The White House was on line. Dr. Sidney Eccles's voice crackled through the earphones.

"Art? You there?"

"Yeah, Sid, we just got in."

Through the open hatch, he could see the long black fuselage of the reconnaissance plane emerge from behind the hangar. A tow vehicle dragged it toward the strip.

"You got it, then?" Eccles's words were curt.

"Yes, we got it."

"Well." The physician's voice sounded tired. "Get the stuff here as soon as you can."

Von Porten felt sudden anger. They'd gone through hell—a costly, dangerous, absolutely incredible hell—and Eccles sounded like they were faxing junk mail. "That's a damn cold greeting, Doctor," he said.

"I'm being practical, that's all. This could be the last night, you understand? The case is just too far along for anything to help." Eccles seemed to have trouble paraphrasing. "To tell you the truth, I've never had much faith in what you're bringing in. But," his voice held no hope, "I guess it's all we've got."

He became businesslike. "Now, what do we have?"

"Nine ccs of a solution that smells like something out of a very old, diarrhetic crocodile."

"Nice imagery, Art, but come on, what *is* the substance?"

"I haven't the faintest idea. You think I carry a laser spectro-scope?"

"Well, what did Babcock tell you?"

"He didn't tell me anything and he didn't give me anything. He's dead. He carried a vial of the stuff in his rectum." With a silent grimace, Von Porten recalled the musical clatter of the vial hitting the deck as Babcock's sphincter muscle had relaxed in death. Somehow, the glass container had not broken.

The radio was silent. Von Porten could visualize Eccles with his gold pen poised over his notes, trying to understand.

"Oh, my God." A throat-clearing sound came through the earphones, then, tentatively, "What's the dosage?"

"A half cc twice every twenty-four hours, I think."

"You *think*? Didn't he tell you before he died?"

Von Porten groaned and the helicopter pilot turned to stare at him. "Sid, someday I'll give you the whole story, but right now, hear me out and don't interrupt. Babcock didn't tell me anything. He wanted to keep the serum for his own glorification. Now listen—"

"I can't believe this! Then, how in hell do you know the dosage parameters—"

"Damnit, shut up, will you? I had a few minutes with a nurse who worked with him." He winced at the memory of Sylvia

Kruloff. "A fine woman. I questioned her at length about the ingredients, but she didn't know a thing. She had never even administered the medicine—Babcock always did that—but she *thought* a half cc injected every twelve hours was about right, and friend, that's as close as we're ever going to get."

He looked out the hatch of the helicopter at the sparkling waters of the Pacific. He had to make Eccles understand very clearly his next words. There could be no misunderstanding.

"Now, you get six ccs of the nine—no more. You understand, Sid?"

"Six? Hell, that's only twelve doses!"

"You use one milliliter more and I'll hold a news conference when I get back. You understand me? The rest is an analysis batch that belongs to the human race, and don't you forget it."

The shriek of powerful jet engines blanketed the coast from Nanakuli to Ewa Beach. The Blackbird sped down the runway. Von Porten waited for the sound to fade.

"Tell your principal the package is on the way."

Washington, D.C.

4:42 P.M. Saturday, October 1

"I assume you've been practicing a look of dignified grief." Yvonne spoke from the depths of her narrow Louis XVI bed as she sipped a delicate Pekoe Souchong. Even though it was late afternoon, she still wore a silk dressing gown.

Pyle looked annoyed. "You know, my dear, cynicism doesn't become you." *Nor does anything else,* he wanted to add. But she was in one of her moods and it would be pointless—even harmful to his euphoric state of mind—to aggravate her.

"All that cloak-and-dagger shit gone to waste. Now Moody is going to slip away peacefully, exactly as he would have done had you kept your hands off." A giggle escaped from the pillows' depths and he looked at her sharply. She had been drinking something besides tea. Could he ever be completely happy— really, totally satisfied? Here he was, within days—hours, even— of achieving the highest goal that man could strive for, saddled with a harridan of a wife who drank too much.

Well, after a decent interval as president, perhaps a divorce might be in order. Quiet and dignified, of course—an amicable agreement with a liberal settlement, say, of ten or fifteen million, plus some property. Yet, it was funny—just formulating the thought made him uneasy. That old feeling. Every time he got to the point of even thinking about divorce, the awareness struck at his core. He would . . . well, miss Yvonne. She was the only person he knew who spoke honestly to him, without fear or compromise or hope of reward. Younger, far lovelier women could be his for the asking, but where would they be if he were still only an accountant at Acme Paper Mills? No, Yvonne had her faults, but she was a known quantity. Her loyalty was beyond question. He was sure of it.

He poured himself a second scotch from the bedroom liquor stand. Usually, he limited his predinner drinking to one, but this evening might be very special. Louis had reported that the plane known as *Sucker One* was overdue. His White House contacts had informed him that Moody was sinking fast, so his defeat at the hands of Moser and Collines yesterday morning now seemed inconsequential.

The wall intercom buzzed softly. Pyle answered, "Yes?"

"Sir," the butler's voice was unctuous, "there's a man calling."

"Who is it?" An uncomfortable feeling began to replace the scotch-induced glow.

"He declines to give his name, sir, but he says it's urgent."

He was convinced now that it was Louis. He waited for the code word. The servant continued, "He says he's an old friend."

Pyle set his glass down carefully. It *was* Louis, and work lay ahead, no doubt about it. It all came down to this, the last few hours of Simon Moody's life. Even now, the president might be sinking into a coma from which he would never awaken. So, should the plan that he and Louis had developed be used, or should he let nature take its course? Every plan, of course, carried risks, and the odds were ten thousand to one that the medicine, no matter how powerful, was too little and too late.

His thought processes were interrupted by that damned giggle.

"What's so funny?" he said over his shoulder.

"It's just the idea."

"What do you mean?" He stopped, his hand on the doorknob.

"You." Her laughter came close to hysteria. "Having an old friend."

Furious, he stomped down the hall. God, she could be a trial at times.

CHAPTER TWENTY-ONE

Dr. Junzo Fuchida left the officers' *benjo* and climbed to the second floor of the ancient, stone-walled building that served as the camp hospital. On the landing, a narrow, arched window facing Manila Bay admitted a northwesterly breeze. He stopped and permitted himself a fantasy. Perhaps this same air had blown across the tiled roofs of Kyoto where his young wife dwelt, swooping down to caress the tendrils of hair at the nape of her slender neck, picking up the scent of jasmine she loved so much, and wafting it a thousand miles across the Pacific to tantalize him.

The coolness felt good on his moist face, but it carried no perfume, certainly not of jasmine—only the sharp scent of the prisoners' outhouses built against the wall of the old University of Santo Tomás. He wrinkled his nose against the penetrating and too-familiar smell. Reluctantly, he dropped his gaze from the distant blue horizon to the long lines of gaunt men and women shuffling urgently toward the evil-smelling structures. He sighed. Another outbreak of dysentery. Disgusting. The Spanish friars who had established this university—when was it, three and a half centuries ago?—would be shocked to see it now.

Senior physician of Santo Tomás Internment Camp was a miserable position in a miserable climate—no glory, no promotions. He could never satisfy these Caucasians with their delicate stomachs and their endless whining, and he had long ago stopped trying. Neither could he satisfy the camp commandant, Colonel Saburo Kozono, but he *had* to keep trying.

Still, he ruminated as he walked down the wide corridor toward his office, things could be worse for him, such as a reassignment to the Kwantung Army in Manchuria, with its scorching, dust-filled summers and winters that froze the mercury in thermometers, treating the occasional Soviet prisoner. They were filthy subhumans, those Russians—virtual animals. He shuddered at the recollection. No, this wasn't bad. The Americans and the few interned Europeans were at least reasonably civilized, although they tended to complain about the food— which was admittedly bad—and the medicine, which was worse. The big, ungainly Westerners should be grateful for what was available, such as old Santa Catalina convent here on the university grounds, now converted into the camp hospital.

The sound of an angry female voice speaking English echoed from the admissions office down the hall. Sinking into a chair behind his desk, Dr. Fuchida hoped his young assistant would be able to handle whatever was causing that ungodly squawking. He simply could not understand how American men permitted their women to speak as equals, demanding this and that without regard for the proprieties that should exist between the sexes.

His hope turned out to be fruitless. Multiple footsteps sounded on the aged timbers of the corridor, closing inexorably upon his office. There was a knock, and Dr. Naohiko Shiga's worried face appeared in the doorway.

"Sir," he said hastily. "The American nurse, Captain Crane, insists upon talking to you."

Fuchida's lips compressed into a thin line. The woman was a nuisance. Almost daily, she came to the hospital making impossible demands.

"She is the one who will not permit her . . . male friend to be brought to the hospital?"

"Yes, sir. She is afraid of contagion."

"I suspected as much," Dr. Fuchida said. "I'm busy, Shiga. Tell her there is nothing we can do for her."

Dr. Shiga bowed and had started to withdraw when a muffled sob came from the corridor. With a look of pain on his young face, Shiga hesitated, then tried again.

"Dr. Fuchida, she is concerned about the infection developing in this man's stump." He licked his lips nervously. "I have examined him, and it is quite bad. He has a high fever and the sepsis is spreading." Shiga lowered his voice as if the woman could understand Japanese. "Sir, we do have a small supply of prontosil remaining."

Fuchida glared at his underling. Damn this contemptible weakling! Three years of medical education in the United States had destroyed the manly fiber required by every member of the Imperial Armed Forces.

"That drug, Shiga, could save the life of one of our own soldiers—a warrior who could fight again for the emperor. Would you waste it on an enemy who will probably die anyway? You're a fool and maybe worse."

In the doorway behind Shiga the woman appeared, tall enough so that her head topped the young doctor's. Fuchida had seen this Captain Crane before. Before her capture she might have been attractive to men of her race, but eight weeks of prison food and the scorching heat of Manila had left her a virtual scarecrow. It was evident to Fuchida that she had tried to make herself presentable this morning. Her khaki shirt and shorts were clean and her hair combed, but perspiration and high emotion had dampened her clothing and plastered the red curls against her skull. Her arms and legs were thin, half-white, half-red with sunburn. An ulceration glowed angrily on one ankle.

Fuchida jumped to his feet. "Get her out of here," he ordered.

The young doctor turned and said something urgently in English, but the woman pushed him aside. Advancing on Fuchida she spoke rapidly, insistently, tears mixed with sweat streaming down her face.

Even though he could not understand what she was saying, the continuing flow of words made him angry. Moving toward her, the senior physician pointed menacingly toward the doorway. "Get out, woman! Get out!" he screamed at her. Shiga, his face pale, attempted to lead her away, but she shook him off and continued to plead her case, her bony hands pressed imploringly together.

Dr. Fuchida had heard enough. He grabbed the woman's arm and pushed her roughly toward the doorway, surprised as he touched her at her fragility. She stumbled and nearly went down, but regained her balance and faced him once more, outrage in her blue eyes. Swallowing hard, she again shouted at him.

Craaack! Fuchida's open hand lashed across her cheek. Captain Crane stumbled back against the door frame, her cheek flaming red from the blow. Again and again he struck her, his fury building with every slap. He would have continued to hit her had she not collapsed unconscious on the floor of his office. Shiga, the weakling, knelt by her side.

The light from the candle was inadequate. Dr. Shiga moved it away, took a flashlight from his pocket, and handed it to Captain Crane. Almost reluctantly, she focused the beam on the suppurating stump of Kogan's left arm. Shiga looked closely. It was as he had thought. Infection was spreading up the man's shoulder from its source under the skin flap. Kogan grunted with pain as the doctor's fingers pressed against the yellow-purplish swelling. Pale pink blood mixed with pus dripped onto the mat. The foul odor of putrescence filled the small room. Septicemia had set in with a vengeance, moving up into the shoulder region to destroy Shiga's hope that a second amputation would eliminate the corrupted flesh. Without drugs or antibiotics, there was nothing to stop the infection from continuing its invasion of the body.

Shiga took the flashlight from the woman and snapped it off. She watched his face for a hopeful sign, but she was really grasping at straws. Her medical training must tell her what she did not want to accept.

The patient stirred, his cheeks bright with fever and a sunken, withered look around his eyes. Somehow he managed a twisted grin. "How's it look, Doc?"

"Could be better, Mr. Kogan." Which was profoundly true. It also could hardly be worse. At the rate the infection was spreading, the big, gaunt man lying in the makeshift tent would be dead in a very few days.

"This morning I heard you say the word *prontosil*, Doctor," Marie said, her words coming rapidly. "Do you have any? Oh, dear God, please let us have some."

The doctor shook his head. "We have a very small amount, but Dr. Fuchida will not permit it to be given to a prisoner."

"But to save a man's life..."

"I'm sorry. I cannot disobey orders." He sat back on his heels. "Besides, the drug is a very basic medicine. At this stage..." He did not finish the sentence.

The tent flap opened. Norris Sinclair, his six-foot frame crouching, entered. Bearded now, with his brown hair in tangles, the PhilPak executive had lost the fleshiness that had been so noticeable at Del Monte. He knelt by the foot of Kogan's pallet, then nodded to Shiga.

"Glad to see you, Doctor," he said. "How's the patient?" Without waiting for a reply, he grabbed Kogan's ankle playfully. "How ya feel, Joe?"

"Fine, Norris," Kogan answered, his voice a croak. "Just fine."

"Good." Sinclair nodded agreeably, but his face remained concerned. He glanced at Marie and the Japanese doctor. The silence in the tent extended uncomfortably.

Dr. Shiga rose to his feet, his head scraping the top of the tent. "I will have to leave now," he said. "Mr. Kogan, I'll drop in again tomorrow night."

"I'll walk a ways with you, Doc," Sinclair said, then turned to Marie. "It's cooler out, my dear. Why don't you come along and get some air?" She looked down at Kogan doubtfully, but he nodded for her to go along.

Outside the tent, Marie followed Sinclair and the doctor to the old disused water fountain with its sculpture of a brooding Saint Thomas Aquinas. It was still early evening and the muted hum of voices rose from tents and ramshackle huts strewn haphazardly about the walled campus. Across the bay to the west lay the black bulk of Bataan, unlighted and at peace for now. What a distance she had traveled, in time and miles and emotions, since the high euphoria she had felt scrambling aboard the PBY that would fly her to freedom. Now she was back within a dozen miles of her starting point, struggling hard to stay alive. For Joe, the man she loved, the struggle could be nearly over.

Norris Sinclair laid a big hand on her shoulder. "I'm sorry," he said. She bowed her head in anguish, unable to speak. "Doctor," he continued, "is there any way we can save him?"

"I'm afraid not," Shiga answered. "He needs medicine we don't have."

"What kind of medicine?"

Marie stirred. "Norris, we call them the new wonder drugs. Sulfa. They might have enough potency to stop the infection."

"I agree," Shiga said. "Sulfanilamide, or better, sulfapyridine could do it, I think."

"Can you get them?"

There was a trace of acerbity in Shiga's voice. "I told you, Mr. Sinclair, that we don't have them. As far as I know, there isn't a single dosage available in the entire Japanese army."

Sinclair looked thoughtful. "Sulfa . . . what?" he asked.

Shiga looked at him curiously. "Sulfapyridine."

Sinclair pulled a small notebook from his pocket. With the stub of a pencil poised, he said, "How do you spell that?"

• • •

Marie, her bruised face hidden in the shadows, hardly looked up as Dr. Shiga parted the canvas flaps. He knelt beside Joe's side and felt his pulse. There was no need to check for fever. The man was burning up.

"He's been in a lot of pain today, Doctor," Marie said.

"I assumed he would be." He took an envelope from his pocket and slipped it into her hand. "I brought a little veronal. I wish I could have gotten more. Use it when . . . things get too bad."

Kogan's eyes opened and took a few seconds to focus. He attempted a smile at Marie, but it didn't quite come off. A spasm of pain hit and his lips drew back to flatten against his teeth. It passed and he released his breath explosively. Marie leaned forward and wiped his face with a wet cloth.

"Dr. Shiga brought something to help with the pain, dear." She continued to bathe his face.

"You've been using the hot compresses?" Shiga asked.

She nodded. "Every four hours."

The doctor looked at her closely. "You need rest. Have you anyone who can help you?"

"My friend, Lieutenant Kruloff, has been coming in every day, but she is now sick herself. Could you take a look at her?" Sylvia had been able to spell her so that she could sleep some during the day. But her old friend had fallen ill, victim of one of the camp's most prevalent diseases. In just the last week Marie had watched Sylvia rapidly weaken. Almost overnight, it seemed, her marvelous skin had begun to blotch and the firm tissue of her body shrivel.

"Lieutenant Kruloff?" He shook his head. "Ah, yes, I have seen her. So far I have been unable to tell whether her dysentery is amoebic or bacillary. I have administered some sodium sulfate . . ." Dr. Shiga left it at that. "If only," he continued, feeling Kogan's pulse again, "we could get out of this heat—move this camp to Baguio, in the highlands. What a help that would be."

Marie watched Shiga as he hovered over Joe, waiting for him

to do something, to suggest something else. He shrugged his shoulders helplessly.

Marie jumped and gave a little scream.

Without warning a parcel had flown in through the tent flap and hit with a thud beside Joe's pallet. Norris Sinclair followed it in, breathing hard, his dark brown hair rumpled, as usual, but his mouth smiling under a spiky mustache.

"Whew!" he exclaimed. "Good timing. Glad to catch you here, Doc." He pointed to the package. "Open it up."

With flying fingers, Shiga tore the wrappings off, exposing two brown cardboard boxes with typed labels. Holding them close to the candle, Shiga muttered, "This is difficult to believe—an American pharmaceutical company? Sulfanilamide powder— twenty grams. Ah, that will help." He picked up the other box, read the label, then with an incredulous hiss, reread it. He looked up at Sinclair, his face filled with wonder. "The magic bullet," he said softly. "I have heard of penicillin, but I never thought I'd see it. Where . . . how did you get this? No, don't tell me." He turned toward Kogan on his hands and knees. "Please," Shiga spoke to no one in particular. "Give me a little time to think about this."

Later, outside the tent, Marie finished wiping her eyes. "Oh, God, Norris, it's a miracle. How were you able to do it?"

"Simple enough, really." He grinned, and she could see the rebirth of an executive's pride that had been forcibly suppressed by imprisonment. "It's common knowledge that American submarines are supplying guerrilla bands on Negros, Leyte, and Mindanao with all sorts of supplies, including medicine. Excess stuff finds its way to the Manila black market. I bought the medicine through the wall."

"Oh, of course," she said, disbelieving. "Just like that. Norris, there isn't a peso in the whole camp."

"We've got pesos," he said. His expression turned serious. "Thanks to the reputation of PhilPak. Look." He pulled out his small notebook and riffled through the pages. "I write out a promissory note for the pesos I need, based on 'the full faith and credit of the Philippine Packing Company,' and sign it. Works like a charm."

"How much did you pay for . . . that package?"

"A mere bagatelle." He smiled.

"How much? Tell me."

"One thousand pesos."

Her eyes widened. "Five hundred dollars! Oh, Norris."

"Joe's worth far more than that." He chuckled. "This is only the beginning. Of course, after the war, Del Monte Foods is going to have quite a tab to pay."

Two Years Later —

August 17, 1944

A few ragged figures moved listlessly in the heat, but for most prisoners, midday in August was a time to hunker down and suffer the cruel temperatures passively. Faint breaths of hot air stirred dust-covered weeds and the few surviving bougainvilleas. The tents of two years ago had disintegrated under sun and wind. What remained of the canvas went into huts built from nipa grass and scrap lumber.

In one of the hovels, Marie Crane lay back on a thin cotton tick and tried to smile.

"I forget, Joe. When does the cooler weather begin?"

"Not long now. A few weeks more." He shot a glance at the sliver of steel blue sky showing through the pulled-back canvas roof of the hut. He rinsed the cloth in the water pan and wiped the sweat from her forehead, brushing back her matted hair, then held to her lips a cup of water he had boiled. She drank gratefully and raised a thin hand to touch his bearded face.

"Thank you, General," she said, making the little joke that always brought reproof.

He responded with a half smile and warning shake of his head.

He was *Mister* Joseph Kogan and had been since they had entered the camp. As an army officer he would have been shipped off to Cabanatuan or O'Donnell, but civilian status meant he could stay with Marie. Now, more than ever, it was important for them to be together. The feverish red of her cheeks and the emaciation of her body under her sweat-soaked shift frightened him. The wasting was an all-too-familiar prelude to death at Santo Tomás. He *had* to take care of her, to try to save her as she had saved him. The struggle and the nursing and the worry of that effort had exhausted her, leaving her pitifully vulnerable to the diseases of the camp. Month by month for more than two years, her health had deteriorated until she could barely walk. Now they were two scarecrows whose love had deepened over time, transcending the physical attractiveness they had long ago lost. Marie's thin body weighed less than a hundred pounds, and Joe was gaunt and stringy—a bearded, one-armed pirate of a man.

She stirred restlessly, her bony hands picking at a thread on her garment. "Joe, you know we won't have much more time together, don't you?"

"Hey," he said reprovingly. "Come on. That's nonsense."

"No, it isn't. You're the one who told me I'd die in this place, remember?"

God, yes, he remembered. He was never free of those words he had shouted to her while racing for the plane. Mike Witkowski had uttered them first when he had read her death sentence off the VAX 8800. What could he say to her now? They'd been through this before, but he knew how much she needed reassurance. "Computers make mistakes," he said, lowering his voice. "Believe me. They'll get blamed for everything that goes wrong." And he added, to build her spirits, "Some day you'll see."

She shook her head. "No, I won't. And you don't believe it, either. Bea . . . poor, dear Beatrice went right away. She didn't have a chance." She pointed to the scruffy suitcase in the corner. "Every time I look at her little blue hat I think of her—"

"Maybe you should get rid of that hat."

"No!" she said fiercely. "Bea gave it to me. It means a lot to me. I want to be buried wearing it."

"All right, all right," he said soothingly, leaning forward to wipe her face. "But stop thinking about dying."

"I can't help it, Joe. Sylvia Kruloff died more than a year ago. Leona Saunders is terribly sick. Oh, God, Joe—"

He deliberately interrupted, not wanting the emotional strain to sap her remaining strength. "You know," he said with elaborate nonchalance, "I think it's time you and I got married."

They had never spoken of marriage, because to Marie, who was convinced that she would never survive internment, a life after the war was a dream never to be realized. And marriage at Santo Tomás was strictly forbidden by the camp commandant. They had never even been lovers, nor could they live together, for cohabitation was prohibited even between husband and wife. Each of the huts in "shantytown" had a large section of the side wall opening on hinges, making the interior subject to inspection by the guards. But the major obstacle to sex was pregnancy. The previous year, four married women had become pregnant. Colonel Kozono had immediately sent the husbands to Los Banos, a harsh work camp inland. There had been no more pregnancies.

Now Kozono was gone. Three weeks ago, a younger commandant, a Major Hata, had taken over. According to the grapevine, he was an improvement over his predecessor. It was rumored that he might even permit cohabitation and new marriages, although no one knew for sure. But the important thing for Kogan was to find something to take Marie's mind off dying, to boost her spirits, to instill in her the will to live. Marriage might not make her well, but it would help.

She managed a smile. "Where will we go on our honeymoon?"

"I mean it. I want us to be married."

She sighed. "Oh, Joe, it's impossible."

He leaned forward, fanning her with a palmetto frond. It suddenly became very important for him. Anything was that might give her the strength to carry on. But it had become more than that. He couldn't imagine life without her. She was his closest friend, his confidante, his love. The high point of their days was the precious hours they spent together when Joe came to bring her news of the camp, and they talked endlessly of the past and the future. Marie's curiosity about a world he knew well, but she would never see, was inexhaustible. Her eyes would go wide as he talked of the new technological marvels in entertainment, communication, and transportation. He tried to explain the new morality—or lack of it—the crime in the streets, the Cold War and McCarthyism, the assassinations of the young president and his brother, the criminal stupidity of Vietnam. He watched her face go from disbelief to dubious understanding when he talked of the rise from ashes of defeat of Japan and Germany, and of the international power realignments, and of the Great Change in eastern Europe and Russia. The next fifty years, he told her, was a time of incredible events and changes that had never been matched in the history of the world.

"I'm so glad you were . . . are a historian, Joe," she would say. "You make it come to life. It sounds so wonderful, yet so scary. I'm not sure I'd want to . . . well, maybe it's better that I die here."

"No, no," he would answer her. "It's an exciting time, it really is. You will hate some of it, but you will love most of it. Marie," he chuckled, "it's something you can't afford to miss. Trust me."

But all of his entreaties and arguments and promises failed to penetrate her pessimism. This was why he argued so strongly this afternoon. He had to give her something to distract her.

"Let me try," he said. "The new commandant, Major Hata, is supposed to be a different sort. Maybe I can talk him into approving our marriage."

"Yes, and you could talk yourself right into another beating, too." She took his hand in both hers. "You want to do this before I die, don't you?" Tears trickled down her pale cheeks. "Darling, I've dreamed about it so many nights, but really, we can't be any more married than we already are. I love you, and you love me—we've proved that over and over. Why else would you hang around with an ugly hag?" She tried to laugh, but it became a

Kogan ignored her words. "Please. For me," he pressed.

For a long time she remained silent, one hand thrown over her closed eyes. Finally, she asked, "Does it really mean that much to you?"

He leaned forward and kissed her cheek. "I'll be back," he said.

The little officer with the neatly trimmed mustache returned Kogan's bow with a slight inclination of his head. Major Saburo Hata had come to the camp three weeks ago, and since then, to everyone's surprise, conditions—at least in small ways—had slowly improved. Although not many prisoners had contact with the new commandant, it was known that Hata was a reservist, a former professor of English at Tokyo University. It was said, perhaps more in hope than in certainty, that he lacked the brutal military ethos of the army officer class.

At any rate, Kogan found that the major spoke the language perfectly.

"I have looked at your record, Mr. Kogan," he said, indicating a folder on his desk. "What there is of it, which is very little. I am really surprised. According to this, you were a civilian visiting a friend, one Norris Sinclair, an executive of Philippine Packing Company, when the war began. A few months later, you were wounded and captured by our forces while trying to get aboard a flight to Australia." He raised his eyebrows and looked at Kogan.

"That's right, sir."

"Yet the record also shows that you were wearing an officer's uniform when captured."

Kogan's answer was casual. "Fog of war, Major. I habitually wore khaki trousers, for comfort. My civilian shirt—a very nice Brooks Brothers model, I might add—was cut away because of my wound."

Major Hata tapped the folder thoughtfully. "I see," he said. "Well, this does contain a statement from Norris Sinclair—interned here, as you know—confirming what you say." He laid

Major Hata tapped the folder thoughtfully. "I see," he said. "Well, this does contain a statement from Norris Sinclair—interned here, as you know—confirming what you say." He laid the folder to one side. "You assert, then, that you have never had military training, never attended, for instance, the Staff and Command School at Leavenworth?"

Kogan didn't like the way this interview was going. This small-statured officer was sharp, and he was digging into a dangerous area Kogan thought was long behind him.

"No, sir. Never even went through boot camp."

"Boot camp?" Hata looked puzzled, then his eyes brightened. "Oh, yes. Recruit training. Well...we'll come back to that later." He put the folder to one side. "So, what is the purpose of this visit?"

Kogan told him, then waited, his muscles tensed, for the reply.

Hata seemed in no hurry to respond, one way or another. "Would you like tea, Mr. Kogan?" He rang a tiny silver bell and spoke rapidly to a stocky enlisted orderly, then turned back to Kogan. "You understand, I hope, why Colonel Kozono permitted neither marriage nor cohabitation among married prisoners. This policy of celibacy was implemented to keep Santo Tomás from becoming a giant nursery that we are not equipped to handle. Yet," Hata eyed the ceiling reflectively, "I can understand the hardship that prolonged celibacy imposes. I am seriously considering rescinding the policy, but I need more time for study."

The door opened and the orderly appeared with the tea tray. Setting it on a small, lacquered table, he bowed and withdrew. Hata poured as he talked.

"So you see my problem, Mr. Kogan. If I approve this marriage, I imply to the others that cohabitation is also permitted them. Right now, I am not prepared to go that far, which means that your marriage would be only a sham. After the ceremony, you and your wife would have to return to your respective beds."

Kogan sipped his tea. Its taste was delicious. Perhaps it was because his taste buds had been deprived of anything good for too long. "Let me explain, Major," he said. "We are not asking for sexual union. Captain Crane is not well. No, let me be honest. She is . . . she is . . ." To his horror, he found the words stuck in his throat. Tears welled up in his eyes. *My God*, he thought, *I'm about to break down and cry.* He fought desperately for control.

Hata stepped around his desk quickly and poured more tea. Handing the cup to Kogan, he said, "I think I understand." He kept talking, as if to give Kogan time to recover. "I am sorry for her condition. Westerners do not do well in this execrable climate. I wish we had more medicine to give you—and better food." His eyes swept over Kogan's emaciated frame and rested on the empty sleeve. "Has your arm mended?"

Kogan was grateful for the time he needed to pull himself together. "Yes, sir," he answered. "Some time ago." The stump was still occasionally tender, but Norris Sinclair's medicine had stopped the infection and permitted the arm to heal.

Hata returned to his desk. "Well, if the circumstances you relate are true—and I have no reason to doubt them—I see no objection to the marriage." He nodded and placed his hands across his small belly, looking like a beneficent Buddha. "You may marry any time you wish."

"Thank you, sir," Kogan said, manfully concealing his delight. He had learned the value of stoicism. The tea was gone and he assumed the interview was over. He rose to go and was preparing to bow, when the major again picked up Kogan's dossier.

"Uh, Mr. Kogan, as to your military background. It seems strange that a civilian such as yourself is reputed to be an excellent military strategist."

"I don't understand." He had a glimmer of what Hata was driving at, but he had to make sure.

"From what my informants have told me, your analysis of the war in the Pacific has been masterful."

Oh-oh. Now he understood what had happened. During the last two years, he and his fellow prisoners had formed a council to serve as a gathering house for information about the progress of the war. Once or twice a week, huddled over a tattered map of the Pacific, listening to clandestine radio broadcasts, they laboriously charted known positions and speculated on future operations. As the blue lines across the Pacific grew longer, and the red positions withdrew, the time seemed ever closer when rescue would come. But only one person in the camp knew exactly when that would be, and Kogan couldn't tell. What he had done, though, as cautiously as possible, was to fill in the gaps that broadcasts and Filipino friends were unable to provide. Always phrasing his comments as opinions, he had predicted how the army, navy, and the marines would fight their way back. In the beginning, he had said he "thought" it would be slow going because America would pay more attention to defeating Germany than to Japan. Later he "believed" that once the United States mobilized fully her industry, progress would come much faster. Then it was his "opinion" that movement across the Pacific would be along two major axes—a South Pacific thrust and a Central Pacific offensive. He "felt" that the method would probably involve bypassing some island bastions while assaulting others.

At first, his fellow prisoners argued with him, advancing their own points of view, but as reports proved him right time and again, the sessions became little seminars in which others put forth their opinions and then listened respectfully as Kogan "speculated."

Someone, he thought as he considered Hata's statement, had talked too loudly.

"Major, I've made a few lucky guesses, that's all."

Major Hata smiled. "You are too modest." He walked to the large map of the Pacific on his office wall and picked up a pointer. "Three months ago, American forces took New Guinea. One month ago, Guam was recaptured and Saipan occupied." He pointed to the map. "Now your bombers have struck Formosa, and Leyte Island right here in the Philippines. Such bombing is usually the signal for an invasion." Hata leaned on his bamboo pointer. "Now, Mr. Kogan, what is your guess? Will the next assault come at Formosa, or at the Philippines?"

Kogan grinned. "Gee, Major, that's a tough one. I wouldn't want to hazard an opinion."

Hata tossed his pointer on his desk. "I suspected that would be your answer. But I assure you that Imperial Headquarters does not revise its plans simply because a prison camp major extracts an opinion from an American civilian. No, it was only for my own edification." He looked at Kogan keenly. "Would you care to humor me?"

Kogan shook his head.

Hata sighed. "Oh, well. It is no secret that we are losing this war, even if the lordly shoguns at headquarters refuse to admit it. I suspect that if you can survive long enough on the appalling slop we feed you, the time will come when I will bow low to you, sir." He seemed suddenly diminished, his small frame shrunken inside his uniform.

"So much wealth wasted, so many lives thrown away on a dream. We thought we could dominate all Asia, become a world power, speak authoritatively at international councils. An impossible, tragic, misguided ambition. Our future, I am afraid, will be a return to our past—a small island empire of rice paddies, posturing samurai, and..." his expression was rueful, "...Madame Butterflies."

"Not necessarily, Major."

Hata's brows arched in surprise. "Really? Why do you say that?"

"Once there was another small island nation that by trade alone became the world's greatest power."

"Ah, England. Yes, you have a point." He pursed his lips. "However, Japan has a strong military tradition. Given the choice, I'm afraid we'd rather conquer than buy and sell."

"I'd be surprised if your military tradition isn't knocked into a cocked hat after this war."

The major hastily picked up a writing brush. "What's that? Into a c-o-c-k-e-d hat," he muttered while writing. "Very good." He laid his brush down and straightened. "And so you think that by trade alone, Japan could rise again?"

"For what it's worth, that would be my guess."

Hata nodded, his eyes narrowing speculatively, then he became businesslike.

"Very well, I appreciate your comments. So, Mr. Kogan, once the marriage ceremony is performed, please report back to this office with your bride so that we can make the proper notation in our records."

Kogan bowed and moved to the door. With his hand on the knob, he turned back. "Major," he said, "if it's any help in deciding whether married couples should live together, I can tell you this—no more American babies will be born in Santo Tomás."

Almost instantly, Major Hata understood. His face paled. "Are you telling me what I think you are?"

"Of course, you can take that as an idle comment," Kogan said.

It was as if Hata had not heard him. "That soon?" he muttered. "It will be over that soon?" The major seemed to get a grip on himself. "Really, there is absolutely no reason I should believe you. How could you possibly know?" He paused and bit his lip. "But I assure you, Mr. Kogan, that you frighten me."

Frequently at this time of the year, the evening wind from the southeast quickened to blow some of the heat away, so they scheduled the marriage at sunset. But what Joe and Marie had hoped would be a quiet little event became a major happening, a respite for others from the boredom of the camp.

Women turned Kogan out of the hut as they prepared Marie. One internee, a professional hairdresser, washed and set the bride's hair. Bathed, manicured, and wearing a patched dress donated by a friend, Marie, with a bouquet made up of three hibiscus blossoms set in feathery acacia leaves, was ready to be wed.

Kogan's wedding preparations consisted of a shower, shave, and clean khaki. Then he stood with a gaunt Norris Sinclair at his side as Marie walked slowly down an open-air, weed-strewn aisle created by well-wishers, smiling shyly at him. The dress hung on her wasted body, but for the first time since internment, she wore makeup, expertly applied, and startlingly effective against the white of her skin. Perched on her head was the little blue pillbox of a hat.

The only hat in all of Santo Tomás.

Kogan thought she was beautiful.

Norris, at the appropriate moment, handed Kogan a gold band bought on the black market. Slipping it on Marie's finger, Kogan noted with pain how much too large the ring was. It literally hung on her finger.

The ceremony was conducted by a navy chaplain who managed to inject some ribald humor into the occasion. Guards on the walls turned their heads in surprise at the rare sound of raucous laughter and applause.

Then it was over. In accordance with the chaplain's stern command to kiss the bride, Joe lifted the tiny veil. He wrapped his arms around the thin body of his wife for the first time and kissed her. She clung to him, her eyes closed against the parchment pallor of her face. Joe felt the weight of her body as it collapsed against his. Marie had fainted.

They carried her into the hut and laid her down. Norris Sinclair pushed worried friends out while Joe bathed her face and arms. After a few minutes her eyes opened and focused on him.

"So sorry, Joe, to be so weak," she said. "Imagine, fainting at one's own wedding."

"Understandable. I'm known as a power kisser," he said, leaning forward to touch his lips to her cheek. Later, a few friends tiptoed by to congratulate them and offer a cup of bootleg wine. That was the extent of their marriage celebration.

Very early the next morning, while there was still some coolness in the air, they went to the commandant's office, walking slowly, Joe half supporting her, husbanding her strength. She looked up at him.

"Now that we're married, maybe you'll be kind enough to tell me how long before American troops get here," she said.

Kogan didn't answer. There was a reason he hadn't ever told her. In the spring of 1942, the consensus among prisoners was "several months" before rescuers arrived. As each month passed, the date was pushed back, but it was always "just a few more months." Had he told them in the beginning that it would be three more years, many, would have curled up and died. Some did anyway.

"Please, Joe, tell me," she pressed him.

He shook his head. "It won't be long." It would be almost half a year. His heart ached with the realization that unless he could somehow make her believe that she would survive, Marie would not live that long.

They bowed to Major Hata, who had come out of his office to offer his personal congratulations.

"Ah, let me see," he said, taking the roster book from his clerk. "Yes, we will write in a new name—Mrs. Joseph Kogan— and scratch out Captain Marie Crane." Kogan stiffened with shock. The words that Hata spoke meant something, but it took a moment for him to make the connection. Suddenly he was back at Del Monte, standing beside old *Sucker One* listening to Witkowski read a computer printout: "*Sorry, Joe, but Captain Crane is not on the list of repatriates after the war.*"

Now he knew, and the hair on his scalp prickled as he listened to the soft sounds of Hata's brush on paper. For a moment, the old office with its moldy furniture, mahogany doors, and white-washed walls whirled about him, delighting him with his new knowledge. Involuntarily, his hand stole to Marie's and he gripped hard—too hard, he saw from her momentary wince, but she quickly smiled up at him, her blue eyes awash with fatigue and sickness.

Then it was over and they walked out into the hot sunshine

of Kogan's bright new world. They were still in the shade of the building when he stopped.

"February 5, 1945," he said.

"What did you say?"

"February of next year. That's when the First Cavalry Division will break down the gates."

She looked up at him, her expression uncertain. "Why, dear husband, after all this time, are you telling me?"

Laughing aloud, his first real joyous laugh in a long while, he reached out and cupped her face in his hands. "Because you're gonna be here, Mrs. Joseph Kogan, to greet the First Cav, even though Marie Crane won't be. You understand? Do you really understand? Honey, I told you computers could screw up."

As comprehension slowly dawned, she put her bony arms around him and held on tight.

═══ CHAPTER TWENTY-TWO ═══

Twenty Years Later —

Baguio Highlands, Philippines, 1965

The mansion sprawled along the crest of a mountainous spur extending from the flank of Mount Ambuklao. Pristine white with Ionic columns marking the entrance, it glowed like a huge pearl against the deep-green foliage of the Baguio highlands. Built two years after the war by a Manila hotel man whose tastes outstripped his income, it had been purchased in the mid-1950s by Joseph Kogan and his wife, Marie. In the years since, refurbishing and improvements to the property had far exceeded its original cost.

This morning was cool and a lean, gray Kogan wore a jacket with its left arm pinned up as he rallied with Carlos, a muscular Filipino tennis pro. Bouncing a ball with his racket, Kogan balanced it adeptly on the strings for a second, then tossed it into the air. *Whaack!* His service caught the service line and Carlos had to lunge to return it. The rally went on strongly for some time before Kogan netted a ball.

From courtside, Marie, with a bandeau around her red hair, wearing white slacks and a chartreuse sweater, laughed and applauded. "Bravo, Rod Laver. Now, come have a glass of orange juice. Alfred is going to be here any time."

Kogan waved his thanks to Carlos and picked up a towel as he came off the court. Age had roughened his strong features and left only a few iron-gray strands across the tanned skin of his head.

"Yeah, the boy wonder's probably been on the road since six." He glanced around. "I tell you, honey, it's time for the company to get a helicopter." Wiping his face, he pointed eastward. "We can put a helipad out on the ridge, away from the house."

Clarita, a middle-aged Filipino woman, handed him a tall glass of orange juice. He took a gulp and continued. "Cut travel time between here and Manila from four hours to . . . oh, less than an hour."

She smiled indulgently. "You are so spoiled," she said.

He kissed the top of her head as he sat down. "Touch of gray amid those fiery locks, my dear," he said.

"Will you stop that?" Marie complained. "I had more than a *touch* of gray twenty years ago when we left Santo Tomás. If it wasn't for my hairdresser and her magic bottle, my hair would be completely white." She leaned toward him and patted her curls. "Come on, now, what do you think? Shall I let it go?"

Kogan chuckled. "Since those silver strands were mostly on my account, it's up to you." He reached out and caressed her cheek. "You really want my input? I say let it go."

She looked out across the gorge of the Abra River, where the cloud shadows were racing down the mountain slopes. "I don't know," she said with mock seriousness, speaking to the distant peaks. "This is a major decision. We'd better sleep on it." He followed her gaze. Of all the places in the world they had traveled to, he loved the unspoiled beauty of the highlands best. He thought of something.

"Oh, incidentally, Alfred is bringing someone with him."

"Really?" She indicated mild surprise. "That's unusual, isn't it?"

He watched her carefully. "The man represents a Japanese firm. His name is Hata."

Marie sipped her orange juice. "Any particular reason why he's coming here?" Her eyes widened. "Joe! I know that name. Wasn't the commandant at Santo Tomás named Hata? It couldn't be the same man, could it?"

"Hardly. Same name, all right, but a different man. I had our law firm in Tokyo check. This Hata is in his early thirties." He stretched and yawned. "But yes, there is a particular reason to have him here. Nothing to do with his name, though."

The shiny new 1965 Cadillac limousine effortlessly climbed the winding, black-topped road. Alfred Thayer Hill, Ph.D., Princeton, 1959, drummed the expensive briefcase resting on his knees. He had worked for Pacific Development three years now and he knew that most of his peers—that is, young economists working in multinationals—envied him. Although he could not take the time to check, Alfred believed that he was very close to his first million, perhaps even past it. His career was pretty much assured, and his relationship with the legendary, publicity-shy Joseph Kogan comfortable, although occasionally aggravating.

First of all, there was the secrecy involved. The name Kogan must never be connected with Pacific Development, Ltd. Norris Sinclair, a very nice old geezer who spent most of his time traveling and collecting art, was listed as president, but he had no real authority.

Try as he might, Alfred could never uncover any reason for the layers of legal stratagems created to mask Kogan's ownership, but he had been told, in unmistakable terms, that were he to violate the dictate, he wouldn't be able to get a job peddling newspapers on a Manila street corner.

His other complaint was more fundamental. Alfred was, after

all, Kogan's chief adviser on investments and he worked hard at it. The old man was intelligent—very sharp, indeed—but economics and finance were not his strong points. Quite often, when Alfred explained to Mr. Kogan the technical details of a potential acquisition or trade, he was certain they simply went over his head. Sometimes the boss would drum on the table with his fingers while his eyes wandered around the room or fixed on something out the window. Usually, though, he heard his young assistant out with great courtesy. When Alfred would ask, patiently, if he should go over some part of the deal again, Kogan would smile and say no thank you, Alfred, you've been very helpful.

Then Kogan would make the decision, sometimes in accordance with Alfred's recommendation, and sometimes the exact opposite, never giving any reason. Okay, that was his prerogative. But to Alfred, the really scary element in working for Pacific Development, Ltd., the part he had trouble admitting even to himself, was that Mr. Kogan was always right. Not *usually* right—*always* right. It was uncanny. He seemed never to make a mistake. Well... that might be an overstatement, for just last month the old man had passed on an opportunity to buy several undervalued buildings in downtown Saigon. When Alfred pointed out with irrefutable logic that the United States was now in charge in Vietnam, and that the future there could hardly be brighter, Kogan's smile had snapped off. His joviality had disappeared. The blunt, weather-beaten features turned icy and his eyes shifted to some vision far beyond the walls of the boardroom.

"Not one dollar of our money will ever be invested in that country," Kogan had said.

Alfred had never seen the old man react like that before, but he realized, with a little prickling of fear, that he was not ever to mention it again. Still, he reflected, thinking back on the incident, maybe in just a few years he'd have the courage to point out to Kogan the chance he missed.

As the Cadillac slid beneath the mansion portico, Alfred assayed a smile at the little man riding with him, although it was an effort. Part of his resentment of this Japanese petitioner was

that the boss had agreed to the meeting against his own recommendation. A letter signed "Osachi Hata" had arrived three
weeks ago, requesting an interview with any senior executive of
Pacific Development, citing an investment opportunity. In his
weekly meeting with Kogan, Alfred had said the Japanese possessed nothing the West wanted. Let him go elsewhere. To his
surprise, not only had Kogan said yes, he had added that he,
himself, would meet with Hata.

It was pretty obvious that the Japanese did not quite appreciate
the coup. One of the few exchanges during the long ride from
Manila had substantiated that.

"I had rather hoped, Mr. Hill," Hata had spoken apologetically, "that I might have an opportunity to speak with the president of the company, Mr. Norris Sinclair."

"He's out of town," Alfred had said shortly. It was true. Sinclair
was somewhere in the Loire Valley, he'd heard, trying to acquire
a couple of old French Masters that had come on the market.

The car reached the crest of a long climb, passed through a
rocky cleft, and eased down to cruise through the bowl of a valley.
White clouds, their edges darkening, rested on the mountains
ringing what resembled a Swiss vale. The view seemed lost on
the Japanese.

"This Mr. Kogan, sir," Hata had said. "He is of sufficiently
high rank to make decisions?"

"Yes, Mr. Hata." Alfred smiled at the question. "You may be
sure of that."

Mr. Hata needed money desperately. That was what he had
come for, but Alfred was going to see to it that he left empty-
handed. He was positive that this time, Mr. Kogan would see it
his way.

"Tea, Mr. Hata?" Marie asked.

Hata seemed to half rise when either of his hosts spoke to him.
"Yes, thank you very much," he said too quickly in his precise,
heavily accented English, "that would be very nice, Mrs. Kogan."

Clarita served tea. Kogan handed her his empty orange juice glass. "Sweeten that with a little vodka this time, will you?"

Alfred decided to get this one over with quickly.

"Mr. Hata." Alfred turned suddenly to the Japanese, causing him nearly to spill his tea. "What is your proposal?" It was not the approved way of doing business on the Pacific Rim, but he wasn't in the mood for the protocol of endless preliminary chitchat.

With a glance at Kogan, Hata slid forward in his seat and cleared his throat. It was obvious to Alfred that the Japanese had carefully rehearsed what he was about to say.

"Sir, we are trying to build a car for the Japanese—a small, economical car much in the same mold as the German Volks-wagen. We would like—"

Alfred interrupted. "Why not import the Volkswagen? It's been quite a success in the United States."

"It is far too expensive for our people, sir. And it is important to Japan that we develop our own car industry." Although a cool breeze swept across the patio, Hata mopped his brow with a large handkerchief. "We would like someday to have a car good enough for export to other countries."

Alfred glanced at Kogan to see if he, too, was amused by the words of the Japanese. But the boss's face registered nothing. Disappointed, Alfred said, "Not to the United States, surely."

With an apologetic glance at Kogan, Hata nodded. "Yes, someday. We have already sold a few to Americans."

Alfred laughed. "That's true, Mr. Hata, and I've taken the trouble to check on your car. Let me be candid. It has the style of a packing crate, the thousand-cc engine has no acceleration, it won't start in cold weather, and you've had a miserable sales record with it." He turned again to Kogan, hoping to see his diligence approved. But the boss's face might have been made of stone. He kept his eyes steadfastly on the Japanese.

Hata set himself more firmly in his chair. He placed his cup carefully on the table beside him and pulled a folded document from an inner pocket. "What you say, Mr. Hill, is absolutely correct. The car's deficiencies are set forth in this . . . prospectus,

I believe you call it." He leaned forward and handed it to Kogan, who tossed it carelessly to Alfred. "We are working on an entirely new engine in the hopes of producing a car without deficiencies—one that both Japanese and less affluent Americans can drive with enjoyment." Although he spoke with vigor, Alfred noted that Hata's smile lacked confidence. "This requires money. As you know, sir, that is why I am here."

There was silence around the table as Clarita set a tall, frosty glass at Kogan's elbow. He sipped it and smiled approvingly at the servant.

"Pardon me for asking, Mr. Hata." Marie spoke up. "But is your name an unusual one in Japan?"

Surprise and a measure of relief showed in the carmaker's face. The conversation had veered away from the danger zone into more traditional channels.

"I would say, Mrs. Kogan, that it is neither common nor uncommon. It is perhaps..." he bowed slightly to Alfred, "less common than Hill in your language, and..." he smiled at Marie, "found more frequently than is Kogan."

Marie returned his smile and stirred her tea. Kogan watched her, understanding that she had more to say and pretty sure of what it was going to be.

Mr. Hata's next words gave her the opportunity. "Are you acquainted perhaps with another of the Hata family?"

"No," Marie answered. "Not really. Forgive my questions, but was your father in the Japanese army?"

Hata shook his head. "No, I regret to say that he died while I was still a child." Then he smiled. "Ah, but I had an uncle, Saburo Hata, who was a major in the army." His eyes narrowed in thought. "Yes, I recall that he was here in the Philippines as commandant of..." Hata's voice left him and his face paled as he looked at his hosts. His eyes came to rest on Kogan's empty sleeve.

"...of Santo Tomás Internment Camp?" Marie finished his sentence for him.

"Yes, Santo Tomás," Hata whispered. After an agonizing moment, he asked, "Was your husband an internee, Mrs. Kogan?"

"We were both internees, Mr. Hata."

Hata put his cup down carefully and wiped his lips. He continued to stare at the tile of the pool deck as though it might help him reach a decision. Then he picked up his hat, got to his feet, and bowed low. "I am aware of the sufferings experienced by Americans confined at Santo Tomás. I can only express my sympathy for yours. Now, if you will excuse me, I will take my leave."

"How much, Mr. Hata?" Kogan spoke to him for the first time.

"Sir?" Hata stopped, surprised.

"I said, how much money do you want to borrow?"

"But, sir, after experiencing what you have, you must have much hatred for Japan . . . and the officer who administered Santo Tomás."

"Your uncle was there only three months. And let me tell you something. If the officers who commanded before and after him were standing where you are, Mr. Hata, I would happily heave their asses off this cliff. No," he continued, "neither my wife nor I have any complaints to make against Major Hata. On the contrary, he gave us permission to marry."

Relief flooded the industrialist's face. "That is incredible, sir, absolutely incredible." For no discernible reason, he bowed again, but remained standing.

"Sit down, please," Kogan said.

Hata complied quickly, but kept his hat in his hand.

"I repeat. How much, Mr. Hata?"

The Japanese licked his lips and took a deep breath. "We would like very much to get a million and a half."

Kogan remained silent, his face revealing nothing.

At the risk of falling to the ground, Hata edged farther forward on his chair. "However, sir, we could perhaps make do with one million."

"I'm sorry, but that is out of the question—" Alfred started to put the nail in the coffin.

"How about five million?" Kogan bounced a tennis ball between his feet.

"Five million? Five million dollars?" Hata's mouth dropped open.

"Mr. Kogan," Alfred protested vehemently. "You must be joking."

"Sir," Hata said hurriedly, "that is wonderful, very generous. We will be able to do everything that we planned and more." Then his smile became fearful, as though a prize might be snatched away. "We can repay on a five-year schedule, or . . ." he added hesitantly, "we can transfer to you a substantial block of stock."

"We'll take the note. Five years at eight percent." Alfred spoke with resolution.

"No, Alfred," Kogan said just as wearily. "We'll take the stock."

Hata got to his feet and bowed several times in succession. "Mr. Kogan, on behalf of our workers, I wish to express my deepest appreciation for the confidence you have shown in us."

Kogan got to his feet and the two men shook hands. "There is one thing, Mr. Hata, that I must insist upon," Kogan said, his eyes fixed on the smaller man's face. "You are never to mention to anybody that I was involved in this, or that you even met me. Is that clear?"

If Hata was perplexed by Kogan's words, his face did not show it. "That is clear, sir."

"If you feel that you cannot keep this pledge, our business is concluded as of now."

Hata bowed. "I understand, Mr. Kogan. You need have no worry on that score." He picked up his briefcase and hat, but he had something to add.

"Perhaps, sir, if we work hard and diligently, Nissan Motors will be able to repay you and Mrs. Kogan for the sufferings you experienced at Santo Tomás."

"I'm sure of it," Kogan said.

CHAPTER TWENTY-THREE

Looey yanked open the door of the helicopter fitted with float landing gear, and struggled into the right-hand seat. The pilot, a slim-framed Asian named Tran Duan, greeted him nervously. Looey responded nervously. Things were not going well.

He buckled himself in and pointed to the radio. "Any calls?"

"No, sir." The pilot's accented English was excellent.

Looey checked his watch for the twentieth time since he had left Pyle in northwest Washington. The Blackbird should be coming in any time now.

"Rockets ready?"

"Yes, sir." Tran's slim brown hand fussed with the controls. The noise of a car engine came from a nearby alley and his head swiveled in that direction with a catlike alertness.

Looey overlooked the young man's jitters. He was, after all, new to this kind of game, with its dangerously high stakes, but quick to learn and capable—with the proper tutelage—of becoming a true professional. Before hiring him, Looey had done his homework on the Vietnamese. Tran Duan had flown against the Khmer Rouge in Cambodia, but when Vietnam had pulled out of that war, he had defected, flying his helicopter across the Chinese border and handing it over to the military. As a reward, he had been given a Chinese passport, a sum of money, and freedom to travel.

From that point on, the young pilot had sold his considerable talents as a flyer and ordnance expert to the highest bidder on the international market—Angola, Afghanistan, Honduras—to whichever right- or left-wing movement met his price. A month ago, Looey had learned of Tran's availability and had hired him in expectation of just such a contingency as this. The vice president had agreed that as a cover for Tran's activities, he could be employed as a mechanic in charge of Pyle's personal automobiles.

Working with a compatriot that Tran vouched for, the two Asians, in a locked shed at this isolated landing field in Maryland, had accomplished the excruciatingly difficult task of installing remote-firing M-159 rocket pods on the sleek Aerospatiale 355 Twinstar.

"Sir?" Tran interrupted Looey's thoughts.

"Don't be so formal. Call me Looey."

"Okay." Tran's smooth, tanned hands toyed with the controls. "Looey, I do not know about this job. Who are we shooting down? I know the jungle well—that is where I fought—but here..." He gestured. "Over this big city, I am uncomfortable."

Looey interrupted. "You are doing the American people a great service, remember that. You must leave the rest to me."

Tran didn't seem satisfied. "Will this great service you speak of be so viewed by the authorities?" He muttered the sarcasm with a glum face.

Looey laughed. He really liked this slim youth. "Of course," he answered, "I guarantee it."

Tran did not seem to respond to Looey's reassurance. "There is something else. I have worked here for nearly a month. There is always activity of some kind here at the field. I have seen no one tonight."

Looey was getting a bit jumpy himself, though not about the solitude, which he considered a bit of luck. But the Blackbird should be in by now. Why hadn't the call come in from Andrews? He leaned forward and checked the wires leading to the demolition pack and mentally reviewed the plan. It was typical Looey, simplicity itself.

At a point over the Anacostia River, six miles from Andrews Air Force Base, they would intercept the White House helicopter. At two hundred yards, the 2.75-inch rockets could hardly miss, and the seven projectiles in each pod gave a redundancy that put to rest any thought of failure. After the shattered craft had spun into the waters, Tran would turn at high speed and fly northeast along the river, setting their helicopter down near an old ferry crossing. Looey would toggle the demolition switch, and in 180 seconds, five pounds of Czech semtec would reduce the helicopter to tiny fragments. He and Tran would then drive into the night, using separate cars parked nearby.

Looey could stand the wait no longer. He picked up the radio and transmitted. "Hello, Fox two, this is Fox one." Nothing. He repeated the call.

"Hello, Fox two, come in." What had happened? His mind refused to consider a slipup.

It was doubtful that Looey could have heard the response had there been one, for at that moment a Bell JetRanger with Secret Service markings roared in and hovered thunderously directly above their smaller Twinstar.

"Move it, Tran!" Looey screamed. "Let's get out of here!"

Tran Duan's hands darted over the controls with magical swiftness, but it was already too late. Three more identical craft had dropped down into position—one directly in front, the other two flanking the now immobilized Twinstar. Men lunged from the craft and pulled the Twinstar's hatch open.

As rough hands grabbed him and yanked his Walther HP from its holster, Looey tried to bluff.

"What is the meaning of this?" his voice croaked. But he knew it was useless. The illegal rocket pods, though still under canvas, gave them away. One man jerked Tran roughly from his seat and hustled him away; the other handcuffed Looey's hands to an overhead stanchion.

"What are you doing?" A cold, icy finger began to play up and down his spine.

With practiced movements, the man whipped a length of nylon cord from his pocket and tied Looey's legs to the seat posts. His hand hesitated only briefly, then found the plastic cover for the demolition switch, raised it, and toggled it on. The red light glowed.

"*No . . . you can't!*" Looey's screams were drowned as the helicopter overhead thundered off.

The man smiled at Looey, patted his shoulder in a sympathetic way, and ran toward one of the flanking craft. With a roar, the other helicopters departed, leaving Looey sitting in the quiet darkness watching the digital numbers roll back.

Standing behind a hangar some fifty feet away, Tran Duan pinned his gold Secret Service badge on his windbreaker and glanced at his watch. When he spoke to his companion, his accent had diminished considerably. "Time for the fireworks."

From far in the distance, the sound of an explosion reached them. "Beautiful," Tran said, checking the time again. "Right on the button. That ought to make all the networks."

His companion, an older agent, jerked his thumb at the Twinstar sitting in the darkness. "Our friend should be getting a little antsy about now."

"Not yet." Tran put a restraining hand on the man's shoulder.

They watched the dim image of Looey twist frantically inside the Twinstar as he tried to free himself. "We'll give him a little extra time to reflect on his sins." He waited another minute, then, whistling cheerfully, he walked to the helicopter.

Saturday, 8:12 P.M.

Pyle watched the forty-two-inch screen in his study avidly. A newscaster was discussing the new trade bill, when he stopped and picked up a paper laid at his elbow. As he read it, his professional suavity wavered. He glanced at someone off camera for confirmation, then looked directly into the camera, his face very serious.

"Ladies and gentlemen, I've just received an important news bulletin."

Hurriedly getting up from his desk, Pyle moved closer to the TV.

"Just moments ago," the announcer said, "a helicopter exploded and burned over the Anacostia River." He hesitated, then hurried on. "The craft had apparently departed from Andrews Air Force Base just prior to the explosion. There are reports—and I wish to emphasize that they are as yet unconfirmed—that the helicopter was *Marine One*, the presidential craft. At the present time, there is no indication that the president or any member of his family or staff was aboard at the time. Please, let me repeat—"

Pyle clicked the TV off. Standing straighter, he walked the length of his study several times, deep in thought, his face content. The odds had really been excellent throughout this whole business. Even if this serum they were bringing in *was* effective, Simon Moody was too far gone for it to have done him any good. Still, he never liked to gamble. Better safe than sorry. An old cliché, but one he had always lived by.

A helicopter landed on the helipad of the White House. Pass-more, escorted by two agents, jumped out and ran toward the ground-level entrance, clutching a steel box to his chest.

Rodale knocked at the bedroom door. Lillian answered and he entered the darkened room. She stood at the president's bed-side looking down on Simon's pale face, the dim light from the shuttered window silhouetting her upper body, creating a vague, madonnalike image. As his eyes grew accustomed to the shade, Rodale could make out the president's waxy face and closed eyes. For a heart-clutching moment, he was afraid that what he had to say might have come too late. Then the president's eyes opened, the bright blue dulled. Very, very slowly they settled on Rodale, and around the cracked lips he detected a faint move-ment that might have been a smile.

In a hushed voice Rodale answered Lillian's unspoken ques-tion. "It's here. Sid is preparing the first injection."

She looked down at her husband. "You hear that, darling? They've brought back B-juice."

Moody licked dry lips and tried to speak. Lillian quickly filled a glass with water and lifted his head, watching him swallow painfully. He expelled a breath and crooked a finger. They both leaned closer.

"How did the ... expedition ... go?"

Lillian looked askance at Rodale, who patted the president's hand reassuringly. "Mission accomplished," he said heartily. Even though he had a thumbnail account from CINCPAC of the depressing details, the last thing he wanted was to upset

Simon. "I'll tell you all about it . . . well, later," he said. Moody's brows set firmly and he shook his head disapprovingly.

"All right," Rodale said. "I don't have much, just a sketchy account passed to me by Admiral Edwards. Nothing seemed to go as planned. They ran into a lot of problems—"

Moody raised a shaking hand. His voice was a husky whisper. "I'm glad Kogan was . . . along. He could handle things."

Rodale took a deep breath. He'd never lied to Simon, and he wasn't going to start now. "Yes, it *was*. We owe Joe Kogan an enormous debt." He looked up at Lillian. She nodded acquiescence. "Simon," Rodale said, "I'm sorry to have to tell you this, but he didn't come back. As I understand it, Joe was killed as he was getting aboard the plane."

The president's eyes closed and one gaunt hand made a fist. His chest heaved with the effort to breathe.

A rapid knock came on the door and Dr. Eccles entered, with Beth Diego following, bearing a medical tray. Eccles grasped the president's wrist and quickly felt his pulse. Muttering under his breath, he very deliberately picked up the hypodermic needle and held it at eye level. It contained exactly one-half cc of a greenish fluid.

"Make a note of the time," he instructed Beth. Rolling back Moody's sleeve, he swabbed his arm and poised the needle over it.

The president stirred and his lips moved. "You're wasting it, Sid."

"Be quiet," Eccles ordered, and spoke words he didn't believe. "Your miracle is here." With that he injected B-juice into the president's bloodstream. He handed the hypodermic back to the nurse, eyeing the green scum adhering to the inside of the glass body.

"Don't dispose of that syringe," he said to Beth. "The residue could be valuable. Send it over to our lab. I want every speck recovered."

Pyle had breakfasted alone, drinking more coffee than was good for him, and except for a slice of toast, pushing aside the food. The morning papers only repeated what was essentially the TV broadcast of the evening before, along with an inconclusive follow-up ("Pending further investigation by both the FAA and the FBI, the White House has not yet confirmed..."). He was starved for information and there was nothing he could do about it. When things like this happened, vice presidents didn't call the White House—just the reverse.

What the hell had happened? Why hadn't Looey reported in? Maybe he couldn't. Perhaps he was being too closely followed, or.... Pyle shuddered involuntarily as he considered that Looey might have blundered into the arms of the law.

Unable to control his impatience any longer, Pyle left the house through the French doors leading to the swimming pool, and headed for the old carriage house that had been converted to a garage. He wandered in on the very long chance that Tran would be there. If so, whatever had happened to Looey, or wherever he was, Tran Duan might provide the answer.

"Good morning, sir." Tran smiled at him from across the gleaming hood of a Daimler. Pyle expelled his breath. He couldn't remember being so glad to see someone. Outwardly controlling his emotions, he waved to the Vietnamese.

"Let's go for a little stroll," he said casually. It was best they be in the open when they talked. He doubted that Bill Passmore would bug the place, but one never knew.

"Whatever you say, sir." Tran capped a can of polish and headed for the lavatory. "If you please, I'll wash my hands."

"No, no," Pyle said with a touch of irritation. "Don't bother."

An early autumn tang in the air made the superheated days of two weeks ago only an unpleasant memory. In the distance, the Potomac glittered through a gentle mist that had the smell of fall. It was a good day, Pyle mused as he and Tran stood beneath an

oak and looked out over the broad expanse of Washington, seat of
government of the United States of America, the most powerful
political entity on the planet, the prize for which he had worked
and schemed so long. It was coming to him—he could sense it.
Nothing the young Asian by his side could tell him about the
events of last night would change that. Tomorrow, or within a day
or two more, Spencer Pyle would be president. Looey? Even if ar-
rested, he wouldn't talk. He was smart enough to know that no
prison could hold him. A presidential pardon would see to that.

"Tell me about last night," he said.

The indelible smile on Tran's face grew broader. "There is
really very little to tell, sir. We were waiting when the helicopter
flew over the river. One pod of rockets was all that was needed.
The rest of the operation went as planned. However . . ." A frown
replaced the smile.

"Yes?"

"What a waste! To have to destroy our wonderful Aerospa
tiale."

"Never mind that. What about Looey? I haven't heard from
him."

"Really, sir?" Tran's eyes widened. "That surprises me. We left
in separate cars after the operation was completed." His smile returned. "Well, Looey carried out your instructions successfully.
He probably feels it is wise to—how you say it, lay low."

Pyle shifted his position. By squinting, he could see a small
white block of a building surrounded by green just at that point
where the Potomac veered to the south. It was not too far as the
crow flies—perhaps three miles. It was a million miles for the
scruffy accountant in the Worcester paper mills thirty years ago.
But to hell with that sentimental crap. He'd let some hack write
it all up in the biography he was planning.

Everything should be perfect today, yet something nagged at
him. It was a drain on his nerves to be this close to the White
House, both in time and distance, and yet have to wait as the
hours dragged by.

Rodale walked down the hall toward the president's bedroom, his mind racing ahead of him, excited yet fearful of what he would find behind that closed door. He remembered last night. Moody had just had his third injection of B-juice. Eccles had come out of the bedroom, and the usually worried lines of the physician's face had seemed changed—for the first time Rodale could recall in more than four months, there seemed to be a spark of hope there.

"I dunno, Marty," he had said in response to the chief of staff's unspoken question. "I've just never seen anything like it. Three shots of that crap and a man who was literally taking a step across death's doorstep appears to have stopped with his foot in the air." He rubbed his jaw thoughtfully. "Let's be a bit more professional. His condition seems to have stabilized."

"It's working, then?"

Eccles's natural caution reappeared. "Welll," he stretched the word to its maximum. "Seems to be, but I still can't rule out a placebo effect. For so long now, Simon's life has been wrapped up in hoping and praying for this B-juice, and now that it's here...well, you just don't know. He may be willing himself to feel better. The power of the mind can be an awesome thing."

"I'd like to see him."

"Not now. He's sleeping—peacefully, thank God—and his body needs all the rest it can get." Eccles had looked up at the big man and squeezed his arm. "Come around tomorrow. We should know if it's really helping him by then."

This was tomorrow.

He knocked and Lillian opened the bedroom door. One look at her and Rodale had his answer. Her face was flushed with suppressed excitement.

"Marty," she said, her voice just above a whisper, yet urgent. "He's better, he really is. Come take a look." She took him by the hand and led him to the bed.

At first Rodale was disappointed. Simon simply lay there, his eyes closed, his hands folded over the counterpane.

"Do you see it?" Lillian asked.

See what? Except for the slight rise and fall of his chest, the man could be dead, waiting for the mortuary crew to pick him up. Still . . . yes, there was something different about him. At first, Rodale couldn't decide what it was. There was a little more color in his face, true. The gray had softened to a paleness that had a touch of rosiness, perhaps of life . . . but that was it! For weeks he had watched Simon Moody slowly dying, each day a small but inexorable progression toward the grave. Now—he grinned in relief and put a long arm around Lillian's shoulders—the slide toward death had been stopped, maybe even reversed.

"By God, I think you're right," he said softly.

"We'd better go," Lillian said. "He mustn't be disturbed." She seemed to have trouble pulling herself away; her hand unconsciously smoothing the bedspread. The chief of staff shot a sideways glance at her. These months had drained her, stealing some of her youth, drawing indelible lines around her eyes and mouth, sapping her vitality, but never her will. For this incredible lady had never given up. She had fought on ferociously after all the rest of them had surrendered to fatalism, and she had won. It showed in the loving, possessive smile she bestowed on the supine figure. Her hand reached out and touched Simon's shoulder with a butterfly caress.

She gasped and clutched at Rodale's arm. The president's lips moved and curved in a faint smile. His eyes opened and focused on them.

"Hey, you two," the voice was a whisper, but his eyelid drooped in an unmistakable wink. "Hang in there."

Thunder roared and lightning streaked across the sky, illuminating for an instant the whiteness of the Executive Mansion, all gleaming wetness from the battering of the early autumn storm. The shrubbery and small trees along the curving drive tossed violently as a limousine with the flag of the vice president of the United States pulled underneath a porte cochere.

A White House usher stepped forward and opened the car door. Wearing a black raincoat and an expression of respectful concern, Spencer Pyle walked up the steps and looked back at the extensive grounds, darkened now through some power failure. "If you lived here, you would be home now." The phrase reverberated in his mind. It wouldn't be long now. He even appreciated the wind and the rain. A good writer could take this setting and make high drama from it, describing how it was that high officials hurried through the stormy night to the side of the sick president. There, as tensions rose in Europe and around the globe, and after much solemn soul-searching, the decision was made to relieve Simon Moody of the heavy burden of his office, transferring it to the saddened but able vice president, Spencer Pyle.

"Mr. Vice President." The usher interrupted his thoughts. "If you will come this way."

Meanwhile, on the second floor

of the White House

The chief of staff left the elevator first, then, with a touch of Old World courtesy, reached back to assist Barbara McShane, the chunky secretary of Health and Human Services. Fred Tannahill, secretary of Agriculture, stepped out to join them. Otherwise, the corridor was empty.

"An incredible sight, Marty," Tannahill said. "He's coming back, no question about it."

McShane nodded her agreement. "I wouldn't have believed it if I hadn't seen it. I'll bet Lillian is walking on air."

"You betcha," Rodale said. "When she's not turning cartwheels."

McShane poked a carmine-tipped forefinger into the chief of staff's chest. "I want complete details on the cure, Marty," she said, "and soon."

"Barbara, you'll be the first to know, I promise you, but as I explained, we're talking ultra super-duper top secret on everything pertaining to it, for obvious reasons. But we'll keep you in the loop all the way."

Passmore's stocky figure appeared at the end of the corridor. His hand gestured downward emphatically. Rodale nodded receipt of the message.

"Okay." He turned to the two cabinet secretaries and spoke rapidly. "Pyle is at the east entrance. Get down there and meet him in the lobby. You know what to say, and a lot depends on how you handle it. Bless you both."

The usher assisted the vice president in taking off his raincoat. An especially powerful bolt of lightning caused the bulbs in the crystal chandelier to dim momentarily.

With a nod of thanks, Pyle turned to find two cabinet members approaching. That surprised him a little. He had visualized a bedside scene where everyone would see Simon at the same time, recognize his debility, nod gravely, and give a modest obeisance to the man who was going to take over.

"Fred, Barbara." He shook their hands gravely. "Have you seen the president already?"

Barbara McShane touched a handkerchief to her eyes. "We have. Oh, God, Simon is ... well, how can I say it? He's ..." Her voice broke.

"Can I have a couple of words with you, Spence?" Tannahill

asked. He took Pyle's elbow and led him a few feet away, out of earshot of the two Secret Service agents posted unobtrusively near the entrance. "Let me give you a little advice." The secretary lowered his voice and peered around cautiously. "If I were vice president, I'd make myself scarce—at least for the next couple of days. It would look better, you know what I mean?"

Pyle's face turned morose. "Golly, Fred, I was praying he might have taken a turn for the better." He, too, glanced around discreetly. "Uh, tell me, is he really that bad off?"

Tannahill shook his head sadly. "Mr. Vice President, let me just say this. You might as well forget about that letter. We'd be wasting our time signing it a second time." He took Pyle's hand in both of his and shook it warmly.

"May God watch over you," he said. He took the elbow of the secretary of Health and Human Services and proceeded toward the door and a waiting limousine. Pyle stood watching them, then gestured to one of the agents.

"Would you inform Mrs. Moody that I regret not being able to keep my appointment to see the president." With that, he left hurriedly.

Washington, D.C.
Tuesday, October 4, 1944, 11:45 A.M.

The phone rang and Yvonne's maid answered it.

"For you, ma'am," she said, and left the sun room.

"It's me." Pyle's voice had a note of urgency.

"Where have you been? Where are you?" Yvonne asked.

"Hiawatha Club. Communing with nature."

"You're in Michigan? You haven't been up there in years. And for God's sake, why? You hate the outdoors."

"Except for the goddamn mosquitoes, it isn't bad. Look, I'll be back in a couple of days." He chuckled. "If not before." The line went silent for a moment. Yvonne could picture him running things through his mind.

"Oh, yes," he continued, "better alert your hairdresser. You're going to be photographed a lot next week. Be prepared to gaze lovingly at your husband." He waited, as if expecting a comment.

"Get yourself a golden retriever," she snapped.

He started a retort, "Now listen, damnit," then apparently thought better of it. Finally, he said, "Uh . . . any news?"

She knew what he was asking. She'd kept the TV on constantly since she had gotten up, waiting. But there had been no announcement—not the slightest indication that the end might be near for the president of the United States.

"No," she answered. "Nothing."

"I don't get it. By this time, I expected—"

Yvonne interrupted. "I know what you expected. Why didn't you tell me you were going? Why pick this time to go?"

"Looks better, that's why. Got the idea talking to Fred Tannahill yesterday. Had Tran fly me up." He laughed softly. "History, my dear—we all should study it more. Teddy Roosevelt was out of town when McKinley was shot. And Coolidge—old Cool Cal—was out of town when Harding died. Now look," Pyle's voice became confidential. "Couldn't you call Lillian Moody, say . . . just for a little social chat? Then call me back."

"Forget it, you goddamn ghoul." She slammed the phone down.

The president leaned forward as the First Lady plumped up his pillows. He looked down at his breakfast tray with an expression of distaste. "Jesus, for the first time in months I have an appetite and I get Cream of Wheat. How about some bacon and eggs?"

Lillian laughed, a delighted sound. "Doctor's orders, lover, so stop whining. That stomach of yours has got to get reacquainted with food."

Moody took a spoonful. "Not bad," he said. "But pass along the word I want something a little more exotic for lunch. Hey, Marty," he spoke to the chief of staff, who leaned against the wall, watching him with an amused expression. "I'm going to get on my feet this afternoon—do a little walking, get measured for some new threads. Eccles said it was okay."

Rodale pushed his cuff back to check his watch. It was almost time. The British ambassador had spoken to him yesterday to ask if it would be convenient for the prime minister to phone at ten. It was going to be all right. Yesterday, Simon's voice had still been husky, but this morning the rich baritone had almost completely returned.

"That's good, sir—"

He was interrupted by the soft ring of the phone beside the president's bed. Lillian stepped forward quickly and removed the tray. Moody put his hand on the phone, then grinned at them. "Want to hear what he has to say?" He pressed the speaker button and picked up the instrument.

"Yes."

The chief White House operator spoke, her precise diction filling the room. "Mr. President, the prime minister of England is on the line."

"Good morning, Mr. Prime Minister," Simon said. "How nice of you to call."

"And a good afternoon to you, Mr. President." The clipped

accent was softened by a Welsh intonation. "I hope I'm not disturbing you."

"Not at all, sir."

"Good." There was a slight hesitancy, then, "Mr. President, since our change of government here, we—that is, you and I—haven't had a chance to meet face-to-face. I want to tell you personally how really much we're looking forward to seeing you in Brussels on the nineteenth."

Rodale, listening carefully, detected an ever-so-slight upward inflection on the last three words. What it meant, of course, was that the prime minister had asked a question: was Simon coming or not? Were the rumors true or false? Is the president of the United States all right? Is he still going to be president on the nineteenth?

Moody caught Rodale's eye and winked. He had also spotted the fishing expedition. "That's very kind of you, Mr. Prime Minister, and may I say how much Lillian and I are looking forward to meeting you and your lovely wife."

"That's very kind of you. Needless to say, Jenny and I feel precisely the same." The prime minister cleared his throat. "Uh . . . I know, Mr. President, that our respective position papers are in general agreement on DOE, but I wanted to reaffirm to you my personal support for what you have set in motion. As you are doubtless aware, there may be a few conferees who question whether the multipolarity developing in Europe and the Middle East isn't more dangerous than the bipolarity of the past."

Moody glanced at Rodale, then rolled his eyes heavenward. "With your help, Mr. Prime Minister, I think we can dispose of those arguments."

An embarrassed little chuckle crossed the Atlantic. "Excuse the pedantry, sir—I really didn't call you to talk shop. Just wanted to pass along my enthusiasm for DOE and my optimism for the future."

"I can't tell you how much I appreciate that, Mr. Prime Minister. Tell you what. If I may make a suggestion, why don't we both just happen to arrive in Brussels a day early? We can impose on my ambassador there for a quiet little dinner before we get started on the talks."

The answer came back immediately. "Wonderful idea, Mr. President—absolutely first-rate. Jenny will love it." The relief in the prime minister's voice was too real to miss. "It's a date, then. Mr. President, it has been very nice talking to you."

"Nice talking to you, sir, and thank you again." Simon started to replace the receiver, then jerked it back to his ear. "Mr. Prime Minister? Still there? Good, I'm glad I caught you. I wonder if you would do me a great favor? Would you withhold from the press . . . oh, say, for the next twenty-four hours, any announcement that we have spoken?"

Friday, October 7, 1994, 10:35 A.M.

Lillian spoke quietly into the phone. "Mr. Pyle, could you come to the White House as soon as possible? It is quite urgent." She replaced the phone and smiled mischievously at Rodale. "He's coming at a gallop."

11:10 A.M.

The vice president's limousine pulled up under the west portico and Spencer Pyle got out, pulling the coat of his dark suit down and adjusting his tie. He climbed the steps quickly and found Lillian Moody in the lobby, dressed in a black *grain de poudre* dress without jewelry. He advanced upon her, hand outstretched.

"Mrs. Moody . . . Lillian, my dear, I got here as quickly as I could."

"I appreciate that, Mr. Pyle," she said, her face somber. "Please come with me."

She led him to the elevator, but instead of going up, they went down. "I don't understand," Pyle said. "This isn't the way to the Family Quarters." Lillian sighed and dabbed at her eyes. She led the way down the hall toward the west wing and stopped before a set of double doors.

"But this is the Oval Office," Pyle protested.

"Yes," Lillian answered, and opened the doors.

Simon Moody looked up, smiling. He was sitting on the edge of his desk, a slice of Danish in his hand. A beautifully tailored suit of glen plaid accentuated the slimness of his body. Handing a paper back to Dale Haskins, director of the Office of Management and Budget, the president popped a bite into his mouth, wiped his lips, and waved at Pyle.

"Glad to see you, Spence," he said, his words muffled by the pastry. "We're having a dickens of a time with this budget proposal. How about lending us a hand?" He slipped off the desk and flopped down in his chair. Then he gazed solicitously at the vice president.

"Say, there, you're not looking well. Sit down and let me get you a glass of water."

"Simon's putting on a great show, Marty," Lillian said as she strolled with the chief of staff on the South Lawn, "but get those people out of there soon. He's still got a long way to go before he's completely well."

"I'll take care of it."

"What's going to happen now?"

Rodale stopped and rubbed his long jaw. It had been one hell of a hectic week and he was tired. He was sleeping better, though. In a few more days, after things had settled down, maybe he and Stephanie could get away to the house in Maine for a week or two.

"Well, there's the good and there's the bad. We're getting a package together asking Congress for a supplemental appropriation to fund the analysis and research needed to replicate

B-juice. It'll be open-ended as far as money's concerned. The sky's the limit, even if we have to sell a fucking carrier group to Saudi Arabia. The Philippines government has informally indicated complete cooperation—Negrito translators, University of Manila botanists, armed forces support, the whole ball of wax. It'll be a multinational effort. Art Von Porten is on his way out there now to head it up."

They started back toward the White House. "It's all suddenly so wonderful," Lillian said. "The world seems renewed, full of promise." Then she sighed heavily. "How I wish Joe Kogan were here. I'd just like to tell him how grateful we all are to him."

"Well, I suspect he knew you would be, right from the beginning." He laughed softly, as if remembering. "And I don't really think he'd appreciate the accolades. Kogan never struck me as a man who enjoyed taking bows."

"I guess you're right." They walked a ways farther in silence. "The sad thing is that he truly never wanted to go. He had his life planned, he had a girlfriend . . . oh, dear me." Lillian's eyes widened. "I must call her. God knows what I'll say."

"I can have someone take care of that."

"No," she said firmly. "It's my job. I think Joe would appreciate it. You know, Marty, I believe he had a feeling, a premonition, that he wouldn't come back."

"Did he tell you that?"

"No, but I sensed it." She turned to him, and Rodale saw that her eyes were filled with tears. "Oh, damnit, it's so unfair. Joe Kogan was so close to getting aboard the plane and coming back safely."

She touched a handkerchief to her eyes, then shivered and unconsciously clasped her breasts in an almost defensive gesture. Rodale noticed.

"Touch of fall in the air," he said. "Shall we go in?"

She turned and faced the autumnal haze drifting across the greenery leading down to the river. She seemed to be listening to something other than the oscillating rumble of traffic coming from the Ellipse.

"No," she said softly. "I'm glad summer's gone. It's been a loathsome time, with all we had to go through. I'm not cold. And I'm happy, for the first time in ever so long. I tell you, Marty, for the rest of my life I'll love days like this. They'll always remind me of getting out from under a cloud of despair that seemed to go on and on." She glanced down at her breasts and trilled a small, self-conscious laugh. "I was just thinking of the terror millions of women go through every day when they feel their boobs. Maybe from now on, if we're lucky..." Her voice dwindled off.

"Well." Her tone indicated a change of subject. "You said there was good *and* bad. What about the bad? We're talking Spencer Pyle, I assume."

"Yeah. We're not in a good position there. I don't have to tell you that this B-juice thing is going to be tough to control. Simon says he's going to make a clean breast of his illness in a nationwide hookup. Fine, I'm all for that. But the public is sophisticated enough to realize that something extraordinary must have happened to pull the president through, and they—particularly the medical community—are going to want to know what it was. Maybe we can do enough damage control to handle that temporarily, *but*..." Rodale stopped and placed a hand on Lillian's arm, turning her to face him. "Here's the problem."

"You don't have to hit me over the head with it," she answered, moving along the path again. "Pyle's attorneys will have a field day with *Sucker One* and B-juice. They'll accuse Simon of endangering the world for his own selfish interests, maybe even risking losing the panacea everyone has waited so long for."

"Yep," he agreed. "Not to mention conspiracy, illegal use of government funds and equipment, and official misrepresentation. They'll say that in a noble effort, Spencer Pyle tried to put a stop to these malefactions."

"So, what do we do? Tell him he's been a naughty boy and forget it?"

The chief of staff shook his windblown head doubtfully. "I don't know." He glanced in the direction of the Oval Office. "But right now, in conformance with your instructions, I'm going to get Simon the hell out of there."

CHAPTER TWENTY-FOUR

The vice presidential limousine moved smoothly down Pennsylvania Avenue, the chauffeur sliding the big car adroitly through heavy traffic, but Spencer Pyle gripped the door strap of the car with a hand that was white-knuckled. What had gone wrong? The explosion over Anacostia River, the news reports, the silence from the White House—had they all been faked? Even the—*Jesus Christ!*—the talk with Tran Duan. Could that son of a bitch have set him up? If so, then who was he? His mind veered away from the probabilities.

The last half hour had been the absolute nadir of his life. He had walked into the White House as vice president, prepared to commiserate with the First Lady, offer his assistance, and eat humble, grieving pie through the funeral ceremonies. The inauguration, the speech—he'd already roughed it out. Perhaps a week or so later, he'd address a joint session of Congress, indicating his concern with the economy. Going off triumphantly to Brussels, fighting off the doves there, reversing this denuclearization crap, easing the world back toward confrontational diplomacy and big defense budgets was next. And in doing so, by God, he'd stop the slide of the United States into a second-rate power. That's what he'd expected.

What he got was the sight of a goddamn ghost. Simon Moody sitting confidently behind his desk in the Oval Office, a breezy greeting, and a cup of coffee handed to him that he was afraid to lift to his lips because of his shaking hands. He had been close to retching, and his brain had shut down operations. He remembered mumbling something inconsequential in response to the president's jovial but veiled conversation. He recalled getting to his feet, his knees knocking, to excuse himself on some flimsy pretext. He had only the vaguest impression of stumbling down the corridor, head bowed for invisibility, nearly bumping into unseen people uttering unheard salutations, grateful finally for the cool air under the portico as he fumbled his way into his car.

Now, speeding toward home, he was intensely conscious of the Secret Service car following close behind. Were they protecting him or spying on him? He opened his mouth and took deep, calming breaths. He needed to reestablish control, to think again, to plan, to use all his faculties in order to survive. First of all, he must consult his attorneys—but wait, that would mean confessing his complicity in the SUCCOR affair. Right now he mentally drew back from that step. Later, he might have to take it.

There was only one person in the world he wanted to talk to now—Yvonne. He leaned forward and spoke to his driver. "Step on it. I've got to get home." He picked up the car phone and hurriedly dialed.

Simon Moody plucked a silken strand dangling from the sleeve of his pajamas, rolled it into a tiny ball, and flipped it away.

Then he groaned. Looking up quickly at the concerned faces of Passmore and Rodale, he smiled reassuringly. "Not to worry. I feel fine." He frowned again. "But I dunno, it doesn't seem right to let that Transylvanian scumbag get away scot-free."

"He won't, Mr. President," Passmore interjected quickly. "In return for his cooperation, he'll get a reduced sentence—maybe five years instead of twenty."

Rodale leaned against the walnut newels at the foot of the presidential bed. "We've got a real explosive situation here, Simon. If we can't nail Pyle solid, he'll blow us all out of the water. Right now we've got Tran Duan's word against his—a Vietnamese against the vice president. I wouldn't give a nickel for our chances. Even though we wired Tran before that little tête-à-tête two days ago, the words on the machine could be twisted around by clever lawyers, and believe me, Pyle will have the best. I haven't practiced criminal law in years, but even so, I think I could make a case that Tran and Pyle were talking about something quite innocuous."

"Shit!" Moody banged a fist softly against the counterpane. "So we wire whatzisname, this Looey, and try to get something really incriminating."

"Yes, sir" Rodale said. "Something so blatant Pyle's own mother would convict him."

"I'm not looking for a conviction," Moody said. "I just want enough leverage so that I can force him to resign and keep his mouth shut about B-juice."

"We'll get it, sir," Passmore said. Rodale winked at the agent. The plan was all set to go. All they needed was Moody's approval.

The president pursed his lips dubiously. "We're not dealing with some dummy, Bill. This Looey has got to have a real sweet story, or Pyle's going to be on him like a terrier on a rat."

"We understand that, Mr. President," Passmore said. "So it's important that we move fast. My guess is that right now the vice president is pretty much in shock. We'll have a lot better chance if we can get to him before he regains his balance."

"You're sure this character isn't going to screw this up? I

understand he's worked with Pyle for a long time. Maybe there's some residual loyalty there. He could give us away."

Passmore's face was confident. "Looey doesn't know what the word *loyalty* means, Mr. President. Besides, there was never any love lost between the two."

"Can we go on this, Simon?" Rodale asked.

Moody nodded. "Get cracking."

"Lemme see if I got this straight." Yvonne's words came slurred as she overcarefully set down the glass of orange juice that Pyle figured contained three or four ounces of vodka. "Moody is okay? He's better? The stuff they got worked? Whooee!" she chortled. Then she went into a fit of coughing, and reached for a cigarette. "Maybe, by God, I can smoke all of these I want and die of plain old age."

"You're missing the point." Pyle tried to keep the annoyance out of his voice. "My interdiction operation failed. If either or both of my people were picked up and start talking, I could well be on my way to impeachment and a long stay at a federal prison." He was angry, with good cause. In the middle of the worst crisis of his life, he found her not yet out of bed and heading toward a monumental drunk. He had gotten over his shakes and recovered some of his equilibrium, and now he wanted intelligent, no-nonsense advice.

"Ha!" She spat the syllable out and blew smoke at the ceiling. "What's important to you doesn't mean shit to the human race. Tell you something else. If it ever gets out you tried to stop this medicine, federal prison is gonna look pretty good to you. It's the only place you'll be safe."

He hadn't thought of that. His scowl didn't fade, but a glint of respect crept into his eyes. Even drunk, she was one smart cookie. All hyperbole, of course, what she said. With his money he could find sanctuary in any number of out-of-the-way places, but her words pointed up a salient fact. Unless this thing was handled just right, he would end up making Judas Iscariot, Hitler, and the Hillside Strangler seem lovable.

The phone at her bedside rang softly. Three times meant that none of the staff was available to answer. Yvonne picked it up.

"Yes?" She listened, her expression changing. Some of the liquor-induced vacuity left her face as she handed him the instrument.

"Pyle here," he said.

It was Looey. "Take a drive," he said. The accented words were cold. "No chauffeur. Use the Jaguar. Drive to Dumbarton Oaks Park. Once you get inside the park, drive slowly until you see headlights blink behind you. Then pull over."

"Wait a minute," Pyle said. "What's going on?"

The phone clicked in his ear.

"That was him, wasn't it?" Yvonne sat up straight against the pillows, her eyes now focused and alert. "What did he want?"

"I don't know. I'll find out when I get there, I guess."

"Don't go. Spencer, I don't like it. This could be trouble." He stopped then, looking back at her with surprise. She used his name only when deadly serious and wanting his attention. "Damn you," she continued with the old rancor back in place. "I told you to lay off, but you wouldn't listen, would you? You had to have a sure thing, a one-hundred-percent guarantee that you'd win. And now it's blown up in your face."

He stopped listening. It was another harangue, an I-told-you-so tongue-lashing that interrupted his own thoughts. For some reason, the call from Looey had strengthened him. The other side was making the first move, but so what? He had always been a great counterpuncher.

What was she running on about?

"Spencer, will you pay attention?" She leaned forward, the contents of the forgotten glass spilling on the sheets. "For God's sake, don't go any further with this. Call your attorneys, level with them, they can save you. Make them earn that colossal retainer you pay them. Please don't let this man drag you down with him."

He smiled, but it was an effort. He would go to his law firm only when all other avenues were closed. To do otherwise would be to admit that he had been beaten. Well, he had failed, but he wasn't beaten.

"Stop worrying," he said. "I know what I'm doing." He left the bedroom and walked down the hall. Faintly, from behind the door, he heard her call out his name again. He almost went back, but he was anxious now to see this thing through.

Looey had been kind to Pyle, he thought. By designating the park for a rendezvous, he had given the vice president one last chance of driving toward the White House. He chuckled at the irony. Besides, when the car came out of the Naval Observatory grounds it would be turning right, toward the lights of the city. It was human nature, he had discovered, that when people are faced with danger, they seek not a place to run, but a place where there are lights and warmth and other humans, even if only strangers. That the vice president felt himself faced with danger, Looey had no doubt, even as he too felt danger. The only difference between them was that Mr. Pyle, in his money-insulated world, was not accustomed to fear, while Looey, whose natural milieu was a perilous subworld, felt almost comfortable.

Looey had been told that four government sedans would be stationed along Massachusetts Avenue, two north of the exit from the Naval Observatory grounds, two south. As Mr. Pyle's Jaguar pulled into the sparse traffic on Massachusetts, Looey followed, keeping a half block behind. The two government sedans placed to the south fell in behind him. Although he gave all his attention to keeping Mr. Pyle in sight, he knew the other sedans were convoying behind—a bit of good old American overkill.

It would be just a few minutes before they reached the park. Looey adjusted the recorder strapped to his body. He had asked the Secret Service technician for a German make that he had used often in the past, but the man only grunted as he attached a Japanese recorder. It was a good machine that could pick up a whisper twenty feet away, but its voice-activated mechanism was too noisy for Looey's tastes. Still, street sounds should be sufficient to mask the noise. Now, all he had to do was make Mr. Pyle say the right words.

The Jag had gone nearly three-quarters of a mile and was approaching the Dumbarton Oaks turnoff. Looey waited for the brake lights to flare, but the car kept on going. What the hell? Had Mr. Pyle missed the turn, or had he passed by deliberately? Looey gripped the wheel, his nonchalance shaken. On over Rock Creek and past the parkway, the Jaguar continued on down Massachusetts for another mile. It stopped at a red light at R Street. Looey had anticipated the red and let a car drift in between his and the vice president's. The light turned green, the left turn signal on the Jag blinked, and Mr. Pyle proceeded on down R. He had deliberately ignored Looey's orders. Well, that was Mr. Pyle for you. He gave orders, he didn't take them.

Looey leaned back and kept his Chevy Lumina a couple hundred meters behind the gleaming car ahead. A turn on New Hampshire, another five minutes, and they were into an upscale neighborhood of broad streets and mature trees.

The vice president slowed as if looking for something, then he turned into a side street with widely spaced lights gleaming through the thick foliage of trees. The car moved hesitantly, almost stopping, then speeding up, then slowing down again. *Damn amateur*, Looey fumed. Nothing marked a car as an intruder in an area more than this kind of erratic driving. The sedan finally pulled over to the curb and parked. The brake lights flashed briefly before the headlights turned off. Looey cursed in fluent Czech. Was the man insane? He had parked right under a streetlight, and directly in front of a large, well-appointed home, every window glowing with interior lights! Mr. Pyle was supposed to possess a very superior mentality, but—Looey's mouth curved in a contemptuous smile—take a financial wizard out of his element and he becomes a child. Or, the thought struck him, could the vice president be afraid to meet him in a darkened park?

In a sense, though, it might be to the good. Frightened men

babble freely, and under stress, even so high an official as Mr. Pyle was not immune to saying things he would later regret. All Looey had to do was to say the right words. The agent Passmore had worked up a little script for him to follow.

Feeling very confident, Looey pulled over and parked some fifty feet to the rear of the Jaguar. Walking with the casual swagger of a man of the neighborhood taking a constitutional, he approached the passenger side of the car. Before reaching for the door handle, he looked back down the street. A car stopped, then parked. Two agents had arrived on the scene. A following car continued on toward Mr. Pyle's car. It would pass them, Looey knew, make a turn, and park facing the other direction. That would make four agents, and one of them was probably the estimable Mr. Passmore.

He reached for the handle of the door and pulled it open.

Looey was totally unprepared for what then happened.

From the interior of the car, a loud, frightened voice cried out. *"What do you want?"* Looey felt, rather than heard, the recorder click on.

"Get out of here!"

Ah, well, now he understood. There it was, just twenty-four inches away—a large-caliber pistol pointed at his chest. Why had he not thought of that? Stupid, stupid, stupid.

The voice, even louder, shouted, *"Put that gun away!"*

The darkness of the car vanished in the white light of the explosion. Once before he had been shot, but it was a 25mm in the leg that seemed only to sting, compared to this sledgehammer battering that picked him up and dropped him on the seat. It was over, his life ending violently, as he had always expected, though he had not expected it to be taken by a man who had hired him. He felt himself drifting toward a black, pain-filled depth from which he would never return. But wait, what was happening? Someone lifted his hand, and he felt cold metal placed in it. Ah, yes, Mr. Pyle, the little man he had badly underestimated, was planting a gun in his hand, fumbling and cursing as he crooked Looey's finger around the trigger.

The darkness finally closed around him, but even as he welcomed it, he still sensed voices shouting, lights flashing, and tires squealing.

The street became bedlam. Sirens shrieked and motors roared as Secret Service sedans homed in on the vice president's car. Bill Passmore, his automatic drawn, leaped from the lead sedan just as Spencer Pyle backed unsteadily out of his car, still holding his gun.

"Mr. Vice President, are you all right?" Passmore didn't wait for a response. Over his shoulder he yelled, "Move a car in here close. Get a spotlight on the interior of this vehicle!"

Pyle squinted in the glare, but continued to stand as if mesmerized by what the spotlight revealed. Blood splattered the leather upholstery and blotched the windows. Looey's body lay facedown, stretched across the passenger seat, one hand gripping an automatic pistol.

Passmore gently disengaged a weapon from Pyle's hand and passed it to another agent. That action seemed to release the vice president from the spell that gripped him. Beads of sweat covered his forehead and upper lip. Shaking visibly, he turned to Passmore.

"Thank God you're here, Bill. I just can't believe what happened. That madman was going to kill me."

Passmore placed a reassuring hand on his shoulder. "Take it easy, sir. Don't say anything now. We can get a statement later."

"No!" Pyle nearly shouted the word. "I'm telling you! The bastard was out to get me."

Passmore didn't seem convinced. There was a note of irritation in his voice as he leaned over and peered at the body. "Nothing to worry about now. You recognize this man?"

"No! Never saw him before in my life. Good God, I was just driving—"

"Isn't it unusual for you to drive yourself, sir?"

"Yes, but I didn't want to bother my chauffeur for this short trip. I came here to talk to Bob Waller, my press secretary." Pyle gestured at the big house. A man and woman had come out of the house and stood looking down at the scene below. Agents held up their hands, warning them to stay back.

"That's Bob up there now." Pyle turned back to the car and pointed at the body sprawled on the seat. "This man, whoever he was, must have followed me."

A voice, accented and weak, came from the interior of the car. "Mr. Pyle..."

Instantly, Passmore reacted. He lunged forward, trying to shove the vice president aside, but Looey's bullet had already smashed Spencer Pyle's skull.

$=$ EPILOGUE $=$

President Moody stuck his head through the door of the second-floor dining room. Under the magnificent eighteenth-century crystal chandelier, the table, with a flowered centerpiece, glistened with silver and fine china for eight. Martin Rodale leaned against the door frame, peering over the president's shoulder.

"By the way," the chief of staff said, "Collines's nomination has been reported out of committee in both houses. Only a couple of dissenting votes."

Moody nodded, his eyes still on the elaborately set table. "When does it go to the floor? I want Gould installed soon. I don't like being without a vice president."

"Next Thursday, I understand." Rodale placed a hand on the president's shoulder and squeezed. "Hey, you're the picture of health. What's the rush to get a new vice president?"

The president walked to the table, picked up a crystal goblet, and held it against the light. "Yeah, I feel great," he said, polishing away a smudge with a napkin. "But these are perilous times. There are a lot of crazies out there. Now that we've got a start on disarming Europe, maybe we can do something about our domestic arsenals."

He set the goblet down and looked around the table. "Seems a little formal," he said dubiously. "I don't want this to be a wake."

"We'll keep the wine flowing," Rodale said as he followed the president out and down the hall. "If worse comes to worst, you and I can always do our famous impression of Ken Galbraith explaining supply-side economics to Reagan."

"Speaking of economics, refresh my memory. What exactly did the crew get out of this?"

"Not an awful lot, sir, considering the risk and what they did for us. Quarter of a million apiece, tax-free, plus an insurance policy. John Hortha's estate will receive an additional million from that."

"How about Kogan's money? What do we do with that?"

"Hadn't given it any thought. Guess we'd better return it to your contingency fund." The lofty chief of staff glanced down at the president in a message of shared understanding. He added, "In light of the circumstances."

They had nearly reached the sitting room at the west end of the hall when Rodale checked his watch. "They'll be arriving soon."

Longford held the First Lady's chair for her, then took the one to her left, glancing at the place card—BRIGADIER GENERAL JASPER LONGFORD, U.S. AIR FORCE. Across from him, Martin Rodale had the chair to Lillian's right. President Moody presided over the opposite end of the table. Admiral Jefferson Edwards, chest ablaze with medals and sleeves heavy with gold braid, sat at his right. Betts, Witkowski, and Hiraga filled the other seats. Longford thought his old crew, particularly Betts and Witkowski, looked a shade uncomfortable, but maybe that was because he'd never seen any of them wearing suits and ties.

President Moody nodded to Lillian, and she, in a soft green wool dress, her creamy throat adorned with a topaz necklace in an antique gold setting, smiled brilliantly at her guests before speaking.

"Simon and I are so pleased that you could all make it this evening. We only regret that Dr. Von Porten and Dr. Eccles could not. As you know, they're both in the Philippines working terribly hard on that special project that you all have made possible."

As the First Lady's words continued, soft and touched with an accent that blended so well with the setting, Longford's attention stayed with that phrase, "special project." How long, he wondered, would it be before the public would be brought in on the massive effort now underway? Not until they'd achieved success, he'd been told. And how long would that be? "God knows," Von Porten had said just before he left. "Pray for us."

"...but this evening is not," Lillian was still talking, "just to get you here for a dinner. Simon has something for you." She smiled at the president.

"Well, yes and no," Moody said. "We do have a little something to give you, but you don't get it until after dinner. That way, you see, even if the food's bad, you're beholden to stay right through dessert."

Moody's lighthearted remark set the tone for the dinner, and Longford noticed that even Betts and Witkowski basked in the warmth and genuine friendliness of the president and the First Lady. As he had expected, Lillian Moody was fascinated by the flight through time.

"I simply can't imagine anything more exciting," she said to the circle of faces. "What *was* it like back there?" The question got no response other than bashful grins. No one wanted to tackle that.

"How stupid of me," Lillian said, and laughed lightly. "Let me get specific. Mr. Betts, did you see any difference in the people of fifty years ago?"

Betts's seamed face sobered. The First Lady wanted to know and he was going to try. "Not really, Mrs. Moody. They were just like us. They smoked more, and listened to different music, but I guess they had about the same feelings we do. They were scared. Hell...heck, *we* were scared. But they looked about the same." He eyed Lillian's short hairstyle. "Women wore their hair different...but don't ask me to describe it."

That got a general laugh. The president spoke. "That reminds me of something my professor of medieval history once said. He said the foot soldiers who marched all the way to the Holy Land during the Crusades probably looked pretty much like the soldiers slogging across the Normandy beachhead. People don't change very much, I guess." He glanced at Longford. "I do notice a small change in you, Jake. Congratulations on your promotion to brigadier." He raised his glass and they all drank to the new general.

But Lillian was not to be denied. As the dinner progressed and the courses came and went, she questioned and prodded until every one of the crew had described what he had seen and felt at Del Monte. As dessert was served, she had another question.

"This nurse, Marie Crane—the one Joe Kogan was willing to give his life for. What was she like?"

Jake answered. "I'm sorry, Mrs. Moody, none of us knew Captain Crane. We saw her, of course, that last morning, while she struggled to get aboard the plane, but other than telling you she was tall, red-haired, and very pretty, I can only add that she must have been a fine woman, because although he never said so, I think Joe truly loved her."

•　　•　　•

The dessert dishes had been cleared away and coffee served when Longford leaned toward Lillian and made the observation that he would have stayed right through to the chocolate cheese-cake even if the president had not promised them a little surprise.

"You're such a sweet-talker, General," she said, "I'll pass that on to the kitchen."

Then, as if in response to an unheard signal, the dining room door opened and a sober-faced young major entered bearing leather-covered boxes. At a nod from the president, he quickly laid a case at the elbows of Longford, Betts, Hiraga, and Witkowski. Two more were laid by the president's side. The aide then departed as quietly as he had arrived.

"Gentlemen," Moody intoned. "If you'll open the cases, each of you will find a Medal of Freedom inscribed with your name." He waited until the boxes were opened. "Regrettably, the action for which you are receiving this medal has not yet been engraved thereon. It will not be, of course, until the ongoing work is successful. Each of you therefore has a choice. You can take the medal home, show it to your friends and family, and say, 'Don't ask,' when they want to know what you did to get it." Chuckles rippled around the table. "Or," the president continued, "you can leave them in our custody. But...I did want you to know how highly I value what you have done for me and for the world."

"Mr. President," Admiral Jefferson Edwards's voice boomed. "I'd like to pay special homage to the boot general we've got with us tonight. From what I hear, Jake Longford did a job of flying that would curl your hair. If he hadn't, old *Sucker One* would never have come back. I think we all ought to drink to that."

"Hear, hear," the president murmured as they stood and drank. Before they sat down, Hiraga raised his glass and extended it toward one of the unopened cases.

"And to Johnny Hortha—we all loved him. God rest his soul."

After they had seated themselves, Moody picked up the remaining leather case. "One left, gentlemen," he said.

Longford pointed to it. "He was our leader, sir. May I propose the toast?" He leaned forward, ready to rise. The president shook his head.

"No, General Longford," he said.

Longford tried to conceal his shock, but his face gave him away, for Moody quickly extended his hands in a forgive-me gesture.

"Hear me out, please. General Longford, a toast to the leader who did not come back would be most suitable," the president said. "But first I want you to listen to me. I have a rather strange tale to tell you. I confess it is the principal reason I chose this evening to have you here. The story may even be a little disquieting, but nevertheless, I think it should be told." He waited while Charles and the maid poured more coffee.

"I'm going to begin by recalling for you the fact that I first ran for Congress in 1968. I was twenty-eight, running on an antiwar ticket that didn't go over well with a lot of Maryland big shots, so I didn't have much support in the way of campaign funds. Things weren't going well and I was pretty much reconciled to defeat when a large contribution—the maximum permitted by law—came in from an executive of Pacific Development, Ltd., an investment company with a San Francisco address. I'll mention the man's name, Jonathan Cross, though it's not important to my story. With the contribution from Mr. Cross, I was able to hire a larger staff, buy TV time, newspaper ads, and become Congressman Simon Moody. Naturally, I wrote, thanking Cross profusely, and received a terse little note of acknowledgment in reply.

"Two years later, being an incumbent, I had an easier time getting reelected, but nevertheless got a second welcome contribution from Mr. Cross. Again I thanked him, obliquely inquiring as to why my candidacy was getting such nice financial support. Again I received a short letter containing vague platitudes about how pleased he was to be able to support my political ideals.

"This financial support continued over the next twenty years while I went from the House to the Senate, and finally received the nomination for the presidency. You recall, I'm sure, how close a race that was. The demand on me and my backers for campaign money was overwhelming. We were being outspent three to one by the opposing party. Even Spencer Pyle's sources of help had run dry.

"I had, of course, gotten the usual maximum contribution from our friend in Pacific Development, but in the later stages of the campaign, when we were really strapped and needed several million immediately, I felt I had to turn to him. So I called Jonathan Cross. This was the first time I had ever spoken with him. It was rather a bizarre conversation. I explained the situation and said that although I knew that he, as an individual, could not legally contribute more money, I'd be eternally grateful if he could give me the names of friends or associates of his from whom I might solicit funds.

"He was polite, but curiously disinterested." The president chuckled. "I told you this was a strange conversation. Here was a man who had supported me wholeheartedly throughout my political career, and now, when everything was at stake, showed no fire, no zeal, no real concern for my situation. Cross said that he would try, but could promise nothing. I hung up, terribly disappointed. Two days later, to my delighted surprise, a batch of envelopes arrived by special messenger and was dumped on the desk of my campaign manager. Each envelope contained a check. Each check was the maximum an individual could contribute. Each contributor, we later discovered, was connected in some way with Pacific Development. For the next few days the money continued to pour in."

The president paused and sipped his wine. He looked around the table. All eyes were on his face. Moody continued.

"I can see that I'm *not* boring you. So let me ask you this: does any one of you have any idea why I'm telling you this story?"

Longford watched the others. Witkowski became intensely interested in policing the crumbs beside his dessert plate. Admiral Edwards shrugged his shoulders. Betts shook his head slowly. Hiraga stared at the president, his face impassive, but his eyes glowed as though he had glimpsed something far distant, but wonderful. As for Longford, the question itself had become the answer. He felt the hair begin to stand on the back of his neck.

"Yes, Mr. President," he finally said, "I think that perhaps I do."

Moody nodded, smiling slightly in satisfaction. "Let me go on. With the additional money, we won, of course. We sent out the routine letters of appreciation to all contributors. And just as routinely, the contributors appeared on the doorstep of the White House with hungry looks, asking for ambassadorships, judgeships, favors, exemptions, and all the other good things they believed I had the power to bestow."

The president's face grew sober. "Except for the people from Pacific Development. They wanted nothing.

"By now, I was completely intrigued. An executive whose name I barely knew, who worked for a company in which I had no interest, had taken on a paternal role toward me and my career." Moody chuckled as he toyed with his wineglass. "*Paternal* is really not the right word," he added. "Most fathers don't provide unlimited funds without giving advice, whether wanted or not. None of this had happened. There were no suggestions, no demands, no requests—no congratulations, even. For more than two decades, except for the money, there were no communications of any kind. You can, I'm sure, understand why I was determined to get to the bottom of this.

"But it was not to be. Just about then—early last spring—the first symptoms of my cancer struck, and from that time on, my every waking moment was taken up with staying alive and holding on to the presidency. And, my friends, you here, along with Kogan and Von Porten, became my saviors."

Moody grinned benignly at them all. "Gentlemen, I see empty wineglasses." He motioned and Charles stepped to the buffet and picked up a wine bottle.

The president added, "I personally would like more coffee."

"Mr. President," Admiral Edwards rumbled, glowering fiercely at Moody, "you're not going to leave us hanging by our fingertips, are you, sir?"

"No, Jeff, of course not." He waited while his coffee was poured. "Let me go on. A week or so ago, Marty was reviewing our agenda for last spring, trying to catch up on the things we had been forced to postpone." The president turned to Rodale. "Tell them what you found out."

The chief of staff cleared his throat and began diffidently. "Almost the first thing I ran across was the notation to check on Jonathan Cross and Pacific Development. Knowing that Simon had been intensely interested, I thought of asking the FBI to investigate. But deciding that the company was probably multinational, I put the CIA on the task. It didn't take long. The company turned out to be legitimate, as was Cross, but as we had begun to suspect, the San Francisco office was only a subsidiary of the headquarters, which is based in Manila. Other branches are located in Singapore, Tokyo, and Hong Kong. I was surprised to hear that Cross himself was only a middle-level administrator, certainly not one who could command the sort of instant obedience that had produced the money we needed. The president of Pacific Development turned out to be a man in his late seventies, a Norris Sinclair. The CEO is Alfred Thayer Hill, who is quite a bit younger—middle fifties, as I recall."

Longford held up a restraining hand. "Excuse me, sir," he said, "but that name, Norris Sinclair, is familiar. I met a young man with that name at Del Monte. He was an executive with PhilPak—the Philippine Packing Company. He was on his way to be a guerrilla against the Japanese, as I recall."

The president smiled broadly. "Small world, isn't it?" He chuckled and picked up the story. "Well, let me go on." He leaned forward, both elbows on the table, his face ruddy in the candlelight. "The CIA report also mentioned, almost apologetically, the existence of a rumor—a story that had become almost a legend in the Far East—to the effect that the real power behind

Pacific Development, Ltd., was a shadowy figure, anonymous and reclusive, a man who would have made Howard Hughes seem positively gregarious.

"All right. Marty called the director and told him that rumors were a lot of fun, but when the president asked for information, he wanted facts, and was that clearly understood. The director said it was, apologized profusely, and the CIA went back to work. Two days ago, we got a photograph from the Far East. The report accompanying it said that it had been taken in Manila eleven years ago and acquired from a source with a ninety-eight percent reliability factor. In the language of the report, 'Subject purported to be founder and head of Pacific Development. Name still not ascertained.'"

President Moody rose from his chair and stretched, arching his back. He walked to a sideboard beneath the wallpaper scenes of the Revolutionary War, picked up a large envelope, took a photograph from it, and returned to the table. He handed it to Longford.

With a tremor in his hand, Longford angled the photo to catch the light, and squinted. It showed a busy street scene with cars and people in the background, presumably in downtown Manila. In the foreground, a large car was parked at the curb, with a chauffeur, back to the camera, holding a car door open. A man, stoop-shouldered and grasping a cane in his right hand, had emerged from the car and was caught by the lens as he walked toward the building. A wide-brimmed panama hat covered white hair and cast his face in shadow. The left coat sleeve of his light-colored suit was tucked into the coat pocket.

"Well, Jake?"

Longford looked up at the president. He understood what Moody wanted him to say, but he wasn't ready. Not yet.

"May I pass this around?" Moody inclined his head and Jake passed the picture to the other crew members. Each looked at it and wordlessly passed it on. Lillian picked the photo up, gave it a quick glance, and dropped it. Longford got the impression she had seen the picture before. He looked at Moody.

"It could be Kogan."

The president glanced at the others. "What do you think?"

Betts's face was set in stubborn lines. "The only thing I see there, sir, is a real old man with one arm."

"Larry," Hiraga spoke gently. "It's the only explanation for all that political money being sent by Pacific Development. Kogan wanted to make sure that Moody—sorry, sir—that President Moody would make it to the White House."

"Could Kogan be that old? My God, we were with him less than a month ago."

"Wrong. We were with him fifty-two years ago. Now, how old was he when we went back—midforties? That would put him in his eighties when this picture was taken." Hiraga picked up the photo. "Looks about right."

It *was* about right, Longford conceded, but he'd seen Joe fall forward on his face, blood gushing in torrents from his arm, the nurse trying desperately to stem the hemorrhaging. Was it really possible for him to have survived?

"I don't know, Mr. President," Longford said. "I wouldn't have given a nickel for Joe's chances when we saw him last. To think he lived on—"

"He did, Jake," Witkowski said, then turned to Moody. "May I tell him, Mr. President?"

"Of course. You see, Jake, after receiving this photo, we got in touch with Mike at the Archives and asked him to search the records to see if a Major General Joseph Kogan was captured and survived POW camp." He nodded at Witkowski. "Okay, tell them what you found."

"I thought it would be simple. The records are all computerized. I quickly went through Bilibid and Cabanatuan and Davao and O'Donnell in the Philippines; then the Formosa camps, the Japanese camps, and even the one in Manchuria where General Wainwright was imprisoned. Nothing. Then it occurred to me that the Japanese had interned American army nurses at Baguio and Santo Tomás on Luzon. If Joe *had* survived and wanted to stay with Marie, the only way for him to have done it was to assume a civilian identity. Sure enough, a Mr. and Mrs. Joseph Kogan were released from Santo Tomás in 1945."

"I'll be damned," Longford said softly. He turned to the president. "Is the old boy still alive, sir?"

"I was damn well going to find out," Moody answered. "I had our ambassador to the Philippines deliver a personal letter from me addressed to Kogan, care of Pacific Development, Ltd. With that kind of horsepower behind it, we were sure the letter would get through, wherever he was."

"Did it?"

The president laughed. "If it's all right with my dear wife, I'll let her answer that one."

Lillian laid her slim hand on Longford's arm. "The answer, Jake, is yes, the letter was delivered." She held out her hand and Rodale slipped a folded sheet of paper into it.

"I believe," she said, "the best way to answer your questions is to read the reply that is addressed to both Simon and me." She unfolded the letter, glanced at it, and then looked slowly around the table, her gaze touching the face of every crew member.

"This is from Marie Kogan." Lillian swallowed and blinked her eyes rapidly. "Here is what it says.

Dear President and Mrs. Moody,

I have received your letter, Mr. President, addressed to my deceased husband, Joseph Kogan. I am taking the liberty of answering it because I think I can tell you what you want to know.

I am addressing this to both of you, because my beloved Joe has spoken of you both so many times over the years that I feel we are friends, and if this is presumptuous, please forgive an old woman.

Four years ago, Joe died in his sleep at the biological age of ninety-three. His only regret at the last was that he did not know whether the flight made it back. So what a blessed relief it was to get your letter and to know, finally, that it had. Except for John Hortha, I never met any of that gallant group of men who flew back to my world with my husband. Please, if you have a chance, speak to them of my deep admiration and respect.

You mentioned the work that Dr. Von Porten is engaged in on the Bataan Peninsula, about ninety miles south of here. The accommodations there are primitive and the weather can be wretched. I would like to make a suggestion. The home that Joe and I built here in the Benguet Mountains is very large and very empty and the weather is delightful. I offer the estate to Dr. Von Porten and his associates for whatever use they can make of it. I will also have Pacific Development provide on a daily basis as many helicopters as are needed to transport people, material, and equipment between Bataan and here.

I am old, but I once was a nurse. Please let me help. God bless you both.

Marie Kogan

"Jake," President Moody said, "I believe you were saying something about a toast."

ABOUT THE AUTHOR

A Marine Corps infantry officer from World War II to Vietnam, C. F. Runyan served in Japan, Okinawa, Korea, and the Philippines. After retiring as a lieutenant colonel, he taught American history and modern military history at Grossmont College in San Diego, where he lives today. He holds the bachelor of science and master of arts degrees from the University of Maryland, and is the author of *From the Delaware to the Mekong: A Military History of the United States.* He is currently at work on a second novel.